Dearest Clementine

USA TODAY BESTSELLING AUTHOR

LEX MARTIN

Copy edited by RJ Locksley
Cover design by Najla Qamber

May 2024 Special Edition Paperback

ISBN 978-1-950554-22-5

To my husband Matt, who has always encouraged me to write, and to my two little bears...

You are my happily ever after.

Foreword

My dearest lovely readers,

I can't believe it's already been ten years since I first published *Dearest Clementine*! To celebrate, I put together this special collection that has exclusive bonus content.

This edition is for the readers who reached out to me over the years to let me know how much this book meant to them. This is for those who wanted a little more spice, those who wanted more from Gavin's perspective, and those who asked for more Jenna and Ryan.

At the end of *Dearest Clementine*, you'll find an extended (and steamy) epilogue and a super sweet bonus scene from Gavin's point of view.

I also included a prequel for Jenna and Ryan fans. *The Girlfriend Games* is an angsty 30,000-word novella that will make you laugh, (possibly) cry, and definitely swoon. If you're new to the Dearest series and want to read everything in order, you can flip to *The Girlfriend Games* and read that before *Dearest Clementine*, but each can be enjoyed as a standalone.

I've also included a playlist and an author's note at the end to detail some of my personal connections to this story.

From the bottom of my heart, thank you for ten years of book love. I hope you enjoy!
Love,
Lex

Playlist

Back To Black | Any Winehouse
Love Song | Sara Bareilles
You Know I'm No Good | Amy Winehouse
Out of My League | Fitz and the Tantrums
Kiss You Inside Out | Hedley
Stay With Me | Sam Smith
Daylight | Maroon 5
How To Save A Life | The Fray
Numb | Linkin Park
Hanging By A Moment | Lifehouse

Dearest Clementine

"It is never too late to be what you might have been."
- George Eliot

Chapter 1

My pen traces mindless circles in the margins of my journal as I stare out the window of the dusty common room.

This is what I've needed to find my footing, I think as I fight the nerves taking root in my stomach.

Down the hallway, the sound of squeaky wheels is punctuated by a groan and a thump as luggage hits the floor.

"Wait, what will happen if there's a fire? We're on the eighteenth floor," one girl says, her vowels long and polite. A Southerner.

A deep male voice reassures her. "I know it's a hike down those stairs, but don't use the elevators. The last thing you want is to get stuck between floors. I'll check each room to make sure you've evacuated."

I can't make out the rest of the conversation until two girls shuffle by the lounge.

"Holy shit. Our RA is hot!" a girl in a sundress tells her friend as she lugs an overstuffed duffle bag. "I wonder if he has a girlfriend."

"He's a senior or a grad student, dork. He's not going to be interested in *you*," the other one says, her accent softening her words.

Hitting on the resident assistant, the upperclassman paid to keep an eye on all of the kids in the dorms, was never my thing. My RA freshman year, Tao, was five two and into Jesus. Not my scene.

I can't imagine who would want to be an RA. Tao was always rushing some poor slob to the hospital with random broken bits. I'll never forget the look on his face when he found my friend Sarah passed out, piss-drunk, with a broken ankle. How she managed to vomit on all four walls of her dorm room before she went down is beyond me.

Tapping my pen, I shift in my seat.

I've spent the last three months trying to get in the zone, grappling with ideas, but I only ended up with a journal full of manic-looking drawings.

This has to fucking work.

I breathe deeply, the smell of stale Cheetos assaulting my nose.

If I can get into a writing routine again, I can do this. I've done it before.

I keep telling myself the same crap, hoping something clicks. All summer, I've tried to be positive, and trust me, that's no easy feat.

My knee starts to jiggle, and just as I'm about to go into full-out crisis mode, a voice startles me.

"Darlin', now *you* don't look like a freshman."

Turning slightly, I see him in my peripheral vision, leaning in the doorway. The RA.

"That's because I'm not," I say flatly.

"So what are you doing in Warren Towers? I mean, why would you willingly hang out here? I get paid to be here. What's your excuse?"

He's joking. I get it. But I'm not in the mood.

"Just looking for some white noise," I say, returning to my journal. I feel his eyes on me, and my face starts to heat. "Look, I'm not some creeper if that's what you're getting at. I just need a little inspiration."

I jot down random words, hoping something can pull me out of my writing coma: suitcases, hot RAs, condoms, diet Coke, donuts.

Trying to ignore the intensity of his stare, I gaze out the floor-to-ceiling windows.

I've always loved this view. Boston is alive with color, rich with the burnt sienna of brownstones that bake in the August sun. Walls of ivy ripple in the breeze off the Charles River, making me wish I could go for a run.

Nostalgia tugs at me as I think about how much has happened since I lived here freshman year. I got the idea for my book in this very seat three years ago. And I'm hoping like hell I can do it again.

A quick glance at the clock feels like a punch to the gut. At this rate, I'm never going to figure out my next book if I can't get in the zone. And I *have* to get in the zone. No one will pay my bills if I don't, and Boston University doesn't exactly have a soft spot for poor little rich girls. Because on paper, I'm silver-spoon-up-my-bum wealthy, the daughter of two Fortune 500 assholes. Unfortunately, my parents never got the memo they're supposed to give a shit about my life.

Who knows what I did to piss them off? It's immaterial at this point. The bottom line is I need money. *Pronto.*

I have one thing on my side. On a good day, if the stars align and the fates agree, I can write my ass off. Which helped at the end of my freshman year when I received the letter from the bursar's office noting that I owed a cool twenty grand.

It's ironic that my novel, which highlighted one of the most humiliating moments of my life, helped pay that bill.

I haven't been able to write anything on par with *Say It Isn't So,* my one and only book, the lucky ticket that bailed me out of debt. But I guess I haven't had to. What started off as maudlin ramblings in my diary that I shaped into a narrative somehow jumped up the charts and became an indie bestseller.

The RA clears his throat, pulling me from my thoughts. "And you thought you'd find inspiration here, a freshman dorm?"

I don't have to look up to know he's grinning.

How the hell do you hear someone smile? my inner voice quips.

He chuckles. "Are you having any luck? Finding inspiration?"

Finally, my eyes sweep up, and my stomach instantly lurches. He's tall with dark, shaggy hair that flops in his face. Intense green eyes stare back. *The girls were right. He* is *good-looking.* He smiles a dazzling, megawatt grin, and my chest clenches at the thought that he probably has lickable abs.

Oh, for the love of God, Clem, get a grip.

I bite my lower lip until it stings, and my eyes dart back to my journal.

"No," I say, wishing I had more time to write. "No luck with inspiration."

My jaw clenches as my pen returns to drawing circles. Ignoring the hammering of my heart that I hope has everything to do with my looming tuition bill and nothing to do with Henry Cavill's doppelgänger, I flip through the pages in front of me, desperate to find something that will help me get my shit together.

He shifts in the doorway.

"I'm Gavin, by the way."

"Nice to meet you," I say half-heartedly. My body, on autopilot, starts to pack my stuff even though it's too early.

Shit. Fuck-it-all-to-hell shit! *You can't go. You don't have anything figured out yet!*

"And... you... would... be?"

"Leaving." My inner voice sighs at me. *Always such a bitch, Clem.*

"Yeah, that's not what I meant." He sounds amused.

I swing my messenger bag over my shoulder.

"I know what you meant," I say, glancing up as he blocks my exit.

He's taller than I thought... and built...

The fact that my heart beats even faster the second I smell his citrusy cologne pisses me off. I pride myself on being a modern girl, one who doesn't need a man, especially if all he'll do is break my heart. So the idea that this guy and his little smirk give me kamikaze butterflies aggravates me more.

I let out an exasperated sigh as I wait for him to move out of the way, my eyes traveling along his bulging bicep, which strains against his t-shirt.

Stop. Checking. Him. Out.

I shake my head at myself as I scoot around him and head for the elevator. I press the button and wait all of three seconds before I punch it again.

"You know, you're on the eighteenth floor. This could take a while," he says behind me. "I'm guessing you probably have more than enough time to tell me your name." He chuckles again, apparently undeterred by my fuck-off vibe.

This doesn't mean anything. Just because you didn't get an idea today doesn't mean anything.

Nerves jumble my stomach, and I half consider taking the stairs when the elevator doors slide open and relief floods my chest. I don't know why I have to get away from here right now, but I do.

I get in and turn around. Obnoxiously sexy RA guy is leaning against the wall with his arms crossed over his broad chest, watching me. Our eyes meet, and he raises his eyebrows.

As the doors start to close, I feel a twinge of guilt.

Ugh. Fine.

"Clem. My name is Clementine."

The doors close, but not before I catch him grin.

* * *

The musty smell of our apartment building blasts me in the face as I trudge up the stairs. Everyone is standing around the wagon-wheel coffee table, and Jenna hovers protectively in front of her garage-sale find with her hands on her hips. Her shoulder-length blonde hair is pulled up in a spiky ponytail and she has a smudge of dirt across her cheek.

"Clem, help me out here," she says in her sweetest South Carolinian drawl. "Do you think this is hideous? Because I don't. I think it has personality."

Harper is standing next to Jenna silently begging me to side with her. She removes her glasses to rub the bridge of her nose before she swats at a loose strand of dark auburn hair dangling in her face. I'm lucky to have her as my in-house shrink. Her father is a world-renowned psychiatrist, and she'll be one too someday.

I've been roommates with Harper since second semester of our freshman year after neither of us could stand living with our original roommates in Warren Towers. That's when we got matched up with Jenna, who's a creative writing major like me. By some fluke sophomore year, our little trio ended up in a coveted apartment on Bay State Road, which rocks the most amazing brownstones. We've been living together ever since.

Aside from Harper and Jenna, people here don't know me, the real me. They don't know I stand to inherit a shit-ton of money. Between the trust fund and the holdings from my grandfather, the amount is staggering. But I don't like how people look at me when they think I'm some trust-fund baby.

Besides, the money isn't mine, so I don't want it. Especially if it means groveling to my mother. Because that will never fucking happen.

Harper clears her throat to catch my attention, and I remember that I'm supposed to be the enforcer.

"Jenna, we don't have much room in our new place," I say, hoping to let her down easily. "Our common area is pretty small this year."

I don't tell her that we've wanted to burn her table all summer.

"Babe," Jenna's boyfriend Ryan says with a look of resignation, "why don't I take it for now? I'll put it in my garage, and you can get it next summer." As much shit as I give him, deep down he's a great guy. "Besides, we've made some good memories on it." He waggles his eyebrows at her, and I have a deep desire to hurl.

"Gross!" Harper yells. "Why can't you two limit your sexual activity to the bedroom like normal people?"

"I can't help it if I have a hot girlfriend." Ryan leans over and kisses Jenna, and she giggles like a love-struck teenager.

Fortunately, the buzzer rings, which gets him bounding over boxes and out the door to pay the pizza guy. After scrounging around for some paper plates, we congregate on the bare floor in the living room.

By the time we're done eating and the food coma starts to set in, the task of moving all of our crap to our new place on campus seems daunting.

A weary Harper holds up her cup of soda. "Here's to our senior year." We all raise our drinks. "To Ryan, may he sell out all of his concerts." He winks, his stage swagger evident in the upward tilt of his chin. "To Jenna, may she be just as pleased in the bedroom but less vocal." Jenna shoots her the finger but laughs. Harper turns to me and grins. "To Clem, may she write another bestselling book."

Her words send twin pangs of hope and fear through me as I pray that I can finally break my dry spell and do it again.

Ryan tips his cup toward me. "You ever gonna let me read that book of yours?"

That's an easy answer.

"I'm thinking no." I arch an eyebrow at him, and he feigns disappointment. Yeah, like he really wants to read my Young Adult chick book.

Jenna interrupts to finish our toast. "And here's to Harper, may she be wrong about all of my Freudian slips!"

Laughing, we clink our cups.

Jenna pauses mid-toast to wave her hands, sloshing soda all over the floor. "Don't forget that Ryan's show is tomorrow night at Euphoria." Jenna is the ultimate groupie, standing in the front row to eye-fuck her boyfriend, who's the lead singer of Tragic Paradox. "They got a new guitarist, and he's really amazing."

She leans over to kiss Ryan, which goes from a sweet peck on the mouth to something more, eliciting groans from Harper and me.

As Ryan starts to pull away from the kiss, he cops a feel.

"Are you always such a pervert?" I ask, giving him what I consider a withering eat-shit look, one that only makes him smirk. The fact that he just grabbed Jenna's breast doesn't faze her at all. Public groping is something she has gotten used to, like getting frisked by the TSA.

He's still looking at me with a big, stupid smile. I shake my head. "You're immune to my powers, huh?"

"Guess so." He shrugs.

"I never could scare you."

"No, but you scare the shit outta all my friends." He scruffs my hair like I'm a kid, which has me seriously thinking about punching him in the kidney. "Why you so mean, Clementine?"

I lean back and shrug. "If you can't stand the heat, stay the fuck out of the kitchen."

"You just need a worthy adversary." He has that look in his eye. This guy never gets the message.

"No, and don't go trying to set me up with one of your sorry-ass friends."

"Clem?"

"Yeah?"

He cocks an eyebrow. "Don't take this the wrong way, but are you a lesbian?" Before I can scoff, he raises his hands defensively. "Because it's okay if you are. I won't judge you, and seriously, that would be pretty hot."

"Fuck off, Ryan."

"I think you'd be less tense if you had sex, maybe just once."

"Who says I haven't?"

It always goes here. I catch Harper's eye, and she makes a face. She knows how much I hate this.

"Clem can't help that most men don't meet her standards," Jenna says as she clears away our paper plates.

"Thank you." It's not like I've never dated. I merely gave up trying to find someone who wasn't a shithead. Or a cheater. Or a stalker. Yeah, guys suck.

Ryan frowns. "I've been with Jenna for a while, and you've never had a boyfriend in all of this time. That's fucked up. All my friends are dying for a shot with you, and I like to think that pairing you off with someone is good for the gene pool."

He's ridiculous. There's nothing special about my genes. I'm a little on the short side with long, blondish-brown hair and blue eyes. People say Jenna and I could pass for sisters, but where her hair is silky and smooth, mine is longer and wavier. If I wanted to look as good as Jenna does when she rolls out of bed, I'd have to spend half the day under a blow dryer. No thanks.

The biggest thing I have going for me is that I love running and rock climbing, so at least all of my parts will stay in place for a while.

Ryan points at me with a sly grin.

"The fact that you never date must mean you kind of hate men, right? Well, except for me."

He makes a puppy-dog face, and Jenna coos at him. *Good lord.*

"I don't hate men. I hate *predictable* men." I'm not sure what's gotten into Ryan tonight. He knows better than to mess with me.

"You should come with a warning label, girl," Ryan jokes. "Mishandling could result in injury or death."

"Yeah, let's start with yours," I say as I mock-punch him in the stomach.

* * *

Bay State Road is lush with maple trees and ivy, the perfect setting for a postcard to send home. That's if I sent postcards home.

Exactly one block from the heart of Boston University is our brownstone for the year. Although I'm exhausted and the street is crawling with students and double-parked with cars, standing here looking at our new place has me practically bouncing on my toes with excitement.

Harper, Jenna and I bound up the stairs and throw open the door to our new place.

"Let's figure out where everyone goes." Harper has her no-nonsense face on.

Our apartment, which is at the top of a four-story walk-up, has a little more space than the other suites in the building, but it's still a glorified dorm.

In the front is a small common area, which is lined with two single-occupancy rooms and one double. I eye the bathroom. Four girls sharing one bathroom is never fun.

"Dani is rooming with me," Jenna says, "so the double in the front is mine."

She stays with Ryan most of the time anyway, so she doesn't really need privacy.

I'm glad I'm not the one stuck with the new girl. That's the drawback of living on campus. Even though it's convenient, the lottery system doesn't care that we wanted to live as a trio and randomly assigned us a suite that housed four students. We then could wait to get assigned some random person or scramble to find someone ourselves. Jenna swears we'll love Dani, but I'm reserving judgment because you can never be too cautious. Especially in my position.

I try to live under the radar because the press would love to splash my family's name across the tabloids. It's happened with my twin brother Jackson a few times, but Jax relishes the limelight because it means he can get laid whenever he wants.

But I make it my mission to live a quiet life, even if it is a little boring at times. Because Lord knows I've seen enough drama.

Quiet is how I like it, so I used a pen name when I published my book—because there is no way I can lay claim to the fiasco that inspired that novel.

Harper looks to me, and I shrug. I've paid for a single, and although that'll be a stretch for me financially, I can't write while someone is watching *Glee* in the background.

"You can take whichever room you want. As long as I don't have to live with Eva Richardson ever again," I say as Harper laughs.

My freshman year roommate Eva, a snarky sorority girl, made my life hell, but she's also the reason I ended up with Harper later that year.

Footsteps echo along the hardwood floors, and we turn to find Ryan groaning.

"Fuck. You girls couldn't get a room on the first or second floor?" When he reaches the top of the stairs, he heaves the boxes to get a better grasp.

"Drinks and dinner are on us tomorrow night," I say, grabbing the top box out of his hands. "Besides, this is the price you pay to date one of the most gorgeous girls on campus. You get to be our grunt on moving day. Man up, buddy."

He sighs, then nods. "You're right."

Okay, so maybe *all* guys don't suck.

Chapter 2

The next day I'm sore from moving, like I've been dropkicked by a medium-sized farm animal, which is why I'm not excited to go to work. I'm one of the assistant managers at the campus bookstore, a coveted position among students as it gets you discounts on books, clothes, and, most importantly, coffee. My store is three stories high, takes up half a city block, and has everything from a Barnes & Noble and Starbucks to dorm room essentials and apparel. Eager parents can outfit their kid's crappy room, pay out the ass for textbooks, and top it off with a goofy coffee mug for grandma.

I love my job. Most days. It keeps my head busy, preventing me from crawling into a cave, which is always my go-to response when I'm stressed. But this is the busiest time of the year.

With school starting in a few days, I have to deal with the overflowing storage room, but I need the money because I'll be damned if I'll call my mother for help, so I caffeinate with a double latte, preparing myself for the work ahead of me.

Selling my book has gotten me pretty far, but attending one of the most expensive schools in the country, which is located in one of the most expensive cities in the country, has been tough financially. My mother pays for my brother's tuition, but at least he's down the road at Boston College, so I don't have to see daily reminders of his preferred status in our family.

I type a quick text apologizing to Jenna for needing to skip out on Ryan's show, and I promise to pitch in some cash to buy the guy a few drinks to thank him for moving us.

Jenna writes back: *I understand. Wish you were coming tonight, though! Wanted you to meet Murphy, the new guitarist. Very cute.*

Laughing, I respond: *Stop trying to set me up!*

Jenna: *Your vagina is going to close up, and you'll need surgical assistance to use it again.*

Me: *Don't worry. I have insurance. And battery-operated accessories that don't cheat on me or stalk me. Can't beat that!*

Okay, I don't have insurance. Or a vibrator, and I feel a tad guilty for lying, but Jenna doesn't totally get why I don't like to date, and I don't have the energy to have that conversation. Again.

Jenna: *Fine. I'll let you off tonight on ONE condition.*

Me: *?*

Jenna: *I get full license to plan your bday next weekend. CARTE BLANCHE!*

Me: *You drive a hard bargain. If I say no?*

Jenna: *You have 10 minutes to get your ass here for the show.*

Me: *You're a pain in the ass. Fine. Bday it is.*

Jenna: *Love you! Don't work too late.*

Shaking my head, I tuck my phone away and get down to business. When I finish dealing with the inventory, it's after midnight. Kenmore Square is bustling with hordes of students headed to Lansdowne Street, which houses a dozen bars, but when I turn down Bay State Road, the block leading to my building is dark. Two street lamps are out, and I can't help but quicken my pace until I reach my door.

I'm relieved to see Harper curled up on the couch talking on the phone when I walk in.

"Are you the only one here?" I ask as she hangs up.

"Yeah, Jenna went back home with Ryan because you know how they get after shows," she says, rolling her eyes. "Dani went out to eat with her friends."

Grabbing the corner of her blanket, I tuck myself in next to her, and we stare at the muted television. At some point, we're going to have to deal with the boxes that are still stacked along the walls, but I'm too tired to consider it. Now that I'm sitting, my legs are numb, and exhaustion starts to spread through the rest of my limbs.

"How was tonight?" I ask.

"The band was great, but Kade the giant dickhead wouldn't stop hitting on me."

Kade is the band's drummer. He's the son of some politician, and he's used to getting his way. Guys like him with money and power and no fear of society's parameters are dangerous, something I've learned the hard way.

"That sucks."

"I don't care how scrumptious I look. The next time he puts his hands on my ass will be his last."

Harper doesn't have Jenna's overt beauty, but she's striking in her own way, and she's one of the few people I know who's comfortable in her own skin. Plus, she's a psych major and doesn't mind digging around in my brain until I stop with the crazy.

"That guy is such a douche. I don't know why Ryan is friends with him."

She straightens in her seat. "But the new guitarist is a sweetheart. And so cute!"

"That's what I hear." I haven't met this guy yet, but he already has Harper's attention. That says something. "You gonna dump your boy toy for him?"

"You know it!"

* * *

I. Am. Such. An. Idiot.

Reaching into my bag, I pull out my class list. I shoved it in there in May, and quickly forgot about it. I scan my classes: Greek & Roman Myth in Literature, Psychology, Romance Novel-Writing, and Applied Math.

I held off three years to do two things: take my one math requirement—because I'm mathematically challenged—and enroll in what I anticipated would be my favorite writing course, Young Adult Novel-Writing with Professor Golding. She was out on maternity leave last spring and isn't teaching the course second semester, so this fall is the only chance I have to take it with her. I hoped the class could help me cultivate ideas to write my book.

My stomach plummets as I read the list again.

Being the genius that I am, I'm only now realizing I accidentally signed up for Romance Writing.

Visions of Professor Golding taking me under her wing quickly vanish. The odds of her class having room for one more student is about as good as finding a street in Boston that doesn't have a pothole.

Young Adult Writing is taught by one other professor, and I placed a restraining order on him freshman year, so hell would have to freeze the fuck over before I'd consider taking another one of his classes.

I had all summer, all damn summer, to figure this out, but I didn't think to look at my class list, other than a cursory glance, to make sure it was correct. I must have seen the "novel writing" part and thought I was set. Shit.

It takes staring at my registration sheet and the online catalogue of classes for ten unblinking minutes to realize that the course numbers for Young Adult and Romance Writing are nearly identical. But the Sunday night of Labor Day weekend is not the time to figure this out because there is nothing I can do until classes start.

Fuck!

By 10 a.m. on Tuesday, I'm in need of alcohol. Shots. Maybe tequila. I'm not a drinker, but the sight of students standing in a packed classroom trying to get into Golding's YA course has me feeling defeated. I double-check her office hours and decide to see her after class and head off to Romance Writing.

I roll my eyes. I hate romance novels.

I'm so screwed.

* * *

I'm ten minutes late, but at least I make it. I scurry in, ducking as though that might make me invisible, and sink into one of the last open seats. The room is huge and almost overflowing, which is strange considering only creative writing majors should be in here.

Professor Marceaux is strolling the front of the class, clucking her tongue as she surveys us. Before I get a chance to look at the syllabus, she calls on a student who has her hand up.

"So what's the difference between *Fifty Shades of Grey* and romance?" a girl in the front row asks.

From the sudden chatter that erupts, I get the impression this is on everyone's mind. Am I the only person who hasn't read *Fifty Shades*?

Marceaux pauses mid-step. "Excellent question. First and foremost, Ana, the main character in *Fifty Shades*, is considering whether or not she wants to be Christian's submissive, so the whole story revolves around this sexual conflict, which places it firmly within the erotica genre. Let's also consider diction. In romance, we say making love or maybe having sex. For my taste, we won't say *fucking*," she says, making the whole class laugh as she wags her eyebrows.

Oh, Jesus. Do we have to talk about sex? Can't romance be about unrequited love and angsty looks? Maybe a little drunk fondling in the coat closet?

The professor has a thick French accent, and as she struts

across the front of the room, she pushes her tortoise-shell frames up to the top of her head. She clucks again. "Along those lines, I wouldn't write penis or clitoris. You will need to make up some fun euphemisms for those words."

Students start muttering and a few girls giggle.

Why the hell do I need a fun euphemism for the word penis? I never plan to write that word. Ever.

I feel ill.

A guy sitting next to me nudges my elbow.

"I could help you out with that," he whispers, smirking. "You know, with the euphemisms."

"Go to hell, jackass." It only takes a minute to pack my bag before I storm out of the room. The professor mumbles something as the door swings shut behind me and laughter erupts a second later.

When I get home, my head is pounding. In the late afternoon, when Jenna walks in, her eyes bug out when she sees me.

"Holy Christ, Clem, what was up with you in class today?"

"What class?" I pull one leg up underneath me and sink deeper into the bench seat by the bay window.

"Romance. You didn't see me waving wildly to you from the other side of the room?" Her arms flail around as though I need a demonstration.

"Oh my God, are you taking that too?"

"Yeah! Why did you run out?"

"Are you kidding? I'm not taking a sex-writing class."

She frowns. "That's not what it is. You missed the rest of the professor's explanation. She said in romance, the sex comes secondary to love. Sex might be part of it, but it's really about the bigger story of growth."

I drop my head into my hands and rub my throbbing temples.

"What happened to that Young Adult class you were dying to take?" she asks as she shuffles through the room.

Groaning, I close my eyes. "I made a mistake when I registered for classes last spring and accidentally selected Romance."

"Bummer." She pours a cup of coffee and settles next to me in the window nook.

I crack open my eyes and glance up at her. "Jenna, I'm not the kind of person who comes up with fun euphemisms for body parts. That's just not me."

"Well, maybe this is a sign, y'know, to try new things and be bold."

It's my turn to frown. Bitchy I can do, but I'm not sure about bold. The last time I did something truly bold was freshman year, and what resulted still scares the shit out of me.

Maybe that's why I still can't write.

Jenna elbows me, trying to coax a smile. "Cheer up. I'm cooking up something really fun for your birthday this weekend."

"Fine. As long as it doesn't involve euphemisms for the word penis, I'm game."

Disappointment sags her face. "Well, that's no fun."

Maybe not, but it's safe.

Chapter 3

I have no idea for my book and no YA class. I keep waiting for more bad news because crappy things always seem to happen in threes.

I begged Professor Golding to let me take her class, but she merely handed me the waiting list, which was two pages long, so I swallowed my pride and apologized to Professor Marceaux for bolting from her lecture. I told her I had a sudden emergency and left out the fact that I nearly died when she said clitoris.

Which now has me thinking of euphemisms for the word clitoris. Like nubbin, bean, bud, button.

Oh my God.

An unwanted image comes to mind. *He reaches between her delicate thighs and strokes her throbbing nubbin.*

Jesus. Someone shoot me if I ever write that in a book.

Accepting that I'll be taking a freaking romance-writing class this fall means a trip to the bookstore. I duck in, hoping to make it out before I get harangued into working, but when I get to the counter, out of the corner of my eye, I see *him*. Fucker-from-hell.

A drum beats fast in my chest, echoing through my body.

Barely able to catch my breath, I do the first thing that comes to mind and dive under the register.

I don't think he saw me. *Please. Go. Away.*

The girl manning the register returns from her break. Her shoes bounce in front of me two seconds before her big brown eyes are in my face. One of her eyebrows quirks up as she tries to understand why her boss is hiding under the counter. I hear Jason Wheeler, my freshman-year writing professor, talking on the other side of this counter.

I whisper, "Becca, if you call attention to me, I will crack your femur with my teeth."

She stares a moment, her other eyebrow rising to meet the first, before she backs up and straightens so that I only see her feet again.

"Hi, Professor Wheeler. Is that all for today?" God, she's chipper.

"Yes, thank you, love." Hearing his voice, all smooth and velvety and full of shit, makes me want to vomit. Or kick him in the balls. Or kick him in the balls and then vomit.

The register beeps as Becca scans Wheeler's items.

"Do I know you, dear?" he asks. *Here we go.*

Becca giggles. "I had you for British Literature a few years ago. I'm surprised you remember."

"You're too lovely to forget." *Hurl.* "Are you an English major?" She must nod because he says, "Excellent."

"How was your summer?" she asks, shifting back and forth on her feet.

"I spent it in London. It was wonderful. I just got back a couple of days ago."

Becca laughs in that innocuous way people do when there is nothing funny.

Wheeler mumbles something I can't quite hear before he says, "Come see me if you ever need help with anything. I'd be more than happy to assist you." *What a skeeze.*

I've known he was returning to teach here this fall, but

nothing has prepared me to see him. When I look down, I'm rubbing my wrist. I close my eyes and take a few deep breaths to regain some composure, and when I open them, Becca is crouching in front of me again.

"He's gone, although I don't know why you'd want to avoid him. He's gorgeous! I had the biggest crush on him freshman year."

"Sorry I threatened to crush your femur." Not that I actually intended to wrap my jaw around her thigh. "He and I have some bad history."

Her mouth puckers. "Oh, he gave you a bad grade, huh?"

"Something like that." *No, nothing like that.* Once my paralysis wears off, I shake my head. "Becca?"

She ducks down to look at me again.

"It wasn't because of a bad grade." I swallow, trying to ignore the lump in my throat. "He's a bad guy. He's... dangerous." I want to tell her more—I want to tell her to stay away from him—but the words don't come.

She looks at me as though I'm speaking a foreign language. A couple of girls approach the counter, their chatter breaking the uncomfortable silence.

Becca glances up at them quickly and then back down to me. "I don't know what to do with that, but okay."

Before I get a chance to explain why I'm acting like a lunatic, one of the customers asks her where to find a bedside TV remote caddy, and Becca saunters off to find the item.

I'm not sure how long I sit there trying to steady my breathing or my trembling hands. The recurring sound of an incoming text finally draws my attention: *Don't forget the Saran Wrap!*

Jenna's message reminding me of the errand I need to make is the icing on my fucked-up day.

I wait ten more minutes to be sure Wheeler is gone before I take off, but with each step, a headache pounds behind my eyes. I should go to the gym, which will help with the tension, but first I have to fill the fishbowl.

No, not with aquatic animals.

"My doctor called in some gingivitis cream," the elderly man in front of me says to the pharmacist as I wait in line at CVS.

How bad can it be to buy condoms? It's a staple, like bread or milk. So it's a little piece of plastic that covers a man's ween. I shouldn't be embarrassed, right?

Jenna realized our fishbowl of condoms was empty this morning and nearly went into cardiac arrest, and she was too slammed today to refill the stash, so I told her I'd buy them. It's Friday after all. I can't let the penis situation reach DEFCON One and leave my roommates in the lurch. No peen shall go unhelmeted on my watch.

I take a deep breath, ignoring the sweat collecting under my arms.

Ugh, it's hot in here.

What's worse than buying rubbers is I have to ask for the jumbo box behind the counter. Not the economy-sized box, but literally jumbo, so Ryan can wear them. Jenna and her boyfriend hump like sex-starved dogs in heat, and since we've heard how ginormous he is from her porno screams, I have to go the extra mile and request the Goliath of condoms.

When it's my turn at the counter, I push my shoulders back. *I'm a modern girl. I can do this.*

"I'd like the jumbo box of Trojan Magnum Extra Large." I say quietly, the words foreign on my tongue.

The pharmacist's eyebrows raise marginally as she reaches behind her for the big shiny box. *See, not so bad,* I tell myself. Until I hear the whistle behind me.

"Sweetheart, where have you been my whole life?"

I tense a second before I roll my eyes.

"Really? That's the line you're going to use?" I mumble. Barely glancing back at the two guys behind me, I reach into my bag to pull out my wallet.

"Aw, come on, sugar. Don't give me the cold shoulder. I have a thing for girls who stay well stocked." The creepy snicker behind me makes the hair on my arms stand up. "You know, if you want to check these things for quality control, I could do a fitting for you. I hear I'm an excellent specimen."

I hand money over the counter and turn around. The dude is tall and built, like body-builder big. I widen my eyes and get closer to him, batting my eyelashes like the bimbo he clearly thinks I am. I bite my lip as I check him out, taking in his broad shoulders before my eyes travel down *there*. I let out a shrill giggle, turning my eyes back up to him with a small grin.

"That's really nice of you to offer because you're *so* built."

He smiles broadly, like this is nothing new to him.

"You must lift weights every day, which must mean you have to be, um, compensating for *something*, so these babies," I say, proudly shaking my box of ribbed, lubed rubbers, "are probably *way* out of your league."

It isn't until Douchebag's friend starts cracking up that I realize the sidekick looks familiar, but he's wearing a baseball cap pulled down tight, so I can't get a good look at his face. Shit. *Where do I know him from?*

After a second, I realize I don't care and sigh at the nimrod hitting on me. He's looking a little pale, and his smile has faded. Douchebag grumbles, "Bitch," under his breath as I toss my bag over my shoulder and walk out.

I shake my head. *Someone should tell him that's not an insult. Especially if it keeps jackasses like him away from me.*

* * *

"You're high off your ass if you think I'm wearing this." I turn in front of the mirror. Jenna's skin-tight silver dress leaves nothing to the imagination. With a low back and scooped neckline, the outfit leaves me bare. "No way."

Even when I pull out my ponytail, hoping to use my long, thick hair as a shield, I'm still revealing too much.

"Aw, come on!" Jenna is in full pout mode. Her hazel eyes are wide and pleading. I immediately liked Jenna the first time we met when she told me I had broccoli stuck between my two front teeth. Girlfriends who are straight shooters are hard to come by, but I still have a hard time believing that the tissue paper delicately wrapped around my body is appropriate to wear in public.

Jenna pokes me in the shoulder. "You totally blew us off last Saturday. You said I had carte blanche this weekend. Carte. Blanche."

"Is dressing me like a streetwalker one of your goals?" My hands trail over the thin fabric, and I squirm thinking that people will see me in this outfit.

"If it makes you feel any better, you look amazing," Harper says as she flops on my bed. "Only you could pull that off. You have a killer bod. Plus, the color of the dress makes your eyes look more gray than blue."

Jenna points to Harper. "See, she would never lie. Please keep it on! You said you didn't have anything to wear. I can't return it, and it doesn't look quite right on me. I thought it looked great in the store, but when I got it home I realized that it makes my skin look green. You somehow look tan, though. I hate you. Biotch."

I can't help but laugh. But she's right—I don't have anything to wear.

Propping my elbow on my hip, I scoff. "Shut up or I'll cut you." She giggles while I crane my head around, checking out my rear in the mirror. "Well, before I go out in public like this, I have to know what our plans are."

"We're going to Ryan's for dinner, and Jax is joining us!"

Jax is my other half. We were born three minutes apart. That Jenna has managed to pry my twin away from his soccer team and his flavor-of-the-month is impressive. We haven't been close in a while, but I still try to make it to his games.

Jenna bumps me with her hip. "Then we're going dancing, and I might also have an activity planned." She has her hands clasped, and she looks like she's going to start clapping from the excitement.

"Girl, you've gone through too much trouble. I don't even like celebrating my birthday. You know this."

Her eyes bug. "You and Jax are turning twenty-one. This is huge! We're doing this right, and that means you need to look hot because it's your night."

I turn to Harper. "Are you sure I'm not going to be arrested for solicitation?"

She laughs and shakes her head.

"Fine. Let's do this."

* * *

I'm stunned by the spread of food and the fact that the house is overflowing with a weird collection of people—a few I know from work, Ryan and some of his band, and several groupies. It gets stranger when my brother and half of the Boston College soccer team saunter in. I should have worn my "friends don't let friends go to BC" t-shirt. Boston University kids take this shit seriously.

"Hey, geek," Jax says as he shakes off his date and leans over to hug me.

"Hey, loser." Hugging him back, I grin. "I haven't seen you since the Fourth of July. I thought you'd been abducted by one of your Russian supermodels."

"I wish. Been busy with soccer."

Jax reaches out to hug Jenna and Harper. After catching up for a few minutes, Jenna pushes Jax and me to a table that's set up with a dozen shots.

"We need to toast the birthday twins!" Jenna shouts, and everyone cheers.

Who are all of these people? Looking around, I see Kade, Ryan's drummer, talking to someone who looks familiar. The guy is tall, kind of rugged-looking. He's wearing a dark flannel shirt over a fitted t-shirt, and he's handsome, drop-dead gorgeous, actually. That admission has me suddenly very interested in the vodka to settle the surprising flutter in my stomach.

Jenna leans into me and grins. "I know you don't usually drink, but you're going to want to have a couple of these before we start my game."

Before last spring, I couldn't drink. Alcohol and anxiety meds don't mix. But now that I'm pharmaceutical-free, the idea of doing shots to blunt the edge of whatever humiliating game Jenna has in store for me is appealing, so I reach for a shot.

"Bring it," I say, clinking my glass with my brother's and throwing it back.

"Did Mom or Dad call you?" Jax asks as we move toward the living room, waiting for Jenna to announce whatever crazy antics she has planned for tonight.

"No." Do they ever? I think my brother keeps asking, hoping for a different answer. "Did they call you?"

"Nope. I talked to Mom a few weeks ago, and she said something about a dog show, so maybe she's out of town. And dad... Well."

It's a lovely idea, that our mother is busy traveling, but we both know that probably isn't the case. And our father is like the amputated limb we keep hoping will grow back. The truth is they're both bona-fide assholes, more interested in work and prize-winning dogs or car shows than their kids.

"I want your schedule so I can come to some of your games."

When we were growing up, I was the only one who went to see him play. Our parents never made it. He won all kinds of awards and medals and a full ride to Boston College, and our parents probably don't even know what position he plays.

"I'll email it to you." He clears his throat and shoves his hands in his pockets. "You know, uh, Daren still asks about you."

My eyes narrow. "Don't go there." He gives me a look, and I exhale in irritation. "Why do people assume I'm still in love with him?" I say under my breath. "Jax, that's history."

"Is it? Because you haven't dated anyone since."

"Could you say that a little louder? I don't think the people in the backyard heard." Turning to glare at my brother, I swirl my next shot in the glass. "He slept with my best friend after I apparently made him wait too long to have sex. Excuse me if I have some trust issues."

He cringes, but before he can respond, Jenna interrupts my tirade to announce she has something special planned for us.

"So the birthday girl has to wear this candy necklace, and she needs your help, fellas, because she doesn't get her roommates' awesome birthday gift until y'all *eat her candy*." Jenna giggles, and as the realization of what she wants me to do settles in, I decide I might need to strangle her with my bare hands. Jax looks at me and laughs as Jenna turns back to him. "The birthday boy, who some of you might know as a star soccer player from BC, has to get twenty-one kisses. Girls, if you give him a kiss, you'll need to put one of these heart stickers on his shirt or it won't count."

My brother, eager to get started with the game, spots a pretty girl and wanders off. As I turn, Kade strolls toward me with a predatory look in his eyes. *Shit.* He's going to ask me out again. When does this guy ever learn? His father owns half of the state, and he simply wants me as another acquisition.

"Clementine, you look breathtaking tonight," he says as he runs his hand through my hair. "So infinitely fuckable."

I glare at him as I swat his hand away.

"Save your breath, Kade. Haven't we had this conversation

before?" I start to walk away, but he grabs my arm so hard I think he's going to leave a bruise.

"Go out with me. I promise I'll rock your world. I've been dying to taste your *candy* all year."

Where did he learn how to talk like this? Douchebags-R-Us?

"Sorry, but we have a problem." I square myself up to him. I'm only five five so he towers over me, but I'd like to emphasize what I'm about to say. "Assholes aren't my type. And in case you missed the memo, you qualify as an asshole." With that I wrench my arm free and stalk off. God, that guy makes me want to take another shower.

As I head for the table of booze, I come face-to-face with Tall, Dark and Rugged, who has his hand in his pocket as he leans against the wall.

"I know you," I say, reaching for the Absolut as I try to place him.

"Yes, you do." *Oh, he has a sexy voice.* A small smile tugs on his lips, and I have to tear my eyes away from his mouth.

"So, can you refresh my memory? How exactly *do* I know you?"

"Darlin', you're gonna break my heart by not remembering me."

Fighting the chill that runs down my arms when he calls me darling, I shrug, turning to my shot glass, which is my new best friend. He has the slightest Southern accent. *Why am I even thinking about his accent... and his mouth... and those full lips?* I shiver, wondering where my steely resolve to avoid good-looking men has gone.

Jenna scampers up to me and grins.

"Clem, this is Murphy, Ryan's new guitarist. Murphy, this is my fabulous roommate, Clementine."

Apparently satisfied with her introduction, Jenna disappears into the crowd as my eyes pass over Mr. Hottie. I'm using the excuse of trying to figure out how I know him, but the truth is I'm honestly intrigued by how handsome he is. Dark, wavy hair, perfect sun-kissed skin, breathtaking green eyes, broad shoulders. *Wow. Wow. Wow.* I find myself licking my lips.

After a moment, I shake my head. "That's not your name."

He holds out his hand.

"That would be Gavin Murphy. It's lovely to formally meet you, Clementine."

As I return the gesture, it comes to me.

"You're an RA at Warren Towers."

He grins, and it's adorable. Dimples peek out, and I force myself not to stare. I'm starting to think that maybe coming out tonight wasn't such a bad idea, but then he opens his mouth again.

"And you buy extra-large condoms."

As the blood drains from my face, I yank back my hand. "What?"

He's laughing, and I'm ten kinds of mortified. It takes me a second to place him.

"You were with that dickhead at CVS," I croak.

He laughs. "I was actually just standing in line. I have no idea who he was except to say you have probably put him in therapy for having small junk."

I don't know if I'm feeling vulnerable because it's my birthday and this is the most alcohol I've consumed in years, but the window of possibility I initially felt toward him instantly slams shut. I narrow my eyes at him and smirk.

"Well, spare yourself the effort because I doubt you'd make the cut either," I say, downing my shot and walking off. *Asshole.*

Twenty minutes later, I'm talking to my brother on the back porch when Harper grabs me. "I need to warn you. Jenna plans to do some karaoke before we go to the club."

"Okay," I say slowly. "Jenna can't sing, so this should be fun."

"She's not the one who's going to sing. She plans to make you take the stage."

"Shit. I don't think I'm drunk enough for that."

Harper laughs as she looks around the back yard, which is littered with random partygoers. "You have a great voice, so pretend you're in the shower, and imagine everyone is naked. I mean, except for your brother 'cause that's gross."

Jax raises his eyebrows.

I laugh. "That *is* gross."

"There is nothing gross about me being naked," he says.

Harper rolls her eyes at my brother and then nudges me as she whispers, "Pretend like I didn't tell you anything because Jenna has been working really hard to make all of this a surprise. I just didn't want you to get overwhelmed."

"Thanks. This should be memorable."

Jenna must be psychic because she beelines it to us, grinning like a guilty cat.

"One more little thing up my sleeve, birthday girl!" She loops her arm through mine, dragging me back to the living room.

Out of the corner of my eye, I see Gavin talking to his friends. A tall redhead is leaning against him, laughing provocatively. She whispers in his ear as she places her hands on his sternum, and something hot churns in my chest.

He seems so at ease and confident. I bet he's the kind of guy who has it all planned out—his career, the perfect wife, a two-story Cape Cod and a Golden Retriever. He'll probably end up with someone like that girl who's all curvy and flirtatious and leggy.

When he tried to talk to me, I was my usual sweet, charming self. He made a joke, and I bit his head off. *Typical.*

Screw it. Why the fuck should I care who he talks to?

He looks up, and my eyes dart away.

"My girl Clem is going to kick off the karaoke," Jenna yells, shaking me out of my haze as she shoves a microphone into my hand. "What do you want to sing?"

I shrug and tell her to pick. *You Know I'm No Good* by Amy Winehouse starts up. I grin. She knows me so well.

As I sing, I feel his eyes on me, and when I hit the chorus, I have a fleeting surge of bravery and look his way.

That's right, Mr. Perfect. I'm talking to you. Because I'd never fit in your perfect little world.

I don't know what I expected his reaction to be, but the corner of his mouth pulls up into a crooked grin just before I look away. Suddenly, I think I'm more nervous from that one little interaction than singing for a room full of people.

When I'm done, everyone is so quiet I can hear the clock on the wall, and I'm starting to wonder if I sounded like ass when everyone starts yelling and clapping.

Damn. Maybe I should do this more often.

Chapter 4

Being jostled around does not feel good. Not. At. All.

I remember leaving Ryan's and heading to the club... and then dancing under the swirly lights... and doing more shots...

"She's hammered. Shit."

I hear people talking about me like I'm not standing here right in front of them. Okay, I'm leaning on someone, but it's pretty close to standing.

Jenna is talking, but she sounds muffled. "... I was planning to go home with Ryan, and Harper already left for her boyfriend's place. Crap. I didn't think she'd get wasted. I've never seen her drink this much."

"I can take her home," a familiar male voice says.

"Really?" It's quiet except for the ringing in my ears from the club. I'm jostled again, and then I hear the jingle of keys. "I'm trusting you not to violate my best friend or run off with her. She'd better not show up on a damn milk carton."

"Don't worry. Drunk girls aren't my thing."

The world shifts as my arm is lifted off one person's shoulders. Then I'm in the air.

"You're pretty light. Hold on, darlin'."

* * *

He smells so good. My nose is up against his neck, which is warm and smooth, and I want to snuggle.

"I never drink," I murmur against his skin. When I open my eyes, I realize we're in my living room, and I'm in Gavin's arms.

"Yeah, I can tell. Clementine, which room is yours?"

I point in what I hope is the right direction. A door opens, and then he's setting me down on the bed, and my arms are empty. The room tilts, and through my alcohol-induced fog, I realize I liked being held by him.

"Don't go. I'm cold. You're warm, and you smell good."

He chuckles as his eyes pass over me. "You sure you want me here? You gave me a serious fuck-off vibe tonight."

"I just do that. I'm broken." I fall back into my bed. He reaches over and pulls off my shoes, and I curl up as he drapes a blanket over me. The room starts to spin.

"Why do you think you're broken?"

I like his voice. It's so, so sexy.

"Because I have pieces missing."

"Where'd they go?"

That's easy. "To BC."

He laughs again and tucks a strand of hair behind my ear. "They ate all the candy off your necklace," he says softly.

"That was gross. One guy licked me. Asshole."

He's quiet, and then I hear him groan. "Clem, don't tell me about guys licking your neck." It's funny that he would care. I just met him.

"You didn't have any candy."

"I wanted some."

"Really?" I'm so tired, I can't help but yawn.

"Yeah."

After a few heartbeats, I realize what I want to tell him. "You know, they weren't for me." He's quiet. He probably hasn't a clue what I'm talking about. "The condoms were for the fishbowl."

"The fishbowl?"

I want to explain how we have a communal fishbowl of condoms, and Jenna was having a penis emergency, but the words don't come. All I can do is shiver.

"I'm cold and the spinning won't stop," I say. There's silence again, and I wonder if he's left, this beautiful man I watched all night, pretending to ignore. But the mattress sinks as he scoots into my narrow bed behind me, pressing his muscular body against my back. He reaches around my waist, and I relax into his warmth and close my eyes.

"I'm sorry I was an ass earlier," he whispers into my ear.

"What do you mean?" He's right here, but it's like we're talking in a dream. Maybe I'm asleep, and I'm dreaming, and for once in my life I can say what I feel.

"The condoms. I knew they weren't for you. Every guy on campus knows you don't date. I was, uh, trying to be funny. I didn't mean to offend you."

I don't know why, but I giggle. "No, I have one gear. It's bitch mode."

"I've never heard that before."

"That I'm a bitch?"

"No, your giggle. I like it."

The spinning starts to subside. In the darkness, Gavin's deep breaths are hypnotizing, and the rhythm steadies me.

"I remember you too." His mouth is still against my ear, and the heat from his breath makes me shiver again.

"From Warren Towers?"

"No." He fits against me, his broad shoulders pressed against my back and his arms wrapped around mine. This is nice. "Proseminar in Literature, freshman year."

I'm still really buzzed, so it takes a while to jog my memory.

"That was a long time ago and that class was huge. How do you remember me?"

He laughs, and his body moves against me. "You probably don't realize this, but you're hard to forget."

My heart flutters and my breathing hitches, and I hope he doesn't notice, but based on his small laugh, I'm guessing he does.

"Clem, don't worry. You had a lot to drink tonight. You probably won't remember this conversation tomorrow."

I somehow doubt that. But the spinning starts again.

"Gavin?"

"Yeah."

"If I do, if I do forget, will you remind me?"

The only answer I get is his arm pulling me closer to him.

* * *

When I wake up, my bed is empty, and a pang of disappointment hits me before a wave of nausea. I scramble out to the bathroom, ducking my head into the bowl just in time.

My head is pounding, and I want to crawl back into bed, but the thought of that disgusting guy at the club licking my neck last night makes me want to bathe with Lysol. I opt instead to take a shower, but I can't find shit in my room because half of my stuff is still in boxes, so I end up with a towel and a black pair of boy shorts, which will have to do until my hangover subsides long enough to sift through my things.

The shower is painful. Although it feels good to get clean, I think I might hurl again. I lean against the shower wall, shaking and weak, and let the hot water pelt me until the nausea subsides.

Did I imagine Gavin staying with me last night?

Fighting the urge to freak out, I take deep breaths. All the details I know about Gavin tumble around in my head. He's a great musician and an RA. He helps all those clueless freshmen through their first year in college. He spoons. He smells fucking amazing.

I roll my eyes at myself.

I shouldn't let myself think about him. I can't get shattered like that again.

Stepping out of the shower, I pull on my undies and dry my long hair before I wrap the towel around my chest. I wipe off the condensation and stare at my reflection. I look like shit. My eyes are bloodshot, and my skin looks sallow. I take a minute to remove the makeup that's turned me into a raccoon before I open the door to go back to my room.

Suddenly, I'm tripping over something hard. I wince at the sharp pain in my foot. That's when I look up to see three guys sitting on the couch, staring at me, in time for my towel to fall. But I'm frozen, my heart pounding in my chest as my head acknowledges that I'm okay. Just half naked.

I growl. "Who the hell put a fucking skateboard in front of a door? Are you trying to kill someone?" They're still staring at me as I grab my towel and throw it over my shoulder. Storming off back to my room, I yell, "What? It's not like you've never seen boobs before. Get over it."

I slam my door, escalating the pounding in my head.

It's almost noon. Good God, I can't believe I have to go to work today. What was I thinking? Shuffling boxes around my small room, I finally find some clothes, so I grab jeans and a t-shirt.

I hear Ryan through the walls. "Baby, don't get mad, but we saw Clem naked."

"She wasn't naked," another voice says. "Well, not entirely."

Who was out there? Ryan, Kade, and... Gavin. *Fuck.*

A few minutes later, someone taps on my bedroom door.

"Clem, honey, it's me. Can I come in?" Jenna asks, her Southern drawl lengthening around the vowels. The door creeks open, and she pokes her head in. I'm half dressed as she surveys the mess of boxes and steps closer. "Are you okay?"

I press my palm to my forehead. "Sorry I flashed your boyfriend."

She laughs softly, shutting the door behind her. "That's okay. I'm sure you fulfilled one of his fantasies just now." Jenna is so used to the groupies at his shows, nothing fazes her anymore. The only thing she cares about is that he goes home with her. "Can I get you some Advil or something?"

I nod, choking on what I want to say.

"Did, uh, did Gavin stay here last night?" I ask, afraid of the answer.

"Yeah, honey. But he swears he was a gentleman. I think he saw more when you walked out of the bathroom a minute ago than he did all night." She's laughing, and my head pounds harder, which I'm guessing is because I'm blushing a deep shade of red. "He's been really sweet. He carried you two blocks last night and tucked you in bed, and this morning he brought you some breakfast."

My heart constricts. She must see the look on my face.

"Hey," she says, reaching over and hugging me, "don't make this something it isn't. He's a great guy, and he must like you, but I don't think he's going to stalk you or anything crazy."

"That's not it." The sound of blood beats wildly in my ears.

"Can I give you some advice?" Her face is full of concern. "Don't blow him off. I know you're afraid to get close to anyone, but I think he's a catch, and good golly, he's pretty. He couldn't take his eyes off you all evening even though you were giving him your famous cold shoulder."

I press my face into my hand. "I was such a bitch to him last night. Why he'd want to have anything to do with me is—"

"How can you say that? You're a gorgeous woman and a brilliant writer. Don't be so down on yourself. Look, get dressed, and come out and have breakfast with us. I swear the guys won't give you shit about seeing you naked."

Jenna looks like she's ready to go out there and threaten their lives if they turn her into a liar. I crack a smile.

"Hey, I've been meaning to thank you for the party. You outdid yourself. Did Jax get home okay?"

She smirks. "Yeah, some model in a cherry-red Mustang picked him up from the club. I think a photo of it got posted on a gossip website."

I roll my eyes. "Sounds like my brother."

Ten minutes later, when I walk into the living room, everyone stops talking. I planned to be social and eat with my friends, but I can't. My heart is pounding, and I'm breaking out into a cold sweat. My hands tremble at my side, from the alcohol or nerves, I'm not sure which.

"I have to go to work," is all I can muster before Ryan jumps off the couch and grabs me in a giant bear hug.

"Sorry my stuff tripped you, and you flashed us your goodies, but damn, girl, you're hot. You have nothing to be embarrassed about."

I lean back and look him in the eye. "Are you always such a pig?"

"Why, yes, yes, I am." He grins, placing a small peck on my cheek. "And why the fuck am I just now learning that you sing? Jesus Christ, you have some pipes."

"Thanks. That's nice of you to say. And thank you for the party. I had a really good time."

"Watching those guys fall over themselves to eat food off your body was more than worth it. How many asked you out?"

I shrug. Who counts that kind of shit?

"Please tell me you have at least a dozen dates now." He grabs my shoulders and starts to shake me, which makes me groan. Does he have any idea what he's doing to my hangover?

"C'mon, Ryan, you know me better than that." I glance over at Gavin.

"You didn't give out your number?" Ryan asks incredulously. I shake my head. "To anyone?"

"Why would I do a thing like that?" I say, grabbing my jacket. My heart is pounding. I need to get out of here. Now.

As I reach the door, I hear footsteps behind me.

"Wait up, Clem," Gavin says. "I'll walk you out."

* * *

Each step I take reflects the throbbing in my temple.

"Here, drink this," Gavin says as he catches up to me in the stairwell. He hands me a green beverage.

I eye it skeptically. "I'm pretty sure I threw this up about an hour ago."

He laughs, unleashing one of those megawatt smiles, and it ripples through me like a tidal wave. "Trust me, it'll help the nausea." God, he has beautiful eyes. They're green, the color of a dark forest, and rimmed with thick lashes.

Snap out of it, Clem.

"Trust you, huh?" I nibble on my lip before I lean in and sniff. It smells fruity, so I take a small sip, and it tastes like apples with the slightest hint of ginger.

"Okay, this isn't bad."

Gavin's lips tug up further.

His hair is still damp from a shower, and he smells like soap. The morning stubble on his face gives his boyish smile an edge. I find myself thinking about rubbing that face against me to feel the roughness against my skin.

Oh, fuck, I need to get away from him.

I turn and start down the stairs again, and I hear his steps behind me.

Did he go home, shower and come back? I know he only lives a block away at the dorms, but still. He went through too much trouble.

"Did, uh, did you really carry me home from the club?" I ask, pausing to see his response.

He looks away a second before he shrugs. "Maybe."

Shit. I don't know what to do with him. He's all kinds of sexy and sweet, and I desperately want to pull away and hide before we can ever get close. *He didn't even try to grope me last night*, I think, and I was barely wearing anything in Jenna's skimpy dress.

I start to turn, and he touches my arm to stop me.

"I have a proposal, Clem." He sounds all businesslike, which makes me wonder what his major is. I really don't know that much about him except that he carries dumb drunk girls home and doesn't have roaming hands.

I tilt my head, curious about this proposal.

Gavin tucks his hands in the pockets of his black hoodie. "How about we go climbing on Friday at the gym and maybe grab a bite after? But just as friends because I know you don't date."

I almost laugh at the tone of his voice. He might be saying *just friends*, but that's not how he's looking at me right now.

"How do you know I climb?" BU has one of the best fitness facilities in the country, complete with one badass climbing wall that I do a couple of times a week.

He smiles again as his eyes pass over my body, sending another shiver down my back.

"You're in amazing shape, and I'd venture to say that's where you got those killer abs."

My face flushes at the memory of exactly how he saw my abs this morning, and my defenses flare up.

This is too much. He's too much. I'm going to get hurt.

But I don't want to be rude. I know I'm not myself when I'm thinking about letting a guy down easily.

"Can I think about it?"

He seems unfazed and nods.

"Sure, call me when you decide," he says as he starts walking back up to my apartment.

"I don't have your number," I blurt out.

Wait. Why would I point that out?

"Yeah, you do. Check your phone," he says with a grin as he disappears up the stairs.

* * *

Gavin Murphy programmed his number into my phone. I'm sitting at work, wondering if I should be totally flattered or freaked.

I reach for my cell and text him before I take a second to consider whether I should be communicating with him at all.

Me: *How did you know that I'd want your number? A little presumptuous, no?*

He texts me back a minute later: *How could you not? I'm a great snuggler, remember? And I didn't grope you in bed even though I really wanted to.*

Me: *Doesn't mean you're not a perv.*

Gavin: *I'm most definitely a perv, baby.*

I laugh, shaking my head as the evening crew walks in. One of the guys says, "Hey, Clem, that's quite a smile. Someone is in a good mood today."

I shake off my stupid grin and stare down the little sophomore, whose face falls.

"You're late."

Chapter 5

When my professor talks about sex, she sounds like she's purring, but since she's French, I attribute her quasi-animalistic tones to her European roots.

"You must dig deep," Professor Marceaux says as she paces the front of the classroom. "You must get to the core of what makes relationships bloom, what makes them falter, what destroys them."

Cheating. Cheating destroys relationships. Blow jobs from other girls also fall under this category. I blink, and I see an image of Daren, the one that's haunted me for years, where his face is contorted in a mixture of pleasure and pain from whatever Veronica is doing to him.

Marceaux taps the podium.

"First loves are at the core of many romance novels, so you can use your experiences, however wondrous and exciting and painful, as fodder for your manuscripts. The reader should experience the blooming of this relationship with all of its awkwardness and lust and possibly shame. You Americans seem determined to feel guilty about having sex, so explore this aspect if it's been a part of your experience. I want this to be authentic, and as this is a senior writing course, I'm sure you all have adequate personal examples from which to draw."

My experience? *Oh, fuck me now.*

Jenna nudges me and smiles.

"It'll be okay," she whispers.

Marceaux pauses when she reaches the end of the room and stares out the window. "Your semester-long assignment is to write a thirty-thousand-word novella. I want to see a fifteen-page scene by next week, starting with the first time your lovers meet. Show me their attraction, why they can't stay away from one another, and what is keeping them apart." She adjusts her glasses before she turns back to the class. "We'll separate into writing groups to critique. By the way, I can smell bullshit, so don't attempt to pawn off some dime-store romance on me. I want authentic relationships, ladies and gentlemen!"

* * *

When Harper joins me for lunch in the student union, her brows quirk up and crinkle as her watchful eyes appraise me.

"You look upset." She takes a bite of her sandwich and lets the silence settle.

We've always met here. I'd be having panic attacks over how I was going to pay for school or the fact that I thought my professor was a creeper, and Harper and I would curl up in this booth, hidden behind the decorative planter box, and she'd talk me off the ledge. Thank God she's a psych major.

I've only had one other best friend, who betrayed me in the worst possible way, and it took a long time to trust Jenna and Harper, but they never stopped trying. I don't know what they saw in me, but their friendship helped pull me out of the darkness to the point that I don't need to take anxiety meds anymore.

Exhaling a deep breath, I say, "I'm overwhelmed. I'm supposed to tutor tonight, but I have a ton of work to do on my website if I ever want to sell a second book, and people keep emailing me about how *Say It Isn't So* needs a new cover. I guess I need someone to redesign it. And I'm having trouble with my writing class."

She frowns. "Talk to Dani about the cover design. She works in the art lab, and I bet she knows people who do that stuff if she can't."

"I had no idea she was an artist." Peeling back the corner of my Peach Snapple, I realize how little I know about this girl despite having lived with her for almost two weeks. "I'm a sucky roommate."

Harper laughs as she takes a sip of her water. "But you have potential." I shake my head, feeling a little better now that I've unloaded a little. "Don't worry about the writing assignment. You've got this. You're a bestselling YA author, freak."

I don't always believe this, but every month I get statements from Amazon that prove this crazy fact. I think I'm able to sell books, not because I'm creative or original, but because I've been honest about the crazy shit that's gone down in my life. Of course, I wrap it up in a thin veneer of fiction, but my best work always originates from my own experiences. I don't need make-believe when real life is more fucked up. Especially my life.

Honestly, the whole publishing process scares the hell out of me, like with full-out nightmares or bouts of insomnia, but I want to pull up my big-girl panties and move on.

The little pep-talk voice in my head tells me I can do this without Jason Wheeler's help, and I hope that's not just wishful thinking. Because I've only finished that one book. And damn it if it wasn't in part because Wheeler encouraged me every step of the way.

I think that's why I've been struggling with writer's block. Since shit went down with Wheeler my freshman year, I've sequestered myself in a lot of ways, but keeping people at arm's length is what helped me survive. That's the trouble, though. My last two years of college have been quiet. Safe but insulated. With no drama. No cheating boyfriends. No crazy professors. No emotional breakdowns.

But I'm starting to realize that closing myself off has taken its toll. I think that's why Marceaux's assignment has been so difficult. I can write about Young Adult heartbreak because I've experienced it, but I don't know jack about adult relationships.

"Does your professor know who you are?" Harper asks, jarring me from my pensive thoughts.

"No. And I'm keeping it that way. In case I forgot to say it, you were a genius for suggesting I use a pen name. Plus, I was late for that first class, so I missed the whole 'who's been published?' conversation."

"Would it be so bad if she knew?"

My blood pressure rises thinking about that possibility.

"One, I don't want brownie points for shit I wrote three years ago. Two, you know I can't handle people reading *Say It Isn't So* and suspecting all that crap really happened to me. Besides, the fewer people who know I wrote it, the better. If this ends up in the tabloids, I'll die." I shred the napkin in front of me. "And three, it's liberating to be able to write without the scrutiny of people knowing who you are." Or at least it's supposed to be.

Her eyes are understanding. "Tell me what's been so difficult about this class."

With the move and my birthday and classes starting up, we haven't had much time to talk lately, so I unload it all. That I don't know what to write as a follow-up to my first book. That I'd better figure it out soon if I plan to pay my spring tuition. That even if I could use my romance-writing assignment for my new book, it still has to be good. Never mind that I have no fucking idea how to write an honest-to-goodness romance. One-night stands I can do because the emotions don't run deep. But love? Trust? Vulnerability? I'm not so sure I can pull that off.

"Your professor said that? You have to write about sex?" Harper asks, her eyes wide.

"No, but given the examples she's read us in class, I know that's what she's expecting. She wants *intimacy*." My heart sinks as I flick a piece of wilted lettuce from my salad. "Come on, Harper, I know shit about relationships and even less about sex."

Just talking about intimacy has me practically hyperventilating. I take a sip of water and start counting backward from a hundred like my shrink taught me.

Harper puts down her sandwich and grabs my arm, pausing me mid-gulp.

"Relax. I will cut that bitch up if she fails you."

She says it straight-faced, and I start laughing so hard that water comes shooting out my nose. My little prim and proper best friend going hood has me in hysterics, and I stop counting.

* * *

On Thursday night, I get his text: *So. How about it? Meet me at the gym at 4:30 tomorrow?*

I'd be lying if I said I hadn't been thinking about going climbing with Gavin. *Just as friends...* His words make me smile.

I'm so tired of being in hibernation mode. My friends assume I've been denying myself all this time, like I'm into some kind of asceticism, but the truth is I've been numb—numb from my parents not giving a shit about me, numb from breaking up with Daren, numb from my asshole professor attacking me. I just haven't felt anything, and when I have, it's been rage, and the only face I could put on all of this was Clem, the bitch. I can't count the number of people who have gotten in my path and felt my wrath. I'm the youngest assistant manager at my job, not just because I run the campus bookstore like a damn naval operation, but also because the kids who work for me don't want to piss me off.

When I look in the mirror, I don't like who I've become. I mean, at first this was about survival—getting to my next class, making it to work on time, living with strangers—but now that I have the basics figured out, I'm still walking around in my protective shell while life goes on around me. And while the idea of getting close to Gavin scares the living shit out of me, being near him reminds me of a time when I used to take chances and be carefree and be the girl everyone wanted to be around.

Fuck it. I go climbing on Friday mornings anyway. I'll do it in the afternoon instead.

I text him back before I have a chance to chicken out.

* * *

Usually, the smell of the locker room is strangely soothing, but right now it's making me nauseous. Turning back to my gym bag, I pull out a hot pink tank top and black spandex shorts.

Really?

I pack my clothes ahead of time, so I don't have to think about it when I'm rushing around in the morning, but now that I'm meeting Gavin in five minutes, I wish I'd given my outfit a little more thought. This is tight. And revealing.

I start to laugh. *He's already seen me half naked.* Girls scamper around here in sports bras all the time, so I guess this isn't a big deal. Besides, it's hard to climb in baggy clothes.

When I walk out, Gavin is leaning against a pillar, talking on the phone. He sees me and smiles, motioning that he'll join me in a minute. I point toward the climbing wall, and he nods.

As I strap myself into the gear, he walks up, unnerving me with one of those killer grins. *Oh, my God. Is that a chin dimple?*

"Hey," I say, trying to sound collected. "Do you want to spot me or should I ask a staff member?" My hands linger on a carabiner. I get the sense I should hug him, but that's weird. I hardly know him. Except for the spooning.

Ugh. I wish I hadn't thought about that.

Gavin raises his eyebrows and reaches over to grab my rope. He smells like citrus and sunshine, and it makes my mouth water.

"Must you ask, Clementine?"

I've never been turned on by how a guy says my name, but damn, I love how it sounds coming from him. I fight the embarrassed smile that's threatening to spread on my face and duck my head to check my gear.

He nudges me with his elbow, and I look up at him.

"It's nice to see you." His voice is scratchy and deep, and it makes me wonder what he sounds like first thing in the morning.

I swallow. "It's good to see you too."

And, oh my, it is. He's wearing thin black sweats that hang low on his hips and a dark fitted t-shirt that makes me wonder what he looks like underneath. My stomach does a few backflips when his eyes pass over me. *Clothes. I should be wearing more clothes.*

I finally break the silence because not talking is making me more nervous. "Okay, so don't drop me."

He laughs and runs his hands through his dark hair. "I carried you home, remember? I'm not going to let anything happen to you, darlin'."

If I hadn't been anxious before, I definitely am now. Being near him has my insides twisting around like I'm electrically charged.

Forty-five minutes later, I'm drenched in sweat as I rappel down the wall for the third time. I've had to battle to concentrate on what I'm doing instead of thinking that he's below me, possibly checking out my ass.

"You're a beast," Gavin says as he eyes his watch. "This last time up was your fastest. How's that possible?" He looks genuinely impressed.

"I run a lot, so this isn't a big deal. Thanks for spotting me this long. Let's swap."

When he steps into his gear, he puts his hand on my shoulder to steady himself even though there's a giant three-story structure in front of him. I stiffen at his touch, but when he looks up and smiles, I almost forget I'm uncomfortable. Almost.

As he ascends the wall, I must be boring holes into his back with the way I'm staring at Gavin's body. Every time he reaches over to grab another hold, the muscles in his arms and back bulge against his clothes. His shirt rides up, and when he turns sidewise, I can see his taut stomach descending into his sweats. *Holy delicious six-pack.*

I finally break my eyes away, embarrassed, and try to think about something constructive. Like math. I suck at math. I definitely should be more worried about math.

After I spot him for two more sprints runs up the wall, we go our separate ways toward the locker rooms and meet up after quick showers.

"You hungry?" He elbows me gently as we walk out onto the street.

"Starving."

"You want to hang out with me while I babysit the toddlers at Warren, and we'll order some pizza?"

It's Friday night, so Warren Towers will be a zoo with freshmen bouncing off the walls like spider monkeys.

"I have to work on a paper, a manuscript for my creative writing class, and I should really get started on it. I've been struggling to come up with an idea, so I don't know that I'd be good company."

He takes my gym bag out of my hands, combining the handles with his before tossing both of them over his shoulder.

"That's perfect because I have to write an article for the *Freep* that's due tomorrow, so we'll work together."

The *Freep* is the *Daily Free Press*, BU's student newspaper, which makes me realize I have no idea what he's studying. My skin prickles as I think about the tabloids that have printed articles about my brother in the past.

"Are you a communications major?" I ask as we start our trek back toward central campus.

He nods. "Double major in journalism and English. You?"

A knot forms in my stomach as I think about the irony of spending time with a reporter. Before I get a chance to list all the reasons spending time with him is a stupid idea, I remind myself that he's friends with Ryan and Jenna, and they'd never encourage me to spend time with a creep or someone they felt would jeopardize my privacy. Warm fuzzies spread in me as I think about how protective my friends are. I may give Ryan shit, but I know he'd knock out Gavin or die trying if he ever hurt me.

Remembering Gavin asked me a question, I say, "English and creative writing, which must be how we had Prosem together freshman year."

He smiles, and something in those sultry green eyes makes me want to ignore my urge to run and hide. "Creative writing? Is that why you were looking for inspiration?"

I tilt my head, confused.

"At Warren on moving day, when you were all curled up in the common room trying your hardest to ignore me."

I laugh. "Jeez, yeah, I'm sorry. I was trying to get in the zone."

"The zone, huh?" He pauses to let me walk ahead of him when we reach a narrow walkway. "Ryan tells me you're a great writer, that you've written a book and you're working on another one."

I stop mid-step as all the positive feelings I had for Ryan a minute ago take a nose dive. Ryan and his big mouth!

Letting out a humorless laugh, I shake my head. *"He's never read my work*, so I'm not entirely sure how he can say that."

I reluctantly tell him how I plan to turn whatever I write for Marceaux's class into something longer, hopefully my second book. I just leave out the part about how I need to do it to pay my bills.

"So you're actually published?" he asks as we start walking again.

I'm encouraged by the admiration in his eyes and nod slowly.

"That's really impressive, Clem."

I can't help the embarrassed grin on my face. "Thanks, but I'm kind of blocked right now. I have until Monday to figure it out because my fifteen-page draft is due on Tuesday."

He looks like he wants to say something else, but I start talking before he can ask any more questions, like the name of my book or what it's about. Thank baby Jesus for pen names.

"I've been meaning to ask you, Gavin..." I trail off, and he raises his eyebrows. "At Warren that day, why didn't you just tell me you knew me from class?"

He looks down at his feet and shrugs. "I wanted to see if you'd tell me your name."

"Okay," I say slowly. "Did you remember it?"

"Of course."

"But you asked anyway?"

"Yup."

I wait for a better response and finally nudge him. He turns toward me and grins. "I guess I wanted the challenge. Would Clementine Avery tell me her name?"

"That's stupid." I laugh, covering my mouth.

"Yeah, but you did. Now what does that say?" Gavin says as he stares at me, humor flitting behind his eyes.

I fold my arms over my chest. "That you pestered me until I gave in."

He barks out a laugh. "Damn. I thought you were going to say I was so charming you couldn't help yourself."

"Well, there's that." I smirk, and he gently elbows me back.

When we get to his dorm, freshmen are stumbling in and out through the double doors.

"C'mon," he says, like he's not giving me a choice. "Let's go find you some inspiration, and maybe you can peer-pressure me into doing my article."

"Did you just use peer pressure as a verb?"

"God, you make me hot when you talk grammar."

I laugh because he's being so stupid and adorable. He smiles, wrapping his arm around my shoulder and pulling me toward the dorm.

Chapter 6

When we exit the elevators, I'm taken back three years. The smell of expensive perfumes and beauty products permeate the air as half-naked girls scamper from room to room, squealing about their plans to go bar-hopping or pick up guys. One spots Gavin and smiles before she sees me and darts off. The guys' hallway is quiet in contrast.

Gavin walks to his room, the first one on the right after the elevators, seemingly oblivious to the frantic pace of what's happening on the girls' side of the floor.

His door has his hours of availability posted, along with a dry-erase board that has a message written in neon pink that says, "I heart Gavin." I smirk at it before I can stop myself. He sees the note and rolls his eyes and rubs it off with his elbow. Following in behind him, I'm grateful he leaves the door open.

His room smells like him, like fresh laundry and some kind of sexy-ass shower gel. He drops our bags into the chair at his desk.

"Your room is pretty neat for a guy's." Eyeing him curiously, I'm more than intrigued about what else I'm going to learn about him tonight. His desk is organized: a laptop, several reference books, a giant mug of pens, and a board with notes and concert tickets pinned across it.

I get a good look at that coffee cup. It reads, "The past, the present, and the future walked into a bar. It was tense." I try not to laugh. *Oh my God. He's a geek who jokes about verb tenses.*

"Can I get you something to drink?" Gavin pulls out two bottled waters from his micro-fridge and starts to hand one to me, but when I reach for it, he doesn't let go. Instead, our fingers stay coiled together. He stares at me, those dark lashes fanning across his tanned skin, and his close proximity sends a spark through me like fire raging through a forest after a drought. My head twists up to look at him, and he smiles devilishly before he lets go and brushes past me.

Uh, make that a hot geek.

As I attempt to dislodge my heart from my esophagus, I continue assessing his room. Several instruments sit propped against the wall, and I find myself staring at one that looks like a miniature guitar.

"That's a mandolin," he says, picking it up and strumming a few chords.

I listen to the soft melody for a few minutes. "It's crisper than a guitar."

"Yeah. It is."

Chewing on my lip, I make a mental note of the differences in the instruments. "It reminds me of... Actually, never mind. It's stupid."

I start to turn away, and he stops playing.

"Tell me." He looks genuinely interested. My lips twist briefly as I consider what I want to say.

"It reminds me of the end of *The Outsiders.*" His eyebrows raise, prompting me to continue. "After Johnny dies, and Ponyboy finds his letter that tells him to stay gold, like the sunset they saw while they were hiding out. That's like the mandolin. Golden." I pull on the end of my ponytail, eager to find something for my hands to do.

When I glance at him, I can't quite make out what passes behind his eyes, but it makes me nervous, big-lump-in-my-belly nervous. I swallow and make a concerted effort to breathe.

"Your room is very nice, Mr. Murphy. I'm impressed with your organization, especially since you just moved in." I'm relieved to regain my ability to speak.

"I was here all summer interning at the *Boston Globe,* so I couldn't move back home."

An internship before his senior year. Impressive.

"Where's home?" I ask.

He puts the mandolin back. "Connecticut."

"But that's not where you're from." I keep hearing it in my head, the Southern way he says darlin'.

One side of his mouth slants upward in a half smile. "I grew up in Austin, Texas, but we moved when I was eight. How did you know I wasn't from New England?"

"Lucky guess," I say, not wanting to divulge how closely I've been paying attention to him. "Are both parents back there?"

"Yeah, they're teachers," he says, answering my next question before I ask it.

"Still together?"

"Yup, and still in love. It's sweet. And kind of disgusting. They still make out like teenagers."

I laugh at the embarrassment in his face and wonder what it would be like to have parents who actually like each other.

"Where are you from?" He hands me my bag.

"Nowhere exciting. Lexington." A whole forty-five minutes away.

"So you must get home a lot."

"No, never," I say as I peruse the books in his shelves. He has several biographies of famous journalists, a book on Watergate, a lot of classics. Spotting a couple of F. Scott Fitzgerald titles, I smile to myself, but then my heart seizes up when I see a half dozen black Moleskine journals standing at attention. God, this guy is perfect.

"Really?" He looks at me quizzically as he takes off his sweatshirt, which makes his black t-shirt rise, revealing that tantalizing six-pack. I avert my eyes so I don't stare at his bare, muscular stomach with that sexy V that makes me stupid.

I clear my throat. "Haven't been home in three years. Jax goes back, but my mother has a soft spot in her soulless black heart for him."

He's watching me, gauging whether or not I'm joking. He must realize I'm not.

"Are you and your brother close?"

Fighting the urge to shut down at the personal question, I make myself answer.

"We're twins, so I guess we are by default from sharing the same uterus for nine months. He's kind of busy with soccer and girls, so we don't hang out much, but I try to go to his games."

Gavin frowns for a second. "It must be hard being an Avery. There must be a lot of pressure."

So he does know who I am.

I mean, of course he does. He's a reporter. He probably thinks I'm some little rich girl.

I wait, wondering if he'll turn on me and want something because that's always what happens, but he actually looks concerned, like he cares about my wellbeing. Something inside me relaxes, and I shrug.

"It's just a last name. It's not like I'm at the helm of my family's corporation or ever will be. No thanks." If my mother had it her way, I'd be trotting around like a prized pony, wearing something from her fashion line and whoring myself out to the cameras.

Looking to change the subject, I ask, "Are you an only child?" Something about how responsible he seems tells me he's either an only child or the oldest.

"No, I have a little sister who's a senior in high school."

He goes over to his desk as he reaches into his pocket for his phone. He motions for me to grab a seat, so I sit at the edge of his bed.

"What article are you working on tonight?" I ask.

His eyebrows furrow. "A follow-up on Olivia Lawrence, the BU student who disappeared this summer."

It's been one of the biggest news stories on campus all fall.

"I've read those. They're kind of intense. You wrote them?"

"Yeah."

They've been headlining articles since school started. Some have explored theories that she was abducted or possibly drowned in the Charles River. Others have been about her home life and family. One was about the new self-defense classes that started as a result of her disappearance.

I wait for him to say something, maybe brag about how he's on the front page constantly, but he doesn't.

Finally, he sighs. "I've been writing for the *Freep* since the first week of my freshman year, and I've never hated working on a story more."

He grabs a binder out of his bag and rearranges a few things on his desk. "It kills me to have to interview her friends and family. It's so intrusive." He stills, and his shoulders slump. "That part of the job has never bothered me before, but having her mom fall apart on me every time I see her breaks my heart."

Even though I haven't known him long, I want to take him into my arms and comfort him.

"But maybe your coverage will help find her. Maybe something you write will bring her home."

He takes a deep breath and looks up at me with a sad smile that tells me I'm being overly optimistic.

I pull out my journal and a pen from my bag, and I search for something to lighten the mood. Motioning to his guitar, I ask how long he's been in Ryan's band.

"Since June." He motions toward me. "You have a killer voice, by the way."

I stare at him and blink.

"You sang at your party." He says it slowly, almost like a question.

"Oh, that." I shrug. "I sing in the shower..." My voice trails off as I remember tripping and dropping my towel and flashing him my goodies last weekend.

Trying to distract myself from that embarrassing memory, I stare out the window. His room faces the middle tower of dorms, but because he's on the northernmost side of the building, he has a stunning view of the river that runs parallel with the campus. The dark swath of water is calm tonight as it laps against the banks. I love running along the Charles. If I don't climb, that's where I head to unwind, to pound my frustrations and fears into the pavement while the wind whips through my hair.

Gavin orders pizza, and he muffles the phone to ask my preference of toppings.

"Pepperoni and mushrooms?" I ask, unsure of what he likes.

He winks back and places our order. *Damn it, he's cute.*

"You can take off your shoes if you want, sprawl out, get comfortable. I usually write at my desk," he says as he hangs up.

"Are you sure?"

He nods, like he really doesn't care that I'm lounging on his bed. *Okay.* I kick off my shoes and scoot back until I'm leaning against the wall. Thankfully, I just showered, so I'm sporting clean socks. I start doodling in my journal while Gavin flips through some notes and opens his laptop.

After half an hour, the phone rings and he heads downstairs to get our food. A minute later, I hear a soft knock.

"Are you Murphy's girlfriend?" a peppy little voice asks.

A cute blonde girl in boxer shorts and a t-shirt is leaning in the doorway. She looks at me sideways and repeats her question.

"I, uh... we're friends."

She looks at me like I didn't say something right.

I clear my throat. "I'm Clem."

"Because he said he had a girlfriend, like a serious one he's been dating for a few years, and you're *gorgeous*, like the kind of girl I imagined he'd date. But you're saying that's not you?"

I shake my head.

"Huh. Maybe he's dating that tall redhead." Her eyebrows scrunch briefly before she bounds off with her tidbit of gossip.

Who's the redhead? That girl from my birthday party? I hadn't asked Gavin if he was seeing anyone, but Jenna was trying to introduce us, and I know she'd never waste her time if she thought he was dating someone.

"Why are you frowning?" Gavin walks in with a pizza box and soda.

"I didn't realize I was. One of the girls came by looking for you, but I didn't catch her name." I describe her to him, but he seems distracted by the food.

"If it's important, she'll come back."

I want to ask him the question, but my heart is doing all kinds of crazy acrobatics in my chest. I should get this over with because if he has a girlfriend, what the hell am I doing here? I mean, he said "just friends," and okay, he's a cool guy, and we could be friends, but fuck.

"You're doing it again." He's standing there, frozen, with a paper plate in each hand.

"What?"

"Frowning. It's kind of cute, actually. Unless there's something wrong."

"No, nothing's wrong."

Play it cool, Clem. I've been warming up to the idea of Gavin all week, but I'd be lying if I said this wasn't throwing me in reverse so fast I might get whiplash. But the chill settling over me helps to clamp down on my emotions.

I motion toward the hall. "She mentioned your girlfriend,

which makes me wonder if I met her the other night at the party and didn't realize it."

He grins so wide it catches me off guard. *Okay, that's not the reaction I was expecting.*

"I tell the kids I have a girlfriend so they leave me alone."

I'm so relieved, I want to laugh. He's still grinning like an idiot. "What?"

"You. You were jealous." He's looking at me like he knows exactly what I was thinking, and I want to crawl under his bed. Maybe even under the building.

"No, I wasn't. We're *just friends*, remember?" Throwing his own words back at him, I smile coolly.

I don't think he believes me.

"Here. Eat up," he says, ignoring what I said and handing me a plate of pizza. "You need to replenish after kicking my ass on the wall today."

"Whatever. I think you held your own." I reach for a slice and take a bite. My stomach is growling. I glance out the window again, mesmerized by the lights of the city and the dark river below. That's when it hits me.

"So do girls hook up with their RAs?" I turn to look at him. His eyes are wide, and I realize maybe he thinks I'm insinuating he's done this, so I shake my head before he misunderstands. "Because that would make for an interesting story. A freshman girl who falls in love with her RA, but they can't be together, so they sneak around."

"Oh, um, yeah," he laughs. "It happens. Obviously, it's not supposed to, but it's not illegal or anything. The girls in Warren are eighteen or older. But it's definitely scandalous when it does go down."

I drop my pizza and open my journal to a fresh page and start writing.

Forty-five minutes later, I'm still at it. I'm lying on his bed with his pillow tucked under my chest as I lean forward to scribble down ideas. Finally, after I've jotted down all of my initial thoughts, I close my book and curl up. I haven't written like that in so long. I feel weightless and a little buzzed from the euphoria of breaking through and being able to write again.

Gavin is sitting at his desk, but he's turned his chair around and is staring at me. Why is he staring at me?

"Was that the zone?" he asks.

"Hmm?"

"I think you were in the zone. I asked you at least five things, at which point you mumbled something back that was completely incoherent."

I grin. "Yeah, that was the zone. Sorry, I didn't mean to ignore you. Sometimes I'll write all night if I'm on a roll." Seeing my uneaten pizza, I groan. "No wonder I'm famished." I take a few bites. "Have I told you how much I love pizza?"

He seems happy that I'm eating, and I'm so thrilled to be writing again, I have a hard time not smiling around a mouthful of food.

"So now you have your idea, and you're all set."

Sighing, I pull off a mushroom and pop it in my mouth. "I wish. This is a romance novel-writing class. I've been writing Young Adult. They're different." I roll my eyes at myself, my good mood tempered by how difficult this has been for me.

"So you throw in a few kisses." He laughs, and I know he's joking.

I need to choose my words carefully. I could sound all kinds of stupid if I don't.

"My professor wants us to draw on our own relationships, and that's not exactly my forte."

I look away before I can see his reaction. *Why am I telling him this?*

"But you've been in a relationship before, right?" he asks hesitantly. Before I can respond, he shrugs. "I'm sure you could pull it off."

Groaning, I take another bite. "Theoretically, that's true. But my one significant relationship did not have a happy ending, and I don't date. You know this about me." I tear apart a piece of crust. "Based on the examples we're reading, Professor Marceaux wants hot sex and a happily ever after. I don't do either."

The minute the words are out of my mouth, I regret saying them. Shit. I glance over, and he's grinning. Then he cracks up laughing.

"Clementine, you surprise me. No one ever surprises me anymore."

I look down, embarrassed.

He clears his throat. "Well, if it means anything, I think you could pull both off."

"Pull what off?"

"Hot sex and the happily ever after," he says with a wink.

* * *

Something is warm against my chest, and I have my arm wrapped around a body pillow that's so snuggly, I think I moan.

Wait. I don't have a body pillow.

I'm exhausted, and it takes a few seconds to open my eyes. When I do, I see a blue flannel shirt.

I am wrapped around Gavin's body with my arm over his chest and my thigh over his. And what a body it is. In my early-morning haze, all I can think about are his hard pecs underneath me, and I really want to run my hands down over his abs.

Oh, God.

It's not that I mind being with him because he's fucking hot, but I have no idea how I ended up in the nook of his arm with my head on his chest. I can't get up, though, because the bed is so narrow that my back is against the wall. Glancing around the room, I'm relieved when I see the clock. It's still early.

I try to disentangle myself without waking him, but he sighs deeply and stretches.

"Hey, good morning," he says like finding me in his bed is normal.

"Hi." What do I say? *Thanks for the pizza and the snuggle, but I gotta go?* No, that doesn't sound right. I decide to be direct. "Gavin, how did I end up wrapped around you like a human pretzel?"

He chuckles against me. I'm glad someone is amused.

"You fell asleep, and damn, girl, you're a sound sleeper." His voice is deep and scratchy and pretty damn sexy. He stretches again, his hard muscles flexing beneath me, and yawns. "I tried waking you up, twice, but then I gave up and rolled you over. As for being wrapped around me, I think it's because I'm irresistible. You couldn't resist even when you were practically in a coma." His eyes close, and he's wearing a self-satisfied smile.

My cheeks flame, and I shake my head. Why am I always embarrassed around this guy? It's not like we had sex or anything. We're fully clothed.

A nervous laugh escapes me. "It's good to see you're embracing your modesty this morning, but I have to get to work by nine."

I start to sit up, but he grabs my arm and pulls me back to him, turning and snuggling into me.

"Has anyone ever told you that you look really cute in the morning, especially when you're embarrassed? And God, you smell good." He buries his face in my neck, his breath hot against my skin, and goose bumps break out on my arms. "You want to go for a run with me later this weekend? Maybe tomorrow evening? I'm thinking I might be able to kick your ass, but I'd like to be sure."

Laughing, I say, "You need to be careful what you wish for."
And clearly, so do I.

* * *

Sneaking up the stairs to my apartment wearing yesterday's clothes gives me a moment of pause. *Maybe everyone is still asleep.* I turn my key quietly and open the door to find Jenna and Harper.

"Thank God you're okay," Jenna yells as she rushes toward me, enveloping me in a hug.

Harper watches me with a raised eyebrow. "Do my eyes deceive me or are you doing the morning-after walk of shame?"

"Ha, Harper, ha!" I pry Jenna's arms off me and ignore the heat rising to my cheeks. "Yes, I stayed at Gavin's but only because I fell asleep on his bed, and no, we didn't have sex."

Jenna, who was looking so hopeful at the mention of Gavin's name, deflates like a balloon. "There I was thinking he had popped your cherry."

"Jesus, you're getting as bad as Ryan." Jenna likes to think of me as some kind of born-again virgin. "Yesterday we went climbing, and then we did homework. That's it."

"When are you going to give us some juicy details?" Jenna is pouting. "That boy is too delish for words, and this is all you have for us?"

"I thought you were madly in love with Ryan. Why are you scoping out Gavin?"

She cocks her head toward me, her messy ponytail hanging sideways. "Holy shit. You're jealous!" Jenna giggles like a fool.

The bedroom door behind her opens, and Dani, our youngest roommate, stumbles out. Her thick, dark hair is twisted up into a bun. Hot pink tips stick out in a crazy disarray from her hair tie.

"What's going on?" She rubs her eyes as she surveys the three of us. "Hi, Clem."

"Hi, Dani. Sorry we woke you." I take off my jacket and reach into the mini-fridge for some OJ before I turn back to my audience. "As much fun as this has been, I have to go to work. I've been meaning to ask if you guys still have any textbooks you need. I have to buy them to get my discount, but you can pay me back."

Dani looks suddenly very awake, but she stays quiet.

"Jenna? Harper?"

They shake their heads. I turn to Dani, who is fidgeting. She obviously wants something. I feel bad that I've hardly uttered two words to her since we've met. I should be friendly even though it's not one of my noteworthy qualities.

"Dani, what do you need? Write it down, be specific, and include your cell number on it, so if I have any questions, I'll call you, okay?"

She gives me a shy smile and nods.

After a quick shower, I get dressed and come out to find Dani's note with a list of three textbooks.

"Hey," Harper says over my shoulder, "that was nice of you to help Dani. A little unlike you, but nice. Clementine Avery, I think you're showing your soft underbelly."

"Shut up. I'll shank you in the kidney if you tell anyone about this."

Harper's laughter bursts through the apartment.

"Here I was thinking you'd gone soft."

Maybe I have.

Chapter 7

One thing is clear. This is a terrible idea.

I stare at Gavin's text: *Run with me tomorrow. I'll even let you beat me.*

Running is too personal. It would be like doing our laundry together when we only just met. Working out like that—side by side, measuring our strides to match one another and finding that perfect pace—is more bonding than I'm ready for.

Distance. I should create some distance.

I decline his offer. I even include a smiley face so I don't sound bitchy, which frustrates me more because he has me using emoticons like a twelve-year-old.

After a long shift at work, made longer by random thoughts about Gavin, I try to buckle down and write, and although I have an outline, my characters don't feel right. I'm missing something. I might be able to eke it out if the teaching assistant grades my submission, but once we get into critique groups, my peers will tear this up. Never mind that this will never cut it as material for a full-blown novel.

I'm so frustrated that I go for a jog. It's dark outside, and I know it's not smart to go alone, but my roommates are out, and I have too much pent-up energy. The moon is bright, and the sky is clear. I blast music and run until I'm numb.

As I slow to a walk when I reach my block, a flyer for Olivia catches my eye. Glancing up and down my street, I try to ignore the creepy sensation that I'm being watched and hustle to my apartment.

* * *

The next morning, Harper pokes her head into my room. "We're headed to Ryan's later. Want to come and do some laundry with me? Jenna is going to show Dani how to make those awesome grilled cheese sandwiches."

"Ryan doesn't mind that we use him for his washer?" Glancing at my overflowing hamper, I know I should take advantage of the offer.

"As long as we bring his girlfriend, I don't think he cares."

I agree, packing one load of dirty clothes along with my laptop and journal so I can work. Dani and I pile in the back seat while Harper drives, and Jenna takes shotgun. Harper mentions my book cover problem to Dani as we cut through campus.

"You don't need a designer. I can do a cover for you," Dani says as she roots around in her purse for some gum.

"Really? Because I suck at that stuff. Do you think you can track down a stock photo for it? Oh, and do you know anyone who designs websites? Mine is in serious need of a facelift."

She unwraps the gum and pops it in her mouth. "I could take some pics for you, and I definitely have friends who could do your website."

"That would be huge! I will totally pay you for the work you do on my cover."

Dani shakes her head like the idea offends her. "No way. You're my roommate. It's, like, against the code or something."

I glance at Jenna in the front seat, who nods like I'm an idiot for not knowing that Dani is so cool.

"Okay, if you're not going to take my money, let me buy you some art supplies 'cause I know that shit is expensive."

Dani smiles and offers me some gum. "Deal, but I want to read your book. Jenna says you're a great writer."

I kick Jenna's seat in front of me, and she gives me the finger. I chew my lip as I think about it.

"All right, but you're sworn to secrecy. I write under a pen name, and I don't want that getting out. And when I say secrecy, we're talking blood oath or I get your first child."

Dani laughs but agrees, and we brainstorm different cover concepts. Ten minutes later, I'm feeling better about life.

"This is so huge, Dani. Thank you. My publicist has been on my ass to redo my cover and website for ages."

Her eyes widen. "Wow, you have a publicist?"

"Since I'm an indie—I'm not with some big publishing company—I pay her by the service she provides, but she's really good at getting blogs to review my book and helping me get traffic on my blog so people can read excerpts from other things I'm writing." *Like half-written books.* I scowl at my inner cynic and return my attention to my roommate.

Dani and I talk non-stop until we reach Ryan's, and then we each grab a load of laundry and trudge across the yard. As I amble up the steps to Ryan's two-story house while trying to balance a basket of dirty clothes on my hip, the music hits me first—the Notre Dame fight song and cheering.

"Jenna," I say slowly, "what game is on today?"

Her eyes widen as she processes why I'm asking.

"Oh, I think it's Notre Dame and Stanford." She smiles back reassuringly, but my heart is still racing. At least I'm not in full panic-attack mode. Those used to strike all the time for almost no reason at all. But I'm tired of Daren still qualifying as a reason.

When we walk in, Ryan comes up and plants his face on Jenna's.

"Get a room," I say as I push past them.

"That's actually a great idea," Ryan says, laughing.

"You two are like drug addicts. It's too early in the day for tongue."

"Clemster, it's never too early for tongue. See, that's why we need to get you a boyfriend."

"If you weren't dating my best friend, I'd take out your spleen for calling me that. Furthermore, I am not a tongue-in-front-of-my-friends kind of girl."

Jenna pushes him off, giggling, and we drop our laundry in the hall. When I get to the living room, I'm surprised to see my brother.

"Hey, loser." He gets up, and I hug him. "What are you doing here?"

Jax is always busy. I didn't think he socialized with guys other than his teammates.

"Ryan invited me over last weekend, so I thought I'd stop by. Heard you girls were making lunch."

"You came for the free food. That makes sense."

He grins and sinks back down into the couch. The rest of Ryan's band is here, including Kade the douchebag, which is his official name in my book. I turn and almost run into Gavin, who's coming from the kitchen with a beer in his hand.

"Hey," I say, surprised to see him.

Gavin smiles and gives me a hug. He does this like we're old friends. I've never really thought much about hugs, but holy shit, this one feels good. I'm immediately flooded with thoughts of those washboard abs. As I press my face to his chest, he smells all kinds of yummy.

He whispers, "You left your Classical Lit notes at my place the other night. If I had known you were coming, I'd have brought them."

That's thoughtful. Butterflies swirl in my stomach like drunk sailors.

I lean back so I can see his face. He hasn't shaved this morning, and his jaw is scruffy. Damn, he's even hotter like this.

"I didn't notice I'd lost them. Thanks for mentioning it."

We're talking, but he hasn't let go of me. *Is this weird?* I still have one hand on his hip, and he has one arm around my shoulder. But friends hug, right? I mean, I just hugged my brother. Oh, but this is so *not* like hugging my brother. Gavin's all warm and sexy, making me think about waking up nestled against him yesterday morning with my thigh wrapped around his.

As my resolve to stay away from him takes a nosedive, I'm suddenly aware that everyone is watching us. Panic rips through me, and I pull back, mumbling something about food and laundry and who knows what else.

I dart into the kitchen as Jenna and Dani start lunch, so I wash my hands and get out the supplies to help them. We bump around in a comfortable silence until Kade starts yelling.

"Clem! Come here!"

I hate Kade even more now that he's seen my nipples. I don't have a clue why he would need to speak to me, but I wander into the living room anyway. The guys are watching the half-time show, which features a preview of next weekend's BC game.

"Isn't this your boy?" Kade asks as a picture of one very attractive Daren Sloan, star quarterback, pops up.

I don't know who thought it was a good idea to explain my connection to Daren, but obviously someone has. The segment features Daren's recent engagement to his "high-school sweetheart" Veronica. I can't help but laugh.

Kade pokes me, and I contemplate breaking that finger.

"Clem, aren't you jealous? You could've married the guy who is probably going to be the number-one draft pick."

I'm almost positive that Kade is going to hell, a thought that nearly puts a smile on my face.

Trying to stand tall, I do my best to seem unaffected. "If Veronica giving him blow jobs our senior year while he was dating me qualifies her as a sweetheart, then I'm a little mistaken about what that word means. And for the record, I've never regretted breaking up with him." I feel blood pumping through the veins in my neck. "He still sends me tickets to his games. I bet Veronica doesn't know that little detail. So really, they're perfect for each other."

Jax looks irritated. "He's never told me he sends you tickets."

"He's your best friend. Maybe you should ask him about it." I turn on my heel and head down to the laundry room. *Breathe. Breathe.*

* * *

My hands are still shaking ten minutes later as I start the load of whites. Or I'm trying to start the machine, but the button is stuck.

"Here. Let me help." Gavin reaches over my shoulder and does this weird twisting motion to the switch, which makes the machine magically start. I must be out of it because I didn't hear him come down the stairs.

"How did you know to do that? Do you do laundry here a lot?"

He's still standing in my personal space.

"No, I don't do laundry here, but it's my house, so I have to deal with the appliance problems."

What?

He sees the confusion on my face and smiles. "It's my grandmother's house, or it was until she died a few years ago. My parents gave it to me, but since I have to live on campus, I rent it out. That's how I met Ryan."

"Oh, that makes sense."

His eyes tighten and his head tilts.

"Are you okay? I'm sorry Kade is being a dick."

He runs his hands through his thick, black hair, and it's going every which way but still somehow looks great.

"I'm fine." Although Kade *is* being a bigger douchebag than usual. "I'm just not used to talking about Daren with anyone, so I'm surprised he knew."

Gavin sighs and rubs his chin. "He's going through some rough stuff right now."

Because I don't care what Kade is going through, I shrug.

He motions toward me. "That sounded kind of intense, what you said about Daren cheating on you."

I nod, not really knowing how much I want to tell him, especially since he's a reporter. But he wouldn't write about something as stupid as my nonexistent love life, would he? Not when he covers serious topics?

He senses my hesitation and pulls me into a hug. "You don't have to talk about it if you don't want to."

Breathing in the scent of his clothes makes something in my heart ache. "There's not much to say. It happened a long time ago." I step back and look up at him warily.

He smiles back and nods. "Okay, well, lunch is ready, and Jenna said to get your ass up there."

We start to walk back upstairs when he nudges me. "You wanna go climbing again on Friday?"

I don't know if it's his easy smile or the fact that he didn't pressure me to tell him more about Daren, but it makes me want to trust him, so I tell him yes.

Chapter 8

The corner convenience store is crammed with students hustling to get to class.

"I'll have a cinnamon raisin bagel, light cream cheese and small coffee," Jenna says, handing the guy behind the counter a ten.

"A banana and coffee." I drop the piece of fruit into my messenger bag and hand over some cash.

"I hate Mondays," I grumble, tired from spending half the night revising the copy on my website. Gagging in the aftermath of the sorority girls who walk by, I wave my hand in front of my face and whisper to Jenna, "And biatches who wear too much perfume."

Jenna elbows me in agreement. "And girls who over-pluck their eyebrows so they always look surprised."

Laughing, I link my arm through hers, and we make our way out onto the sidewalk and wait for the light to change.

I scrunch my face in disgust. "I hate sauerkraut and yappy dogs."

"Yes! And thong wedgies because even though that scrap of fabric is supposed to be up there, it ain't supposed to be *up there.*"

I try not to choke on my coffee as she lowers her voice and cocks an eyebrow.

"And I hate used condoms. The way they sit there all deflated and judgmental, like little reminders of the dirty sex you had the night before."

I snort before I get a chance to cover my face. "Jesus, Jenna."

We trudge across Commonwealth Avenue with the hordes of other students, and we're about to make our way to the Liberal Arts Building when I hear a familiar voice in the distance. Before I realize what I'm doing, I yank Jenna behind a thick row of hedges. She squeals as her knees sink into the moist dirt, and her coffee tumbles to the ground.

"Shhh!" I put my finger over her lips as we huddle like escaped criminals behind a bush.

Over the shrubbery, I hear their steps. The girl's giggle precedes her high-pitched voice. "Thank God you liked my submission. I was so worried it sucked."

"It is simply breathtaking, love. I'm confident you'll be able to publish it, but we can talk about it more after class, perhaps over lunch." His voice wraps around me like a python constricting. I close my eyes as I try to catch my breath.

I wait several minutes so I can be sure they're gone, and then, like a little gopher in one of those arcade games, I pop my head up over the shrubbery to survey the scene.

Satisfied the coast is clear, I inhale several times in relief before I extend my hand down to my roommate who has a *What the fuck was that?* expression on her face.

"I'm so sorry, Jenna! I heard Wheeler's voice and reacted. I didn't mean to shove you into the mud."

She pats me on the back. "You haven't seen him yet?"

"Not face to face, and I'm wondering if I can go the whole year without any meet-and-greets. I already had a close call at the bookstore. Do you think I stand a chance of avoiding him until graduation?"

Her mouth twists as she contemplates my question. She shakes her head. "That dog doesn't hunt."

I stare at her and blink. I *think* she means no.

There's nothing like Jenna's Southern wisdom, but that wasn't the answer I was looking for.

* * *

When the week starts with leaping behind shrubbery, I know I'm in trouble. I fumble through the next few days, sleeping through my morning alarms and running late to classes and work. No matter how much coffee I drink or attempts I make to plan my schedule, I can't seem to get my act together. Wheeler's presence anchors me like lead, and I find myself always looking behind me, worrying if I'm going to see him again.

So all I can mumble as I stare at the red scribble in the margins of my assignment is, "It figures."

A C? Marceaux gave me a C?

"I got a better grade on this than you?" Jenna snatches my submission for our romance-writing class, and the delight on her face is unmistakable. I shoot her a dirty look, and she sticks out her bottom lip like she's sad, which I know is complete bullshit.

"Yeah, it's official now. I'm a loser." I knew this wasn't right when I wrote it.

After flipping through the pages, Jenna sighs. "Her comments are pretty intense."

Harper, who has been half listening to our conversation, shuffles out of her room and drops onto the couch. "What did Marceaux tell you?"

"That my writing feels stilted and repressed. That I need to loosen up." I could have told her that. "But she's not half as tough as our critique groups will be."

Harper frowns. "That sucks."

"I'm just not feeling it."

Jenna jumps up and bolts into her room, calling out, "I have a great idea!" She returns with her phone, and a second later my cell buzzes.

I glance down at my screen. "Jenna, why are you texting me when you're three feet away?"

She smirks. "We're going to play Out-Skank."

"I'm sorry. What?"

"We're gonna help you talk about sex. The point of the game is to see who can out-skank the other. Harper and I are going to send you dirty texts, and you have to write us back."

"Where do you come up with this?" I'm shaking my head as I read her text out loud: *I want you to touch my man-slinky.*

Man-slinky?

I look up at Jenna and Harper, and the three of us crack up.

"You have to write me back. Or else." Jenna waves her phone at me with a grin.

I roll my eyes.

I've never sexted, so I don't know where to begin. Jenna has probably had tons of practice with Ryan. *Gross.*

Finally, I return the message.

Jenna reads it out loud: *I would touch your man-slinky, but I don't like jangly parts.*

She looks up at me and laughs. "What?"

"Jangly. Penises are jangly," I say as though this should be obvious. "They jingle and jangle. I mean, unless they're erect. Ew. There's a lovely word for you. Erect."

"Hey, don't knock it," Jenna says. "Speaking of jingle and jangle, at Christmas I should sell mistletoe for the peen. Bet I'd make a killing."

"You have a serious problem. I think you're obsessed with your man's junk."

Jenna laughs before turning a serious shade of red. "Not as obsessed as he is with my girl parts. That boy is great at oral."

Harper and I groan. I'm too embarrassed to say I've neither given nor received in the oral department. I am admittedly out of my league here.

"Maybe he could give Jonathan a few lessons," Harper says under her breath.

At least I'm not the only one with issues tonight.

* * *

After the climbing wall on Friday—where I don't tumble to my death, offering some hope that perhaps I've broken my streak of bad luck—Gavin and I grab some Thai and head back to his dorm room to work. We're having a conversation about his journalism class, but all I can think about is how his t-shirt kept riding up while he was climbing, showing off that sexy-as-hell six-pack. And that little treasure trail leading south...

"You listening?" he asks as we reach his room.

"Oh, sorry, I was thinking about this horrible grade I got." Lie. Lie. Lie. But I *have* been obsessing about that stupid assignment for the last twenty-four hours, so that might absolve me from being a total lunatic.

When we reach his room, I lament about my professor's comments.

"Can I read it?" he asks, holding the door open for me. Shit. I never let anyone read my drafts except under extreme duress, like threats from professors or overly nosey roommates. He lifts his chin. "C'mon. I'm a writer. Maybe I can help."

"I don't know." I raise an eyebrow. "You're not in my circle of trust yet."

Gavin pretends to be in pain as he clutches his chest. "Ouch. And after we've slept together? Clementine, you're hurting my feelings."

"Shut up." I smack him in the shoulder.

He tilts his head down, staring at me through those dark lashes, and makes sad puppy-dog eyes. Oh, hell. Who can say no to that face? I stick my finger in his chin dimple and sigh.

"Fine. Here." I reach into my bag toss it to him before I can reconsider. "But I'm warning you. You can't laugh at me. I've already told you I don't write this stuff."

I grab some paper plates and serve our dinner as he sits at his desk and reads. I hand him his food and sit on the bed across from him.

During his silence, the axis of the planet shifts and then realigns as I watch him go through my draft. I don't know why letting people read my writing makes me so anxious. And a little nauseous. Okay, a whole lot nauseous.

"This isn't bad," he says finally, "but can I make a suggestion?"

"I'm thinking about dropping the class, so go for it."

"Okay, if this is a relationship between an RA and a girl on his floor, this makeout scene would never happen in the common room because it's too out in the open. You need to make it happen somewhere more secluded."

My eyebrows lift. "Make out with girls on your floor much?"

He laughs. "No, none, but you lived in Warren. Kids run in and out of the common room twenty-four seven. No RA who wants to keep his job is going to make out with anyone there."

"I only lived in Warren for a semester. I don't remember hanging out that much in the common room. It's just where I got the idea to turn some dumb diary entries into a book. I wanted to get something constructive out of the hell I went through."

He runs his tongue over his bottom lip. "So your stuff is auto-biographical?"

Shrugging, I nod. "Loosely. I change the characters' names and the settings and twist around a few details, but I get inspired by what I go through."

He cocks his head and breaks out into one of those brilliant smiles.

"You, uh, you ever gonna let me read this mysterious novel?" He bats those eyelashes again, but even his nuclear level of sexiness can't combat the nausea I get from the idea of Gavin reading my book. *Gavin reading about how Daren cheated on me? With my best friend?* My stomach flips.

"I'm thinking no." I try not to look affected by his overt attempts to charm me.

His eyes narrow briefly before he whispers, "We'll see about that."

He grins, and I sense the wheels turning in his head. *He likes the challenge.*

Crossing my arms over my chest, I try to keep a straight face. We watch each other in a standoff, but then that devilish grin is back.

"Let's go find somewhere more intimate for your scene."

He grabs a basket of folded towels and reaches for my hand, pulling me out into the hall. I laugh as I get dragged because he's acting like a crazy person. We zip down two flights of stairs and down another hall.

The laundry room is dark when we walk in, so he flips on the lights. A row of washers and dryers line both sides of the small room. He opens up a washer and dumps in his basket of clothes.

"Gavin, why are you washing clean laundry?" I can't help the laugh that escapes.

He drops in a few quarters and starts the machine before he turns to me, grinning.

"I'm helping you get *in the zone.* Come here." He wraps his hands around my waist, and I let out a surprised squeak when he lifts me up onto a washer. *I can't believe he just picked me up.* Okay, that's a stupid thought. He did carry me home two weeks ago.

His grip is firm on either side of me as he ducks down to look into my eyes. Even though I lean back, I can feel his minty breath on my face.

"Clementine, I want to warn you." His voice is husky and

deep. "I'm going to kiss you, and you're going to like it. A lot. But I want to be clear that I'm not going to sleep with you, because I want you to respect me in the morning." His mouth lifts up in a wry smile. "This is simply one *friend* helping out another. Okay?"

Wait. Is he serious?

He must sense my apprehension because he rubs his thumb softly across my cheek. "It's just an exercise, to get you into your story. I promise."

I laugh, embarrassed, intrigued, and a whole lot turned on by the idea. He smiles again, but this time it's different. His eyes darken as his hands glide over my hips. My breath catches in my chest.

"Gavin, I don't think—"

He rests a finger over my lips.

"I'm doing this in the name of academics. You need inspiration? You're looking at it. Now shut up and let me kiss you."

Holy. Shit.

Pressing his hand on the small of my back, he pulls me to the edge of the washer and stands between my legs, my thighs now on either side of his hips. He runs his other hand behind the nape of my neck, and I think I'm having an out-of-body experience as his touch leaves a trail of flames in its wake. My mouth is dry, and all I hear is the sound of my heart hammering in my chest. But before I can overanalyze it, he's so close I can barely breathe.

"By the way," he whispers when we're nose to nose, "you should remember that I'm already *dating someone,* so don't get too attached."

And with the reminder that he has a fake girlfriend, he puts his lips on mine before I can tell him he's insane.

Gavin's lips are soft, but firm, and my body reacts, my arms lifting automatically to wrap around his neck. My hands are instantly in his hair, and my mouth opens, gasping from having him up close and oh so personal. He uses the brief opening to swipe my lips softly with his tongue. As he presses in closer, I tighten my thighs on his hips.

Gripping my hair with his hand, he tugs my head back and delves deeper, stroking my tongue with his. And dear sweet Jesus, Gavin can kiss. I'm all kinds of turned on, my body a pulse, a beacon of exploding light. We make out a few minutes, kissing, alternating between these sweet, heartbreakingly slow kisses and hard ones that make me feel like I can't get close enough to him.

I use this opportunity to run my hand along his chest, descending down his hard pecs and ridged abdomen. I knew he was built—I mean, I've seen plenty of his defined body when we work out—but touching him like this has me lightheaded.

And this is not me, losing myself in the moment, but I can't seem to stop myself. Hell, I don't want to stop myself.

The wash cycle stops, the machine stilling beneath me, and he pulls away, leaving me out of breath.

Gavin looks into my eyes, and I try not to shy away, but when he kisses my forehead gently, I melt all over again.

He clears his throat.

"So now, because RAs don't like to get caught making out with girls on their floor, I'm going back up to my room. You should come up when the laundry is done so it doesn't look suspicious, and let's see if you can't get a little more done on your assignment."

With that, he steps back, and I'm under his microscope, his eyes passing over me again. He chuckles and leans into me and whispers, "By the way, you're one hell of a kisser, Clementine." Then he winks and walks out.

Oh. My. God.

* * *

After throwing the towels in the dryer, I can't bring myself to go back upstairs. What the hell do I say to Gavin? Do I even return?

Hell, yes! my little inner voice cheers. But I've never kissed *a friend* like that before. I don't think I even kissed Daren like that. And although Daren and I dated most of our senior year of high school, he never had me throbbing so hard it almost hurt.

Despite the increasing desire to hurl, after I fold the towels I head to Gavin's room. When I get there, he's engrossed in his article.

"Towels are dried and folded." I put the basket back in his closet and walk over to the bed, reaching for my bag. "I'm gonna get going."

He turns to me, his mouth tight. "Why? I thought you were going to write." He gets up, comes over and grabs my shoulders. His head tilts down. "Did I offend you? I—"

"No, you didn't." Beyond that, I can't speak. My mouth is open, but words don't come out. I never understood the concept of someone kissing you senseless. Until now.

He laughs softly. "Clementine?"

"Uh-huh."

"I didn't mean to render you speechless. Here, sit down, darlin'. Eat something. I just realized I made you do laundry, and you hadn't eaten yet." He maneuvers me down onto the bed. I sit, obedient, because it's possible I've had a stroke.

He hands me a plate of food and smiles, returning to work on his assignment as though his tongue wasn't doing a tango in my mouth an hour ago.

After taking a few, slow bites, I begin to relax and reach for my laptop. Although I'm still trying to process tonight and the surprising desire I have to grope Gavin, the words are starting to flow, so I type a few ideas.

Rereading my draft, I can't believe I turned in this turd. I kick off my shoes and open a new doc, working furiously for an hour before I close the laptop and lie back on the bed with my journal.

"How's it going?" Gavin comes over and sits next to me, so I scooch over, turning to face him.

"Better, I guess. I won't know until tomorrow when I read what I did tonight. You were right about the common room, though. How's your article?"

His smile falters. "It's fine. I just want to think about something other than a missing co-ed for a few minutes."

"Are the cops any closer to figuring out what happened to Olivia?"

He pinches the bridge of his nose. "Not as far as I can tell. It's becoming old news, which sounds terrible, but that's how the media works. So I keep trying to find new angles to keep her story in the headlines." He scrubs his face with his hands and sighs. "You want to take a break? Maybe watch a movie?"

"Sure."

"Here," he says, passing me his laptop. "Pick something."

I sit up and scroll through title after title on Netflix. "This is too much pressure. Help me."

He reaches into his closet, pulling out a few pillows, and props them up behind us before he settles down next to me, so we're leg to leg, shoulder to shoulder.

"Do you like horror?" He clicks through a list of scary films.

I shake my head. "I run a lot at night, and that might freak me out. Plus, although I have three roommates, I'm actually at home by myself a lot, so no scary movies."

"Chicken. How about a John Hughes film?"

I'm not in the mood for a girly romance. I used to love those, but not anymore. "I'm not a big fan of romantic comedies."

"Says the girl taking a romance-writing class." He looks at me like I'm a foreign species. "I thought all girls liked chick flicks."

When I shake my head, he scrolls through a few more titles. We finally agree on *The Breakfast Club*, which isn't too lovey-dovey. Fifteen minutes in, I need to editorialize.

"Can I be honest?" I ask. "I always thought Emilio Estevez was kind of a tool in this movie."

"Agreed."

"Can I also say that when I first saw this years ago, that little lipstick trick Molly Ringwald did seemed okay, but now I'm disappointed that her one skill is applying makeup with her boobs. It's an insult to women."

"Can you put on lipstick with your boobs?"

"I have no damn idea." I look down at my chest and press my shoulders together to emphasize the girls. "I've never tried."

When I glance up, he's scoping out my rack, and I elbow him. He snickers as he says, "Maybe that's a skill worth investigating before you criticize it."

I feign concern. "But what if I'm not that talented? I don't think I could handle that letdown."

"I think you probably have all kinds of talents you've yet to discover."

My face heats as I think about what he probably means, and he laughs.

We settle back into the movie, but halfway through the film, I can't keep my eyes open. I've been up since six when I got up for a run because I was so anxious about my stupid story, and now it's almost midnight.

"Gav, I'm falling asleep. I should go home."

"Scoot." He lifts my legs so now I can stretch out on his bed. "I have to write some more. Take a nap."

I don't argue with him. It's a brilliant plan. I curl up on his bed, and he throws a blanket over me.

I'm not sure how long I'm asleep before I hear the light being clicked off, but I'm so tired that when he moves me over and wraps his arm around my waist, it barely fazes me.

"Clem, you smell really good," he whispers into my ear.

My eyelids are heavy, and I start to wonder if I'm dreaming. "You kiss like a rock star."

He laughs and pulls me tighter.

In the morning, my conversation with Jenna runs through my mind, and I think of that word. *Erect*. My professor's directive to find fun euphemisms is now the only thing I can think about. *Morning wood. Boner. Hard-on. Stiffy.*

There's nowhere to go. This morning, Gavin is draped over me. He's like a freaking furnace, and his man parts are trying to poke a hole through my thigh. I try to wiggle out of his hold, but his eyes flutter open.

"Good morning, Clementine," Gavin says, his throaty voice terribly sexy.

"Sorry if I woke you."

I let my eyes adjust to the light. Clearing my throat, I mull over the question that's burning on my tongue. "Gavin, so last night... you were just helping me... as a friend?"

"As a friend." He's wrapped around me, hard against my thigh, warm against my back, and nothing about this morning seems platonic.

"Can I ask... do you have a lot of *friends* that you, uh, help like this?"

He chuckles, his chest vibrating against me before he kisses my neck. "No, darlin'. I don't really have time for many friends, especially since you'll remember I have a girlfriend. I don't want to spread myself too thin."

I roll my eyes.

"Do you have to go to work?" he asks, yawning.

"Yeah, but I have to head home and shower first. If I come in wearing the same clothes I had on yesterday, someone will know I'm a harlot who slept with you."

He snickers. "You should go before you ravish me because then I'll feel cheap."

God, he's such a flirt.

Laughing, I punch him playfully. "You're incredible."

"I know, but the next time you say that, you should add my name, like, 'Gavin, you're incredible,' and maybe throw in a few moans. That would be hot."

"Who are you?"

This guy is fucking with my head, and what's worse is I think I like it.

Chapter 9

I stare at the register and then look back at the girl on the other side of the counter. She drops her head forward, waiting for me to figure out my shit.

"Sorry. Yeah, you need change," I mumble before I finish ringing her up.

This afternoon I've mis-charged three customers because my brain got sucked down a rabbit hole the instant Gavin's lips touched mine. All day, I've debated whether he's merely helping me write my assignment, or if he's in any way serious about me. I'm not sure if I even want him to be serious because being with Gavin is like parachuting out of an airplane… without a parachute.

By the time I get to the student union to meet Jenna and Harper for dinner, it's pretty empty with only a few students scattered around the enormous seating area. Dani joins us, and the four of us spread out at a table.

Jenna pulls out a spiral and a pen from her bag. "I need your help, girls. In my story, my main character has a list of 'deal-breakers,' things that would ruin a guy for her, and I'm stalling out."

"That's easy," Dani says, twisting the top off her juice. "I won't date anyone who wears loafers with tassels or loafers without socks. Or a guy who picks his teeth. Gross."

"Oh, those are good!" Jenna scribbles in her notebook while I peel tomatoes out of my sandwich.

I have to think about it for a few minutes, but mulling over Professor Marceaux's declaration about not using the f-word brings me to a realization.

"I hate when people say, 'Let's make love.' It makes me cringe for some reason, the same way I hate guys with clammy hands or hairy chests. Yuck." Gavin's chest is fairly hair-free… except for that sexy trail on his lower stomach that leads south. He switched t-shirts at the gym the other day, and I nearly had a coronary.

I wedge a fallen piece of turkey back within the two slices of wheat bread and take a bite as Jenna laughs and scribbles. "You're so right! If Ryan told me 'let's make love,' I'd kick him in the gonads."

Snorting out a sip of soda, Harper tries not to choke. "That's kind of harsh, Jenna. Ryan might need those some day."

Twirling her pen through her blonde hair, Jenna rolls her eyes. "Of course I'd never kick Ryan in the family jewels. Oh, you know what I *really* hate?" Jenna cocks an eyebrow. "Crotch-scratchers, especially when they do it right in your face as though it's not obvious they're reaching for their frank and beans. What is it with guys adjusting themselves? You don't catch girls randomly rubbing the vag."

We're laughing so hard a study group two tables down shoots us dirty looks that make us laugh harder.

"Save room for the chips and queso, ladies," Jenna says, jumping up to get some napkins and a soda refill. She's decided to turn this into a girls' night, which is sounding better and better.

As I watch her cross the cafeteria, Wheeler strolls in. My mouth goes dry and my heart pounds. Flying into panic mode, I search for a hiding place, but I don't have time because he's already seen me.

Shit. Shit.

The girls see my expression and turn to look.

"Who's that?" Dani asks.

I clear my throat, hoping the few bites I've eaten don't come back up. "My old professor, Jason Wheeler."

"He doesn't look old."

Clad in jeans, a button-up and a black blazer, he looks like a J. Crew model.

"He's not. He's thirty."

"He's really cute." Dani tilts her head while she watches them. "But should he have his arm around that girl? She looks like a student."

Harper looks at me for a split second before she answers. "That's kind of what he does. Have you seen him recently, Clem?"

"No." I swallow to quell my nausea. "I've seen him, but he hasn't seen me." *Because I've hidden.* And dragged Jenna down into the dirt with me. And threatened a co-worker with bodily harm.

And now he's walking straight toward us. *Fuck.*

"Clementine Avery." My name. That's all it takes to suck the air out of my chest. "So good to see you, love. How have you been?"

Fine, since you stopped stalking me, asshole.

I take a deep breath.

"I'm well, Jason. And yourself?" My voice sounds confident, which surprises the hell out of me. I glare back at him, and he smirks. My stomach is roiling with a rush of adrenaline. It's a bitter cocktail of hatred, fury and fear.

"Very well. I've been teaching in London for the last two years," he says pointedly, "and working on my new novel, which I think you'll appreciate." A shadow seems to cross his face, and I shiver. "This is my new protegée, Briget. She's working on a brilliant book right now. It's fabulous. Similar to your novel, but with more depth."

Ah, he's here to insult me.

Turning to Briget, I ask, "Has he told you what he'll want for his services?" I really don't want to mess with this guy, but he's being such an arrogant prick, and the words are out of my mouth before I can stop myself.

Brigit toys with a lock of her short black hair as she appraises me.

Wheeler's eyes harden. I never noticed how cold his eyes were until it was almost too late.

"Well, this has been lovely," he says, breaking the silence. "It's good to see you. You should come by during office hours so we can... catch up." His eyes narrow on me as he speaks, and I can't fight the chill that crawls over my skin. Then he puts his hand on the girl's back and ushers her away.

I blink several times to clear my blurring vision.

"What the hell is he thinking?" Harper whispers as we watch them disappear out the back of the cafeteria.

I don't know. And that scares the hell out of me.

When we get back to our apartment, I beeline it to my room and change into a pair of sweats and a tank top. It's been half an hour, and I'm still trembling.

I trudge into the living room and am surprised to see Ryan and Gavin on the couch. Jenna is in Ryan's lap, and Dani is fiddling with the TV.

"I didn't know you guys were here." God, I really need to be more observant. *I would have put on more clothes,* I think, noticing my hot pink bra strap hanging off my shoulder. I have my room-mates to thank for my sudden increase in sexy underwear. That candy necklace game on my birthday got me one big-ass box of Victoria's Secret.

Shrugging up the strap, I return to my room and throw on a

flannel shirt, but my hands are still shaking too badly to button it up. I give up and walk back out.

"Why is everyone upset?" Ryan asks.

"How do you know we're upset?" Harper, our in-house shrink, is always curious to see how someone's brain works.

"Because you told Jenna you wanted to do facials, and you have an armload of girlie comfort food. Chips and queso, right?"

"Damn it, he's good," Harper mutters, taking the cheese out of the convenience store bag and popping it into the microwave. "We had a rough night. We ran into Professor Dickhead, and he tried to talk to Clementine."

Ryan's brows knit on his forehead. "But doesn't she have a restraining order on him? Can he do that?"

I rub my throbbing temple. "Guys, no one cares about this crap. Let's change the subject."

"I care." Gavin's voice cuts through the awkward silence. "What happened? Who's this guy with the restraining order?"

"I'll explain," Jenna says, sensing my discomfort. She looks to me to make sure I'm okay with this, and I shrug.

She takes a deep breath as though she's trying to decide where to start. "Clem was in Professor Wheeler's writing class freshman year, and he helped her edit her first book that fall. He was great at first, really encouraging and positive. But we all know Clementine is beautiful, and he fell for her, hard." *Ugh. Must she embellish?* "But our girl wasn't interested. She thought of him as a friend, a mentor. When he wouldn't take no for an answer, he started stalking her—waiting outside her dorm at night and lurking in the alley. Totally creepy shit."

I sit in a chair and try to focus on my breathing to stave off a panic attack.

Jenna waves her hand. "So this went on for a while until one night when he decided he had waited long enough."

Swallowing back the lump in my throat, I look down at my fuzzy socks, carefully avoiding Gavin's stare.

Jenna sighs with relief. "Fortunately, Wheeler didn't rape her, but she got pretty banged up. By the time the cops got there, he was gone. The worst part is that police said they couldn't do anything but put a restraining order on the asshole because Wheeler claimed he was with his parents, who vouched for his whereabouts. Without any evidence, the dean's hands were tied too. Wheeler's family basically built that new wing on the library, and you know how things like that always work out. He was on sabbatical for a while, but just returned this fall. And the restraining order has expired, but since he has no criminal record and has exhibited 'good behavior,' the cops won't renew it."

Hearing Jenna tell it with her Southern drawl, it almost doesn't sound *that* bad. I lift my head, and all of my friends are staring at me. *Okay.* Judging by everyone's expressions, I guess it does sound bad.

"Don't look at me like that. I'm fine." I blow a strand of loose hair out of my face.

"Your parents must have been so upset," Dani says.

I don't miss the look that Harper and Jenna share.

Laughing weakly, I shake my head. "My parents didn't give a shit. I doubt they even listened to my messages."

Gavin runs his teeth over his bottom lip as he studies me. "Is that why you stopped coming to class? Just before winter break of our freshman year?"

I nod slowly, my eyes dropping to the floor. "I took a leave of absence."

"Is it hard, seeing him around campus?" Dani asks quietly.

"He avoided me that spring when I came back, thanks to the restraining order, and then he left to teach abroad. This is the first time I've seen him since freshman year."

"And he waltzed up to you tonight like nothing happened?" Ryan asks, incredulous.

"Pretty much."

"You know what I can't stand about him?" Harper asks. "How he smells. It's kind of a sweet cologne." She makes a gagging sound.

"It's not a cologne. He smokes clove cigarettes. Even if I had liked him, that would've been a deal-breaker."

Harper says, "Oh, and he has a new girl. She's young. Looks like a freshman. Of course." The more Harper talks about it, the more pissed she sounds. As my roommate that spring, if anyone remembers what I went through, the nightmares I had, she would. "Someone should warn her that he's a psycho."

"I thought you didn't like to toss around that word," I say. She's always lecturing us about casually using clinical terminology.

"In this case, it's probably accurate."

* * *

Gavin hugs me on the way out. As I pull away, he stops me, placing his hands on my shoulders. "You shouldn't run at night. It's not safe. Promise me you won't do that." I roll my eyes. "Clementine…" He says it slowly, like a warning.

"Fine. I won't run at night." Jeez.

He still has his hands on my arms, and I'm waiting for him to let go. Instead, he pulls me to him and kisses my forehead.

"I'll call you tomorrow," he says, walking out behind Ryan, who has decided to get Jenna a Taser because Wheeler has him freaked out.

When I turn around, Jenna, Harper and Dani are staring at me.

"So, are you guys, like, dating?" Dani asks.

"Yeah, I'm kind of curious myself," Jenna says, smiling.

I don't know the answer. Gavin did say he was only helping me write my story.

"We're just friends." That's the safe answer.

Jenna scoffs. "Girl, what I saw was not a 'just friends' kind of look." Fanning herself, she waits for me to explain.

I follow the grain of the hard wood floor with my toe. "We've been studying together. That's it."

Jenna grabs my arm and yanks me to the couch, dragging me down to sit next to her. "We need details, Clem. You've been holding out on us."

Harper and Dani scurry over to join us.

"There isn't much to tell. We've gone climbing a couple of times, and he's given me some suggestions on my story."

"You showed him your writing?" Harper looks shocked. She knows I don't show anyone my work, especially early drafts.

I nod, and her eyes widen.

"I only showed him that draft I turned in to our romance class. He's a writer, too, and since he works as an RA, he's had some good insights." The girls look confused, so I explain the general premise of my book. When I'm done, they still look perplexed.

"But you've also stayed at his place, too, right? What, twice?" Harper asks.

"And don't forget the night he stayed here." Taking count, Jenna holds up three fingers.

"Before you get all excited, we literally just sleep."

Harper and Jenna look at each other and laugh as though I'm lying.

"Why do I get the sense there's something you're not telling us?" Jenna asks. "Come on, Clem, spill it! I can see it in your face. You're a terrible liar."

Since I don't date, I don't ever have any juicy stories. The last time I talked about kissing a boy, it was Daren. And the friend in whom I confided, Veronica, was busy hooking up with him behind my back. I swallow back a rush of unexpected emotion and try to explain what's going on with Gavin.

"Okay, something *did* happen last night, but when you hear the whole story, you'll see he was merely helping me with my assignment."

Now they're totally confused. I reach for a cold nacho and

reluctantly share how he was helping me connect with my characters and get into their mindset when we made out in the laundry room. I add that when he asked me to go climbing with him he had emphasized *as friends.*

"Holy shit, Clementine." Jenna jumps up off the couch and does a little victory dance like she crossed the finish line of a race. "He likes you! Like, a lot!"

"No, he doesn't," I snort.

"Gavin Murphy has a legion of groupies who come to the shows, and he's never really shown any interest in them. But when he talks to you, he looks like a starving man eyeballing a steak." She stares at me as she taps her chin with one finger. "It probably doesn't hurt that he saw you naked." She giggles and shimmies suggestively.

"What? When did this happen?" Harper asks.

Shooting Jenna a dirty look for bringing it up only makes her laugh harder.

I blow out a breath. "It wasn't deliberate. I walked out of the shower and nearly killed myself on Ryan's skateboard, and my towel fell. And I wasn't completely naked. I was wearing boy shorts."

Talking about all of this makes my heart race, and I start biting my nails.

Harper grabs my other hand. "Okay, guys, let's leave Clem alone. She looks like she wants to crawl under the couch." When I glance up, she's grinning. "Relax. He seems like a great guy, and you're right. You guys probably are just friends. This is good!"

She's in clinician mode. I can tell by her voice she's trying to not scare me.

It's too late.

Chapter 10

Popping a pill is so tempting.

My hands shake for an hour after I get up on Sunday morning. I haven't had a nightmare in over a year, but seeing Wheeler yesterday has churned up my worst fears: his hands tightening on me, those words he growled in my ear, the terror that I wouldn't be able to stop him. And the worst part—not being able to scream. Instead, the panic coils in my gut, writhing like a snake that can't strike.

The pills help me relax and detach, but I want to get there on my own. The downside of the meds is my lack of feeling, how numb they make me. Maybe it's good to feel, even if it's to be afraid. At least it's real.

I lace up my tennis shoes because, if I'm not going to medicate, only one thing can help me off the ledge. And like a soothing balm, each stride helps melt the fear.

In the afternoon, as I'm stepping into my room after my hour-long run, my phone rings.

"What are you doing?" Gavin doesn't say hi. I don't know why, but this makes me laugh.

"I'm waiting for Harper to get home so she can help me with

some homework." I kick off my shoes and reach into my drawers to grab a change of clothes.

"What do you have to do?"

"You had to ask." I groan. "Don't laugh, okay?"

"I won't. What is it?"

"Applied math." I'm waiting for him to make fun of me. After all, I'm a senior taking a freshman course.

"You're in luck. I'm great at math. I'll help you with your assignment if you proof my new article."

"That doesn't seem like a fair tradeoff. You haven't seen how much I suck at math."

"It's okay. I help all the kids on my floor. We'll pretend it's another scenario in your book."

Warmth spreads in my belly.

"Ah, so my *book boyfriend* is coming over to *tutor* me? Why didn't you say so?"

He's grinning. I can tell. "Exactly. So it's almost as though you don't need the help at all. Your character does. What's her name anyway?"

"Samantha. The RA is Andrew."

"I think I should get a hotter name, like Ian or Aiden."

"Hold the phone, Romeo," I snort. "These are *fictional* characters. I happen to get inspired by life, but it's not like I directly transcribe my conversations with people straight into my stories."

"Whatever you say, Clementine. Only make sure you include the part where you say I kiss like a rock star." He's laughing. Grateful he can't see my embarrassment, I drop my head into my hand. "I'll be over in ten."

"No, give me half an hour. I just ran and need to take a shower."

"See, that's too much information. All your *book boyfriend* is going to do is fantasize about that for the next thirty minutes. That and those little black shorts."

My face must be scarlet right now. "What black shorts?"

"The ones you were wearing when you flashed me."

I nearly drop the phone.

"You make it sound like I did that on purpose. I didn't know you were in my apartment. I tripped. The towel fell."

"And it fucking made my year, darlin'." He pauses, and I don't have anything to say to fill the silence. "I'll see you in half an hour."

When we get off the phone, I'm grinning like an idiot.

* * *

Gavin follows me to get my books. "You unpacked," he says as his eyes scan my room. The boxes are gone, finally.

I glance around, hoping I didn't leave anything embarrassing out. My bed is made, my purple comforter tucked under two down pillows. On my beech desk sits my laptop, a small stack of textbooks, a short silver vase with a handful of blue and black pens, and a framed photo taken last winter of Jenna, Harper and me, arm in arm as we huddle in the snow.

He leans in to read some of the Post-Its on my cork board, and my heart beats a little faster.

"Favorite quotes?" he asks.

"Yeah, I know they're silly, but I can't seem to part with them."

He's quiet, his eyes skimming across the rainbow of squares. Reaching out, he touches my favorite. I swallow, wishing he hadn't stopped on that one. *They slipped briskly into an intimacy from which they never recovered.*

He smiles over his shoulder. "I love F. Scott Fitzgerald too. Which book is your favorite?"

"*This Side of Paradise.*"

"Most people say *Gatsby*, but I have to agree with you."

It would be so much easier to ignore how attractive Gavin is if he didn't love my favorite book.

As he steps back, I reach over the desk and grab my assignment.

"I have an idea. Pack up your stuff," he says.

I stop, taken aback by how sexy he looks leaning against my chair. His dark hair is going every which way, and his tall, muscular body fills my vision.

Finally, I regain the ability to speak. "I thought we were going to study."

He tugs on the hem of my t-shirt. "We are, but we can kill two birds with one stone. Let's go to the library. I have a scenario for your book." He grins, making stupid little flutters ripple in my stomach.

"Can we do my math first? I might not be able to concentrate after you try *helping* me with my book." Part of me is embarrassed to admit that, but it's the truth.

He laughs, nodding, but the heat in his eyes makes my blood pulse faster.

Once we've worked on my math assignment on the main floor of the library for an hour and a half, I pack my stuff and lay my head on my bag. Concentrating with him looking over my shoulder every ten seconds has been unnerving, but at least I finally understand the work.

"See," he says. "Not so bad. I told you I'm a good tutor."

"It's true. You are. And very modest."

"Modesty is overrated. C'mon."

I've only barely grabbed my bag when he reaches for my other hand and pulls me up.

"Where are we going?"

"The stacks." He turns to wink at me before he drags me like a little rag doll.

"What's that?"

"Baby, you haven't made out until you've made out in the stacks."

I try to stifle my laugh, but I still get a dirty look from a librarian. *And he just called me baby.* Gavin pulls me into the elevator so hard that I stumble right into him. I'm about to apologize for being a klutz when he wraps his arm around me as he reaches over to push the button for the fourth floor.

"You've never heard of the stacks? Really?"

Ignoring my heart rate, which has accelerated like it's doing a lap at the Indy 500, I shake my head. "No, never. What is it?" He smells so good. This close, it's intoxicating.

"It's where the library stores its main collection, but it's also where all of the hot makeout sessions happen on campus. I'm guessing an illicit affair with your scorching hot RA should have at least one hookup in the stacks."

He smirks, and those dimples come out in full force.

"So now you're my 'scorching hot RA'?" I attempt a look of incredulity, but it's tough when I'm wrapped up in his arms.

"Yeah. That's me. And you're my innocent little freshman who is dying to get in my pants."

And there's a total look of satisfaction in his face that makes me want to take down him down a peg or two.

So I laugh. "What else do I want to do to you?"

He looks down, a mischievous grin spreading. "I don't know, but I'm eager to find out."

I don't have a chance to respond because as the doors open, Gavin grabs my hand and pulls me through a few aisles, and we twist and turn until we're in what must be the farthest corner of the library.

"These are the stacks." He reaches out one hand as though he's making a formal introduction, and I'm about to ask what the big deal is when he turns around and pushes me up against the wall.

I gasp, surprised.

His hand pins me above my heart, which is pounding as he leans in so close I can feel his breath.

He pauses and raises his eyebrows, and I know what he's asking.

I only need the briefest of moments to realize I'm not scared, not with him, not now, and I give him a small nod before his mouth crashes into mine and we pick up where we left off in the laundry room.

I'm immediately lost in his touch and taste. Gavin runs his hand along my back before he fists my hair, and my heart thunders in my chest.

He has the most amazing lips, the kind I want to bite. And in the spirit of inspiration, I decide I should.

I break the kiss long enough to take his bottom lip between my teeth. I look up at him as I gently tug, and I'm glad that he has his arm wrapped around my waist because the scorching look he gives me makes me weak.

He pulls back and stares, his thumb lightly brushing over cheek. Our breaths mingle in the short distance between us, the sound of each intake of air filling the silence.

Suddenly, he growls and pulls me closer, parting my lips with his tongue. The slight stubble on his chin rubs my face, and I run my hands up his broad shoulders and through his hair, pulling him tighter. He grabs my waist, and I'm in the air for a split second before I land on top of a small bookshelf. He nestles in between my thighs, and I yank on his shirt, wanting him closer.

Wrapping my legs around him, I press myself into his hard body as my nails score down his back. He grabs my ass and rocks against me, and I can't help the moan that escapes me.

I don't know how long I'm adrift in his kiss, but as I begin to wonder how smart this is, making out in the library, we're interrupted.

"Ahem." The sudden sound makes me jolt back, and I turn to see a very irritated librarian with a cart of books he apparently needs to shelve. I laugh as Gavin slides me off the bookcase. He grins as he grabs my hand, pulling me behind him as we run down the aisle and back into the elevator.

I'm still breathing hard from our little makeout session and laughing from getting caught when he turns and anchors me against the wall with his hip, bracing his hands on either side of me. Judging by what's pressed up against my stomach, I'm not the only one turned on.

"Uh, you excited to see me?" I say coyly.

"You have no fucking idea." He leans down and gives me the sweetest, softest kiss before he breaks away when the door opens to the main floor.

Dear lord.

* * *

I sit at my desk, thinking about how to capture what happened in the library. I touch my lips, which are swollen from having my mouth pressed against Gavin's like my life depended on it. Trying not to overanalyze what's happening between us, I focus on channeling the emotion of being with him. His touch. His delicious scent. His smile. I close my eyes and allow myself a reprieve from my cynical inner voice and try to enjoy the rush of the last few times we've hung out.

When I open my laptop, the words begin to flow, and I can see my characters—how they fall in love, their sweet embraces, their impassioned stares. It's like my head has been uncorked, and everything is tumbling out so fast, my fingers can barely keep pace. It's exhilarating, and my heart races with the possibilities.

It isn't always this hard. Well, that's not exactly true. I started writing as a form of therapy so I could deal with all the bullshit of breaking up with Daren. When I wrote my first book, I knew how it would end, how the characters would evolve, and roughly how they'd get there. This is different. I don't know where this story will go, a thought that briefly douses my elation.

Somewhere around 4 a.m., I collapse in bed.

The alarm the next morning is painful. When I dress for class, I realize I've probably spent the last twenty-four hours obsessing over Gavin so I can write. I can feel it already, how I open up to him, how he gets me to take chances, how I'm willing to go outside my comfort zone for him.

This is dangerous. I could get hurt.

I keep waiting for the panic to set in, the panic that has tortured me throughout college and kept me from getting close to anyone. For once, it doesn't.

Chapter 11

The edges of the leaves are starting to change. In a few weeks, the street will be full of wild, chaotic color. Even the air this morning is crisp. It won't be long before I'll need to wear more than a light sweater or hoodie. The thought makes me frown because I don't have money to go shopping.

When I reach for my mail, I see Student Accounting Services Office on the top envelope. My fingers hesitate at its edges. *No, rip it off, like a Band-Aid.* I tear through one side and pull out the letter. My eyes skim over the words until I find what I'm looking for. I have to take a deep breath when I see the amount because right now there's no way in hell I can afford it.

Money wasn't an issue when I chose this school. I loved the campus and the programs and the fact that it was so close to Boston College and Daren. Between a few academic scholarships and my track scholarship, I almost had a full ride. My parents seemed pleased with my plans when I told them I wanted to attend Boston University, so I never thought I'd be scrounging to pay tuition every few months.

But that was before my father left for that European merger

and decided that living on another continent was better than living with us. Before my mother had that meltdown because I wouldn't model her overpriced clothes. Before both of them forgot I existed.

The ache in my chest reminds me that I still care too much.

They taught me how to shut out people. How to be cold. Closed off. Distant. Apparently, being a bitch is my only inheritance.

When I get to work, I find a mountain of invoices to process. Somewhere in my dreary afternoon, I step out of the office and run down to Starbucks, which is nestled in the corner of the first floor, next to the Barnes & Noble.

The guy behind the counter is new. He reminds me of a cocker spaniel, all perk and happiness as he hunts and pecks on the register. When his trainer Sarah sees me, she pushes the kid out of the way to take my order.

"The usual, Clem?" Sarah asks, her ponytail bopping on her head.

"Yeah, thanks." I reach over the counter to grab my coffee. "By the way, your team did a great job last week selling the promo drink. You'll be entered in the raffle for the gift card."

"Cool!" she says with a big grin.

"There you are." My manager Roger waves for me to follow him. He has a major crinkle in his brow, so I'm wondering what got broken. I make sure the lid on my drink is secure and run to catch up, but instead of leading me to the home department that has the glass knickknacks that are always getting smashed by the dumber-than-fuck frat boys, he leads me to Barnes & Noble. When he stops, I do a double take.

On the new shelf reserved for indie favorites sits my novel. Until now, I've only sold ebooks, so seeing the actual hard copy in a store is making me drunk with glee, but I try to stay calm.

Running my fingers over the glossy purple cover of *Say It Isn't So*, pride swells in my chest. I got it done, in print and in stores.

Well, a few stores. I touch the book again, my thumb running over the letters like they're little gold nuggets. I don't care what people say online. I still love the cover. The broken heart locket was mine, and nothing can symbolize what happens in my story any better.

"I can't keep these on the shelves," he says as he taps on my book.

It takes me a second to realize he's not just talking about my novel, that he's referring to all of the titles in the indie section.

"This was a damn good idea, Clem," he says. "I'm glad you suggested it."

I had the good luck of tutoring Macy, the owner's daughter last semester, and when we got talking about books, I mentioned the need for an indie shelf at the bookstore. And I *might* have shared my favorite titles with her, one of which *maybe* was my own.

But she didn't know it was mine. And neither does my boss who's staring at it.

Unease takes root in my stomach. *Is it possible Roger found out?*

My boss scratches his belly absentmindedly.

Trying to appear casual, I school my expression. "Um, how do you know I suggested it?"

He grins like he's in on some big secret. "Because Macy's dad told me." He taps the shelf. "And since the titles are such a hit, I'd like to get a few of these authors to come for a book talk next month. I've heard back from everyone except the publicist for Austen Fitzgerald. With the best sales in the city, you'd think she'd give me the time of day."

The frustration in his voice makes me feel guilty, but I can't tell him the truth, that I'm Austen Fitzgerald, a pseudonym I came up with by combining the names of my two favorite writers, Jane Austen and F. Scott Fitzgerald.

My publicist hates me because I won't interact with fans beyond Twitter and a few social media networks, but I've put too much of myself in that book to lay claim to it publicly. I figure that's why I pay her, but apparently not enough because she should call Roger back or at least let me know what he wants.

I'm relieved it's selling, though, because I have to scrounge up a crapload of cash to pay the tuition bill that threatens to kick my ass out on the street.

I motion toward my book. "Let me try calling her publicist. At the very least, maybe I can get some signed copies."

"Good idea!" Roger is only forty, but he marches around here like a grandpa, always worried about sales and figures and schedules. "Corporate is crazy about you. They want you as a full-time manager when you graduate."

"I thought they only hired MBAs for those positions."

"That's true, but they love all of your suggestions and how you incentivize the staff." He tilts his head. "I've been meaning to ask why no one ever calls in sick on your shifts."

I smirk. "I tell them if they call in sick, I'm going to fire them and they'll end up working as a media assistant setting up overhead projectors and presentations for classes, but they'll screw it up and everyone will laugh at them, which will eventually give them a complex that will require intensive psychotherapy."

He crinkles those eyebrows again, obviously unsure whether I'm telling the truth. I shake my head and laugh.

"Roger, I buy them shit every month they're on time. Out of my own pocket. Sometimes it's from the gift cards I get from those efficiency rewards corporate sends out."

I've had practice with that sort of stuff. Like the online raffles I do for free giveaways of my book and autographed bookmarks that feature the cover of my novel. I even write people personalized notes as some of the characters in my story. Fans seem to love those the most. One woman even sent me a new locket after I blogged about how my broken necklace ended up on the cover.

His eyes widen. "You spend your own money? Really?"

"Yeah, but usually the kids are happy taking home the crap we give away after a promotion is over, so it's not so bad. It's better than dealing with their bullshit when they have hangovers."

He scratches his head. "Can I clone you?"

I pat him on the shoulder. "I'm not sure that technology is available yet, so you're going to have to settle for a box of signed books from Austen what's-her-name."

Roger smiles, and the wrinkle in the middle of his forehead smoothes.

"How do you know so much about business and marketing?"

Debating how much to tell him, I opt for vague. "My parents own a few businesses, and I paid attention."

"Hmm," he says thoughtfully. "Anything I know?"

"No." *Um, probably,* I think, watching a couple of sorority girls decked out in clothes from my mother's fashion line saunter by with the brand name emblazoned on their asses.

On my way home, I'm still floating from seeing my novel in the store when I get a dirty text from Jenna. Relieved no one can see this over my shoulder, I laugh at her message: *I'm hard for you, baby. Come relieve the pressure.*

I have to think about this for longer than is probably necessary.

Finally, I write back: *Should I use my hand or mouth?*

Good lord, I can't believe I sent that to someone. Where in the world did she learn how to play this stupid game? Out-Skank. We should box up this idea and sell it as a drinking game.

Gavin texts me, asking if I want to study later this week. Thinking about him turns my insides to liquid. Molten liquid. Those green eyes. Those damn long lashes. Ugh, those lips. I'm mid-fantasy about making out with him in the library when Jenna sexts me again. I'm so busy being aghast at her naughtiness that I nearly plow through a group of professors.

After a few apologies to the elderly gentlemen I nearly trampled, I write her back: *I want to lick your body up and down.*

A minute later, I get another text from Gavin: *Really? And where would this licking begin exactly?*

Holy. Fucking. Shit.

I just sexted Gavin.

I have to close my eyes to regain my equilibrium. Smacking my forehead with my palm for being such an idiot, I rifle off a quick text to Gavin to explain my roommate's insistence that we play this stupid game.

He writes back: *Haha. I didn't have you pegged as a sexter. But if you need practice, baby, I'm always available ;)*

Mental note: Must not space out when sexting.

* * *

Being surrounded by the smells and sounds of the library makes it difficult to concentrate. All I can think about is making out with Gavin in the stacks. His lips on mine. His hands running along my back and in my hair. The way he tastes. How I ache when he presses his body against me.

"Earth to Clem!" Harper whisper-shouts. My eyes shift to her, and the look of exasperation catches me off guard.

"Sorry, I can't seem to focus here." I give her an apologetic smile. Right now, I don't even think I can spell my name.

"You love studying in the library," she says, her face twisted in confusion.

I'm usually the epitome of efficiency when I'm here, but now that I've groped Gavin among the books and felt his hands all over me, homework is the last thing I want to think about. God, he's so—

She snaps her fingers in my face, making me jump.

"There you go again. What's going on?" She taps her pen as she waits for my answer.

Before I can respond, I hear a familiar voice behind me that makes my heart race.

"Hi, ladies." Gavin places his hands on either side of my chair and leans in to kiss my cheek. *Oh shit.* My stomach does a free fall out of my body.

Harper says hi as a wide smile spreads across Jenna's mouth.

"Hey, Gavin, just trying to help Clem with this problem," Jenna says, pointing to my newest math dilemma, "but she can't seem to concentrate. It's like all of a sudden the library distracts her."

I hear him chuckle behind me.

"Hmm. We got a lot of work done here the other day," he says with amusement in his voice.

I brave a look at Jenna, and she raises one eyebrow. "Then maybe you should join us so she'll pay attention." I glare at her, and she smirks. "You should know that Clem doesn't do public displays of affection, so if you got anything more than a hug out of this girl, you deserve an award."

I kick her under the table, and she yelps.

Jenna is right, though. I don't do PDA, or at least I never did before Gavin sauntered into my life. I never let Daren kiss me in public. In fact, I barely let him hold my hand.

Gavin squeezes my shoulder. "As much as I'd like to join you guys, I could use your editing skills."

I momentarily forget my embarrassment and turn to find him looking unusually tense. His hair is in disarray as though he's been running his hands through it all day. It reminds me of what he looks like first thing in the morning, which makes me think about kissing him. And having him press up against me in the stacks. And how I'd like to do that again. Soon.

He slides a few sheets of paper in front of me. "Would you mind proofing this? My deadline is in an hour, and I have another story to cover."

It takes me a second to shake off my lust-filled haze, but I agree and reach into my bag for a pen.

"I need to make a phone call, but I'll be back in a few minutes," he says. I nod and turn back to his article.

Jenna and Harper are all aflutter about Gavin, so I tell them to shut up a few times so I can understand what I'm reading. He's never asked me for anything, and he's been supportive of me and all of my writing hangups. The least I can do is give him feedback.

The headline reads, "No New Leads In Missing BU Student's Disappearance."

I plug my ears with my fingers to drown out the chatter. The article describes how Olivia Lawrence was an English major, a senior who spent the spring semester abroad, and she had just returned for the Fourth of July when she jumped on the T and was never seen again.

The article quotes one of her friends who says she traveled to Europe because she was looking for inspiration.

"'She loved writing Harry Potter fanfiction and was working on her own story that featured a young girl who was trapped in a mystical world,' her friend Anthony Levine said. 'Olivia thought the old-world charm of England would be the perfect backdrop for her book.'"

I jot down a few notes, and as I'm finishing, Gavin walks back up to our table.

"What's the verdict?" he asks, brimming with an intense energy.

"It's really good. Amazing, actually." He smiles, and his green eyes warm with flecks of gold.

"How did you track down people in England?"

"Most of them are back now. Her sister hooked me up with some of Olivia's friends online, and I did a little digging on my own to talk to two of her professors."

"Your lead is really tight and everything flows well. The only mistake I found was this attribution," I say, pointing. "I'm guessing it's a copy-and-paste mistake."

He reads over my comments.

When he's done, I turn to the last page. "My other suggestion is to switch these paragraphs because this one is a more powerful way to end the article."

He runs his teeth over his full lower lip. "You're right." He takes my pen and scribbles a few notes in the margin.

"Is that for the *Free Press*?" Jenna asks. If she leans over anymore, she'll be in my lap.

"No, the *Globe*." He's still scribbling in the margin of his article.

"I didn't know you still worked for the *Globe*," I say.

"I wasn't, but the editor from my summer internship was impressed with what I've been doing for the *Freep* this fall. So now I work for both."

Gavin runs his hand over the back of his neck, his head obviously still in his assignment.

"Wow, that's awesome!" Jenna gets a few angry looks from the people near us. I'm so impressed with Gavin I don't know what to do with myself.

Kade walks up behind Gavin. "Dude, you done?" He doesn't say hi. He doesn't even try to be cordial. I roll my eyes.

Jenna greets the douchebag, and they talk about an upcoming gig.

Gavin checks his phone and leans down to me. "I'll call you later, unless you want to *text me*," he says with a wicked gleam in his eye as he kisses my temple. Remembering my embarrassing Out-Skank moment yesterday, I put my hand over my face to hide. I hear him laugh behind me as he and Kade take off.

I don't know how long I sit there thinking about him before Harper clears her throat. She smiles briefly before a look of concern crosses her face.

"I have two questions," Harper says hesitantly. "Have you had any panic attacks... about him?"

I shake my head, a small grin spreading. She smiles in return and reaches over and punches me lightly.

"Good. Now, for the really important question. Where can I find myself one of those? Does he have a brother?"

"Right?" Jenna might be in a relationship, but she appreciates eye candy when she sees it. And that boy is most definitely eye candy. Not to mention one hell of a writer.

* * *

Jenna and Harper run off to different study groups, and I head home, but when I get to the center of campus, my feet grind to a stop.

The crowd in Marsh Plaza is silhouetted by the setting sun as hundreds of candles wink in the breeze. It's a rally for Olivia. A man in his early fifties, wearing khakis and a gray sweater, is standing on the second steps of the school chapel.

"She's out there, and she needs your help," he says, his voice thick with emotion. "We want to get her home safely, and her mother and I want to remind you of Olivia's story so you don't make the same mistakes. Don't walk around campus or this city at night alone. That was Livvy's mistake."

My heart breaks listening to Mr. Lawrence. The way he talks about her like she's alive. Like she's coming home when she's probably long gone.

The man struggles to continue before he holds his hand over his face. His wife wraps her arms around him. I avert my eyes, feeling bad they have to share this heartbreak in front of what must be three hundred people.

On the other side of the crowd, I spot Gavin quietly interviewing a few students. He looks in his element. So commanding and compassionate. Pride swells in me as I watch him cover the story, one that means so much to him.

A few feet away from me, a small news crew has set up, and a tall, slender student with long, dark hair talks into the microphone.

I can barely make out her words over the sound of the wind.

"Authorities are asking the public for help. If you have any information about the disappearance of Olivia Lawrence, please contact the number on your screen. I'm Madeline McDermott for *BU News*."

I'd never willingly stand in front of a camera like the broadcast students. That takes so much courage. I'm pretty sure I'd stutter or make some totally humiliating Freudian slip.

Turning to go, I stop abruptly when I come face to face with Brigit. We appraise each other briefly before I clear my throat.

"Hi, Brigit. How are you?"

She looks surprised we're speaking, but then her eyes tighten at the corners.

"It's Clem, right?" Her voice is cold and clipped.

I nod and give her a sympathetic smile. There's no reason we should be enemies even though that's obviously what Jason wants. She has no idea what she's getting herself into, no idea who he is.

I should warn her.

I hoist my messenger bag higher on my shoulder. "How is the writing going? I had a hard time getting that first book done." Okay, I've had trouble getting the second one done too. "Is your book fiction?"

She lets the question hang in the air and bites her cheek as her eyes shift to the ground.

"I'm, uh, a little stuck."

I shrug. "I'm working on a romance novel right now, and I'm pretty sure it probably sucks. It would help if I liked romances." I can't exactly come straight out and tell her Wheeler might try to cop a feel between edits. "I got a C on my last assignment."

The tension in her shoulders starts to ease with my admission, and she tells me her book is about something that happened to one of her friends when they went on spring break.

Talking to Brigit isn't as hard as I imagined, but she reminds me of a sparrow, ready to fly away at the first sign of trouble, so I don't push.

I offer to send her a pacing guide I got from one of my writing classes, and I scribble my email on a ripped corner of notebook paper and hand it to her.

"Thanks, Clem," she says, smiling, looking a little surprised that I'm trying to help her.

"I volunteer in the tutoring center if you ever want a second pair of eyes to edit something." Or need a few tips to avoid sexual harassment.

Chapter 12

Crouching in the chip aisle of the convenience store to grab a bag of Doritos is the only reason I overhear this conversation. I'm not an eavesdropper. Generally.

"He was such a good lover," a girl with a throaty voice purrs on the other side of the aisle. "And he was so *huge*." Someone giggles. "I don't know why we only had sex a couple of times. Whenever I see him I want to..." She whispers the last part, but I can only imagine what she says.

I bite my lip, embarrassed to be listening in on this personal conversation. I should get my artificial flavor fix and walk away, but I'm rooted in the aisle like a great oak.

"Why did you ever break up? He's fucking hot," the friend, who has a thick New York accent, says loudly, only to have the other one shush her.

"Tammy, shit. Could you be any louder?"

I guess everyone has a friend like that. The loud one. My eyes travel to the Doritos, and I decide to splurge and get a large bag for my roommates. I straighten up and pivot to the opposite wall of goodies and hunt for something chocolate.

"I'll get him back. We were good together. I think he's dating someone, but whatever. He simply doesn't know he needs me. Yet. And if he thinks he can blow me off, he has another thing coming. No stupid bitch is going to stand in my way."

Junior Mints would be really good melted over popcorn, which we already have at home. This evil idea blossoms, and I grab a box.

With an armload of junk food, I round the corner and collide with a whirlwind of crimson.

"What the—" An angry redhead glares at me as my snacks go flying.

"I'm so sorry." I try not to laugh at my clumsiness, but the chick doesn't look amused. In fact, she pales as she watches me pick my snacks off the floor. *She looks familiar. Really familiar.*

The friend nudges Angry Red, but she doesn't say anything. In fact, she watches me pay for my items, and I sense her eyes on my back when I leave.

* * *

A few hours later, my phone buzzes, and I'm expecting another ridiculous sext from Jenna—she's been sending them every five minutes from the other side of the apartment—but it's Gavin.

I have to babysit the children tonight at the dorms. Come keep me company.

We're supposed to go climbing again after classes tomorrow. I'm so tempted to hang out with him, but I'm not sure if that's smart.

Me: *I have to write.*

Gavin: *Do it here and bring some food. Chinese?*

I debate this for a good ten minutes while we banter back and forth. I haven't been able to stop thinking about him all week, and I'm starting to get worried. Something about Gavin makes me warm and fuzzy and mildly euphoric.

Shit. This is bad.

But he won't take no for an answer. He says he's going to

starve, and the next time I'm drunk, I'm going to have to find some other amazingly strong man to carry me home. *Jeez.*

I write him back: *Fine. Since I'm your friend, I'll bring you dinner.*

Gavin: *My friend whose ass looks amazing in those little black shorts.*

What?

Gavin: *Kidding. Kind of. Get over here.*

Me: *Bossy! Give me half an hour.*

* * *

I groan, frustrated, and close my laptop. I've been trying to write for the last forty-five minutes, but the details keep tripping me up.

"What's wrong?" Gavin asks as he leans back in his chair. Tonight, he's writing an article about the need for greater security on campus. Chinese food cartons litter his desk. I'm in my usual spot, stretched out on his bed.

This is going to sound dumb. "I was debating whether I want the love interest, Aiden, to be a flowers guy."

"What do you mean?"

"Is he the kind of guy who gives flowers or not? Romantic or tough guy? I'm still working out my character sketches." I groan. "I should have this figured out by now."

His eyebrows arch. "Well, what do you like? Do you like getting flowers?"

I draw a blank. The problem, once again, is that I have no experience in this area.

Laughing, I say, "I have no idea."

"This should be easy. When a guy brought you flowers, did you like it?" I hear the humor in his voice.

If I make this admission, he's going to think I'm a total moron. He puts his pen down and turns to face me.

"Clementine, please tell me someone has given you flowers."

I can't outright lie to him. I guess I could, but this seems like a stupid reason, not that there's ever really a good reason to be dishonest.

I shake my head slowly. "Not that I remember. I guess I'm having a bit of a dry spell, but see, that's what happens when you don't date. No dating means no flowers."

"What about Daren? Weren't you guys pretty serious?"

"Yeah, but I grew up with him. We made mud pies together, and I crawled in his window with a handful of worms. I don't think he saw me as the kind of girl who liked flowers." I tap my pen on the top of my laptop while I mull it over. "But I think I'd like flowers. I mean, who the hell doesn't like flowers?" I smile. Talking about this character stuff is helpful. I open my laptop and start typing again. "Thanks, Gav. I'm obviously making this too hard. My professor is right. I do need to loosen up."

My phone buzzes with a text from my brother. Reading it makes my stomach tighten and the happy buzz from writing disappear.

"Uh, no," I murmur to myself as I type a message.

"No?" Gavin asks.

"Jax wants me to go home and pack." I shake my head.

"Pack what? I thought you didn't go home."

"I don't." I chew on my nail as I think about it. "My brother wants me to pack up my bedroom because my mother is about to demolish it and put in a workout room or a walk-in closet or some other unnecessary luxury that will help distract her from her rich-people problems."

When I finish responding to Jax, I toss my phone back in my bag, and I look up to find Gavin staring.

"So are you going to do it?" he asks.

Will he think I'm a freak if I tell him the truth? That I don't care? I decide on the truth, or a small version of it at least. "I told him not to worry about it, to let her throw out my stuff."

Gavin's eyes look heavy with questions, but he doesn't ask, and

I don't offer to explain my fucked-up relationship with my mother. He returns to writing his assignment. I like that about him. He knows when to back off.

After another hour of work, he stretches and gets up from his desk. "Baby, have you eaten enough?" he asks as he gathers up the cartons of food.

"Yeah, thanks." *There it is again. Baby.* I watch him for some recognition of this term of endearment, but he's tossing paper plates into the trash and straightening his desk.

My heart is beating erratically. *It is one word, for God's sakes.* I am a total spaz. Glancing at the clock, I realize it's getting late. Maybe this is a good time to head home.

I close my laptop and crawl off his bed. "I have math at eight in the morning tomorrow, so I should get going."

He grins as he walks over and wraps his arms around me. I drop my head on his chest, closing my eyes, relishing the feel of him.

"Your favorite class," he says, his voice deep and almost melodic. I grin against him. "We're still on for climbing tomorrow?"

"Yup."

"Thanks again for editing my article the other day. Where did you learn about leads and attribution?" Gavin asks as he rubs my back.

"I wrote a few articles for the high-school newspaper. Nothing special, but I learned the structure and a few terms."

"You're handy." He looks down and smiles, his eyes shadowed by his long eyelashes.

"Glad I could help. I think it's only fair after all of your expert makeout tutelage."

"Speaking of which, I have a few thoughts for you," he says, leaning down and rubbing his nose against mine.

"Really? I'm all—"

I can't finish because his mouth is on mine, and as we're kissing, he pushes me up against the door. Shoves me, actually, and it's hot. His body is warm and hard against me. Tracing my hands along his strong shoulders, I think about how he scooped me onto the washing machine like I was weightless. I love these arms. There is something so safe about being wrapped up in Gavin Murphy, like I can forget everything when I'm with him, the past, the hurt, the humiliation.

I thread my fingers through his thick, soft hair as our kisses grow deeper. His tongue tangles with mine, sending a bolt of electricity to my core, and I don't want to stop to breathe. After a few minutes, he groans and parts from me.

"If I don't stop now, I won't let you go home." He leans down for another kiss, this one soft, tender. He lingers against my lips for a second and then runs his nose against my jawline, stopping so he can gently bite my earlobe.

I am a nuclear explosion. Fucking Chernobyl. My face is flushed, and parts of me pound like a gavel.

"Have I ever told you that you're irresistible?" he whispers as I tilt my head to give him access to my neck. Yes, kiss my neck!

"No, I think I'd remember that." I have chills running through my body from stem to stern, and I know I have to leave this minute before I give into what I really want to do. "You're pretty damn sexy yourself."

"Let me walk you home," he whispers into my ear.

"No, you have work to do, and I live a block away."

He holds me tighter. "I don't want you walking around by yourself this late at night."

"Campus security has never been tighter. I promise I'll be okay. I'll head straight home." I look up at him, getting lost in those hypnotic green eyes. "I'll call you as soon as I get in."

He sighs, nodding slowly before he presses his lips to my temple and murmurs, "Goodnight, dearest Clementine."

Chapter 13

It's been a hectic few days, and I hate to admit this, but I need my Gavin fix. He had to cancel our usual Friday workout at the gym because he had a last-minute assignment for the *Globe*, and we couldn't grab lunch on Saturday because I had to work a double shift. But this morning he mentions he's hanging with Ryan, so when Jenna invites me to do laundry at her boyfriend's house, I can't resist tagging along.

Ryan's band is sitting around the kitchen table when we arrive. Kade sees me and rolls his eyes, and I resist the urge to drown him in the kitchen sink. Is it my imagination or is he a bigger asshole than I remember?

Poker chips are strewn about, and a few empty pizza boxes litter the counter. I walk up behind Gavin, who looks up at me and smiles so brightly, I feel like I'm bathing in the sun. He's standing up to hug me when his phone buzzes.

"Babe, can you hold my cards for a second?" he asks, kissing me on the cheek before he runs off to take the call. I look at the hand he left me, which I quickly hide against my shirt. When I glance up, everyone is looking at me.

"What?"

Ryan's mouth drops open dramatically before it slides into a grin.

"I see you and Gavin are getting along."

"Yeah, we're friends."

"Friends with muthafucking benefits!" he yells. All the guys start laughing.

"Why do you make everything sound so lewd?" I ask, narrowing my eyes.

"Because Gavin is my boy, and he deserves lewd, a whole lot of lewd, like all up in his face."

Oh, Jesus.

Jenna, who must have caught the last part of this conversation, walks up and leans in to whisper something in his ear. He looks down and nods.

"Sorry I'm giving you shit, Clem. I'll shut up now."

Gavin walks back in, tucking his phone in his pocket before he slides his arm around my waist, pulling me into his lap as he sits. Everyone is staring at me—again—except for Ryan, who is trying hard not to smile as he becomes very interested in his hand. I'm sure I must be crimson by now. The only thing keeping me on Gavin's lap is the fact that I haven't seen him in several days, and, God, I miss his touch.

"Ante up, bitches," Ryan says, throwing in some chips.

Thankful Ryan is switching gears, I reach into my bag and pull out an envelope and hand it to the cute guy I'm sitting on.

"I thought I'd ask if you wanted these before I give them to Ryan."

Gavin reaches around me to open it. "BC vs. USC tickets?" He turns to me. "Seriously?"

"Yes, compliments of one Daren Sloan. They're good seats too. Fifty-yard line, second row."

He angles his head toward me. "You weren't kidding about him sending you tickets?"

"I would never joke about that," I say, brushing a strand of hair out of his face.

"So he's been sending you tickets to every home game for three, going on four years?"

"Something like that."

He frowns, getting an adorable crinkle in his forehead.

Ryan sits up in his chair. "You're giving the BC tickets to this asshole? Clem, *remember* who moved all your crap for the last two summers." He tosses his cards on the table.

I chuck a pretzel at him. "If Gavin wants, he can take you with him. I didn't know you were such a football fanatic, Ryan, or I would have given you all the other tickets I threw out."

Ryan groans again and slams the table, making everyone jump. "You threw them away? I would have killed to see last year's BC/Notre Dame game. Do you have any idea what these tickets are worth?"

I roll my eyes.

"No, and I'm not interested."

Ryan looks like he's going to yank his hair out by its roots. I've never actually seen him so unhinged before. I watch him, curious if he's going to yell at me some more when Gavin tosses the envelope across the table.

"Relax, man," Gavin says, shooting him a look. "You can have the fucking tickets. Just stop freaking out at Clementine."

I start to stand up, but Gavin tightens his hold, pulling me closer. Part of me is mortified to still be on his lap in front of a room of people, but the other part is excited as hell to finally see him.

Twenty minutes later, when I finally get around to tucking a load of laundry into the washer, a pair of hands grip me around the waist, making me scream.

"Damn, baby, you're jumpy." Gavin chuckles, turning me around to kiss my neck. "Your heart is racing."

"You scared the shit out of me!" I smack his chest and he grins.

His eyebrows lift as he peeks over my shoulder. "Hmm. Delicates," he says seductively. "I'd like to get to know your delicates." He ducks back down to nibble on the spot just below my earlobe. He's so delicious my legs might give out.

After a moment, he groans, stopping to press his forehead against mine. "I have to go finish up an article and babysit the freshmen. Want to join me later?"

"I'll think about it," I tease as his lips descend on mine.

"Good. Because Aiden misses the fuck out of Samantha," he mumbles against my mouth, using my fictional characters to make me laugh.

I have to say the feeling is mutual.

* * *

Gavin is stroking my hair, and I'm nestled against his chest as we watch *Sons of Anarchy* on Netflix. I definitely could get used to this.

"I'm sorry Ryan was such a prick today," he says as the credits roll.

"It's okay. I feel bad I didn't give him the other tickets. I've always thrown them away as soon as they arrived and never thought about it."

"Still, he shouldn't have lost his shit that way."

"He's a good guy. He didn't mean anything by it."

I'm playing with the drawstring on his hoodie when the door flies open, slamming against the wall, and the little blonde girl I met a few weeks ago runs in.

"Jesus, Carly, ever heard of knocking?" Gavin asks as we get up.

"Sorry, sorry!" She covers her eyes like she's afraid she might see something she shouldn't. "Marnie is having a seizure or something. Hurry!" She turns and runs out.

I grab my phone, and Gavin and I bolt after her. When we

reach her room, the first thing I see is a bowl of soup that's been dropped in the center of the room. Marnie is sprawled next to the noodles and bits of vegetables, her legs splayed at weird angles as her body shakes. Gavin ducks next to her as I dial 911.

"She has epilepsy," Carly says as Gavin rests Marnie's head on a pillow.

"911. What's your emergency?" a voice says into my ear.

"I need paramedics at 700 Commonwealth Avenue, eighteenth floor of Warren Towers, building A. We're in room…" I pause to glance at the number on the door and relay the information before I explain Marnie's medical condition.

Carly is starting to cry, so I put my arm on her shoulder when I get off the phone.

"Marnie's going to be okay. You got us really fast. Does she have any medication for this?"

Carly shakes her head and sniffles. "Not that I know of."

When the paramedics arrive, they load Marnie on to the stretcher. She looks pale and a little glassy-eyed. Gavin walks next to her, holding her hand. He looks over to me, and I wave bye. He motions that he'll call me later. Nodding, I turn back to Carly, who is still sniffling.

* * *

Forty-five minutes later, I am definitely in the seventh circle of hell. One girl is braiding my hair while Carly and another perky brunette dab a honey-yogurt mask on my face. Jenna would be in heaven.

It can't get any worse, though, right? Then One Direction blares from the speakers, reminding me that I should never ask that question.

I'm wondering how to politely duck out of this as I turn and see Gavin leaning in the doorway.

"Clementine?" He chuckles as he soaks in the scene.

"Yeah. Don't ask."

Carly bobs up and down on her toes and claps her hands. "We *love* Clem. Can we keep her? She's so beautiful!"

"Ladies, she's not a pet. Stop pawing at her. Clementine has to get up early tomorrow. I'm going to steal her, but if you're good, she might visit."

They giggle. A few minutes later, I walk out of Gavin's bathroom, wiping my face with a towel.

"Thanks for getting me out of there. They were upset, so I suggested manicures because that's what my roommates like to do when they're stressed, and the next thing I know I was being coated in honey and yogurt. I'm still a little sticky," I say, trying to wipe off a bit of goo on my neck.

"I'll be the judge of that," he says, pulling me to him and placing feather-light kisses across my face. When he reaches my jaw, I tilt my head to the side, letting him nuzzle against me.

"Mmm. Found a spot." His soft kisses stop as he takes a small lick up my neck. *Oh, shit. That was hot.* "You taste really good," he whispers.

His mouth migrating across my collarbone makes it difficult to think coherently. "I don't know how I ended up as their guinea pig." I'm starting to pant. Fuck.

"They. Wanted. A perfect specimen," he says between kisses.

My knees are weak, and I'm about to push him onto his bed and let him touch me any way he wants when a loud knock on the door makes me jump.

"God, that scared me," I laugh, nerves shooting through me like my parents just caught us, an idea that gives me pause because of course my parents don't give a shit.

Gavin opens the door and an older guy is standing there with a clipboard.

"Incident report for the lucky RA," the man says cheerfully as he hands over a stack of paperwork.

I know this is going to take a while, so I grab my bag. "I'm gonna get out of your hair so you can take care of this."

Gavin smiles grimly, and I wink back before heading home. I'm not even on my street yet when he texts me.

Gavin: *Can I finally take you on a proper date? I'm warning you, though. If you say no, then Aiden is going to ask Samantha out, and she has to say yes.*

My throat tightens as I think about his request. *Relax. It's a date. He's not asking you to elope.* I laugh at myself, at how ridiculous I'm being.

Me: *My book boyfriend is so demanding!*

Gavin: *Pick you up on Friday at 7.*

I laugh at his presumptuousness, that he assumes I'll agree. But do I really want to decline? No. I want to spend time with him. In fact, I love spending time with him. I write back: *I guess I could use some more inspiration...*

Glad no one can see the idiotic grin on my face, I duck into my building. When I get into my room, his incoming message buzzes my phone: *Wouldn't want you to run into another dry spell.*

Me: *So really, this is in the name of higher learning.*

Gavin: *Funny you should mention that because you're my favorite subject. I could study you all day.*

His flirtatiousness makes me smile wider.

I love that about him, which is weird because for the past three years, I've ignored every guy who flirted with me. Every single one. But Gavin is different somehow. Sexy but sensitive. Strong but gentle. Easygoing but somehow intense. He can turn me inside out with one look, one touch, one kiss.

The second I get home, I get another text from him asking if I got home safely. God, a girl could get used to Gavin Murphy.

I'm lonely in my bed without him, which makes me wonder how far I'll let things go on Friday night, an idea that both thrills and terrifies me.

Chapter 14

This may be the worst coffee in town, but it's fast and cheap and ready right now. I'm putting the lid on my twenty-four-ounce cup of joe when someone steps up next to me.

"Hey, sexy."

I whirl around to see Gavin.

He laughs at the look on my face. "Not used to guys trying to pick you up while you're getting your coffee fix?"

"Shut up, goofball. You scared me, whispering in my ear like that."

He smiles and wraps me in a hug in the middle of the convenience store, and I try to sniff him without looking like a total creeper. I don't know what shower gel he uses, but it makes me want to lick him.

"Where you headed?" He keeps his hand on my waist.

"The tutoring center. Don't worry, I'm not out trying to pass myself off as a math whiz. I edit essays."

My therapist suggested tutoring last year to help me be more social because, apparently, I need help in this area.

"What a relief."

Before I can respond, he pulls me to him and kisses me on the forehead. I smile a big, toothy grin, and I'm sure I look like an idiot, so I bite my cheek to rein it in.

"I hope Marnie is feeling better. Is she back from the hospital?"

"Yeah, she'll be okay. She hasn't had a seizure in a while, so I think that scared her the most." We pay for our drinks and walk out to the street. "You were pretty awesome last night. I meant to tell you."

"What are you talking about? You're the one who handled the whole thing. I only did facials."

"Clementine, come on. Carly was in tears when I left, and when I returned, she was having a blast. You're really good in a crisis."

"No, I think that was a first."

He walks me to the liberal arts building, but before he leaves for class, he ducks his head toward mine, leaving us practically nose to nose.

Gavin drops his voice just above a whisper. "We still on for Friday?"

My heart thump, thump, thumps in my chest. "If I say yes, does this mean you're going to woo me with more than take-out Thai?"

"I'm going to break out my best moves. I promise."

In this light, his eyes have golden flecks amid the green. "Honestly, I don't know if Samantha is ready for it. She's a little on the shy side." I swallow and look down except he takes his thumb and lifts my chin so I have to look him in the eye. *Thump, thump, thump.*

"It's okay. Aiden can be very persuasive." And before he turns to leave, he plants a kiss on my mouth, lingering on my lips as he says, "I'll call you later."

I watch him walk away, wishing I could rewind the last ten

minutes of my life so I could see them play out again. And again. In slow motion.

Floating a good twelve inches out of my shoes, I dart into the tutoring lab. The large room is ice-cold, and my Converse squeak on the tile floor, causing a few students to pop their heads up to stare at my offending shoes.

Behind the volunteer desk is Kade, shuffling through his backpack.

Shit.

I knew he tutored economics and other boring-as-hell subjects, but I've usually had the good luck to avoid him. His hair is a mess, and he looks like he slept in his clothes.

I clear my throat. "What happened to Gina?" She usually coordinates all the volunteers.

He glances up and rolls his eyes at me before tossing a clipboard across the desk.

"It's nice to see you too, Kade," I mutter before I pencil in my name on a few open slots for next month. Gone is my fluttery, Gavin-is-so-adorable giddiness.

"You shouldn't wait until the last minute," Kade says, not bothering to look at me. He turns to the computer and curses under his breath as he reaches over to pull out the paper tray on the printer.

"Some of us have to work for a living." I expect some snarky comment, but instead he types something on the keyboard. "I had to wait for my schedule at the bookstore before I could sign up for October."

After restacking some neon pink paper, he slams the tray back into the machine, making me flinch. Jesus, what's gotten into him?

"Are... are you okay? You're acting more assholish than usual."

I wait for his comeback, which usually entails some kind of reference to us having sex. We've had this kind of relationship since sophomore year when I met him through Ryan. Kade is the kind of guy who is nice until you turn him down, and then he's a dick-stick, looking to unleash his wrath on the poor girls who dare to think he's not the biggest catch on the Eastern Seaboard. And since I unequivocally turned him down the first time, he's been a raging prick to me ever since.

The printer starts to churn again.

"Leave it on the desk when you're done," he says, motioning toward the clipboard before he turns his back to me.

I grab my bag off the counter and start to sling it over my shoulder when I catch a glimpse of his computer screen and see a familiar face. *He's printing missing posters.*

"Kade," I say softly, "do you know Olivia?"

He stills and takes a deep breath before he turns to face me. "I'm not in the mood for this, Clem, and yes, I know her."

His face looks pained, his mouth a tight line, his eyes full of emotion. We've never shared any fun or easygoing times despite having the same circle of friends, but I know that look. After what happened with Professor Wheeler freshman year, for months, every time I stood in front of a mirror I saw a similar expression.

Even though Kade has never done me any favors, I have a hard time walking away. This must be what Gavin meant when he said Kade was going through a tough time.

Lowering my voice, I say, "Can I help you post those up around campus? I have to get to class right now, but I can probably put some up this afternoon."

He looks up, surprised, and clears his throat. It takes him a second to respond. "Yeah, that would be great."

I take a stack of fliers and start to leave but can't. Rubbing the back of my neck, I turn back and inch toward his desk. *Be an adult, Clementine.* In my head I try to ignore every insult he's ever given me, every dirty look, every rude remark. And there have been a few.

"There's one more thing." I crouch in front of his desk so we're eye level with each other. "I feel bad leaving you like this. I know we've never gotten along, but I don't see why we can't be friends. I want us to have coffee tomorrow, okay?" He looks dubious. "You can even pretend we slept together, and I was the worst lay ever."

He cracks a smile.

"I have seen your tits. Let's not forget."

And just like that, the asshole is back. I smirk and let him have his dig. At least he's not thinking about Olivia.

* * *

Kade is sitting at a small table in the corner of the coffee house when I walk in the next morning. He already has a cup in front of him, so I order a latte and sit across from him.

"I put up those flyers all over West Campus yesterday evening. Do you have any more? Because I ran out."

His eyebrows are knitted tightly on his forehead. "Thanks. That's great. I can get you some more."

I pop open my drink, toss in two packets of sugar and stir. "How do you know Olivia?"

He sucks in his lips briefly and shakes his head. "How else? I asked her out last year, we dated a while, I was a dick, and then we stopped talking."

I tilt my head as I stare at him. Kade's hair is spiked up and forward into his face. His fierce hazel eyes peer back at me. He's handsome, there's no doubt about it, but the second he opens his mouth, girls want to slap him.

"Kade."

"Clem."

"Have you ever tried being nice?"

His face twists into a half-smirk. "Says the pot."

I take a sip of my drink. "Touché. But I'm *trying* to be a nicer person. Thus, here we are, drinking coffee together despite the dozens of insults we've swapped." He's wearing a t-shirt and jeans and a rustic-looking brown leather jacket. *Better than that just-rolled-out-of-bed look he was rocking yesterday.* "On paper, you are a catch. You're good-looking, you're smart, and when you're not being a dick, you're kind of funny, not that I would ever give you the satisfaction of laughing at one of your jokes. Why do you have to be such a jerk all the time?"

He raises his eyebrows. "You think I'm good-looking?"

"That's what you got from what I just said?" I give him a look, and he shrugs. "I'm trying to be helpful. Trust me, I'm not interested."

"Yeah, I know. You have that thing going on with Murphy."

I don't know how to answer that, so I ignore the comment. "I think there's more to you, but you never let anyone see it. If you make a deliberate attempt to *not* piss off girls, you might find that they like you for more than a month or two. It's a crazy concept I have. Try it out."

"Fine." He rolls his eyes at me, but he's fighting a smile.

"Tell me about Olivia. I've read a couple of articles about her. She spent last semester in England?"

"Yeah, but she traveled all over Europe before she returned." He looks like he wants to say something else but doesn't.

"What?"

He shakes his head. "This is going to sound weird."

"Try me. But don't be an asshole."

Kade laughs, and it's good to see a full-fledged smile on his face. "Livvy reminded me a little of you. She had this long brownish-blonde hair, and she loved to write. But she wasn't as opinionated as some people I know," he says, deepening his voice melodramatically.

"Me? Have opinions? Puh-leese." I fold over a sugar packet until it's the shape of a triangle. "She was an English major, right?"

"Yeah, she could read a novel in a night. It was really fucking annoying. You would have liked her."

The way he talks about her in the past tense doesn't escape me, and my heart breaks a little.

"She sounds like a great girl. Do you talk to her family?"

"Her sister. She's really fucked up over this. Norah had convinced Livvy to come home for the Fourth of July weekend since they always partied it up together." Kade twists the mug in his hands.

"Have you talked to Gavin about her? You know he's been writing all of those articles for the *Freep*, right?"

"Yeah, we've talked, but I don't know anything that could help him, and I don't want to be quoted in the newspaper. I hate how people come out of the woodwork to get attention when shit like this happens."

That right there makes me warm up to him a little more. When my family is in the tabloids, people I don't even know talk about me like we're best friends.

Maybe Kade's not such a huge asshole after all.

"I know what you mean." I stir my drink a few times, not knowing what to say. "I'm sorry, Kade. I really am. Please call me if I can help put up flyers or make posters. Whatever you need."

He nods. "The thing is, I pushed her away. For the life of me, I don't know why. Livvy put up with my shit, she was beautiful and smart, but I had my head up my ass."

"But what happened to her wasn't your fault."

Frustration and remorse lurk behind his eyes. "She decided to go abroad after we broke up. She was pissed at me."

Okay, I'm doing a suck-ass job of giving this guy a pep talk. "Look, people break up all the time. You're not the first guy to piss off a girl. Trust me." He smirks. "She might have had the time of her life in England. What happened to her when she got home isn't any more your fault than her sister's."

He stares at the table. "Do you ever feel like you don't like who you're becoming?"

I laugh, and his eyes dart to mine. "Kade, honestly, you're frightening me. I never thought I'd have anything in common with you, but to answer your question, yes. What you said basically encapsulates most of my college experience."

"I thought you were perfect." He makes a U shape with his hands, and I flick my football made from a sugar packet toward the goal. Of course, I miss.

"About as perfect as you."

He rubs his chin and grins. "I've never told you this before, Clem, but you're a cool girl."

I smile back.

"Thanks. You're not too bad yourself."

Chapter 15

The sun is shining; the wind off the river is a perfect forty-five degrees; my heart is aflutter with thoughts of Gavin; Kade and I have called a truce; and my professor likes what I've written. I dare say the feeling I'm experiencing is called happiness.

"You biotch," Jenna whispers when she sees my grade on our last submission. "You got an A on your last submission?"

I nod, shushing her. Professor Marceaux is doing her daily strut. That's what I call it. The focal point of this woman's body is her hips, which she points to the far reaches of the earth as she walks. It reminds me of the catwalk models do, but this is more organic somehow, like she was birthed from erotic sculptures that infused sexuality through her all the way down to her toes. Watching her as she passes out the revised syllabus, I realize she'd make a great character. Inspired, I jot down a few notes in my journal before I lose the vision.

I'm marveling at my good turn of luck, at my ability to take things in stride, at how far I've come, when it all comes crashing down.

Clenching my eyes shut, I try to get a grip before I totally freak out. Jenna's quick intake of breath tells me she sees it too. When I open my eyes, my name is still there on the paper in front of me. My roommate nudges me, and when I turn to her, the lump in my throat rises.

"Our class is critiquing your book." Her words, a mixture of praise and worry, seize the very core of me.

I nod infinitesimally, barely able to breathe.

* * *

I'm hot and sticky. I smell. Running hasn't purged me of all my nervous energy, but it's helped. I've been pumping myself with positive thoughts for the last hour. Harper is always telling me the fear of a situation is worse than the reality. I hope she's right and that I don't pass out in the middle of class or piss my pants next week when we critique my book.

I open the door to our apartment and stop short. Gavin and Ryan are hanging out with Jenna and Dani.

"Hi, guys." I wave, embarrassed that I look like crap, but the grin on Gavin's face damn near makes me forget my name.

"Good! You're back!" Jenna proclaims. "You looked pretty pissed when you left, so I wasn't sure if you'd be out running a marathon. You have time for a quick shower before the pizza gets here."

Gavin gets up to hug me, but I put up both hands to stop him. "I'm sweaty."

He grabs me anyway and whispers, "Not a problem in my book, darlin'." I crack a smile. "Is everything okay? Why were you upset?" His eyes are full of concern as his hands grip my shoulders.

"It's a long story. Can I tell you later?" I'm just starting to get a handle on everything, and I don't feel like rehashing it right now.

He nods, kissing my forehead and then smacking his lips. "You're salty."

I laugh, pushing him away. "I warned you."

When I emerge from the steamy bathroom fifteen minutes later, I grab a slice of pizza and sit next to Gavin as Harper walks in the front door.

"Look who I found loitering outside," she says. "This bum claims he's your brother."

Behind her, Jax struts in carrying a large cardboard box. I haven't seen him since that horrid afternoon at Ryan's house. Jax's hair is longer than he usually keeps it, but he's tanned and sleek like a panther, brimming with that overconfident edge he's always had.

"Hey, loser," he says, placing the box on the coffee table next to the pizza.

"Hey, yourself." As I eye the box, a knot forms in my stomach. I stare at my name on the side, written in my brother's blocky handwriting. "I told you I didn't want this."

I get up and walk to the micro-fridge to grab some paper towels. My brother sighs at me. It's one of those long, drawn-out sighs that reminds me of our mother.

"She was throwing away all of your shit. I know you don't care about it now, but you might someday." Rubbing the back of his neck, he laughs as he turns to my roommates. "You'd never know this girl was prom queen." I give him a look, and he shakes his head. "Wait, you were homecoming queen too."

"Jax, I never cared about that," I say, ducking into my room. Although homecoming was fun, I only got voted prom queen because everyone felt sorry for me. It was so fucking humiliating. My face gets hot thinking about it.

My brother follows behind me and grips the top of the doorframe.

"Exactly. That's why you were so popular."

Rolling my eyes, I say, "I was popular because I was dating the 'star quarterback.'"

My brother ignores my sarcasm. "That's not why. Clem, before all that shit went down with Daren, you were the coolest girl I knew. You were the party. You could make anything fun. I miss that girl. I miss my sister."

"Yeah, well, that makes two of us," I say grimly.

Jax is quiet, and I don't remember why I came in here, but seeing my brother in the doorway, blocking my exit, makes me claustrophobic.

He clears his throat. "You know, Daren still feels really bad about what happened."

I glare at him. After all this time, my brother *finally* wants to talk about it? "Why are you telling me this? Do you still think I'm hung up on Daren?"

"I don't know. You haven't dated anyone since high school, and I know you loved him. I just want you to get over it and have a life again. I mean, you stopped running track, you never go out, you hardly have any friends."

I've decided that my brother is a certifiable asshole. I throw up my hands in frustration.

"What do you even know about me, Jackson? I *lost* my track scholarship, so I've had to work my ass off to pay for my tuition. My professor attacked me when I was a freshman. I'd say I'm doing pretty damn well considering."

His blue eyes widen, and he stammers, "I... I didn't know any of that."

A gaping silence settles between us. I don't bother bringing up how my freshman-year roommate freaked out on me because of my brother and his man-whoring ways.

"What do you mean your professor attacked you?" Jax looks pale, and his jaw is clenched.

I shake my head, my chest flooded with the dark buzz of panic. This is how an attack starts. I suck in a few deep breaths, forcing myself to focus on my brother's scuffed shoe.

"Fucking hell, Clementine. Who is this asshole?"

My eyes shift up. The vein in Jax's temple is the only movement in his tightly coiled body.

"Forget about it. There's nothing you can do." Or could do. Even if Jax had known back then, the end result would have been the same, right? "I'm fine now." Not so much back then.

"Why didn't you tell me?" The pain in his voice cuts through me.

My heart sinks at the answer. Does he really want to hear this? Can I even say it? I lick my dry lips.

"You didn't back me up with Daren." The words are a whisper. "Why would you care about this?"

Jax winces, and I keep going. "Our parents didn't seem to care." The laugh that escapes me is tinged with resentment. "You know, they don't pay for my shit like they pay for yours," I say, eying his perfectly cut leather jacket.

Sweat breaks out on my forehead. I wish he'd leave and take that damn box with him.

My brother always thinks he has the answers. We used to be so close. Inseparable. But now, as I stare at a face I know as well as my own, I realize we haven't known each other for a long time.

"Jax, if you think what happened with Daren is what broke me, you don't know me at all."

"Then what was it? What happened? Is it what went down with your professor?"

I tilt my head, wondering how my twin can be so clueless. "The people I trusted most betrayed me. Mom and Dad... and you."

His eyes narrow. "How? How did I betray you? Because Daren is my best friend?"

Jax wants to go there? Fine.

I take a step closer to him and look him eye to eye, my heart beating in my throat. I try to speak, but nothing comes out. Taking a breath, I try again.

"When did you find out Daren was sleeping with Veronica?"

His eyes dart away as a mixture of emotions—anger, guilt, shame—cross his face. He swallows.

"Exactly. You knew, and you didn't tell me." *Dick.*

He closes his eyes. "I almost broke his jaw."

My head snaps toward him. "What?"

"I almost broke Daren's jaw when I found out." His eyes are still closed.

Thinking back to that spring, I remember Daren getting injured at a training camp the week before I broke up with him.

"He said he got hurt in a scrimmage."

His eyes slide up to meet mine. "Yeah. A scrimmage with my fist."

The lump in my throat threatens to choke me. This whole time I thought Jax had known and done nothing.

"Why didn't you just tell me?"

His jaw clenches and unclenches. "You're my sister. Daren is like my brother. Deep down, I had this crazy idea that you two would end up together, and I was afraid to get in the middle. I'm not gonna lie—I was going through my own shit back then, so I know I wasn't the best brother. I didn't notice when Daren started sneaking around with that cunt."

I flinch at my brother's choice of words, realizing for the first time that he hates Veronica, probably on my behalf.

He exhales like he's been holding his breath.

"When I first found out he was cheating on you, I didn't want to believe it, but the rumors wouldn't go away, so I confronted him. And when we were done with that *conversation*, he knew he needed to man up and sort out his shit and talk to you. Only you figured it out first."

I blink back hot tears that threaten to spill over.

"Clem, you must have thought I'd gone on with my friendship with him like nothing happened, but it took a few years to get past it." Jax shifts in the doorway and crosses his arms over his chest.

"And I know he still feels like shit over what he did to you. That helps."

We stand on opposite sides of the room, and I'm too overwhelmed to speak. His eyes fall on the moving box.

"Look," he says softly, "I know Mom has been hard on you, but I think she misses you."

I know he doesn't believe that, but it's the kind of lie we've always told ourselves. *Mom wanted to come to the game, but she had a meeting. Dad missed a flight home from Paris because he got stuck in traffic. They didn't mean to forget our birthday.*

But I'm no longer twelve and in desperate need of their approval, and hearing that bullshit now snaps something inside of me. "She sure has a fucked-up way of showing it. Nothing says I love you like 'take your shit before I toss it on the street.'"

"You're not being fair. You haven't called either of them or gone to see them..." He's saying the right words, but not even Jax can put any conviction behind it.

I should be sad that he talks about our parents as though our father didn't disappear to another continent without a second thought. Or as though our mother is any kind of maternal figure. But I'm too pissed to go along with the charade.

"Are you serious right now?" I've avoided this conversation with him for three years, but now all of my carefully clamped-down emotion is at the surface, hot and bubbling like lava. "Did you ever wonder how I lost my state meet after I won all the others my senior year? How I barely eked out a fifth-place finish when my practice times could have beaten every girl that day?"

Jax shrugs.

"Mom found out I had broken up with Daren that morning. I was walking out the door, and she told me it was my fault Daren cheated on me because I should have slept with him months ago. She said, 'Why do you think I put you on the pill?' Then she said she was late for a meeting and left."

The emotion of this conversation catches up with me, and tears stream down my face.

"So did Daren break my heart? Yes. Did he hurt me by hooking up with my best friend? Yes. But you have no idea how humiliating it is to have the whole school know that your boyfriend is getting blow jobs in the weight room and your own brother knows and doesn't tell you, or that your mother doesn't care that her daughter is dating an asshole."

I put on a sweatshirt and sniffle.

"Jax, I get that you didn't know what to do, but you should have told me. If you had, maybe I wouldn't have found them fucking in his bed."

His eyes widen as more tears fall down my cheeks.

"They didn't know I had walked in. Not that either would have cared."

My body starts to move, and I have only a vague awareness of what I'm doing. The running shoes slip on, and my fingers tie the laces.

Jax clears his throat.

"Clementine, I'm so sorry. For everything, I—"

I get up and push past him into the living room where I come to a dead halt when I see everyone looking at me. Fuck. When my eyes meet Gavin's, I look down. My heart thunders in my chest. God damn it.

"I'm going for another run," I say as I walk out. When I reach the bottom of the stairwell, I'm vaguely aware that someone is calling my name, but it doesn't matter. *Nothing matters*, I think as I head out onto the dark street.

* * *

The living room is quiet. I tiptoe into my room and find Harper asleep on my bed. The creak of my door wakes her, and she yawns before she registers what's going on.

"Hey, you're back. I saved you some pizza. Actually, Gavin did. He wants you to call him. He'd still be here, but he had a late shift tonight at the dorm."

"I'm okay, Harper. You don't need to babysit me." I can barely kick off my running shoes much less eat a slice of pizza.

"I know I don't, but I didn't want you to come home to an empty room." She starts to stretch and then frowns. "Clem, Jax is wrong. You have friends."

The thought that the whole world heard the argument I had with my brother makes me nauseous.

"You guys heard everything?" Maybe I'm wrong. Maybe they only heard snippets here and there.

She nods, looking apologetic. "Your door was open. It was hard to miss."

I smile weakly. "What can I say? Jax and I bring out the best in each other."

"I know you're pissed at him, but he loves you. He wouldn't have taken the time to pack up your stuff and bring it to you if he didn't care. What he did to you in high school was totally shitty, and I get that, but he grew up in the same screwed-up family you did. You can't exactly expect flowers to bloom in the desert."

I grin through my fatigue. "That was some nice metaphorical language there, Harps."

As she gets up, I collapse on the bed, too tired to shower and too numb to care.

"Don't you want to call Gavin?"

"Not really." In fact, that's the last thing I want to do.

"Can I offer my unsolicited opinion?"

I mumble into my pillow, "Will you stop talking if I say no?"

"Probably not." She takes the silence as my acquiescence, but exhaustion prevents my mouth from moving. "Don't shut Gavin out. You tend to cut people out of your life when you get scared or overwhelmed. I think you're afraid of being judged. Give Gavin a little more credit."

"Thanks, Doctor. How much do I owe you for our session?" I should be grateful she's a psych major.

She swats me on the leg for being a smartass. "Clem, we love you."

"I know. I love you too, nosey."

She chuckles as she shuts my door.

Chapter 16

Jax is an asshole. Daren is too. Gavin isn't. But he probably thinks I'm a dumbass after what he heard yesterday.

I want to wallow in self-pity all morning, but I have to drag myself to math at the ass-crack of dawn. I sit in class, taking notes, copying down formulas, but my head doesn't process anything except that my mechanical pencil is running out of lead.

I can't believe Jax thinks this is all about Daren.

Another formula. Scribble, scribble. The professor asks whether we understand the concept. *No.* I nod yes.

In between classes, I take Gavin's call. He says he understands that I don't want to talk about what happened last night, but I'm sure he doesn't get it. How could he? He has a nice two-parent household and younger sister, and they probably all sit around at dinner time and say shit like "Pass the peas!" and "How was your day, dear?"

By the time I get off the phone, I'm not sure I want to see him on Friday. I don't like being put out for display. Harper is right about how I shut out people, but I can't help how I feel. Gavin heard things I've only told one or two people, and I've only known him, what, a month?

Considering it was only twenty-four hours ago that I was marveling at myself in Professor Marceaux's class and thinking my life was so great, I'd say the recent events are about on par with the shit that goes down in my life. How I thought I could change my luck now is beyond wishful thinking. More along the lines of delusional.

After another class, I trudge through campus toward the student union, exhaustion saturating my limbs. Lunch, I need lunch. My hands are trembling, probably from low blood sugar, and my head is so foggy I barely notice that I'm standing next to Brigit as I wait in a long line to pay for my food.

"Clem, how are you?"

I nod politely while I suck down some juice so I don't pass out.

She ignores my grunt and says, "That pacing guide you emailed me is great." She looks surprised I actually sent it to her. *See, I'm not such a bitch.*

"Glad I could help." I offer a weak smile and pop a baby carrot into my mouth.

Her face lights up, and we end up talking about our schedules. She's a sweet girl with big, soulful brown eyes that get even wider when she's excited about something.

"Jason says you're published, that your book is really good," she says as I reach for my wallet.

Wheeler complimented my writing? Not what I was expecting. It doesn't escape me that she's calling him by his first name. It starts that way. Casually. Him asking you to call him Jason, you thinking he's just cool and down-to-earth.

"He's being kind. I'm sure it's horse shit."

She giggles and smiles appreciatively. "I'd love to read it. What's the title?"

Oh, hell.

I pay for my lunch and pick up the tray. Turning to face her, I brace my hand on the counter, still feeling lightheaded. Wisps of her dark hair fall into her eyes, and I shudder to think how much Wheeler could hurt Brigit if I don't do anything.

"Next," the cashier calls out.

Brigit puts her food down to pay and turns back to me. "You write under a pen name, right? I swear I won't tell anyone." She bounces on her toes.

My breath catches, and I feel people move around me as I stand stock-still. A knot forms in my throat, the one that tightens when I think about how much Jason Wheeler knows about me. How he could destroy me. Again.

Internally, I debate whether this is the right decision, telling someone I hardly know. *Wait. Why am I even considering this? I haven't even told Gavin for fuck's sake.*

That lock of hair falls in her eyes again, and she smiles, and there's something so innocent about her expression. Something I want to protect.

Sensing my unease, Brigit sidles closer to me. "Your secret is safe with me. I promise." She holds up her pinky. Her nails are each painted a different color. I look closer and see that her pinkies are purple with little hearts. *Good lord.*

So, yes, I fucking pinky-swear in the middle of the cafeteria and decide she's too cute for her own good.

But as I'm internally debating whether I can actually tell her the name of my book, someone yells her name across the cafeteria.

I turn to catch two girls motioning to Brigit, who huffs out a breath at the sight of her obnoxious friends.

"C'mon, Bridge!" the girl yells again. "Shake your ass!"

Brigit looks mortified.

I bump her with my elbow. "Go on. We'll catch up later," I tell her, relieved at the reprieve. "I'll send you another handout I got in class this week. For your story."

She nods, her smile reappearing, before she trots off to join her friends.

Exhaling, I wonder what the hell I was thinking. I should

know by now that confiding in a stranger is a cardinal sin. I have to find a better way to win Brigit's trust. And I can't wait much longer to tell her about Wheeler.

Grabbing my food, I settle at a table in the corner of the dining hall. Trying to shake off my lingering anxiety, I get out my laptop and grab my journal.

My cell buzzes, and I see a text from Jenna: *I'm wet for you.* Choking back a laugh, I write her back: *Dry off.*

Jenna: *Biotch, you're supposed to play the game!*

Munching on another carrot until I can think of a good Out-Skank comeback, I try to get in a dirty frame of mind. As I punch in the text with my thumbs, I look around to make sure no one can see my screen.

Me: *Dripping wet makes for easy access.*

Jenna: *Want to slip and slide?*

Eyeing a guy's hot dog as he squeezes ketchup on it, I smile.

Me: *Let me sink my meat into your bun hard and fast.*

I'm blushing at my response when laughter bubbling up across the student union catches my attention. A tall redhead is tilting her head back, laughing flirtatiously at something a guy is saying. She has her hands on his shoulders as she leans in to say something obviously only meant for him to hear. They're in a group of mostly guys, but she's only paying attention to this one.

Angry Red. It's the girl I overheard in the convenience store. Except now she's wearing makeup and her hair is done.

She's beautiful. Tall, leggy, with curves I could never have. I know I'm in great shape, but all that exercise means my boobs could never look like hers. I don't know why I'm comparing myself to her. I don't have body issues like a lot of girls, but for some reason I can't stop watching her.

Deciding it's rude to blatantly stare, I grab my sandwich. *Boobs,* I tell myself. *Eating can give me bigger boobs.* Just as I'm about to take a bite, I glance up, and my heart slams to a stop in my chest. Because the guy she is talking to, whispering to, touching, is Gavin.

* * *

The truth is, I have no idea what's going on with Gavin and Angry Red. He and I never said we were exclusive. Hell, we've never actually been on a real date.

It's not as though he can cheat on someone he's not even dating. I bristle at the thought. *He's free to go out with whomever he wants, weirdo.*

It's not fair to judge him based on what happened with Daren, but I'll be the world's biggest idiot if I walk head-on into the same situation all over again. So I go straight to the only girl I consider an expert on these sorts of things: Jenna. After she compliments my Out-Skanking skills, I sit her on the couch.

Her mouth forms a small "o" as I explain what I saw at lunch, but when I'm done, instead of looking adequately horrified, she laughs.

"That's his ex, Angelique," she says like she's relieved. I'm glad someone is because that knowledge doesn't really clarify things for me. Of course the stunning redhead would have a name like some kind of A-list celebrity. Sensing my apprehension, Jenna pats my shoulder. "She's, like, stalking him. He broke up with her this summer, but she won't go away. I think she's an RA too, so they're always forced to do things together, but he's not happy about it. He was complaining to Ryan about it at your party. She's always tagging along, and he's too nice to tell her to fuck off."

Jenna bites her nail as she watches my reaction.

"I guess... I guess I am jumping to conclusions." The more I think about it, the more I realize I never saw his reaction to Angelique being so close to him. He was facing away from me the whole time. I assumed he was into her because she looks like a red-headed version of Angelina Jolie. Yeah, unequivocally gorgeous.

But before I get too far ahead of myself, I tell Jenna what I overheard Angry Red say in the convenience store, and she shrugs.

"You know, you could always ask him about her and see what he says."

Oh dear God, no. After everything that's happened this week, the last thing I need to do is grill him about his ex. *Because that would make it* less *awkward between us.*

It sucks that he knows everything about my love life, and I don't know anything about his, which does nothing to assuage my unease. But in the end, I have no claim to Gavin. He's a free agent, and I'm... well, I'm nobody.

I hug Jenna and shuffle back to my room. I need to stay focused on what matters, so I log on to Goodreads and scroll through my messages. Gavin and I might go to hell in a handbasket, but I have to graduate, which means I need to sell some books to pay the bills. I haven't come this far to screw up now.

Most of my messages are from supportive fans, but when I get to one nasty review about *Say It Isn't So*, I feel nauseous.

"How could the main character Isabelle be so stupid? I don't know how your best friend sleeps with your boyfriend RIGHT UNDER YOUR NOSE and you're clueless. I don't buy the premise of this book. No girl is that big of an idiot. Plus, I can't get over the fact that she goes out a few weeks later and has a one-night stand. She wouldn't sleep with her boyfriend for nine months, but she'll screw some stranger? What a moron."

I'd like to write her and tell her, yes, people are this stupid. I'm living, breathing proof.

I shouldn't let this person's opinion bother me, but it does, which means I have to read her review three more times.

* * *

After class, Harper and I duck into the convenience store on the way home to pick up some half-and-half, a must-have for our caffeine-addicted household. As we reach the counter to pay, she gives me a look.

"What's wrong, Clem? You're acting weird."

Now that I'm standing in one of the shops on the floor level of Warren Towers, I can't stop thinking about it.

"Last Sunday, Gavin asked me out on a real date, and I think I'm getting cold feet. I mean, he's a great guy, but..." There's Angry Red, and Gavin heard my argument with Jax. It's all too much.

"But you don't want to get hurt."

I nod, tears welling up in my eyes, which I blink away.

"I want to bail, but we're supposed to go out tomorrow night, and it would be really shitty of me to cancel on him now, wouldn't it?"

After Harper hands the clerk some money, she turns to me.

"You're going to need to do what's right for you. It's not ideal to cancel tonight, but maybe that's a better option than relapsing into panic-attack mode."

She gets her change, tucks it into her wallet and twists her lips like she's thinking. "How about this? Go see him now—make up a reason, any reason—and if you're still freaked out after seeing him, you can politely back out, face to face. I think having the guts to do it in person makes up for the late notice. On the other hand, maybe seeing him is what you need to relax and be excited about going out with him."

"You're a genius." Hooking my arm in hers, I smile. "But what can I use as an excuse?"

"Just say you thought you forgot something there—a spiral, notes, some lint," she says, nudging me at her joke.

"Okay," I say, taking a deep breath. "Will you come with me? Up to his room? You can get a text or a phone call and have to leave right away, but I could use the moral support."

"Sure."

We walk up to the big glass doors that lead to the dorm. Once we're in the elevator, my heart starts pounding.

"Relax, Clem." Harper tightens her arm through mine. "He's

your friend, right? If you decide to not go out tomorrow night, a friend will understand."

She has a point. *And if I'm his friend, I shouldn't bail.* I'm chewing on this idea when the doors open to the eighteenth floor. Gavin's door is open, but there's no one there, so I knock and call out his name. That's when I hear the music coming down the hall from the common area.

I let go of Harper's arm and walk toward the sound of the guitar. When we reach the big open room, I see Gavin softly strumming, while about a dozen students crowd around, listening. His back is to us, and his head is down. Harper leans on my shoulder as we stand in the doorway listening.

His muscles flex through his fitted t-shirt as he plays. He's such a natural. He plays well, but then he starts to sing, and holy shit, he's amazing. His voice has a gravelly quality to it, but it's also somehow soft and alluring.

Harper nudges me, whispering, "Wow."

Everyone claps and hollers when he finishes. I clap too. Suddenly, the students seem aware that Harper and I are strangers, and their attention on us gets him to turn around. I don't know what I'm expecting, but the grin on his face melts me and the knots in my stomach. My face breaks into a smile. There's something so honest and pure about his expression that it makes my chest hurt. How could I have been avoiding him?

He gets up to hug us, but as he's wrapping his arms around my shoulders, he tilts his head back to look at me. *He's probably wondering what the hell we're doing here.*

"Hey, guys," he says to the students as he grabs my hand and tugs me into the middle of the room. "You need to hear Clementine. Now this girl can sing."

"Gavin, I don't think—"

"C'mon, darlin'. Think of it as payback for all that inspiration." Then he winks at me.

Damn that wink.

I shake my head as I rub the back of my neck. *Pull it together, Clementine.*

Harper is laughing. I'm trying to pretend I'm cool, but I'm sure the heat on my face gives me away.

Gavin repositions his guitar while he gets one of the guys to pull another chair next to his. He motions toward it, and with an eye roll I sit.

"Any requests?" he asks the room. Immediately, one girl shouts Maroon 5. He snickers. "Fiona, that's a little high for me. Hmm..." He messes with a few chords, trying to piece together a tune before he turns to me. "Do you know their song *Daylight*?"

Nodding, I gulp, hoping that sound actually comes out of my mouth when I open it.

He smiles at me, and all of the doubts I've been harboring subside. "Great. The verses are low enough, so I'll sing those, and you can do the chorus, okay?"

"Uh, sure." Glancing around the room, I finally notice the girls are looking longingly at Gavin, or Murphy, as they call him. In the back, I see Carly wave to me. I grin, glad to see her back in her bubbly state.

Gavin starts playing, and I turn to watch him. There's something really sexy about how his fingers work up and down the strings. *But his voice.* Adam Levine is a hard guy to follow, but between Gavin's playing and the way he works the melody, it sounds fresh. I clear my throat, and on the chorus, I start in.

As I sing the chorus, I feel myself blush more. Thinking about the nights we've spent together makes me realize that the pain in my chest, the one that started when I walked in the room, is longing. I've missed him.

My pulse quickens when he looks at me and sings the verse about wanting to slow down time because he doesn't want to leave.

When I come in on the chorus again, he harmonizes, and our

voices meld together. Hearing how right this sounds sends chills down my arms.

I've never sung with anyone other than my roommates when we're driving somewhere, but he makes this easy. I can't keep his eye contact, though—it's too intense—and I look away, but I sense him watching me, along with all the kids on the floor.

The instant we're done, the room erupts in applause. I look at him and smile. "Not bad, Mr. Murphy."

He grins back, that sexy-as-hell smile that is so incredibly delicious it makes my heart flutter. I'm trying hard to keep my breathing in check because being with him has me worked up. I don't know why. I've never been into musicians. Never saw the appeal. I always thought they were too mercurial. Too undependable. Too capricious. But Gavin isn't any of those things. He's a steady, even force who's loyal and good and, dear fucking God, hot.

Still foggy from the rush of that performance, the only thing that stands out right now is that I really, really want to kiss him. Now.

He's about to say something when one of the kids shouts at us. "Why doesn't she sing in your band?"

Gavin laughs and shakes his head. "Clementine has far too much class to sing with us."

"Shut up." I shove him playfully. He grabs my arm and pulls me into a hug, making me giggle.

"Dude, your girlfriend is hot," one of the guys says from the back of the room.

I stiffen, not sure how to respond. We've been playing pretend these last few weeks, and the realization that my emotions might be just the side effect of some fictional flirting dawns on me. What if this is all about Samantha and Aiden, and Gavin's just playing the dutiful book boyfriend? Maybe he doesn't feel the same way.

I start to open my mouth, but Harper walks up, interrupting me.

"That sounded great, guys! I'd love to stay and hear more, but I gotta run," she says, waving her phone as though she got an important message. "See you back home, Clem. Bye, Gavin!"

As she leaves, Gavin pulls me closer to him, and when his lips touch my ear, he whispers, "I've missed you." And suddenly, I don't care that I'm scared by how much I want to be around him, by what he makes me feel, by the things I want to do to him. All I can do is shiver.

Because I've never missed anyone more.

* * *

My chest aches, swelling and stretching with the emotion of the lyrics we sang. When he pulls me into the hall, I want to press my lips to his and run my hands along his fabulously hard body. My heart starts to beat faster as we get closer to his room.

So when Gavin stops in front of the elevators, I'm confused.

"Do you want to grab some coffee with me, and I can walk you home?" he asks softly as he presses the button.

Trying not to look disappointed, I agree. Did I do something wrong?

Gavin is unusually quiet as we head down to the corner coffee shop. He orders a black coffee, and I get a medium latte. We make small talk, but it's uncomfortable and forced, a hundred-and-eighty-degree difference from the intimate moment we shared while singing.

Shit, maybe what happened with Jax weirded him out. Maybe he overheard all of that and thinks I am a big head case.

He stops in front of the steps of my brownstone.

"I'm going to head back," he says, tucking a strand of hair behind my ear.

Finally, I can't stand it any longer. "Are you okay? Did my singing suck?" I joke.

He looks confused, and then he gets that crinkle in his forehead. "No. God, no. I only..." He stares at me a long minute and sighs. "Can I be honest with you?"

This can't be good. My head speeds ahead to all the possibilities. He doesn't like me. He *is* dating Angry Red. He wasn't lying when he said he just wanted to be friends. *Fucking hell.*

I brace myself for the worst. He clears his throat as he watches a car drive by.

"I don't trust myself to be alone with you." What? He's turned to the side, so all I see is his stoic profile. "I'm seriously fucking attracted to you, and I know you need to take things slowly, and I don't want to screw this up, whatever this is, so that's why I'm walking you home and stopping on your front steps. Because I want to be a gentleman."

My heart goes into some kind of arrhythmia. Gavin saying that makes me want him so much more. I take the cup of coffee out of his hands and put it on the step next to mine. Turning to him, I push up on my toes so I can reach up and wrap my arms around his neck. With my body pressed up against his, I look up as a range of emotions cross his handsome face—surprise, confusion, desire —and when we're nearly nose to nose, I pause.

"That's the hottest thing anyone has ever told me," I whisper before I touch my lips to his. It's a sweet, soft kiss even though part of me wants to strip naked for this man. But he's right. I need to take this slow, so I break from him after a minute and smile. Handing back his drink, I wink.

"I'll see you tomorrow. For our date," I say, and I walk inside.

Chapter 17

Nothing seems right. Jeans are too casual, but I don't have anything dressy, and I want to look good tonight. Lately, the only things Gavin has seen me in are sweats and t-shirts, and if he's used to dating supermodel clones, I need to bring my A-game. I eventually relent and slink into Jenna's room to ask her for an outfit.

I end up borrowing a simple black sheath wrap-around dress that's a little low-cut in the front, but it fits well. I even break out the Victoria's Secret underwear my roommates got me for my birthday.

After a hot shower where I do all the requisite grooming, my eyes fall on the fishbowl of condoms. Desire starts to pool in my stomach, and I have to tell myself that sleeping with Gavin on our first official date is not the smartest decision. Of course, I'm hoping we do *something* because after what he told me last night, I'm dying to touch him. I guess there's nothing like saying "no" to build desire.

Slipping on a lacy black push-up bra, I have to admit that Victoria and her Secret have it right. Extra boobage is so worth the cost. Once I'm pushed up in all the right places, I roll on a pair of thigh-high tights and slip into my chunky black heels that were hibernating in the back of my closet.

My long hair, which I usually pull up into some kind of ponytail or messy bun, is in need of something drastic, so I blow-dry it straight. I slide on the dress, and smooth my hands over the beautiful stretchy fabric. For makeup, I play up my assets and emphasize my blue eyes, dabbing them with smoky eyeliner before I smack on some pale pink lip gloss.

"Whoa, Mamma!" Ryan shouts as I walk out of my bedroom. I'm not expecting to see him in my living room, but at this point, I really should get used to the idea that he's a permanent fixture, like a lamp or a poorly trained puppy. "Gavin is one lucky man. Do you know how many of my friends have wanted to go out with you?"

"Shut up, Ryan." I grin, embarrassed.

"It's totally true. They've always looked at me like I was crazy when I told them you didn't date. At least now I can say you have a boyfriend."

I start to explain that Gavin and I haven't defined what we are, but I'm interrupted when Jenna and Harper come out of a bedroom and start crooning that I look great. When Gavin knocks a few minutes later, nerves shoot through me, and I feel like an awkward teenager, unsure of what I should do with my hands or arms.

Jenna opens the door, and Gavin gives her a quick hug, but when he walks in and his eyes meet mine, his smile drops. For a second, I wonder if something's wrong, that maybe he doesn't like how I'm dressed, but then that sexy grin spreads on his face and makes me melt.

"Damn, baby, you look hot."

I let out a relieved laugh before I realize that I'm blushing like a total lunatic. Gavin Murphy has reduced me to a giggling fool.

He looks breathtaking in dark pants, a pin-striped button-up and a dark jacket. Gavin kisses me sweetly on the lips, and I'm grateful his arm goes around my waist because being close to him has me feeling like I'm made out of paper and might blow away. He smells like fresh laundry and a hint of cologne, and for just a second I nuzzle up against him.

Of course, it only takes that brief show of affection to get our friends catcalling. Gavin laughs while I blush more, but when Ryan starts humping the couch, I give him the finger and drag my guy out of my apartment.

We head for dinner at a cozy Italian restaurant in the North End, and after we get seated at a quiet table in the corner, he reaches across the table for my hand and laces his fingers through mine.

"You look gorgeous in that dress. The whole restaurant was staring at you when we walked in." His eyes are piercing, making the fleet of butterflies in my stomach crash into each other.

"That's not true." I look away so he can't see my cheeks flush.

"So you have a hard time taking compliments, huh?" He laughs at me, and I keep my head turned because I know he's going to press this issue. "If I told you that I've wanted to ask you out since freshman year, would that also mortify you?"

My mouth falls open, and I turn to look at him. "Really?"

"It's possible." The corner of his mouth turns up into a crooked grin. He watches a couple cross the room, and he chuckles. "Ever since you told Professor Nevil that you disagreed with his interpretation of *Pride and Prejudice*. He was ranting about Elizabeth being a hypocrite because although she hates her mother's obsession with marrying off the girls, Lizzy marries Mr. Darcy at the end."

He laughs and runs his free hand across his jaw. "You told him that wasn't the point of the novel. You said it was groundbreaking because Lizzy broke social norms to be with someone who outclassed her, that their love helped them overcome what would have shattered an ordinary relationship."

"I said that?" I look at him skeptically. The conversation sounds familiar, but that fall was a blur.

He nods. "Jane Austen has never turned me on quite as much as it did that day."

I laugh, tempted to roll my eyes at him. "She's my favorite author. Well, and F. Scott Fitzgerald."

"*This Side of Paradise*, right?"

Smiling because he remembers that I love this book, I realize how much I enjoy talking to him about literature. "I know the end of that story pisses people off, that the main character went through that whole ordeal, and in the end, he only knows himself—the result is simply self-awareness—but I think there's something to be said for going through hell and coming out the other side understanding your limitations."

I'm tempted to tell him about my stories—the ones that are half-written, the ones I haven't been brave enough to publish—and what inspired them, but the thought of him reading my work and seeing so much of my past is still a little terrifying.

When dinner arrives, I accidentally knock over my purse, and a Sharpie rolls out. I've been using it to autograph books for my boss. Gavin sees it and amusement lights his eyes.

"I once got in a lot of trouble with one of those," he says, motioning toward my pen. "When I was seven, I went to summer camp, and one day I got a brilliant idea for a prank, so I waited until the kids in my cabin went to sleep and then drew on everyone."

I cover my mouth to stifle a laugh. His chiseled features look so handsome as he recalls this memory, the soft lighting creating dark planes of shadow under his cheekbones.

He smirks as I take a sip of wine. "It wouldn't have been such a big deal if I hadn't accidentally used a *permanent* marker on their faces."

"Oh my God!" I nearly choke, and a few drops of wine dribble out my mouth, leaving dots of wetness on the white tablecloth.

"Sorry, this is very ladylike." I wipe away the evidence and cover my face with my napkin, horrified that I've basically drooled all over the table.

"It's okay. I tend to find most things you do adorable."

My mouth opens slightly at his compliment, but he doesn't give me a chance to say anything. "Now that I've shared my embarrassing story, I want one from you."

He twirls a fettuccine noodle around his fork and waits for my answer.

"Hmm." Opting for something safe, I decide to go with a story from middle school. "When I was in seventh grade, I made the mistake of falling asleep early at an overnight birthday party, and when I woke up, one of the girls had frozen my bra in a plastic cup. Her older brother thought it was hysterical. He stood there laughing at me, holding out the frozen bra-cicle for everyone to see."

He laughs, but I hold out my hand. "That may not sound like a big deal, but when you're twelve, and you're just getting boobs, it's horrifying." As I'm explaining, I motion toward my chest, which of course attracts his gaze, making me totally self-conscious, but his eyes make it back up to my face a split second later, a hint of a grin on his lips.

"I can top that. In fifth grade, we got a new teacher, Ms. Holloway, and all of my friends thought she was hot. I didn't really see what the fuss was all about. I thought she was pretty, but nothing worth losing sleep over. But when we came back from winter break, she had gotten a makeover and was wearing this really tight red sweater..."

My eyes widen because I know what's coming.

"Yeah, I guess my fondness for her, uh, *grew* that day."

I snort, and his face reddens a bit. "Luckily, that only happened whenever she wore that outfit, and the next year she switched to a different school, thank God."

"Adolescence is plain embarrassing. Parts are growing,

hormones are raging, and things are coming out of your body that have no business seeing daylight."

Gavin busts out laughing, and I grin back, enjoying that we can share these silly memories.

Our phones are sitting on the table after we shared a few photos from the summer, and one buzzes with a text. He glances at it and grins.

"I think this one is for you," he says slowly, handing me my cell.

It's a message from Jenna, and because it's short, the whole thing fits on my screen as an alert: *Ur hard cock felt good between my moist lips.*

"Holy crap." *Really, Jenna?*

I glance at him briefly before I bury my head in my hands, his laughter ringing out in the quiet restaurant. I wait for my mortification to subside before I attempt to text back.

I stammer, "If I don't write back something... appropriate, she'll send me more." *I'm going to kill her!*

When I'm done typing the message, Gavin raises his eyebrows as he waits for me to share my response. Reluctantly, I hand him my phone.

He clears his throat. "So that represents a blo—"

"Yup," I say, cutting him off. My message to Jenna: :0

Yes, that's our blow job emoticon.

He chuckles, and I give him the finger. "Don't talk to me right now."

His laughter is warm as he reaches across the table and peels my other hand off my face and pulls me around the table, settling me in his lap.

Our waitress, who has been ogling him all night, walks up and stares at us. Gavin has his arms wrapped around me, and I'm still blushing.

"Dessert?" she asks.

He nibbles my neck as goosebumps race down my arms. "Yes,

she's dessert." My face continues to burn as I playfully smack his arm and slide off his lap.

Over a couple of slices of cheesecake and coffee, we talk about our classes, my sex-obsessed romance-writing professor, and all the weird things he's seen as an RA. He seems careful not to ask anything about my family or Daren, which is a relief. I get the sense I can tell him when I'm ready, a thought that puts me at ease.

Actually, everything about our date makes me relax. The way he laughs at me when I'm being a smartass. The way he ignores our beautiful waitress who looks like she wants to devour him for her own main course. The way he holds my hand all night or wraps his arm around me as we walk home.

So when we reach my building, I'm definitely not ready to say goodnight. He stops in front of the steps and tucks his hands in his pockets. The fact that he's trying to respect my need to take things slowly makes me want him more.

I stand on the step above him and pull him to me by wrapping my arms around his neck.

"Gavin," I whisper.

"Clementine." His breath tickles my ear.

"I'd like for you to come upstairs with me." I lean back and look up at him, studying his face—his strong jaw, those full lips, his smoldering eyes. Damn, he's sexy. "I'm not ready for any home runs tonight, but maybe we could go for second or third base?" I keep staring into his eyes as I kiss his lips softly, waiting for him to answer.

"Have I ever told you how much I fucking love baseball?" He leans down to deepen the kiss as I try not to giggle.

God bless baseball!

* * *

The instant my bedroom door shuts, Gavin's hands wrap around my waist. He whips me around and presses himself against me, and he feels so good.

He threads his fingers through my hair, sending sparks through me like a plasma globe.

"Does this mean you'll go out with me next weekend? And maybe the weekend after that?" he asks in between kisses. "And the one after that?"

Dear lord. If he keeps talking like that, I might not be able to keep this from going too far. Somehow, I have the restraint to push him back, but I keep my hands on his shoulders. He frowns at the lost contact, but there are things I need to ask.

"Does this mean we're dating?" I ask hesitantly. Does he think of me as his girlfriend? The thought of that used to terrify me because it means vulnerability and letting someone get close and the threat of getting hurt, but when I think back to Angry Red, it galls me to think of sharing him with anyone.

He chuckles, pulling me closer. "Baby, I hate to tell you this, but we've been dating"—he leans down and kisses my neck—"for a while."

It's difficult to concentrate as his mouth migrates down to my shoulder, and it takes everything in me to stay focused.

"So you haven't... you haven't been going out with anyone else?" His answer scares me, but I need to know.

"Not since I slept in your bed. On your birthday." He says it without hesitation, his breath hot against my skin.

Wow. That wasn't what I was expecting. It's better. Grinning, I start to relax against him when he stops caressing me and looks up.

"Why do you ask?"

I bite my lip. What do I say? *I saw you with that bombshell and instantly assumed you guys hooked up?* Okay, maybe I don't say that.

"I, um, saw you talking to a girl the other day in the student union, and she seemed... comfortable with you."

He tilts his head, obviously confused.

"She had red hair?" I say it like a question to prompt him. I bite my tongue to keep from sharing what I overheard in the convenience store because I really can't be sure Angry Red was talking about Gavin.

I don't mean to bring her up like this, and this is most definitely *not* the way to kick off a heated makeout session, but I guess we should talk about it if I have hopes of this going anywhere.

"Angelique? You saw me talking to Angelique?"

"Beautiful. Tall. Curvy." Glancing down, even with the push-up bra, I'm immediately disappointed with my B-cup. *Jesus, Clementine. Stop being so insecure.*

He angles my chin up with his finger, forcing me to look him in the eye.

"Darlin', that's been over a long time." He sighs, and I see exasperation and fatigue in his expression instead of longing or regret. "Yeah, she wants to get back together, but I'm not interested."

I search his face, looking for any hint of half-truths or ambiguity but find none. I nod, but I'm embarrassed I asked, and I start to look away, but he won't let me. He holds my face between both hands, gently stroking my skin with the rough pads of his thumbs. "She's got nothing on you. Trust me."

That's what it comes down to. Trust. Do I trust Gavin not to hurt me? Staring into his endless emerald eyes, I think I do.

I smile back, the relief in my chest palpable, and I reach up and run my finger over his lips.

"If we're going to do this—date, I mean," I say quickly, realizing how that sounds—"I want to be clear: I don't share."

He laughs, turning and pushing me onto the bed. "Good. That makes two of us." He slides over me and kisses me hungrily. "Agreed. No sharing," he says into my mouth.

As our bodies meld together, my hands roam down his fabulously rock-hard body, along his broad shoulders until they reach those beautifully sculpted abs. Frustrated by the barrier of his clothes, I tug his shirt out from his pants and drag my fingers down his stomach.

I love his weight on me, and I'm reveling in his absolute perfection when I hear knocking on the front door. When it doesn't stop, I kiss Gavin once more and groan. "Hold that thought," I say as I crawl out from under him. After I let in Dani, who had forgotten her keys, I scurry back into my room. Knowing that I can hear Jenna and Ryan screwing from the four corners of this apartment, I walk over to my desk and pop on the makeout mix on my iPod, the one I've been using to write all of my hot hookup scenes in my story.

As Sia's exotic voice comes through the speakers, I turn back to Gavin and kick off my shoes. He's sitting on my bed, watching me. Standing in front of him, I put my hands on my hips as I soak him in.

"I rather like you in my bed," I admit. He is a fine specimen of a man.

His eyes are hooded as he reaches out and runs his hand up my leg. When he reaches the edge of my thigh-highs, his eyes widen briefly and his breath catches. "Do I get to see what's under here?" he asks, his voice deep and seductive.

"If you're very good. Or very bad. I haven't decided which yet." I marvel at how I've become undone and wanton for this man. How I crave his touch.

He licks his lips and pulls me to him so that I'm straddling his lap. My dress pulls up, and the edges of my tights peek through. His hands immediately go there, his fingers lightly skimming my pale skin.

"You know you make me crazy, right?" he whispers as he kisses my neck. His words make my heart thunder in my chest, and I'm aching, everywhere. I've never felt like this before. Needy. Euphoric. Wanting him under my skin.

"I could say the same about you," I say breathlessly as moisture pools between my thighs.

His mouth descends to my collarbone as I rock against the hardness between my legs, making us both groan. I want him so badly, my skin burning against him. Pushing him back onto my bed, I lean down to run the tip of my tongue gently over his lips.

"Fuck, Clementine," he growls, tangling his fingers in my hair and pulling me tightly to him. I'm careening over a precipice, everything in me yearning to know what's on the other side.

I push away and sit up, leaning back to rub the apex of my thighs into him. His eyes flutter closed. There's something powerful about sitting astride him, watching him react to my movements. As I reach out, tracing his cheekbones with my finger, Gavin looks at me, his expression so intense and full of the same desire.

His hands travel up my hips and across my stomach until he cups my breasts. The thrill of having his hands on me like this catches me off guard, and I arch my back, shamelessly forcing my body against his. He pulls down the front of my dress, exposing my bra. Before I realize it, he's unlatched the snap in front, and I'm bare, the cold air giving me goosebumps. I lurch forward a bit, my long hair in my face, almost covering me but not quite.

"You. Are. So. Beautiful." The appreciation in his voice has me trembling. When I lost my virginity, the guy basically hiked up my skirt and went to town. And I allowed that memory to harden me to other men, to think they were all alike.

But this? Feeling cherished. Desired. Worshiped. It's an overwhelming rush. I've always thought getting naked with someone would be embarrassing, but watching Gavin want me somehow makes me more confident.

Reaching down, I slowly unbutton his shirt. When I reach the last button, he sits up, and my hands travel along his muscular chest until they reach his shoulders. The sight of his bare skin makes me want more. So much more.

I push the shirt off him and reach for his belt buckle, drawing it open before I scoot off him so he can slide off his pants. Standing next to him, I remember Ryan's words about Gavin deserving lewd. I don't know that I'm going to go that far, but I definitely feel safe with him, treasured by him, and I want to show my appreciation.

His hand goes to the back of my knees to pull me back, but I stop and reach for the hem of my dress, slowly pulling it up and over my head so that I'm only wearing a pair of black bikini underwear and thigh-highs.

"Damn, baby." His eyes take me in, the hunger in his stare palpable. I let him look, a wolfish grin spreading on his face.

In a heartbeat, he pulls me back onto the bed, flipping us around so that I'm on my back, making me gasp. He settles between my legs, fitting our bodies together, with only his boxers and my underwear separating us. I'm drenched *there* and a little embarrassed by my own desire, but as he presses against me, I could care less.

We rock together, his mouth on my neck like he's tasting me. I almost can't stand what he's doing to my body. I'm on fire everywhere we touch.

His hand travels up my thigh, and as it reaches the edge of my panties, he looks up at me, a question in his eyes. I wrap my arms around his neck to pull him to me, an answer to his unspoken words because, God, yes, I want him to touch me.

As he slips his hand beneath my underwear, sliding across the most sensitive part of me, I moan, arching my back, unable to control myself. His finger travels up and down in a slow, delectable rhythm that has me panting.

I'm so close a few minutes later when he slides in and palms me, and I explode, gripping his shoulders as I come unraveled, shaking and delirious with pleasure.

When I finally stop shuddering, I laugh. I can't help it. I've never let myself go like this. Sure, I messed around with Daren, but I never let him touch me so intimately. I mostly touched him. I don't think I ever really trusted him enough to be that vulnerable.

Gavin watches my expression and grins. "That good?"

If I weren't already flushed with that earth-shattering orgasm, I'm sure I'd be blushing right now. I shake my head a bit, brushing off the embarrassment before I look him in the eye.

"Mind-blowing," I say, still out of breath. He leans down and kisses me gently, and as our lips touch, I know I am gone. I am his.

My hands travel down his chest until my fingers dip into the sculpted V of his hip muscles that I'd love to lick. Hmm, that's definitely headed beyond what I should do tonight. I wouldn't even know how to do *that*, which makes me think I need to sit Jenna down for a tutorial.

Gavin drops his head to my neck, his breath hot against my skin. He groans as I reach under the waistband of his boxers, my palm sliding against his hard, velvety skin. And oh. My. God. My fingers barely wrap around him, which has me all kinds of hot and bothered—again—and, let's be honest, scared, because holy shit, how would we fit together?

My breath hitches in my throat, and it takes me a second to gather myself. *Relax, Clem. You know how to do this.* When I wouldn't sleep with Daren, I got really good at this. But I never wanted Daren the way I want Gavin. This... this is different.

He breathes against me as I stroke down on him.

"Fuck, Clem, that feels good," he murmurs.

His words make me shiver, and I smile. I want him to fall apart. I want to do this to him, for him.

Feeling a little bolder, I pick up the pace as I pull his face to me and kiss him gently before I take his tongue into my mouth and suck. He groans again, and right now I want to devour him whole.

"Shit, I'm going to come." He starts to pull away, but I shake my head.

"Uh-uh. Don't even think about it." I kiss him again, sucking his tongue to the same rhythm as my hand moves along him, and his whole body tenses before warmth spreads against my wrist.

We lie there, quiet, our chests heaving against one another.

"You're so amazing," he whispers in my ear, and I don't need to see his face to know he's smiling.

After a few minutes, once his breathing begins to slow, I start to pull away, but he rolls over onto his back, tucking me beneath his muscular arm. I laugh, wiggling free to grab the box of tissues next to my bed. He peeks up at me as I kneel over him, his eyes sleepy, and he shakes his head.

"I can't look at you unless you want to go for a second round."

I grin, kissing him softly before I snuggle back down against him, pulling a blanket over us. My limbs go limp, and I'm awash in a euphoric afterglow as I fall asleep.

I dream about Gavin and that as we're tangled together he tells me he loves me.

Best dream ever.

Chapter 18

Daylight breaks through my window when I wake. Gavin is draped over me, his face peaceful and relaxed. Nuzzling against him, I inhale his scent. I could stay wrapped up in his arms all day.

"Morning," he says groggily.

"Hi. Did you sleep okay?" Considering we're crammed into my narrow bed, I'm hoping he wasn't miserable last night.

"Hell, yes, I slept well." He chuckles and peeks under the covers before he lets his head fall back onto the pillow. "Feel free to wake me up half naked any day."

I elbow him, and he laughs.

"Do you have to go to work?" he asks.

"Not 'til noon."

My phone rings in my purse, which is by the bed, so I reach over him and grab it. The call is from an unknown number, and when I pick up, no one responds.

"Weird."

"What is it?" Gavin strokes my back.

"This is the third or fourth hangup I've gotten from an

unknown caller in the last couple of days." I shake it off. "It's probably nothing."

I shiver in the cold room, and he wraps his arms around me.

"Want to grab breakfast?" Morning Gavin has the sexiest voice.

I smile. I've heard so many stories of guys who race for the door after they're intimate with a girl. I love that Gavin isn't like that.

"Sure. I'm gonna jump in the shower first."

He groans at me. "Not yet. I'm not ready to let go of you." He wraps himself around me. His hand trails up my waist, making me squirm. "You're ticklish?"

"Maybe. A little. But don't tell anyone."

"I'm learning all kinds of things about you this weekend," he teases.

I cover my face, embarrassed by the sheer number of things to which he could be referring.

He whispers, "You're so damn adorable, I want to bite you." When I peek over at him, his eyes are closed, a smile teasing his lips.

In the light of day, he's even more stunning. Light stubble covers his face, and when he glances at me through those long lashes, I have to bite my lip to stop from grinning. I push him off me so that he's on his back, and I cross my arms over his chest, peering down at him because I want to soak him in. I rest my chin on my arms as he plays with a long strand of my hair. Simply having our naked chests pressed together is almost indecently intimate. And maybe that gives me a certain kind of courage.

"Can I ask you something?" I ask hesitantly. His eyebrows perk up. "Have you... have you been with many women?"

His lighthearted demeanor shifts into something more serious as he studies my face. "Uh, not that many. No. Have you?"

"Been with many women? No. Not many," I joke.

He laughs a little, pressing his palms to his eyes. "I really didn't need new material to fantasize about you."

"You... you fantasize about me?"

He drops his hands and grins at me. "Have you seen yourself lately?"

I look away, embarrassed, and holy hell, flattered. I try hard to focus on my point. "The reason I asked about the women is because—"

"Because we're dating and you have a right to know." He brushes hair out of my face.

"Yes, that, but you're..." *You're good with my girlie parts and something about that makes me nervous.* "You have some skill with those hands, not that I have all this firsthand experience for comparison, because I don't. Not really." Why the fuck am I telling him this? I have no idea. Something about Gavin makes me say things that normally would never come out of my mouth.

"What do you mean you have no experience? Are you saying nobody has ever..."

"I mean, I'm not a virgin, but I've only slept with one guy, and it wasn't Daren. Actually, I never got close to letting Daren get in my pants," I say as I run my finger along his chest. "I think I never really trusted him, and I guess I had good reason not to in retrospect." I could get lost in the ridges of muscle on Gavin's chest. "The second guy was only one night the summer after high school, and the experience definitely was *not* memorable. So to answer your question, no, no one has ever... gotten me there."

He watches me as he reaches up and slowly strokes my cheek.

"Sorry, I don't know why I laid that all on you," I say, frowning.

He threads his fingers through my hair. "No, I want to know about you, about your past. You usually seem like you don't want to talk about it, and I don't want to pressure you."

I'm tired of being so closed off. It hasn't made me any stronger or braver. It hasn't imparted any wisdom or comfort. It's just made me lonely.

I take a deep breath and narrow my eyes at him playfully.

"What do you want to know? If you tell me how many girls you've been with, you can ask me anything."

He grins. "A quid pro quo? Okay, I'm game. Um, let me think about it." He starts silently counting on one hand and then the other and back and forth again as my eyes get bigger. Then he looks at me and laughs. "Kidding."

"Shit, you scared me." I let out a sigh of relief.

"Like seven or eight." He caresses my cheek with the pad of his thumb. "My turn."

I nod, bracing myself for what he might ask.

"Why the one-night stand? Most guys would kill to be with you." His voice is soft and without judgment.

Biting my lip, I think about it. "I didn't like the power it had over me. I wanted to get it over with. Daren acted like it was this huge thing that I wouldn't sleep with him when girls were lining up behind me, and honestly, I wasn't opposed to the act itself. I don't think of myself as a prude, but for me it was more about being *that* vulnerable with someone." I rest my chin on my arms as I trace his collarbone with my thumb. "I didn't like feeling that Daren could use it against me, and I never wanted a man to be able to do that to me again. In the end, I thought it was easier to have faceless sex than to be vulnerable with someone who could hurt me."

Surprisingly, I'm not embarrassed that I shared this bit of my history with him.

His hands gently run along my arms and back. "I didn't think you were a virgin."

"Most people assume I am because I never date."

"It's the way you look at guys. Girls with no experience either look afraid or eager. You looked disgusted."

I laugh, wrapping my arms around him so I can lay my head on his chest and listen to his heartbeat. It's slow and steady, a rhythm that's strangely soothing. After a few minutes, I think of my next question. "Who was your first?"

"My little sister's babysitter, Rachel. I was fifteen, almost sixteen, and she was seventeen."

"Hmm. An older woman. Very daring."

"I'm sure I was anything but daring," he laughs.

I raise my head and look down at him. "If she could only see you now," I say suggestively. "Any of those girls serious?"

"No fair. It's my turn," he says, flipping me onto my back, making me laugh. He wraps his arms around my waist, pressing me tightly to him. "But I'll answer your question. I had a serious girlfriend in high school, but she went to UCLA, so we broke up, and I dated a couple girls in college, but they didn't work out."

"What happened with Angelique?"

He leans down and kisses my neck. "Being with her was empty," he says as he continues migrating south. "She's smart and beautiful but cold."

I tangle my hand through his hair, and as things start getting interesting, someone knocks on my door.

"Clem?" It's Jenna.

"Go away. I'm naked," I yell, making Gavin chuckle.

"You have a delivery. Get your ass out here."

He groans but rolls off me. I sit up, wondering how to cover myself without taking the entire comforter with me. Of course, this is ridiculous as Gavin has already seen me topless. I start to crawl over him, but he pulls me down on top of him.

"You are one fucking hot girl, Clementine," he says, smacking my rear. "I've never enjoyed baseball that much before."

I grin like a lunatic. "Not bad for an in-field triple, huh?"

"And my girl knows her bases. Stop trying to turn me on."

I laugh as I slink out of his grasp. Sitting on the edge of the bed, I brace myself to walk across the room clad in only underwear. *Screw it.* I'm a modern woman. What's the big deal? I get up, fully aware that his eyes are boring a hole through me, and I grab a black t-shirt out of my dresser and slip it on before I head out into the living room, closing the door behind me. Jenna and Harper are sitting on the couch, drinking coffee, and there, on the end table, is the most amazing bouquet of white roses I've ever seen.

"You must have done something right last night," Jenna says provocatively.

They're gorgeous. I lean over to smell them.

"Read the note," Harper says, pointing to a small pink envelope peeking out behind a flower.

I pull the card out from the holder. It says, *Perfect roses for a perfect girl. Love, Gavin.* Emotion catches in my throat, and I almost want to cry.

"It's gotta be good. Look at her expression," Jenna whispers to Harper.

Swallowing hard, I hand them the card. They read it, and Jenna starts squealing. I swear she's worse than any teenager when it comes to this sort of thing. "Holy shit, Clem!"

I start to shush her when Gavin strolls out. He's dressed, but his hair looks like I just bedded him. *Oh my lord.* The mere sight of this man makes me want to lock him in my room for another go.

"Ladies," he says, walking over and wrapping his arms around me.

Harper and Jenna look at each other and grin.

"Morning, handsome," Jenna says in a bedroom voice that makes me laugh. "Didn't know you guys were having a slumber party."

"Baseball, we were playing baseball," he says as he kisses my temple.

* * *

Gavin stands in my doorway, and I lean up and kiss him despite the fact that my two roommates are sitting behind us, watching our every move.

"Thanks for the flowers." I reach up and grab both sides of his jacket. His eyes are so expressive and filled with the same emotions that seem to be pulsing through my veins. "I've never gotten flowers before," I whisper.

"I remember." He places a small kiss on my lips.

"When did you send them? You couldn't have done it this morning."

"Yesterday afternoon." The corner of his mouth tilts up.

"How did you know we'd have a good date?" Oh, God, I hope I wasn't a foregone conclusion. But I don't think that's what the flowers were for. After all, he was the one with his hands in his pockets when we reached my front door.

Leaning down, he whispers in my ear, "I wanted you to have them, no matter what happened last night."

My brief bout of anxiety dissipates with those words, and I can't contain my grin. "You need to be careful or you'll spoil me."

"I fully intend to spoil you," he says, kissing me once more before he leaves. "See you in a bit."

We both want a shower before breakfast, so he's heading home to clean up. When I close my front door, I lean back on it and sigh that deep release a girl can only have after an amazing first date.

"Aren't you glad you didn't cancel last night?" Harper asks as she smells my bouquet.

"Can I just say that my *boyfriend* is dangerously talented in the bedroom?"

Jenna, whose eyebrows dart up when she hears that word, starts freaking out again. "Oh my God! Oh my God! I want details!"

"I need a shower, girls. I am all kinds of dirty right now, and I don't want to be late for breakfast." I duck into my bedroom to grab a change of clothes despite Jenna's protests that I dish. When I get in the bathroom and look in the mirror, I hardly recognize myself. My hair looks windblown, my cheeks are pink, and I look wildly contented despite the mild throb *down there* that started when we were rolling around in bed this morning.

Standing under the hot water, I think about what he said, that he fantasizes about me, and that throb grows. I'm not really one for self-service—I've only done it a couple of times, mostly out of curiosity—but Gavin has flipped a switch in me, and I can't go back. I don't think I want to go back even if I could.

I want him, now, and since he's not here, the memory of him is probably not a bad way to go about this.

Closing my eyes, I think of him—the way his hands caress me, the way his lips brush against mine, the way every part of him is hard muscle—and I let my hands roam my body. As they trail down my wet stomach, my breathing picks up, and when I reach between my legs, I try to imitate what Gavin did to me and place small, slow circles along my sensitive skin. After a few minutes, I have to brace myself against the wall of the shower because it's so intense.

When I'm done, I'm panting and lightheaded and laughing to myself, hoping my roommates can't hear me. *Why haven't I ever enjoyed it like this before? Because, holy shit, this is awesome!*

* * *

I beat him to the cafe, so I grab a window seat facing the dorms and order two coffees, which are being delivered when Gavin walks in, and oh, what a beautiful creature he is. He's wearing a fitted black t-shirt, a hoodie and jeans, and it may only be typical college-guy attire, but I've never seen anything more enticing. How I was not immediately smitten by Gavin Murphy is still a mystery. Apparently, his looks are no secret as several girls turn to admire him when he arrives.

"Hey, babe," he says as he leans in to kiss me.

I'm giddy from his small show of endearment and feeling a little stupid that I've become a hearts-and-flowers girl overnight. Being with him makes me want to kiss nonstop, and I could give a shit who sees. I snicker to myself.

He tilts his head, curiosity in his eyes. Shrugging, I smile back.

"It's nothing," I say, wanting to change the subject before he gets me to confess I could take him on the table if amply prodded.

"Some of the guys from the dorm are joining me in a while. We have to plan activities for the freshmen," he says, checking the time on his phone. "But we have time to eat first."

"No problem. I have to get to work soon. What kind of things do you need to plan?"

"Sightseeing tours, because so many students are from out-of-state, and a Halloween party."

"That doesn't sound too painful."

"No, that's not too bad. It's working out our schedules that's a pain in the ass."

"What do you mean? The schedules aren't already made for you?" I tear open a sugar packet and toss the contents into my mug.

"They are, but we can change them among ourselves—swap days, floors, that sort of thing."

"Swap floors?"

"We have a couple of RAs from our building we can swap with in case of an emergency. We do group outings and social events together, so the freshmen get to know us. My buddy Mark and I have swapped floors a few times when I had a gig with Ryan or a last-minute article I had to write."

"That's so different from my job. If anyone switched sched-ules, I'd skewer them."

"You're in charge of that?"

"My manager is supposed to do it, but he gives me the honors because the students know how pissed I get if they back out."

"So you're the enforcer?"

"Something like that." I laugh at how tough that sounds. "I'm anything but that, but I probably talk a good show."

"You only *seem* like a badass then."

"I don't know that I would go that far." I look up, and he's staring so intensely at me, I blush. "Gavin, stop."

He chuckles. "What? I can't look?" He lowers his voice. "I can't think about you. Naked. Beneath me."

I gasp, "Gavin!" and cover my eyes.

He laughs and reaches over to lace his fingers through mine.

"Besides, I wasn't entirely naked," I whisper, mortified.

He flashes a devilish grin. "You were in my head."

I'm trying not to let my jaw linger on the table when we're interrupted by our waiter who takes our order. I get some fruit and a small omelet, and he gets pancakes. When our food arrives, I smile as I watch him pour the syrup over the perfect squares he's cut into his food.

"Want a bite?" he asks as he holds out a forkful.

"No, thanks." I shake my head. "Boys and their pancakes."

"Hmm?"

"My brother loves pancakes. I used to make them for him every Sunday when we were growing up."

Gavin takes a sip of his coffee, looking like he wants to ask me something.

"What?" I take a bite of my omelet, curious about what he's thinking.

"Have you talked to your brother since he came over?"

I stop chewing. I did tell him he could ask anything. This is what normal people do, right? Share things about themselves. *Except for you because you have the emotional capacity of a garden gnome.*

Fighting the slight twisting sensation in my stomach, I clear my throat. "No, I haven't. I probably should. I know he was being thoughtful by bringing that box over. That's saying a lot about him. Jax is all about Jax, so him taking time to do that shouldn't turn me into a raving lunatic or he'll never want to do anything nice for me again."

It's only now that I'm actually opening up to someone other than Harper and Jenna that I realize how much I've locked away.

Gavin reaches over and strokes my hand. "Don't say that about yourself. You had a right to be upset."

"Anyway, I need to drag my butt out to BC to catch a few of his games, but they're always at the oddest times, like on a Tuesday at four. I think he has a game on Saturday, though. I'm gonna try to go. I can usually get one of my roommates to come 'cause they love ogling my brother," I say, rolling my eyes.

As we're finishing up our meal, a group of guys comes in, and Gavin gets up to greet them. I stand next to him as he goes around, introducing me to his fellow RAs. I meet his friend Mark, who is tall and handsome like Gavin, but not nearly as striking, and Jeremy, who is cute in a nerdy Weezer kind of way. After meeting two more guys, I realize I won't remember any of their names, so I stop trying to keep track. Gavin is all smiles until something catches his eye, making his eyebrows pinch. I turn to see what he's looking at.

Angry Red.

Angelique, who is stunning wrapped up in a burgundy jacket, waltzes through the door.

"I hope you don't mind. I thought I'd tag along," she says to Gavin as though there aren't a group of people with him. She puckers her perfectly painted lips, like she's deep in thought. "You always come up with the best plans, and I didn't want my floor to complain about my activities."

He tenses his jaw as she looks me over, almost smiling but not quite. I must not be the only one who's uncomfortable because everyone is quiet, and as though Gavin senses my apprehension, he rests his hand on the small of my back.

"Hi, I don't think we've met," I say to her since she's staring at me. "I'm Clementine." I paste on a smile.

"Angelique."

Neither one of us continues with the *pleasantries*, and although Gavin says it's over between them, I know she still wants him. Nothing could be more obvious. I wonder if she remembers when I ran into her with all of my junk food at the convenience store. *When she was talking about Gavin and the "bitch" he's dating.*

I start talking on autopilot. "Well, I'm off to work. It's nice to meet you all." Turning to Gavin, I grab his arm. "Thanks for breakfast." He looks down me with an apologetic smile and kisses me on the forehead.

"I'll call you later."

I hate leaving him with Angelique, especially when she looks so damn pleased that I'm taking off. So I decide to give him something to think about. Something that's all me. Leaning up to him, I whisper in his ear. "I thought about you this morning. In the shower."

His head whips toward me, and I grin, lifting up on my tiptoes again to kiss him on the lips before I leave. Because I want Angelique to understand that Gavin is *not* available.

Chapter 19

The roses smell divine, but they're also making me a little crazy, enveloping me in a constant reminder of Gavin. We both have to work the rest of the weekend, so aside from some flirty texts, we don't have any time to hang out.

By the end of my shift on Sunday evening, I'm restless with thoughts of him. Desperate to regain my sense of balance, I lace up my running shoes and head down for a run by the river. Although it's dark outside, the reflection of the moon on the water fills me with a sense of peace. It's cold outside, but I run until I'm sweaty and hot and purged of the neediness that's filled me since Gavin and I parted ways yesterday morning.

When I reach Bay State Road and the familiar sight of my brownstone, I slow to a crawl, content to enjoy the brisk night and the scent of autumn in the air. That is, until I reach my walkway. There, I pause, caught off guard by a sickeningly sweet odor that makes me shiver. Clove cigarettes.

Jason Wheeler wouldn't be stupid enough to lurk outside my door, would he? I'm sure his parents probably paid a shitload of money to appease the powers that be at this school to let his behavior, for all intents and purposes, go unnoticed.

Shaking my head at my paranoia because, really, there are probably dozens of students on my block who smoke those cigarettes on occasion, I duck into my building.

I'm appreciating how running can make everything right in the world when I open my bedroom door and the smell of flowers hits me.

"Damn it." Flooded with images of Gavin, I'm clouded and anxious all over. Not that thinking about him is bad, but I have things I need to do. And I can't focus. At all.

After a quick shower, I get dressed. Sitting on the edge of my bed, I stare at the bouquet, which takes up most of my desk. The blossoms have opened and make for a chaotic arrangement of delicate petals.

Seeing his name on an incoming text a few minutes later has my insides doing a small samba. His message has three beautiful words: *I miss you.* Deciding that I have to scratch that itch before I go insane, I'm halfway out the door when my phone buzzes again with another three words: *Come see me.*

I don't bother to write back. That would take too long.

I reach his dorm in record time, but the glacially slow ride up to the eighteenth floor has me fidgeting with nervous energy, and I'm gripped with apprehension. I know that intimacy with a man can change everything, and even though we didn't go all the way, I was still vulnerable and shared a whole lot of my naked self with him.

A girlfriend in high school once told me that as soon as she messed around with a guy, she lost interest. It didn't matter how handsome or charming he was, the next time she saw him after they hooked up, she was over it. What if it's like that for Gavin and me? What if his feelings have changed? What if I see him and *my* feelings have changed?

My nerves are about to combust when the elevator doors finally open, and I step out. Part of me wants to sigh with relief... until I see who is leaning in his doorway.

Angelique looks like a predator as she arches herself into a come-hither stance and laughs provocatively. I hear Gavin's voice briefly before she tosses her long red hair over her shoulder.

"Thanks for all your help this weekend," she purrs. "You're a lifesaver. As always. You should stop by my room later, and we can talk about that other assignment." Turning around, she sees me and stops. Her eyes tighten. "Why, Clementine, it's nice to see you again."

I'm so sure.

"Same here."

Not.

In a flash, Gavin is behind her, his expression difficult to read, but then his features smooth, and he smiles at me.

It only takes that fraction of a second for a familiar image to come flooding back to me, the one that had me gasping for breath when I saw it. As though transported through space and time, the only thing I can see right now is Daren and Veronica, tangled together on his bed. Before that moment, I had never doubted their intentions with each other. Veronica complained Daren was too cocky and rude, while he always called her a spoiled brat.

And like a fool, I bought it all.

I swallow, trying to push that thought back. I stammer out the first words that come to mind. "I... I didn't mean to interrupt. Clearly, you're busy," I say, turning back toward the elevator. When confronted with a major emotional trigger like this, I have two modes—fight or flight—and right now, I want to sprint. Actually, I'd like to shove Angelique's face into something hard, perhaps a brick or maybe a shoe, and *then* run. I'm too rattled to stake any kind of claim to Gavin, my brief bravado yesterday morning lost in a whirlwind of past pain. So I push the elevator button repeatedly and close my eyes.

"Hey, baby," Gavin says as he comes up behind me, putting his hands on my shoulders. I stiffen at his touch and fight myself not to shrug him off. "Angelique was leaving. Come on." He takes my hand, and he pulls me past her and into his room.

The door closes behind me. I turn slowly to face him.

"Are you okay?" he asks, his forehead knitted as he studies me.

What do I say? I had a flashback of something that wrecked me, and I'm scared as fuck to relive it? I lick my dry lips and decide to be honest. Because if he wants me, he should know what he's in for.

My heart pounds desperately in my chest while the little voice in my head screams to play it cool. But I can't. I can't play it cool. Not when he holds the power to rip me apart. I take a deep breath.

"Look, Gavin," I say, my voice like ice, "I'd love to be kind of girl who is trusting and secure and doesn't bat an eye when her guy hangs out with his stunningly beautiful ex-girlfriend who still clearly wants to screw him, but I'm not. I used to be those things, but it didn't work out so well for me, so that," I say, pointing out the door to where Angelique was standing, "that is going to be a problem for me." Anger starts to course through me, the blood beating in my ears. "You should know that I'm not a low-maintenance girl, and if you're under some delusion that I am, maybe you need to reconsider whether you want to date me or—"

Before I can finish, his mouth is on mine. "Shut up," he growls against me as he pulls on my hair, making me gasp so he can deepen the kiss. His tongue licks and strokes mine, forcing my body to betray me with a dark desire for him that's overwhelming. "She means nothing."

He reaches down to my thighs and lifts me up to his waist, and I wrap my legs around him. We slam into the door, his hardness pressing against me, which makes me desperate for him all over again. As he kisses me hungrily, my worries start to melt away. I can't be angry at him when he kisses me like this, when I feel his need for me as intensely as my own. I reach up and grip his powerful shoulders and kiss him back.

"Baby," he says as his mouth travels over to my ear and down my neck. "You're all I think about. You're all I want. You have nothing to worry about."

He flexes his hips, and I moan as he presses into the delicate part of me that is aching for his touch. I'm sure it's a terrible idea to use this as a coping mechanism because I know I still need to talk through my issues, but I'm trembling with my need for him, eager to push thoughts of him with another woman out of my head.

"I'm sorry," I pant. "I didn't mean to…"

"Don't apologize," he says, pausing to look at me in the eye. "You don't have to explain yourself. I choose you. I want you."

* * *

When I wake up a few hours later, Gavin's arm is wrapped around me tightly beneath the covers. His room is dark, the only light coming from the moon outside his window. I've never slept naked before, but having his strong, warm body fitted to mine without any barriers except his boxers is heavenly. I love being enveloped by him and the masculine scent of his skin.

I got so close to going all the way with him tonight, but I don't want our first time together to be angry makeup sex. I want it to be purposeful and trusting and not have a damn thing to do with his ex-girlfriend.

I scoot slightly out of his grasp to roll onto my back. His hand reaches for me again.

"Clementine?" His voice is groggy and scratchy and sexy as hell.

"Yeah."

"I miss you when you're not here."

My heart melts at his words because I feel the same way. I have that same void. "I miss you too."

"I think you should stay over more often. We don't have to do

anything physical if you don't want to. I just want to be with you."
He brushes my hair out of my face.

I'm overwhelmed by his admission, by his willingness to be vulnerable with me, because that kind of honesty is so difficult for me. Before I know what's happening, big, hot tears are streaming down my temples.

"I'd like that," I sniffle.

"Darlin', are you crying?" He leans up, resting his weight on his forearm.

"No." I wipe my face with my arm and laugh. "Well, maybe a little. I'm sorry. I don't know what's gotten into me. I literally haven't cried in years. I don't know why I am now." I look down sheepishly.

He tilts my face up. "You're so fucking adorable." He's quiet while his thumb strokes away the wetness on my cheek. "I'd like to amend my earlier statement."

I raise my eyebrows.

"The part about not doing anything physical. We should totally get physical, and you should always sleep naked in my bed."

I laugh, smacking him playfully before he leans down to kiss me softly.

"Can I ask you something?" he says, his lips still on mine, his breath on my skin warm and tantalizing.

"Sure."

"Are you on the pill?"

The question makes me pull away slightly. Were it not so dark in here, I'm sure he'd see the blood rushing to my face. I clear my throat. "No, I'm not, but I... I have an appointment on Wednesday."

"It's not that I want to have sex with you or anything."

"No, of course not." I grin at his playfulness. "That's actually the last thing on my mind too."

"Right. Because sex is so..."

"Passé," I say, reaching up to tangle my fingers in his thick hair.

"Exactly. And your hot-as-fuck little body does nothing for me," he teases as he presses his hard length against my thigh.

"Well, obviously," I giggle.

* * *

With an hour left before I need to get to class, Gavin and I duck into the student union to grab some coffee and bagels and do a little homework. I think we need to be in public more because the only thing I want to study is him.

I curl up on a cushioned bench as he crosses the cafeteria to talk to one of his buddies, and I enjoy the opportunity to watch him unnoticed. He has such an easygoing way about him as he talks to his friend. Where I'm uptight and anxious, he's cool and collected. Where I often feel lost and aimless, he's focused and driven.

He's the shore to my tumultuous waters.

Realizing I have a big, stupid grin on my face, I try to read my assignment even though I want to cross the dining hall and throw my arms around him, but I don't want to let myself be the clingy girlfriend. Last night was bad enough.

But Gavin totally put me at ease, convinced me of his commitment to me, his affection for us. I let out a contented sigh as I glance up again only to flinch because someone is standing right in front of me... smelling of clove cigarettes.

"That was quite a look on your face, love." Jason Wheeler stands above me with a calculating expression that cuts me.

Instantly, I'm out of breath.

"You... you need to leave me alone." I try to sound steady and firm, but the words come out barely above a whisper. I'm not as brave when I'm by myself. "The police said—"

He laughs. It's a haunting sound that turns my stomach. "I'm done with the games, Clem. You know you're my muse. Nothing will change that." He reaches down to stroke a lock of my hair.

Leaning in close until his lips graze my ear, he whispers, "And don't think that you don't need me just as much as I need you."

My vision blurs, my pulse a tornado raging in my ears, and as a full-on panic attack is about to set in, Wheeler jerks away.

"Don't You. Fucking. Touch Her." Gavin grips Wheeler by his shirt and glares down at him. Wheeler's eyes bulge with surprise for a nanosecond before a snide expression slips into place. People around us stop moving and stare, but Gavin doesn't seem to care. An angry vein pulses in his temple as Gavin clenches his jaw.

After several heartbeats, he releases the professor.

In an eerily cold voice, Gavin says, "If you ever touch her again, if you ever threaten her, I will fuck you up."

I've never advocated violence, and nothing about Gavin has ever suggested even the hint of violence, but the look in his eyes is deadly. Wheeler has a smaller build. He'd never stand a chance.

As Wheeler takes a step back, Gavin stretches his hand out to me. "Come on, baby." I place my hand in his, and he pulls me to my feet.

We walk to my apartment in silence, his arm around my shoulders. My legs are shaky, and were it not for his support, I'm not sure I'd be able to move.

When the door to my apartment closes behind us, I start sobbing.

All I can see are flashes of Wheeler trying to hold me down, grabbing me, wanting to hurt me. He grips my neck to slam me against the brick wall, my teeth vibrating from the force. His knee forces my legs apart, and bile pushes up the back of my throat as his hand disappears beneath my skirt to rip off my underwear. I writhe against the wall, the rough surface cutting into my skin. I beg him to stop, beg him to let me go, but he only pauses to smile before he backhands me, and darkness presses in against my vision.

I hear the sound of whimpering.

"Baby, it's okay," Gavin whispers.

I'm shaking uncontrollably when he reaches down and scoops

me in his arms to carry me to my room. He gently places me on my bed and reaches down to take off my shoes before he kicks off his own and crawls in next to me.

He hugs me as I cry into his shoulder. I can't stop. Shivering, I huddle closer. Gavin pulls a comforter over us and holds me until I fall asleep.

* * *

Several hours later, I wake, still nestled next to him. He kisses my forehead. It's dusk outside, our plans for the day shot.

"You missed your class," I whisper, my throat sore from crying so much.

His palm squeezes my waist. "I don't care. I wasn't going to leave you alone."

I lift my hand to rub my swollen eyes when I notice I'm trembling. I need to pull it together. I don't want Gavin to see me when I'm such a mess.

Sitting up, I tuck my legs under me and tilt my head down, my hair cascading around me, creating a curtain to hide behind.

"Thank you." I grab the drawstring on his hoodie. "No one... no one has ever stood up for me like that." I'm choked up saying those words, but I want him to know I'm grateful.

He slowly laces his fingers through mine. "I wanted to rip out his heart through his goddamn throat."

Gavin's eyes look black in the dimly lit room, the planes of his face cast in shadow. My heart lurches in my chest when the impact of how he stood up for me sinks in.

"How did you know he was the one who hurt me?" I swallow, hard, because it's still so raw. Hearing Wheeler talk to me like that, with that smug tone, has images of him on me, clawing at me, rising to the surface.

"That look on your face. I've never seen you afraid before, so for you to look like that... I just knew."

Gavin's words, like the key for a locked box, open me. I'm not sure how it happened, but suddenly, I want to share all the secrets I've tucked away.

I twine my fingers through his. "I've had a lot of bad luck these past few years, but having you in my life now kind of makes up for it. You make me feel safe." I don't know if I'm saying too much, but the words burst out of me. How this man gets me to confess some of my deepest emotions without trying still surprises me.

I realize I'm dangerously close to being in love with him, a thought that fills me with both fear and excitement. But if Gavin wants to protect me, maybe he won't be careless with my feelings.

"Baby, I'll never let anyone hurt you." He reaches for my back, and I sink slowly down to him, not able to resist his touch. He brushes my long hair off my shoulder before he wraps his arm around me, settling my cheek on his chest. His heartbeat resonates against me, like a metronome keeping time, steady and constant.

"Don't you have to work tonight?" I ask, alarmed, remembering his schedule. I'm wrecking his whole day.

"I swapped with Mark, and I don't have to be on his floor until nine. One of your roommates should be here by then, right?"

I nod against him, closing my eyes to breathe him in.

"Or," he says tentatively, "you can come home with me again tonight."

I would love to take him up on the offer, but I will smother this man if I'm not careful. "No, I'm sure you have things you need to do. I don't want to take up any more of your time."

He lifts my chin, gently turning me so I'll look at him.

"You say that like you're putting me out. You're not. There's nowhere else I want to be except right here with you." His eyes glimmer beneath those lush lashes, and he glances down, a shy smile playing on his lips. "This is probably a weird time to ask, but Ryan and I have a show in two weeks, and I know you work on Saturday nights, but I was wondering if you could make it."

He's asking me to see him play. In the last twenty-four hours, he's defended me against my former stalker, staved off my insecurities about Angelique and spooned me until I stopped crying, but this touches me in an altogether different way. My armor melts a little more.

"Yes, of course I'll come."

My manager might die of shock that I'm asking for a Saturday night off, but he'll have to get over it. That's one of the *perks* of not having a social life—staying late on the job to clean up everyone's messes always works into your schedule.

I run my finger along his stubbly jaw. "I hear you're quite the draw. That the girls love you," I tease.

"I don't know about that." He chuckles. "Besides, there's only one girl who matters, and I'd love for her to be there."

I smile, leaning toward him to put one feather-light kiss on his lips. Because he always knows what to say.

Chapter 20

We part in my dimly lit stairwell with a kiss that has me seriously reconsidering Gavin's offer to stay at his place tonight, but I stand firm, opting to throw on some flannel PJs and get some homework done.

My chest aches in his absence, which only solidifies my need to give us some space. I try to pep-talk myself—you know, absence makes the heart grow fonder and all that crap—but it doesn't take the edge off.

Closing the door to my apartment, still a bit forlorn, I realize I should probably schedule a few appointments with my therapist. I haven't seen Dr. Klein since school started, mostly because I needed to save money, but also because I thought I was doing well. But now that everything seems upended, from my new relationship with Gavin to having Wheeler creep around, I'm sure I could use some maintenance. It's not fair to Harper that I'm constantly going to her to help me through all my issues.

Two hours later, I've made a small dent in my workload, and I crawl into bed, only to toss and turn despite my exhaustion. When I eventually fall asleep, I have a nightmare about being strangled and wake up in a cold sweat.

Finally, in the early morning, I dream about playing in the backyard fort with Jax. When we were little, people used to ask if we were brothers. I always thought that was funny because I was never interested in dresses and dolls, which pissed off my mother to no end. I generally preferred traipsing around in the mud with my twin, even if he was a giant pain in the ass.

When I get up, I decide it's time to call Jax. He sounds thrown off to hear from me, but that's probably because he has some random girl in his bed, and talking to his sister at the same time is a tad awkward. I hear her giggle and ask for her underwear. Ew!

I sigh. "Jax, stop being such a whore."

"I know," he admits. "But at least none of them can say I've promised anything." He muffles the phone and tells Casey bye.

"My name is Candy," she says in the background, sounding dejected.

"Jesus! You can't even learn that poor girl's name?" Thinking back to my one-night stand, maybe that's better. I hope that guy doesn't remember who I am. "Listen, I called to make sure you have a game Saturday because I don't want to haul my ass out all the way to BC only to find out the times got switched."

"You're coming?" I hate that he sounds so surprised.

"Yeah. I'm sorry I haven't attended any games this season. I've been really slammed." When we were growing up, I never missed any. Not one.

"I didn't expect you to want to come after our fight."

"I'm your twin. You can't get rid of me that easily. Can you get me three tickets?"

"Definitely. Hey, Orange Juice," he says, using the nickname he gave me when we were kids, "I really am sorry." He pauses to exhale. "I hate that all this shit went down, and I know I didn't handle it well."

"It's okay, Apple Jacks." I haven't called him that in years. "I closed you off too. Let's just move forward, okay? I know I don't say this enough, but I love you, and I want us to be close."

"Wow. You've gone soft on me. What are we gonna to do next? Make friendship bracelets?"

"Fuck you. And stop trying to screw every woman in New England. You're going to catch something, and your ween is going to fall off."

"My ween?" He laughs so loud my ear rings. "See, you just need to find me a nice girl so I can settle down. How about one of your roommates? They're all hot."

"Keep your dirty mitts off them, perv."

When the laughter stops, he's quiet. "Clem, I honestly didn't know Mom wasn't paying your tuition. Let me help."

The sincerity in his voice makes my eyes sting with tears.

I clear my throat. "I don't want your money. I've been taking care of myself for a while now, and I think I can handle it."

I cover the phone to sniffle.

"I knew you'd be like this," he mumbles. I can almost see him shaking his head. "Look, I don't doubt that you can take care of yourself. You're the most capable person I know. But BU is expensive, and it's not your fault our parents are self-absorbed fuckers."

"I appreciate the offer. So much. But I can handle it." I hope.

He sighs. "Okay, but if it gets to be too much, or if you need me to spot you some money for a while, I'm more than happy to help."

"Thank you, little brother."

He laughs into the phone, and I smile. I should call him more often.

* * *

After our date this past weekend and what happened with Wheeler on Monday, I thought Gavin and I were getting close, but he's surprisingly out of touch this week. We plan to meet up for dinner on Tuesday, but he texts that he's slammed and can't make it. I end up calling him because I just want to hear his voice—totally sappy,

I know—and ask if I can bring him dinner, but he says he's eaten. He sounds irritable and stressed.

I'm about to say goodbye when I hear someone's voice in the background before he muffles the phone. For some reason, all I see is red—red lips, red hair, red coat. I get off the phone almost positive he was with Angelique.

My stomach sours as I try to come up with a scenario that would explain why they're together when he has work to do, so much that he won't let me come over. He's never had a problem working on an article when we've hung out in the past.

I don't call the rest of the week. Part of me says I'm a jealous lunatic while the other part of me is freaking out like it's a damn five-alarm fire. After all I've told Gavin, after what he learned from overhearing my argument with Jax, after our nights together, I know I've bared myself to him. And I'm scared. The nasty urge crosses my mind to wonder if he's going to sell me out to the press, especially now that he has so much dirt on me and my family.

Idiot, he is *the press.* I roll my eyes at myself.

I'm tempted to numb myself out and take my pills, and as luck would have it, my therapist can't fit in an appointment for two weeks. The secretary always asks the obligatory, "If this is an emergency..." In other words, if I'm about to slit my throat or jump from a high-rise, they'll move some other crazy person's appointment. Of course, I'm not that batshit, so I take the first available slot and hang up.

When Gavin calls on Thursday, he's obviously preoccupied. Gone is his casual flirtatiousness and that laid-back laugh. He says he's working on a big article, and I let it go at that. If this is about work, I can live with it, but the nagging idea that his ex has something to do with his quick trip to Mars eats away at me.

By Friday when he doesn't ask me to work out with him, I know something is wrong. Like a muggy night that smells of mossy soil before the rain, I sense it coming.

Maybe he couldn't handle me breaking down after that

conversation with Wheeler. Maybe he thinks I really am too fucked up. Maybe he's rekindled things with Angelique. The last insidious idea makes me ill. Whatever it is, whatever has come between us, I'm getting the big brushoff.

When I finish working out on Friday night, I can't stand it any longer. The warning bells going off in my head, the ones that led me to Daren's room the night I found him in bed with Veronica, tell me I should see Gavin face to face, that this will help me figure out what's really going on. Ignoring the pit in my stomach, I steel myself for whatever lies ahead.

Gavin said he would be working late tonight. As I walk home from the gym, I decide to stop by the *Free Press* office, which is down the street from my apartment. When I walk in, a harried-looking girl in overalls and glasses asks if she can help me.

"I'm looking for Gavin Murphy. Is he around?" My voice comes out cool and calm despite my internal turmoil.

She crinkles her nose. "I haven't seen him lately. I don't think I've seen him in at least a week."

"You're here a lot?"

Her shoulders sag, and she groans. "I never leave. Sometimes, I sleep on that futon," she says, pointing behind her.

"Fuck."

"I know, right?" She's almost cheerful because she thinks I'm commiserating with her when I'm wondering where the hell Gavin has been.

Why did he say he was working? I suppose it's possible he's working from the dorms and is emailing his assignments, or maybe he's doing something for the *Globe*. I start to leave, but curiosity gets the best of me.

"Hey, can I ask another question?"

By the time we finish talking ten minutes later, I think I might throw up. As I walk down the street, I watch my feet amble along the sidewalk. I'm so distracted, I end up back on Commonwealth Avenue instead of Bay State Road, and by the time I'm underneath the blue awning of Warren Towers, I've cooked up a dozen hair-raising ideas in my head, and none of them are good.

I mean to go home. I mean to walk away, to close myself off before I get hurt. But I can't. It's like I'm driving by an accident, and bodies are everywhere, and I have to watch. I know that Gavin and I are a train wreck about to happen, and I have to see it happen. I have to know for sure. *Just like with Daren.*

The feeling in my stomach is too familiar. I'm suffocating from the similarities, and everything in me screams that this is the same.

That night, Daren and I were supposed to hang out, and he had been acting strangely all week, so I was looking forward to having a movie night so we could talk. His car drove up and a few minutes later the light from his TV flipped on, casting a blue hue through his window. But he didn't return my texts, and he didn't return my calls. In that instant, I knew something was wrong. I just didn't know how wrong. I didn't know I'd find him in the arms of my best friend.

Shaking my head to clear that ugly memory from my thoughts, I step off the elevator and find myself standing in front of Gavin's door, but I'm scared to death to knock.

"Hi, Clem!" Carly's wide smile greets me. "Murphy's not in. I think he went out of town. Maybe Rhode Island. He was in a hurry when he left. See," she says, pointing to the dry-erase board that reads, *Be back in the morning. Call Mark if you have an emergency at x1333.*

She looks at me sideways, probably wondering why I don't know that my boyfriend has left town and will be gone all night or maybe even the entire weekend. Who knows? I sure as hell don't.

"How are you?" Carly asks, still studying me.

"I've been better." I wander back to the elevators and press the call button.

"I've been wondering if I could ask you a favor." She doesn't wait for me to answer before she continues. "I volunteer for a non-profit at school that helps troubled children. I wanted to ask if you'd perform at our fundraiser. Maybe sing a song or two. You and Murphy can do one together if you want."

I nod absentmindedly. *Gavin has been lying to me.*

Carly hands me her phone. She's talking, but I haven't a clue what she's saying. *Oh, she wants my number.* I stare at the device a second before I can process what to do.

"Do you want to play with Murphy? Should I book both of you?"

"What?"

"Would you like to perform with Murphy?"

"No, definitely not. I... I don't need an accompanist. I play the piano." Or at least I used to in a prior life.

"Okay, cool. I'll call you with the details."

I don't remember saying goodbye. I don't remember walking home. I barely remember walking into my apartment. As soon as I close my bedroom door, I head straight to the top drawer of my desk, pull out the prescription bottle and pop the little pill that makes me numb.

Chapter 21

I sleep well, a side effect from my medicine, and after a five-mile run, I launch myself in the shower where I continue to obsess over last night. Why does some girl on his floor know that Gavin has left town and gone to a different damn state and I don't? Even though my meds usually grind out any remnant of emotion, I find myself crying. What is it with me crying this week? No, I will not allow myself to fall apart over a sexy face and a great body. Okay, he's more than that. So much more, which is why this hurts.

After I change, I find my roommates waiting for me in the living room.

"These shirts you made for us are great," Dani says, holding up a white, long-sleeved thermal t-shirt with a red X. I'm wearing one with the letter J, and Jenna is wearing the letter A.

"Why do you look like someone kicked your puppy?" Jenna asks.

I'm not talking about this right now. I'm going to coordinate the dumb t-shirts that spell my brother's name, paint streaks across our faces and pretend that everything is okay because I'll be damned if I let another man break me.

"It's nothing," I say, plastering a smile on my face. "I'm tired." Reaching into a brown paper bag, I pull out a few tubes of face paint. "Okay, ladies. Who's first?"

When we arrive at the soccer field an hour later, the girls and I grab seats in the front row near the team.

Jax sees us and struts over, grinning. "Shit. You guys went all out. You haven't done the t-shirts since high school."

I stand up and give him a hug. "It's my way of making up for missing so many games this season." Seeing him happy helps numb the bitterness that's welling up in me.

His smile widens as he stares at the letters that spell his name. "X marks the spot," he says when his eyes fall on Dani.

"No, Jax," I whisper, remembering how I used to reserve that letter for whatever flavor-of-the-week he was dating. I tap him on the shoulder a few times to get his attention. "What's the deal?" I ask, motioning to the field. "You gonna win today or what?"

"We'd better. Some pro scouts are supposed to come, so I need to have a good game."

"You always have good games." I playfully punch him in the arm. "Go kick some ass, Apple Jacks."

He grins that slightly crooked smile before he glances up at the stands. This was always the worst part of the game. When he'd look for our parents who never bothered to show up. That's why I came up with the t-shirts and face paints. I wanted to make up for the fact that our parents were such assholes.

At half time, BC is up two to nothing. Jax scored the first goal, and he's having an amazing game. I swear he gets better every season. I head back to the concession stand to get the girls some snacks, which is the least I can do for dragging them all the way to Chestnut Hill. When I get back to the stands, I stop so fast a kid bumps into me, spilling his drink down my arm.

A few feet away, Ryan greets Jenna with a big, sloppy kiss, and Gavin stands next to him. He looks tired, but when he sees me, he grins. It's that beautiful smile that lights his eyes. And it totally pisses me off. All I can do is glare.

"Here are your drinks," I say as I hand the sodas to Jenna and Dani, who must sense the tension because everyone stops talking. Ignoring Gavin, I sit next to Jenna and pull out my phone. I sense Gavin watching me before he walks over slowly and sits on the other side of me. I scroll through my texts.

"What's up, Clem?" Even the way he says that gets under my skin. He almost always calls me by my full name.

"Just checking my messages." I scroll through my phone, the tension building until I think I might burst. "You know, I must be confused because there's nothing in here from you that says you were going to Rhode Island." I turn and stare at him, and for a guy with a decent tan, he looks a little pale.

He starts to say something but stops. Finally, he says, "I can explain."

The air gets sucked out of my lungs, and anger radiates from my pores.

"See, I'm not interested in after-the-fact explanations. Call me crazy, but I tend to prefer truth in the moment."

As if the stars are aligning to ruin my life, I hear another voice, one from both my dreams and nightmares.

"Emmie?"

Only one person on the planet has ever called me that.

Frozen in place with the fear that I might be having some kind of seizure—because why else would I be hearing Daren's voice?—I close my eyes a beat before I open them and turn to find that Daren Sloan is, in fact, a foot away.

Standing at six three, Daren towers over me. His dark hair is hanging in his honey-colored eyes, and he's all epic swagger and devilish charm. The boy I loved when we were kids has grown up. Of course, today is the day I wear face paint. I have two streaks along my cheekbones, like warrior marks. Awesome.

"Emmie, it is you," he says, stepping closer to hug me, lifting me out of my seat.

I stand there, stiff. I haven't seen him since our high-school graduation, and although I've been to dozens of my brother's games over the years, we've never run into each other.

"You've gotten taller," I say finally, which makes him laugh. "What are you doing here?"

"For once I don't have a game or practice, so Veronica and I thought we'd catch Jax's game," he says motioning down to the other end of the stands. My eyes roam to Veronica, who looks willowy and elegant and is apparently ignoring the fact that Daren and I are having a little reunion. When her eyes meet mine, she gives me a small wave.

"Wow. Hell really has frozen over." Feeling slightly light-headed, I blink to make sure I'm not imagining this.

He laughs that self-amused chuckle that always gets people eating out of his hand. "Hey, you look seriously amazing. Damn." He places a hand over his heart. "The girl who got away."

Before I get a chance to respond to his asinine comment, Gavin clears his throat, and even though I'm more than pissed at him, I do the polite thing and introduce them as Ryan scoots closer to me, practically knocking over Jenna.

"Dude, I'm a huge fan." He reaches out to shake Daren's hand.

"Ryan, stop drooling," I say, annoyed. For a guy who is used to being the center of attention when he's on stage, he sure is being a fangirl right now.

"And that was an awesome game last weekend! In the fourth, when you faked it to the receiver but then ran it in for a TD from the twenty-five-yard line? Holy shit! That was insane!"

Daren studies Ryan and nods slightly. "You were the one in Clementine's seats."

Ryan grins, apparently excited to be recognized.

I cross my arms. "About that, Daren. You don't need to keep sending me tickets."

"Are you kidding?" Daren's eyebrows furrow. "When we were twelve, you were the one who convinced me to play football. You said I had a great arm for the game when my parents wanted me to stick with baseball. I'd never be here today without you. So, sorry, you're stuck with the tickets."

I sigh. This is awkward. I feel Gavin's eyes on me like laser beams, which pisses me off more. Like he has anything to be angry about. I'm not the one running around behind his back.

"Okay, well, great seeing you," I say to Daren with a curt wave.

"I just saw your mom last weekend when I went home. She came over for dinner." He tilts his head. "My parents ask about you all the time."

"It's nice that someone's parents care about me. Mine sure as hell don't." Under my breath I mumble, "They named me after a piece of fruit. How much more evidence do you need?"

He frowns.

My friends, who all know the drama of Daren, are avidly watching this exchange, and now, I can almost hear the ice shift in our sodas.

"I'm sorry, honey. Our parents are fucked up," Daren says, pulling me into another giant hug. Shit. Why does he keep hugging me? Then he whispers in my ear, "But I love your name." Again, I keep my hands by my side until he lets go. "It's great to see you." With a smile, he walks away.

I can't catch my breath because Gavin immediately grabs me. "We need to talk."

I yank my arm away. "No shit."

* * *

Before he can touch me again, I spin on my heel, walking down the stands in the opposite direction from Daren. My friends are a blur as I move past them, my heart in my throat as all the things I've wanted to say come rushing back to me.

I trudge through the parking lot, stopping next to the visiting team's bus. When I turn around, Gavin stops several feet away from me. His head is down and his hands are on his hips. He starts to say something but stops. Raking his fingers through his hair, he exhales. "I don't know where to begin."

He still doesn't make eye contact, which is so unlike him. Gavin has always been about being direct and bold. The difference in his demeanor doesn't sit well with me. Now that the shock of seeing Daren is starting to wear off, I'm remembering all the details Gavin has been less than forthcoming about this week.

"What's going on with you and Daren?" he finally asks, looking almost hurt.

My head jerks back in surprise. "Really?" I press my temple with my thumb as I try to stave off a headache. "I haven't seen him in three years. That brief conversation is the totality of what we've said during all of that time. I don't see what possibly could be confusing."

Gavin looks at me like I'm lying. What the fuck?

"He calls you Emmie."

"Was that a question?" I want to rain down accusations about his whereabouts for the last week, and he wants to talk about Daren. "When we were little, he couldn't say my name. He and Jax called me Chlamydia a few times if that makes you feel better."

I wasn't trying to be funny, but the corner of his mouth lifts up slightly before his brows furrow again.

He closes his eyes briefly. When he opens them, he takes a step closer. "Look, I should apologize for this week."

For what? For lying? For blowing me off?

His usual easygoing manner is gone, replaced with tension and fatigue. Dark circles shadow his eyes. My stomach clenches nervously. Where did my Gavin go? The reality that his lies will hurt more than I can bear right now becomes abundantly clear.

I inhale, bracing myself.

"I'm going to make this easy for you. I don't do well with lies, so I'm not going to ask you what was so important that you had to sneak around and do it behind my back." I once broke my mother's Tiffany crystal jewelry box. When it shattered, pieces of glass went everywhere, standing up at odd angles, and each time I reached for a piece, I cut myself. Breaking up with Gavin will leave me injured, but it's better than a singular fatal cut. "I told you I'm not an easy girl to date, and we're obviously in different places, so—"

"You haven't heard me out." He grabs my shoulders gently. "I know this is going to sound crazy, but I need you to trust me. I need time to sort through something."

I must have a sign on my forehead that says sucker. My face twists in disbelief. "You want me to trust you?"

"Yes, I promise I'll explain everything. I just... I need a little more time."

He needs time? To do what, get his story straight? To come up with a believable lie? To find someone who will back up his bullshit? I think I can feel my heart breaking. *You were supposed to be different.*

"So I'm supposed to believe that sometime in the near future, you're going to give me the real reason you blew me off this week and went to Rhode Island without mentioning it to me?"

"Yes," he says without hesitation. In his eyes, I see a mixture of longing and regret, but he doesn't look away or otherwise indicate that he's lying. My mouth is dry. His response to what I say next is crucial.

My heart thunders in my chest.

"Will this explanation include why you didn't mention Angelique is your editor on the newspaper and why you were with her on Tuesday when we were supposed to be having dinner?"

His eyes dart to the ground, his arms dropping to his sides, and with that, my heart sinks.

"No? Okay, how about this one. Did you go to Rhode Island with Angelique?"

Gavin finally looks at me. "Jesus, Clementine." He lets out a cold, humorless laugh. "What'd you do? A background check on me?"

Thank you, Gavin. That's what I needed to let go. "Fuck you." I brush past him, my feet crunching the pebbles beneath me. I can't believe I'm such an idiot.

"Wait. Damn it. Don't go." He grabs my elbow, and I jerk away, whirling around to face him.

"You're a dick. I stopped by the newspaper office because I missed you, not to dig up all this shit." My heart is pounding, and I want to throw up. "You told me you'd never let anyone hurt me, but guess what? You've hurt me. Now leave me alone."

Heat is welling in my eyes. I blink it back, looking away, wishing I could disappear.

"Baby, really, it's not like that. There's nothing going on with Angelique." I turn to look at him, and the plaintive expression on his face tears at me. "I do a lot of stupid shit—I work too much and get preoccupied and neglect my gorgeous girlfriend—but I am not sleeping around behind your back. I swear."

A lump rises in my throat. "If that's true... tell me what's going on."

He groans. "Fuck. I can't, but I promise I'm not cheating on you."

"Goodbye, Gavin." I try to walk past him, but he steps in front of me.

"Clementine," he says, putting both hands on my shoulders. "What... what would it take for you to wait?"

My eyes are glued to our feet. I'm wearing a beat-up pair of blue Converse, and he's wearing a black pair of hiking boots. At times like this, I always notice something mundane. When I broke up with Daren, his right shoelace was untied.

"I don't know that I—"

"Please. What can I do to prove myself to you? That I'm not some giant asshole?"

Any other time, that would make me laugh. But not today. His hands run down my arms, and for a second I remember our nights together, our limbs tangled in the dark, and despite everything that's happened this week, I want to hold on to him. Somewhere in my chest, he's left an indelible mark, a traitorous piece of me I can't get back.

"Tell me something that's true." My voice comes out barely a whisper. I'm not even sure I've spoken at all.

Gavin leans down to get me to look at him and then pulls me tighter. I can smell his skin and clothes, and I can barely stand being so close to him. "I remember you freshman year, the way you came to that first class a few minutes late and sat by the window and stared outside like you had the weight of the world on your small shoulders." His hand runs up the back of my neck, and he grips me closer. "You were the most beautiful girl I'd ever seen. You have *always* mesmerized me." His voice is raspy but reverberates with a kind of conviction that makes me shiver.

My heart is beating erratically, and if I weren't so mad at him, I'm almost certain I'd be in love. I frown, shaking my head, before I lean up on my toes and kiss him softly. It's quick, but I do it before I can stop myself. As I back away, one solitary tear escapes.

"Gavin, I can't be with you until this gets resolved, until I know everything. Come back to me when you're ready."

That's the best I can do.

* * *

My roommates don't say anything as we get in the car and start the drive home. The afternoon replays in my mind over and over again.

When we get to a light, Jenna, who's driving, turns to look at me. She's so preoccupied staring at the sullen girl in the passenger seat that she doesn't notice the light has changed until the driver behind us honks. She shoots him the finger.

Reaching for the radio, I say, "I never realized you had such anger issues, Jenna. That's refreshing."

"There you are. I was wondering who had stolen my roommate and replaced her with Magnet Girl."

"Magnet Girl?"

"Yeah, you attract the hottest guys on the planet and then do your best to blow them off or otherwise ignore them. It's a special power. I've never seen it before. You need a cape and maybe some tights." She shakes her head. "Daren Sloan." Then she whistles.

The desire to cry has subsided, and I'm numb. "You know my history with Daren, so it's not like I'm going to leap for joy to see him. But he looked good. He always looks good." I bite my lip, irritated to be talking about my ex when thoughts about Gavin and Angelique plague me.

"He is one sexy man, Clem," Dani says as she pops her head between our headrests. She looks like she wants to say something else but doesn't.

Jenna cuts off another driver and then glances at me. "Daren is hot, but Gavin is more rugged-looking, and I think that's sexier." When she checks her rearview mirror, she frowns. "You haven't seen Daren since high school, right? Even though he and Jax are BFFs?" I nod, certain Jenna is paying close attention because this is her thing, being a matchmaker and getting into everyone's business without invitation. "How did Daren act so casual? He didn't seem fazed that he screwed around behind your back and the screwee, Veronica, was right there today, twenty feet away."

"That's rich-guy syndrome. He only feels bad for about fifteen seconds before his life resumes as though his influence in my world didn't tilt everything on the wrong axis."

Jenna's eyebrows raise briefly in acceptance before her head tilts toward me.

"Okay, so please explain why Gavin looked like that."

"Like what?"

"Like he was ready to walk through a burning building for you."

Blinking back the heat in my eyes, I roll down the window, hoping the cold air will help me calm down.

"We're taking a break."

"Excuse me?"

"We're taking a break."

My head jerks so hard, for a second I think we've been hit by a car. It isn't until Jenna pulls up the handbrake that I realize she's driven over to the side of the road deliberately.

"Back the fuck up and tell me what happened," she says, twisting in her seat to face me. Dani, who had tumbled backwards when Jenna pulled her guerrilla driving maneuver, tugs herself back up to re-join the conversation.

I shake my head, annoyed that I opened myself up to this. With a sigh, I recount the last week, starting with meeting Angelique at breakfast last Saturday and ending with the argument I had with Gavin. When I'm done, Jenna smacks the steering wheel with her fist.

"You can't take a break," Jenna says as though she hasn't heard what I've been saying.

"She's right." Dani nods. "You'll end up with a Ross and Rachel situation."

My eyebrows quirk up.

"Like on *Friends*." Dani says it like a question. "Rachel wanted a break, and Ross ended up sleeping with another girl because he didn't technically have a girlfriend, but Rachel felt like he cheated on her. Breaks are always bad."

Jenna looks back and forth between Dani and me. "I think I love you, Dani. I couldn't have said it any better."

It takes me a second to speak because the last thing I want to think of is Gavin sleeping with someone else.

"Look, if Gavin hooks up with another girl right now, there's nothing I can do about it. I just can't be obsessing over what he's keeping from me. That shit makes me mental because of what happened between Daren and Veronica." I start peeling the paint on my t-shirt. "This is going to sound crazy, but I don't think he'd cheat on me."

Fuck. I sound crazy, even to myself.

Jenna scoffs. "But isn't that why you're on this ridiculous break? Because you think he's sneaking around with another girl?"

"Yes, I mean no. Yes, I'm afraid that Angelique is making the moves on him, but this is about him not being honest with me. This is about principle."

"Your principled ass is going to lose your boyfriend and send him running into the arms of that bitch," Jenna says, shaking her head again. "Unless, of course, you're sabotaging yourself because you really want Daren back."

I laugh mirthlessly. "Daren and I are *so* over."

"That's what Rachel said about Ross," Dani says, "and then they had a baby."

"Dani, shut up. My life is not a sitcom."

Dani looks nonplussed, and Jenna is grinning proudly at her little protégée.

"Can we go home now?" I ask, wanting to crawl into a hole, preferably a dark one with an endless supply of ice cream.

"On one condition." Jenna grips the steering wheel and waits for me to answer.

I blow a strand of hair out of my face. "I'm not going to send Gavin any sexts, so you can take that off the table right now."

She snorts. "God, you know me well. Okay, sexting aside, you have to come to his show with me next weekend because there are going to be, like, fifty girls dying to get in that boy's pants, and you need to be there to claim your territory, break or no break."

Ugh. She's right. Gavin is only human, and I've seen the groupies who come to their shows, bouncing their silicon boobs all over the place. It's why Jenna has never missed one since she started dating Ryan. It's why she can Out-Skank anyone via text. It's why the things she shouts when they're *together* make me blush. She aims to keep her guy happy. I gotta say it's smart.

"Fine. I'll go. But don't ask me to flash him on stage or wear edible underwear or dance on the bar."

"Omigod. Edible underwear! I might have a pair of those somewhere."

Chapter 22

Diving into work for the rest of the weekend is the best distraction, but as soon as I'm back in my room Sunday evening, I'm weepy and morose. I've thrown out Gavin's dying roses, but I swear the scent clings to everything—my comforter, my clothes, my robe. I can't escape him. I miss him so much it's hard to breathe, but I won't let myself give in. When I can't take it any longer, I cry into my pillow until I fall asleep.

Monday isn't much better. In between classes, I volunteer in the tutoring center, which I'm hoping will help me focus on someone else for a while, but it's empty, so I end up with extra time on my hands to wallow.

Kade stops by briefly to check his schedule, and part of me waits for him to revert to his old asshole ways, but he's surprisingly soft-spoken.

"I have some new flyers to put up. If you have the time." His expression breaks my heart, and I want to give him a hug, but that would be weird.

"I'll make the time. Is it okay if I do it over the next couple of days?"

"Yeah. That would be great." He hands me a stack of neon copies with a sad smile.

The last article Gavin wrote said police found Olivia's cell phone on the T, but authorities haven't been able to get any useful information from it yet.

Kade's eyebrows pinch.

"What?" I ask.

"Olivia's sister Norah wonders if she was stopping off to see some guy she just met."

I see the jealousy in his face.

"Wouldn't Olivia's phone records have that evidence?"

"That's what's so weird. Norah said her sister was talking to some guy on the phone, but her phone records don't show any unusual numbers. Livvy had just gotten home, and they hadn't had time to catch up yet when this happened, so she doesn't have anything concrete."

I think about the dozens of calls I've gotten lately from an unknown number, and my skin prickles. I never answer, and the caller never leaves a message.

"Kade, what if she had a second phone? Maybe a disposable one? I had a friend once who bought a cheap cell while she was in Italy because she was paranoid someone would steal her iPhone."

"I guess that's possible." His eyebrows furrow.

"Hey, you don't know for sure that she was seeing anyone. Don't make yourself crazy thinking about something that might not have happened."

Jeez. That's good advice, Clementine.

He gives me a tight smile and rubs his forehead. "I just don't understand why we haven't learned anything yet."

"No news might be good news. They could still find her." I don't know what possesses me to say this because the odds are against any kind of positive outcome, but something deep inside me wants to believe it's possible.

"Thanks, Clem. I needed to hear that." On his way out, he leans down to hug me, and I wonder if being friends with Kade is a sign of a zombie apocalypse.

When I get home a few hours later, I throw on some comfy sweats and, fighting the urge to mope in my room, wander out into the living room and collapse on the couch.

"It's the birth control pills," Jenna says as she throws me a piece of chocolate. "The reason you look like you want to cry. It's the hormones. You'll get used to it. Eat something decadent to take the edge off."

Or it could be that I essentially broke up with my boyfriend. I peel off the aluminum wrapper and toss it at her.

"I'm afraid to ask, but how do you know I started taking birth control?" This girl should work for the CIA or NSA or some agency that specializes in classified secrets.

"Last week you said you had an appointment at the clinic, and you weren't sick, and the only other reason girls go there is for birth control. It's elementary, Watson."

"Who's on birth control?" Harper asks as she cuts through the living room.

"Goldilocks here," Jenna says, pointing to me.

"Oh, are you and Gavin doing the dirty?" Harper stops mid-step. She's been spending a lot of time at her boyfriend's lately, so I haven't had a chance to fill her in on what happened this weekend.

"Jenna, you're a terrible influence on this girl," I say, shocked that Harper would mutter such a thing. "No, I'm not *doing the dirty* with Gavin. I mean, that was my intention, but we're on a break."

The confusion on Harper's face is immediate. "A break from what?"

"Each other," Jenna says, raising her eyebrows in judgment.

"Why? I thought you two were crazy about each other."

I blow out a breath. "I'm going to work out. I can't handle

having this discussion again." Motioning toward Harper, I tell her that Jenna can give her the gory details.

I grab my workout bag and head out. On my way to west campus, Jax calls, wanting to meet up. When I tell him I'm going climbing, he says he'll join me in twenty minutes.

I've never gone climbing with Jax, and he's rarely shown an interest in hanging out with me on my campus. He mumbles something about wanting to talk. Maybe this is about my run-in with Daren. Curiosity tugs at me like a loose thread hanging off a sweater, so I agree to let him join me.

Because my brother has been known to get sidetracked by a pretty face and a nice rack, I don't bother waiting for him to start my workout. I get one of the staff members to spot me on my ascent. On my way down, I hear a familiar voice and look down to see that Jax has taken over my rope. As he lowers me, a ball of nerves develops in my stomach.

"Jackson, be careful. I don't want to die today." I glance toward the door and see Gavin, Angelique and Mark walk in. My heart beats erratically. God, I've missed him. Gavin looks relaxed as he talks to his friends. *Shit, maybe I have been paranoid over nothing.*

But then, Angry Red reaches over and grabs his arm and laughs, and I remember why I wanted to smash her nose.

Gavin glances up and sees me, a smile crossing his face before his expression abruptly falters. I'm trying to figure out why when I suddenly drop.

I scream before I land cradled in a pair of muscular arms.

"Emmie, you're so light." Daren Sloan is holding me, smiling like this is normal behavior. *What the fuck?* I gasp for a minute, realizing that I only fell a few feet, but it was a few feet too far.

"You two are assholes! Let me down."

I kick my way out of his grasp while he and Jax crack up. As soon as I get my balance, I turn and push him as hard as I can, which doesn't budge him at all. It only makes him laugh harder. Jesus, this is just like when we were kids. Those two would play pranks on me all day long.

A staff member carrying a clipboard walks over. Good, they're going to get in trouble for endangering my life.

"Excuse me. I hate to bother you, but could I get your autograph?" the guy asks Daren, who grins broadly.

"Sure thing."

Motherfucker. I unbuckle my harness and storm off to change.

* * *

After a long shower, I eventually emerge from the locker room, surprised to find Gavin waiting for me.

"Are you okay?" he asks, walking up and wrapping one hand gently around the back of my neck and one on my hip. He does it before I think he shouldn't, that it isn't smart to be close to him, but the minute he touches me, I know he gets it. As someone who climbs, he understands you never joke about dropping someone. It's sacrilege, and this quiet moment says he'd never do that to me.

I nod, looking up at him. His lashes are so dark that his green eyes look almost kohl-rimmed. His touch makes my insides flip flop.

Seeing Jax and Daren walk over makes me start to pull away from Gavin, but he tightens his grip on my waist.

"You ready to go?" my brother asks. He sees Gavin and gives him the guy nod greeting. "Hey, man."

Gavin says hi, but he looks pissed. He turns back to me. "Do you want me to take you home?"

"No, Jax wanted to talk about something. I'll be okay."

He pulls me into a tight hug, and right now I could close my eyes and let the world go by. Although I know people are watching us, I don't want to let go. Remembering what Jenna said about this weekend and all the girls at the show, I realize I can't totally cut him off while I wait this out or there might not be a road back to where we were. As much as I want to be angry about last week, when we're together like this, all I can think is that he's been telling me the truth.

He whispers, "I'll call you later," before he kisses me on the forehead, and I can't help but smile.

On our way to Jax's car, my brother nudges me. "So is that your boyfriend?"

"I don't know. It's complicated."

"Well, if you ask me—"

"I didn't," I say, cutting him off. "What did you want to talk about?"

Jax waits until we're in the car to drop the bomb. "Dad's back from Europe. I'm not sure for how long, but he wants you to come home for a visit."

I sit silent, waiting for the punch-line. When it doesn't come, I turn in my seat, my eyes shifting between my brother behind the wheel to Daren in the back seat. "Is that why you brought your buddy? For protection? Jax, I dare say you've grown a vagina."

Daren starts howling and pounds his fist into Jax's seat. "A vagina! Holy shit, Emmie, I've missed you."

I rub my hand with my face, too tired to be dealing with these two jackasses. "I have homework I need to do, so if that's all you want to talk about, you should take me home."

"Clem, you should hear him out. Dad didn't know Mom cut you off. He feels like shit." Jax starts the ignition and shifts into first.

"Well, it's only taken two years." A well of emotion rises in me. No, I won't get upset up over this. I've worked hard to not care that my parents could give a shit about me. One phone call from Daddy shouldn't get me worked up.

"Think about it, okay? That's all I'm asking." Jax pulls up to my building, and if it weren't for his expression, I would never agree, but my brother rarely asks me for anything.

"Fine, I'll think about it."

When I get out of the car, Daren follows. I think he's going to jump up front, but instead he mumbles something to Jax and shuts the door. I'm more than surprised when my brother drives away, leaving Daren in front of my apartment.

I blink, making sure this isn't a figment of my imagination.

"What are you doing?"

"We need to talk," Daren says, taking my elbow.

What now? I shrug off his hold and put my hands on my hips. "Fine. Talk."

A couple of girls walk by staring at him.

"Not here. Let's go up to your place."

I give him a raised eyebrow.

"I'm not going to try anything, Clementine. I have some things I need to clear up with you, and it's overdue. I'd like to not have to grovel on the street, if you don't mind."

Then he makes that face, the one he used to do whenever he broke something of mine, which was often.

Damn it. He could always get his way.

"You and Jackson are exasperating me tonight. I'm going to let you come up, but I'm warning you now. I'm in no mood, so don't piss me off."

He grins, running his hands through his hair. "Yes, little princess."

Nothing is worse than being patronized by Daren Sloan. I scowl, which makes him laugh. Trudging up the stairs, I let him follow me up. No one is home, which is good because I'm not prepared to explain why I have the star BC quarterback tailing me.

I turn on a few lights and motion for him to sit while I take a seat opposite him, as far away as possible on the other end of the couch.

"You miss me that much, huh?" he asks.

"I'm not trying to make any kind of commentary here, Daren. You wanted to talk, so talk." I grab a pillow and tuck it into my lap in case I need to scream into something or want to punch the football player next to me.

His confident demeanor slips a little, and he takes a deep breath. "I wanted to apologize to you for what happened senior year, for being such a dick to you. Your brother told me what happened with your mom, and that's all kinds of fucked up. I'm sorry. I know you had a lot riding on your state meet, and then we imploded. I didn't know you lost your track scholarship."

I shake my head quickly. "I lost it at the end of my freshman year. Too much shit happened, and I couldn't clear my head. It wasn't you. Not really." Daren was just the beginning of that runaway train.

I'm busy staring at the pillow. It's forest green, which is so much better than kelly green or lime green. I hate lime green. I actually prefer viridian, though, which is green with the slightest tint of blue.

"Emmie?"

Glancing up, I realize he expects me to say more.

I shrug. "Thank you." I say it like a question. "I appreciate it." I realize I'm gripping the pillow so tightly that my knuckles are turning white, so I force myself to relax my hands. "Is that it?"

I'm caught off guard by the hurt expression that spreads on his face.

He opens his mouth but closes it again, an awkward silence enveloping the room. He laughs weakly. "I'm trying to say I'm sorry. You have no idea how many times I've wished I had done things differently."

My chest constricts, and I squirm uncomfortably in my seat.

He exhales loudly. "I liked you so much, Clementine. My God, I thought I loved you."

Nausea ripples through me. Laughing without conviction, I

try not to be overwhelmed. "What do you mean you thought you loved me?" I can't hide the bitterness in my voice.

"We grew up together. You were my best friend. I worshiped the ground you walked on, but you'd barely even let me hold your hand or kiss you in public. I thought I was the only one in the relationship half the time."

"You can't be serious." After everything he put me through, after all the heartache and humiliation, he has the nerve to say this to me?

"Emmie, you held me at arm's length. And I don't mean physically. Once we started dating, you changed. It was like you were afraid to let me get close to you. I would have waited as long as you wanted to sleep together. Fuck, I thought I'd marry you some day, so it wasn't about the sex. You just kept slipping farther and farther from me, and I know I should have confronted you or maybe broken up with you, but I couldn't bring myself to do that. The thing is, I wanted to be with you, but you were somewhere else. This might be the biggest dick thing to say, but it's the truth—I think I started hooking up with Veronica so I could get over you before you crushed me."

He thought he loved me? A few years ago, hearing Daren say that would have been blissful. But now, after all this time, it leaves me hollow. The universe is mocking me with a boulder-sized serving of irony and a giant Fuck You.

I sniffle, only to realize that I'm crying. God damn it.

"Honey, I'm so sorry," he says, scooting over and wrapping his arms around me, and I can't help it—I start sobbing. The dam of tears I'd been holding for him comes pouring out, and Daren lets me cry as he strokes my hair and kisses the top of my head.

"Why are you telling me this?" I hiccup into his shoulder, still not able to bring myself to look at him.

"Because you'll always be special to me. Because I should have apologized years ago. Because I want you to be happy."

Of course, that makes me cry harder. In my mind, I'd built him into this horrible prick. This hurts so much because I know he's right. I've never been good when it comes to admitting my emotions, but I didn't realize that I'd shut him out. My whole life I've been terrified of turning into my mother, who thinks showing emotion is a display of weakness. So what did I do? I bottled myself up in every possible way. And I haven't gotten any better in college, especially when I was on my meds.

"I'm sorry, Daren." I pull myself away from him and wipe my face with the sleeve of my shirt. "I guess you had no way of knowing that I was in love with you, and apparently I didn't know how to deal with it."

I swallow and manage to finally look up at him. He's pale. "You... you loved me?" he asks, echoing my thoughts a minute ago.

Nodding, I offer a grim smile. "Yeah. Should I not have told you?"

"Really?" His jaw tightens, and his hand curls into fist. "Fuck."

This is a mistake. I should have kept my mouth shut. "It was a long time ago, Daren. I'm over it now. I'm... I'm okay."

"Shit, Clementine." He lets out a long, pained sigh. "You might be okay, but I'm not." What does that mean? He pulls away from me, propping his elbows on his knees and staring down at the ground. "I've spent a long time trying to rationalize what I did with Veronica, why I've stayed with her. We've broken up a few times and dated other people for a while, but we end up back together. But the really fucked-up part is that I always come to the same conclusion that she's not right, that... that she's not you."

I reach out and touch his shoulder. "You just feel guilty about what happened between us. You need closure. We both do. We were so young, and neither one of us dealt with this well. Daren, this isn't totally your fault. I played a part too."

He looks up, a flicker of hope in those large hazel eyes. "Do you think you could forgive me?"

"Yes." Of course I forgive him. "Can you forgive me? For being an ice princess?" He laughs and puts his arms around my waist, crushing me against his chest and making me laugh. "If it makes you feel any better, I almost slept with you a dozen times."

He groans and pushes me away, making me laugh more. Eventually, a smile tugs at the corners of his mouth. "You want to torture me, don't you?"

I snicker. "Maybe a little."

"It's okay. I guess I deserve it."

Chapter 23

I wake up for class on Tuesday refreshed. Lighter. Hopeful. While I told Daren I thought he needed closure, I didn't realize I did too.

I consider the possibilities. Maybe I *can* work through my boatload of baggage and come out the other side. Despite the weird weekend I had, I only popped that one pill and managed not to fall apart.

Gavin was too sweet after my brother and Daren had been such douchebags at the gym. When they're together, they revert to being twelve. I'm rolling my eyes thinking about it when my phone rings. Although I need to get to class, my heart races when I see Gavin's name on the screen.

"Hey," I say sweetly, embarrassed that I threw down that ultimatum this weekend. I need to smooth this over. I can't believe I've been so jealous of Angry Red. If Gavin says he's going to explain what happened, I'm sure he will.

"I need to ask you something." The cold tone of his voice is unexpected. When I saw him at the gym last night, there was a tenderness to him that melted me inside and out.

"Okay," I say, trying not to be paranoid.

"Why was Daren Sloan leaving your place after midnight?"

My breath shallows from the accusation in his voice. I don't know why I'm worried. It's easy to explain. Daren and I talked until Harper came home, and the three of us ordered pizza and watched reruns of *The X-Files*.

I'm about to say this, to tell him what happened, but I get a moment of pause as I open my mouth. Apparently, it's okay for him to ask me what I'm up to, who I see, where I go, but I can't ask him any questions. What a hypocrite! A chill creeps through me.

"Well, I'd tell you, Gavin, but I'm going to need some time. I'm sure *you* won't mind waiting."

A half laugh escapes him, but I know he doesn't find this funny. Neither do I. "Just tell me. Is there something going on between the two of you?"

Anger coils in my stomach. "If you tell me why *you* went to another state with Angelique, a girl who clearly still wants to fuck you, I will gladly tell you why Daren Sloan was with me in my apartment until midnight." I can't help it. The evil bitch side of me is pissed. All I hear is silence. "No? I didn't think so."

And I hang up.

Staring at my phone, I don't know what just happened. My hands are shaking, and I'm starting to sweat. *Shit. Shit!* I didn't mean to come off like I had something to hide, but I can't believe he had the nerve to suggest that I'm running around with Daren after I've been so open with him.

Should I call him back?

No, no way. Even though I want us to go back to the way we were, I'm setting a precedent. If I cave now, I'm telling him it's okay for him to do things I can't. That's not the kind of relationship I want. *But damn it, Gavin, how can I want you so badly and be this furious at the same time?*

Glancing at the clock, I realize I have twenty minutes to get to class. I don't have time to lose it now, so I grab my jacket and bag and race out the door. A cold blast of air hits me in the face.

Why do I have to be so stubborn? Why couldn't I simply answer his question? Part of me is practically apoplectic at his double standard and the other half wants to track him down and apologize. The tension is becoming unbearable. Why can't he tell me what's going on so we can stop playing this stupid game?

I duck into the convenience store to grab a cup of coffee. I see Brigit's black bob, and when she glances my way, I wave. She grabs her bagel and walks over. We chat for a minute, and seeing her helps me get my head out of my backside for a few minutes. I still need to have a serious conversation with her about Wheeler, but I'm not sure what approach I should take. If I lay it out on the table the way I want to, I might lose the little bit of trust I've built.

"Clem? Can I ask a favor?" she asks, her bubbly demeanor unusually somber.

Nodding, I try to ignore the fact that this conversation might make me late to class.

Her hands fidget, drawing my attention. Her nails are now a bright blue with little white swirls painted on the ends. "Would you mind taking a look at the first draft of my novel? Jason has been editing it, but..." Emotion clouds her eyes, but she quickly shakes her head. "He's so busy these days, and he's been kind of moody lately, and I thought maybe you could help me with some dialogue."

"No problem." Smiling to reassure her, I can tell it was hard for her to ask me for help.

I reach into my bag to grab my phone, and the neon flyers that Kade gave me catch my eye. I bite my lip, debating what to say.

"Brigit, you just met Jason this fall, right?"

"Yeah, I'm in his frosh writing course."

I nod, wondering where I'm going with this. "He and I haven't had a chance to catch up. Um, was he in London *all* summer?"

She gets dreamy-eyed. "He went everywhere this summer—all over England, Spain, and Scotland. I forget where else. I can't believe Jason's friend loaned him his yacht like that. He has some amazing photos. I'm surprised he hasn't shown them to you yet."

I shrug. "We've grown apart in the last few years because he was teaching abroad." And because he wanted to get in my pants.

My cell buzzes in my hand with a text from Jenna. *Get your ass to class!*

I see the time stamped above the message.

Shit. I'm gonna be late.

"Brigit, I have to run, but I'm happy to read your draft."

We exchange numbers, and after I pay for my coffee, I turn back toward her. "Let's meet up for lunch in a day or two, and I can take a look at your story." Of course, she could email it to me, but this way we can have a serious talk about Wheeler.

I'm out of breath when I get to Marceaux's class, and the room is packed, so I stand near the door and glance around, hoping to find Jenna. I finally spot her, and she waves to me from the fourth row, so I trudge toward her. The aisles are narrow, and I stumble over a guy I've never seen before. He's wearing a plaid shirt and black-rimmed glasses, but despite his geeky exterior, there's something really intense about him. I apologize as I scoot by and try not to trip over anyone else before I settle next to Jenna.

"You ready for today?" She looks concerned.

Why wouldn't I be ready? I submitted what I thought was a pretty strong draft last week, and I have several pages of notes for the upcoming chapters. I think our professor should be pleased. I think I'm even ready for our small group feedback sessions.

Jenna tilts her head toward me like she's waiting for me to get with the program.

"Oh my God. The critique." With the drama this weekend, I'd forgotten we're discussing my book today. Fucking hell.

Jenna pats my hand, seemingly content that I haven't fallen off my rocker and developed early onset Alzheimer's.

Professor Marceaux claps her hands to start the class, and

everyone quiets. She mumbles to herself at the lectern and tilts her glasses up so they're perched on top of her head.

"Today we'll be discussing *Say It Isn't So* by Austen Fitzgerald. Typically, it's considered a Young Adult novel, but it crosses into Romance and more specifically New Adult because the character turns eighteen early in the story, and it also deals with first love and infidelity." She starts her strut across the room. "I chose it because it was an e-book bestseller, one that does not have the happy ending generally associated with YA novels."

Jenna nudges me. My eyes slide from her to the door of the class. My mouth goes dry as Jason Wheeler strolls in.

"I have a special treat." Marceaux holds her arm out dramatically. "Some of you may know Professor Wheeler, a very successful YA author himself. He's written four books, and his fifth is in the late stages of the editing process and should be on bookshelves this spring. Because *Say It Isn't So* is somewhat of a crossover novel— actually, one he suggested—I thought it apropos if he directs this discussion."

Wheeler strolls over, kissing Marceaux European-style on both cheeks. *What a poseur.*

He's wearing a tailored black suit and a pale salmon-colored shirt. If I didn't know what lurked beneath that coiffed exterior, I'd think he was someone to emulate.

Tapping on the podium, he soaks in the sight of the class. In about two minutes, everyone will be eating out of his hand. Thinking back to my freshman year, it was easy to get mesmerized by how he talked about books and poetry. He spoke with such passion, conviction even.

While he's read my book and we've had dozens of discussions about my work, having that acumen pointed at my novel in public makes me ill. Like a distant storm rolling in, I know this isn't going to go well. I don't trust his intentions. I mean, why else would he suggest critiquing my story except to humiliate me somehow?

"Jason, why don't you tell us a little about your next book. I think everyone is dying to know." Marceaux waves him on, letting him take over the class as she settles into a chair behind him.

"This one is a bit of a departure for me," he says, loosening his tie in a faux attempt to look casual. "As you know, I tend to write about coming-of-age themes. My latest novel, which is my first attempt at romance, is more of a murder mystery so the reader pieces together the love story in the aftermath of a tragedy." When the words leave his lips, I close my eyes briefly, fighting the urge to leap out of my seat and run as far away from this man as possible, like maybe to Indonesia. "It's about a girl who betrays her boyfriend and ends up dead. The story picks up after she disappears, when the girl's friends and family realize they didn't know the first thing about her. She had built so many walls that she was nearly unlovable."

I'm having difficulty breathing. His eyes shift toward me, and I know this is a threat. That he means to harm me. He continues. "She was a stranger to everyone but her boyfriend. To him, she was like Dante's Beatrice who should have led him to paradise. After all, he was the only one who knew her, who loved her, who was even capable of loving her and appreciating her brilliance, but her foolishness led her astray, and instead of paradise, she led him... somewhere darker." He chuckles, and the sound rolls my stomach. "I'm going to have to let you read it to see what happens."

Everyone applauds except Jenna and me. She and I make eye contact, and the expression on her face confirms that I should be afraid of Jason Wheeler. Very afraid.

"Thank you. Gracious, you're being too generous," Wheeler says. "It could be total crap." Everyone laughs. "Well, let's discuss *Say It Isn't So*. We can start with something easy before I rake you over the coals." Again, the class laughs. "What did you notice?"

After a couple of comments, someone says, "It seems a little sexually graphic to be YA."

"That's true," he says. "That's one of the noticeable flaws with this story. I think it goes too far."

What? That was something he repeatedly told me he loved. *Of course, maybe he had ulterior motives for encouraging me to describe those scenes.*

"I liked it," Jenna says loudly as she grips my hand. "I thought Isabella's honesty about her breakup with Evan pulled you into the story because of her desperation. They grew up together, and he slept with another girl, practically in her face. I think most girls would go postal over something like that."

I squeeze her hand.

Wheeler's eyes squint slightly as they pass over us, and I shiver under the weight of his stare.

"Perhaps, but don't some of you find that Isabella might be a little, I don't know, pathetic? Especially with that sad one-night stand?" he asks, almost grinning.

Jenna tenses next to me. A few hands go up, but I don't hear what they say because blood is thundering in my ears. The discussion continues, but all I can do is take deep breaths as I try not to hyperventilate. I keep watching the clock behind the podium, waiting for the instant I can leave.

Wheeler's laugh gets my attention, but I haven't been following. He clears his throat. "Perhaps one of the most unappreciated details here is that I have it on good authority that Miss Fitzgerald borrowed several ideas from one of her writing partners."

Holy. Shit.

Jenna gasps as hands start flying up. Marceaux sits straighter, tilting her head at her colleague. Wheeler calls on a student in front of me.

"Professor, are you saying this author plagiarized?"

"I am." He looks so smug up there that I could leap over these seats and strangle him.

There are instances in life when the powers that be push the pause button, and you can see your future before you like an endless road stretching into the horizon. I see this now, realizing that how I react to this situation has a myriad of life-alternating implications, like dominos set up to clatter against one another as they reach the ground in quick succession. Biting back the fury that has taken residence in my body, I struggle to swallow.

He smirks at me. "I know Miss Fitzgerald personally, and I know that she outright stole portions of her manuscript—"

"What the *fuck* are you talking about?" I cut him off, fisting my hands in my lap. Professor Marceaux's head jerks toward me. "I've sat here, listening to you insult *my* novel, the one I wrote when I was a freshman, the one you called brilliant when you helped me edit it."

The class erupts in murmurs, and Marceaux's eyes widen. I know there will be hell to pay for what I'm doing, but I can't stand another minute of this man's insane accusations.

"You know that I have several journals' worth of evidence that prove this is my work, and if my peers are curious, I'll also add that you were the only person who saw the manuscript prior to publication. So unless you're saying that I stole this story from you, you should shut the hell up."

I get up and balance myself against the seat in front of me. Forty pairs of eyes are on me, so I'm hoping I don't faint. Looking up at him and seeing his steely defiance pisses me off more.

"You have some nerve, Jason. You'll be hearing from my attorney." Shit. That means I need to get one.

On my way out, I trip over the same geeky guy. When I get home, I head straight for the bathroom. And throw up. Again and again.

Chapter 24

Someone presses a wet washcloth into my hand. "You okay?"

I can't help the hysterical laughter that comes from my mouth. I've officially gone off the deep end.

"She's cracked," Jenna says to Harper as I stare at their feet, which are clad in neon socks. Why do they have matching socks?

My left cheek is pressed to the cold tile in our bathroom. Rolling onto my back, I stare up at my roommates who stare back. This must be what it feels like to be an animal in the zoo, always being observed and always observing. Any minute, someone is going to start petting me.

Harper crouches down and presses her palm to my forehead. "I don't think she has a fever," she says to Jenna like I'm not here.

I close my eyes. "Everyone knows. It's out there, and I can't make it go back in the can. God damn Wheeler."

"Clem, it'll be okay." Harper grabs my hand to pull me up into a sitting position. I groan, my whole body aching from lying on the floor for the past hour. "I know anonymity is important to you, but there are bigger problems in this world than revealing a writer's identity, like famines, genocide—"

"Human trafficking and sexual cults!" Jenna adds. Harper and I turn to look at Jenna who shrugs. "What? Those are serious problems."

"Okay, point taken." My throat is hoarse from vomiting. After wrapping my neck with my hand to soothe the pain, I try to stand, and my roommates steady me.

"I'm glad you stood up for yourself today," Harper says as she hugs me, but just as quickly, she wrinkles her nose and pushes me away. "You stink. Take a shower."

"He accused me of plagiarism. I couldn't stand there and take it." Noticing a chunk of an undeterminable nature in my hair, I pluck it out.

There are bigger things you should be worried about. What if he tries to hurt you? My hand trembles as I cover my eyes.

"You should have heard her, Harp." Jenna nudges me. "She totally told off that asswipe. It was awesome."

Pressing my hand to my stomach, I say, "We'll see how awesome it is when I have to explain this to the dean. I should call him before Wheeler beats me to it."

Relieved to find that Dean Marshall isn't in today, I leave a message before I crawl into a hot shower. Letting the steady stream beat into my back, I stand there and try to keep it together.

Every molecule in me wants to call Gavin. I miss my friend, and there's no one I want to confide in more. Remembering how he nearly beat up Wheeler last week makes the ache in my chest grow.

But Wheeler's words echo in my head, that my character Isabella is pathetic. Really, that *I'm* pathetic. Because not only did I blow it with Daren by shutting him down, but I ran off and had a one-night stand after we broke up. Ironic that I wasn't opposed to having sex with Daren; I only wanted to make sure I was ready so that he'd respect me afterward, so that I'd respect myself. I wanted to know that he loved me. Instead, I hooked up with John or Sean or whatever the fuck his name was for ten minutes of awkward and somewhat painful sex.

The thought that I'd go crawling to Gavin broken and needy disgusts me. I won't go to him to pick up the pieces of my life. I'll handle this myself. Besides, now that people know I wrote this book, he might not be interested anymore. I wouldn't blame him.

God. Gavin is going to read about my one-night stand for fuck's sake! Although I've told him what happened, it's another thing entirely for him to read a first-hand account.

Mortification spreads in me as I think about what else that book reveals. I poured all of my insecurities between those pages. Every shortcoming and fear. Every humiliating moment as I fell apart over Daren. Every tear shed as my life fell imploded.

Sniffling, I brace myself for the fallout, which I'm sure includes some pissed-off rich people.

I should give Daren a heads-up.

While he's not named in my novel, it won't take a genius to figure out who I'm talking about. I'm sure his parents will be thrilled with my depiction.

I change into some yoga pants and t-shirt, stopping to wipe the steamed mirror with my elbow. "Man up, Clementine," I tell my reflection.

When I step out into the living room, I stop short. Jax jumps off the couch and scoops me into a bear hug. "I'm going to kill that motherfucker."

"Not if I can get to him first." Daren stands up and walks over.

I shoot an exasperated look at my roommates. Jenna loops her arm through Harper's. "We didn't think you should deal with this by yourself, so we called your brother."

"Yeah, I caught that."

"Clem, how is it that you wrote a book and I had no idea?" Jax stares down at me with a hurt expression. How the hell is he so much taller than I am? I'm barely five five while he's at least six feet tall. "Answer me."

"It wasn't a big deal, and anyway, what did you think creative writing majors do?"

Ignoring my question, he asks, "How am I just finding out that you're a bestselling author? And why are you using a pen name?"

Jax lets go of me and starts motioning with his hands. Why does he care that I wrote a stupid book? He's always so wrapped up in soccer and random girls.

My eyes lock with Harper's, and she gives me a sympathetic smile as she drags Jenna back to her room.

"Jax, calm down." Daren places a hand on his shoulder.

I blow out a slow breath. "Daren, you might not be quite as understanding when you read my novel."

He angles his head toward me, clearly not getting my point.

"Okay, both of you, sit. Now."

My brother sighs and stomps over to the couch. Daren joins him. If I weren't in some deep shit right now, I'd laugh that I ordered these huge guys to sit like little boys, and they totally followed my command.

Sitting on the coffee table in front of them, I brace myself for what I need to say.

"Aside from hating being in the tabloids, unlike some people," I say, giving my brother a pointed look, "the reason I used a pen name is because the book is autobiographical. It's about what happened my senior year." I look at Daren. "With us." His eyes begin to widen with understanding. "Before you freak out, you should know that it's fictional—the names and places are different, but it's about a girl named Isabelle who falls in love with the star quarterback, Evan, who cheats on her."

He starts to say something, but I hold my hands up. "It's about how she ran off and slept with some other guy because she thought it would lessen the pain somehow."

Daren winces as my brother groans.

"Shit, Clem. Don't tell me this," Jax grunts.

"Everyone else is about to know, so you'd might as well hear it from me." I grip the hem of my t-shirt and twist it, which will ruin the fabric because nothing that's stretched out that far ever goes back to normal. "It talks about her mother who told her she should have sex with Evan or he'd lose interest but otherwise didn't give a shit. Actually, she cared, but not in the way I thought."

"What does that mean?" Daren sits forward and touches my knee gently so that I'll look at him.

I clench my eyes shut as I think about it. "She said I could learn a few things from Veronica and that I should crawl on my hands and knees and beg you to take me back. Because I'd probably never do any better. And because a Sloan-Avery marriage was great PR. For her. Then she left for a meeting like she couldn't be bothered with my life. And I lost my state meet later that day."

Swallowing so I don't throw up, I wrap my arms around my waist.

"Jesus." Daren stands up and pulls me into a hug, crushing me into his chest. "I'm so sorry, honey. I know your mother is a bitch, but I never realized she'd hurt you like this. No wonder you were reluctant to—"

"Dude, don't fucking say it," Jax says, his hands forming tight fists. "Don't fucking talk about banging my sister."

"Calm down, asshole. I would never talk about Emmie that way."

"So I have a few problems," I say, scooting out of Daren's hold and making him sit again. "Obviously, our parents are going to freak out, but I'm also being accused of plagiarism."

My brother makes me explain exactly what happened in class. After I spill the details, I get to my most pressing concerns. "I have two serious legal issues: the public accusations along with what I suspect will be an academic investigation. I could get expelled if Wheeler somehow convinces the school that I've stolen these ideas from him."

"Don't worry about a thing, babe." Daren whips out his

phone and dials a number. "Prescott, this is Daren Sloan. I need to talk to that libel attorney in your office. No, this is not about me." He covers the phone. "Wheeler is lucky I don't rip his dick off."

"That's... graphic." I laugh weakly as the tension starts to dissipate.

When Jax and Daren leave two hours later, even though I'm humbled that I had to explain this ugly ordeal, the fact that neither of them asked me if Wheeler's accusation has any merit comforts me. They simply assumed I was telling the truth. I smile, knowing that those two are on my side. Maybe I've done something right after all.

* * *

When I wake up the next morning, someone is shouting. Rolling over in bed and placing a pillow firmly over my head does nothing to shut out the noise. Someone yells my name.

I wander out of my bedroom to find Dani pressed up against the front door.

"Dani? What's wrong?" I wipe the sleep out of my eyes and yawn.

"There are *people* here to see you." Her bed-head makes her look like she's twelve. Why does she look so weirded out?

Jenna comes jogging out of her bedroom. "You can't leave, Clem. The press is out there."

"What? Seriously?"

"Come look out my window."

I scurry into her room and peek out through the blinds to see a couple of news trucks. The sight makes my heart race. "Why are they here?"

"You and Wheeler, I think. Ryan says the whole campus is talking about it."

A loud knock on the door jars me from my out-of-body experience.

"Clementine. It's me." The sound of Gavin's voice makes my knees weaken. The thought of him knowing what's in my book churns my stomach.

Jenna takes one look at me and grabs my arm. "You haven't told him what's going on, have you?" she asks in a strained whisper so he won't hear through the door.

I shake my head and remind her of the break.

She smacks me on the side of my head, and her face twists into a scowl when I yelp. "I am not going to curse at you because my momma would say that you never want to hit someone when they're down, but for fuck's sake, Clem, you need to talk to that guy before he gets tired of your shit."

So much for not cursing at me. "Jenna, you think I should've called him yesterday so he could see how *pathetic* I am?"

Jenna doesn't miss my use of Wheeler's word. She turns to me, hands on her hips, and lets out a deep sigh. "Good lord, girl. What am I going to do with you?" The more frustrated she becomes, the thicker her Southern accent gets. "Go clean up because I'm letting him in, and you are going to talk to him. I don't understand how you can go to Daren for help, but you leave out Gavin."

"I didn't call Daren for help. *You* called my brother, and they're attached at the damn hip. Since Daren and I talked the other night and cleared the air, he's been acting like he did before we dated. It was always the three of us since we were little. I can't help that we have that history. He's helping me a lot, and before you give me that look, you should know that *nothing* is going on. I'm not interested in him. At all."

I don't wait for her reply as I shut myself in the bedroom and change. I pull on jeans and a t-shirt and tie my hair into a messy ponytail. A few minutes later, there's a tap on my door.

Placing my hand on the handle, I close my eyes. *You have to stop hiding. Let him in.*

When Gavin sees me, he looks as uncertain as I feel, which unsettles me more, but he's here, now, and my heart thuds faster, quickened by his close proximity. I think back to Monday night when I saw him walking into the gym, laughing with his friends. The realization that he isn't like this with me, not anymore, makes me wonder if I'm even any good for him.

"I guess you heard what happened yesterday." I want to hug him but don't.

He takes a few tentative steps into my room. I'm pained by the distance between us that started with Angelique and wormed its way to Daren. The burden of unspoken things is clearly taking its toll. We are three feet apart, but it might as well be a gulf.

"I did, but I wish I'd heard it from you." His jaw tightens.

The only way to break these barriers, to be close again, is to tell him everything, but he's yet to disclose the secrets he started keeping first. Do I really want to do this? To keep tabulations of past insults? This is exhausting. I don't do angst well.

Maybe I could start by saying something small but honest and see if he reciprocates. I want to take a small step and be vulnerable with Gavin.

"I was embarrassed. I didn't want you to know what I'd written, to see me in that light."

His eyes soften, and he takes a step closer. "I know what it's like to be judged for what you write. For every article I publish, I get an inbox full of hate mail."

"That's ridiculous. I've read your stuff. You're a brilliant reporter."

He shrugs as though uneasy with the compliment. "You've had that advantage." I raise my eyebrows, wondering what he means. He clears his throat. "You know what I've written because I don't use a pen name."

My eyes turn down to the floor. Of course he's known I have a pen name. I told him as much when we first started studying together. I just never told him what it was. Nothing was stopping him from asking. *Unless he was waiting for me to offer it.*

"I wish you felt like you could talk to me." He runs his hand through his hair.

"I could say the same thing." My stupid mouth opens before I realize what I'm saying. He nods slowly, his distance growing.

I think about how he spends time with Angelique. Hell, I saw her walk in with him at the gym only two nights ago, and yet he and I aren't spending time together. I've never thought of myself as a jealous girl, but damn it, I'm pissed.

Gavin exhales and starts for the door, pausing to place a pink square of paper into my palm and kiss my forehead. "I'll talk to you later."

Don't leave.

But I don't say the words. I can't. And then he's gone.

I open my hand to find a Post-It with something scribbled across it. A quote by F. Scott Fitzgerald. *"That is part of the beauty of all literature. You discover that your longings are universal longings, that you're not lonely and isolated from anyone. You belong."*

God, I'm an idiot. He comes here to comfort me and I piss him off. I suck at relationships. I start to go after him but stop at my front door, remembering I have a lawn full of reporters. My situation has garnered enough attention to have a few news trucks parked outside, and yet Gavin didn't ask to interview me or get a story when his specialty is investigative reporting. He never leveraged me for his own advancement. My vision gets blurry, and I blink back the tears, the ache in my chest overwhelming.

I stare down at his note in my hand and wish I knew what to do.

Chapter 25

The best distraction from how screwed up things are with Gavin is to deal with the shitstorm brewing over my book. If I can deal with this myself, maybe I can figure out how to straighten things out with him. Time to make some calls.

The first one is to the dean's office.

After I'm on hold for about ten minutes, a polite elderly-sounding woman tells me Dean Marshall wants to see me on Monday to discuss the allegations made by Wheeler. Her calm, perky demeanor is better suited for taking my lunch order at a 1950s diner than asking me to attend the Spanish Inquisition.

Daren's legal firm hooks me up with top-notch representation, a woman named Kate Peterson. I can hear the disgust in her voice for Wheeler, and thank Jesus, Joseph and the Easter bunny that Daren got me an attorney who sounds like she might tear off my former professor's man parts personally and enjoy it. She says she'll start working on a slander lawsuit immediately.

Gathering up a little more courage, I call my boss Roger who chews me out for not letting him know about my alter ego sooner so I could do some in-store book signings. After grumbling about how his week is shot to shit because I can't come in this evening, his voice softens.

"Look, kid, take the week off so you can deal with school, but you have to promise to do a few promotional events when you get back. That book of yours is a hit."

"Thanks, boss."

"Don't call me that. You know it makes me feel old."

"You are old," I tease.

He laughs. He's taking this really well. Guess I need to address the polka-dotted elephant in the room.

"Roger, I want you to know I didn't plagiarize."

Before I can say anything else, he cuts me off.

"Of course you didn't. Any jackass knows that. Now hurry up and figure all this out so you can get back here and do next month's schedules."

I'm relieved not to have to explain more, and he wishes me luck, offering me more time off if I need it. I start to relax now that everyone in my small circle of friends has been so supportive.

My phone rings for the tenth time in the last hour, and although I've managed to dodge a couple of reporters so far, I know I have to make a statement soon. As if on cue, a familiar name flashes on my cell. I don't get a chance to say hello before Maeve, my publicist, starts in on me.

"I don't think I need to explain my job to you, Clementine, but I'm your liaison to the media. However, if I don't know what the fuck is going on, I can't do my job, which makes me very unhappy." Her British accent sounds amazingly sophisticated even though she's telling me off.

"It's nice to talk to you too, Maeve." I roll my eyes. She can be so dramatic. Of course, I've never made her job easy.

After listening to a few rounds of apologies, she's quiet. "I hope there is no merit to the charges."

"No, God, of course not!" I share what my attorney has said, which seems to assuage her ruffled feathers.

"Great. Now get yourself a few nice outfits."

"Okay," I say slowly. "Why?"

"You need to get in front of this. I made a few calls to the Sunday morning news shows. I'd love to get you out there this evening, but the story will resonate more if you issue your statement during a slow news cycle. So pray there isn't a terrorist attack or natural disaster this week that messes with your PR."

"You want me to do an interview?"

"Interviews. Plural. Or maybe one big one. I'm still working out the details."

My mind floods with fears, but she's right. I have to state my side. It's like being on trial. If I don't do the interviews, it'll seem like I have something to hide. And I don't. Not anymore.

"About that. I have one request."

* * *

After being on the phone for two hours, I'm in a nearly vegetative state when my cell rings again. I should let it go to voice mail when I see that it's an unknown caller, but I accidentally hit accept.

At first, all I hear is music. I recognize it as a Beatles tune, but as the lyrics become clearer, my hand starts to shake. It's called *Run for Your Life*. The evil song about a guy who would rather kill his girl than watch her end up with someone else plays in my ear.

"Did you get that, love?" Wheeler asks with a snicker before he hangs up.

I'm still gripping my phone when I walk out into the living room and find Jenna, Harper and Dani watching an episode of *True Blood*.

"Is it weird that I think Eric Northman was hotter when he was a heartless asshole?" Dani asks.

Harper turns to her with a raised eyebrow, looking like she might launch into a clinical assessment when she spots me. The phone slips from my hand, crashing to the wood floor.

"I... I might need to take off for a few days," I say before I break down, sobbing.

Chapter 26

You've got to be kidding me. The first thing I notice is that my palatial hotel suite smells like lavender and candles. The second is the massive mahogany sleigh bed dressed in a delicate ivory comforter that looks *way* too big for one person. The last detail that sends my wallet into heart-attack mode is that from my balcony—yes, I have a balcony—I have the most stunning view of Copley Square below where dozens of people stroll around the fountain in front of the majestic Trinity Church.

"This can't be right," I tell the bellhop, who sets my small suitcase by the door.

"Ma'am, if you're Mr. Sloan's guest, this is the room." He stares at me like he's waiting for me to say something and itches his collar nervously. *Oh.*

"Shit, hold on." I reach into my bag for my wallet and hand him a five, which I realize is probably a small tip for a five-star hotel, but I'm on a budget.

As soon as the door closes, I dial Daren.

"Are you crazy? This is too much!" I yell the second he answers.

"Do you like it?" he asks with a laugh.

"It's gorgeous." Uh, understatement! Try bridal-suite amazing. Wait, that's bad.

I stop breathing, trying to choose my words carefully. "Daren, I really appreciate your help, but why are you doing this? You know I'm in a relationship, right?" Or kind of in a relationship. Damn it. I don't know what Gavin and I are anymore, but he's where my heart is, and I don't want to give Daren any mixed messages.

"Don't get your panties in a twist. I saw how you looked at that guy at the gym, and I'm not trying to throw my hat in the ring here, but I owe you, and we're friends, right?"

"Yes, we're friends, but this goes above and beyond—"

"You need a place to stay until Boston PD can get back to you about another restraining order, right?"

"Yes, but—"

"Look, I know you don't see your brother often because he's been afraid to put us in the same room together, so if we can put this behind us, maybe the three of us can go back to being friends. Besides, I put you through a lot of shit. I know because I read your book, and even *I* think I was a dick, so look at this as my way to put the universe back in order again. You didn't deserve how I treated you, and if I can do something nice for you once in a while, you should let me. My dad's hotel has great security, and at least I'll know you're safe. Jax has an away game this weekend, and he doesn't want you to be alone, so unless you want to sleep on my couch, you're going to have to deal with it."

"But I'll barely be able to afford your attorney, much less this suite."

"Honey, you're not paying for any of it."

I pinch the bridge of my nose. "Daren, stop. I won't let you throw money at all of my problems. I'll figure out how to pay for my attorney, who's great, by the way. But this suite is too much."

"Emmie, we grew up together. We played in the same crib. You were my first kiss when I was twelve, the first girl to slap me when I was an ass, and the first girl to break my heart. But I also think you've taught me more than anyone I know. You're not some random woman. Now let me take care of this or you'll hurt my feelings."

I roll my eyes at his melodrama. He has this all wrong. I *so* did not break his heart, and I would remind him of this and correct his revisionist history except he keeps yammering on in that Daren-Sloan-rules-the-world kind of way.

"Besides," he says, "you'd do the same for me, right?"

If I were a millionaire like you? Sure. But since my bank account is nonexistent at the moment, you shouldn't look to me for this kind of help any time soon. And I know of at least one person who definitely will not be cool with this arrangement. "Yes, but I wouldn't want this to come back and bite you in the ass with Veronica."

He's quiet, but then he sighs. "Let me worry about her."

I've spent three years trying to block out how Veronica is a c-word, so now, I merely have a general distaste for her, the way I dislike food poisoning or yeast infections.

"I'm not trying to get back at her. I mean, I don't think I'll have her over for lunch anytime this millennium, but I'm not looking to hurt her."

"That's big of you. Now stop wasting my time. I'm a busy man."

I snort. "In your dreams, beefcake." He laughs at me. This is easy, like it used to be for us growing up. "Daren, I *really* appreciate this, everything, but we're even now, okay? This is it. You can't just ride in on a white horse for me again or I'll get pissed."

"I thought most girls lived for that shit."

"Yeah, well, I'm not most girls."

"Emmie, I think we all know that." He chuckles again and tells me to take advantage of the masseuse and day spa downstairs. Good lord, he's infuriating.

* * *

As heavenly as this bed is, I can't sleep. I keep thinking back to how I left things with Gavin earlier today. It's obvious we're growing apart, but I don't know what to do. I would kill to have him here with me in this bed, despite everything we haven't talked about, to have him wrap his arms around me. I feel safe with him, like we can figure things out better together than I can alone.

I want to call Harper or Jenna, but neither one seems to understand why I needed to take a step back from the relationship. Fuck, *I* don't understand it right now.

Maybe I should call him. But it's after midnight, and I don't want to wake him, so I resolve to do it in the morning. Simply making that decision puts me more at ease, enough to finally fall asleep.

I'm up early on Thursday morning and go for a run at the gym downstairs, and as my feet pound on the conveyer belt, I try to plan my day. My empty schedule is uncomfortable, like an itchy sweater that doesn't fit. After learning about the camera crews who stalked me at my brownstone, the dean's office advised me to call my professors to get my assignments and take a brief leave of absence until our meeting on Monday. I'm in no mood for classes or for dealing with any press that might be lurking, so I complied. Plus, at least this way I know I won't run into Wheeler. But I have too much time on my hands, and that makes me nervous.

Around ten, I finally get the nerve to dial Gavin, but the second the phone starts ringing, my stomach twists into a tight knot. He doesn't answer, so I leave a message.

"Gavin, hey, I'm sorry about how we left things yesterday. I... I miss you. Call me when you get a chance."

When I hang up, I realize he doesn't know I'm staying at a hotel or that Wheeler threatened me. *At least you'll have something to talk about when he calls.* The thought almost cheers me. Except he never calls. I write three thousand words on my story, people-watch out my window for an hour, and veg out to two reruns of *CSI*, and my phone never rings.

Curiosity gets the best of me, and like any modern woman with half a brain, I cyber-stalk him on Google. He's been busy. Gavin's had several articles in the BU newspaper in the last two weeks and a front-page article about sexual predators on college campuses in the *Globe* that ran yesterday. That piques my interest.

Apparently, a girl at a nearby college recently got attacked by her ex-boyfriend, but the school didn't believe her because it was a he-said/she-said situation, which Gavin uses to explore how much evidence a woman needs to prove her claims in a situation like this.

That hits close to home. I wonder if he got inspired by what happened with my professor, but he never asked me for an interview. *He must have thought I'd turn him down.*

Eventually, early Saturday afternoon, my phone rings.

It's Jenna. Damn.

She asks about the restraining order, which the police won't reissue because they say there isn't enough evidence to consider Wheeler a threat. The fact that Wheeler sounds like he wants to eat my insides Hannibal Lecter-style doesn't seem to bother them at all, so I call Jax and tell him I might crash with him next week if I can't figure out what to do. And I *really* don't want to stay with my brother. The last time I did, his late-night hookup came waltzing out of his bedroom buck naked and asked if I had seen her thong.

"Are you coming to the show tonight?" Jenna asks, interrupting that unpleasant memory.

I sigh. "Shit. With everything going on this week, I forgot about it."

"You really should come. Remember, stake your territory, mark your man, maybe show him your goodies."

"Jenna, I am not showing him my goodies." I don't know why I say that. Out of principle, I suppose. After all, he's already seen my goodies, but he and I aren't like that anyway. That's not what our relationship is about.

The club is one train ride away, and the B-line will drop me off in front of the venue. Unless Wheeler is lurking in the bushes right outside of my hotel, which is unlikely since no one knows I'm here, I'm probably okay for a quick trip. I have to go because the writing is on the wall: Gavin must think we're over. If he doesn't, that's where this is headed if things don't turn around ASAP.

"Yeah, I'll try to make it." The thought of seeing him makes my insides squirm with excitement and fear, but I need to be a big girl and deal with this.

"Great. I'll make sure your name is on the VIP list."

I wish I had realized the band was playing this weekend. Maybe I would have packed more than jeans and t-shirts. But the idea of gorgeous girls in barely-there fabric draping themselves all over him is enough to motivate me. I can see Angry Red now, shaking her big tits in the front row, and my blood boils.

A quick trip to the mall across the street suddenly seems like a brilliant idea. I need something for the interview my publicist set up for tomorrow morning anyway, so maybe I can kill two birds with my MasterCard.

About two dozen outfit changes later, I drag myself back into my room, toss my packages on the bed and bury myself in the blankets for a nap. Jenna can shop endlessly for days, and I can barely manage a few hours.

Truth be told, I can't wait to see Gavin. I've never seen him perform with Ryan's band, but the impromptu open mic with his students a few weeks ago has me wanting more. He's so damn sexy when he plays the guitar.

With thoughts of that hot man tumbling around in my head, I put my whole heart into getting ready. I straighten my hair, do my makeup, making sure to play up my eyes, and then wiggle into my dress, which I think hugs in all the right places. He liked the outfit I wore on my birthday, and this one is similar, but it's fire-engine red—a bit of a departure for me, but I know I need to pull out all the stops if I want to stave off the hungry droves of women who might be pining for him.

And suddenly, nothing could be clearer. I don't want to lose him. If he says he hasn't been cheating on me, I believe him. That's probably stupid and naive, and I'm setting myself up for heartbreak, but I'm tired of living life on the sidelines, and if I don't take a chance with Gavin Murphy, I think I'll always regret it.

I know my problem. After years of consuming a steady diet of romantic comedies with Jenna and Harper, I think I've been waiting for the big gesture, the one where the guy stands in the rain and declares his love or makes some scene at a football game that ends with the crowd doing the slow clap. It's official. Romantic comedies have ruined my life.

Maybe tonight I just need to tell him how I'm feeling, that I want to work this out. Maybe that will be enough, and he'll tell me what happened with Angelique last weekend. Of course, there's a chance I might vomit before I get the opportunity because I don't do well with these kinds of declarations.

On the bright side, there's never any puking in romantic comedies.

I check myself in the mirror one last time before I reach for the door, but I flinch when a loud knock startles me. Through the peephole, I see two men in black suits. I put the chain on the door before I open it slowly.

One waves a badge.

"Ms. Avery? We're with the FBI. We'd like to ask you a few questions about Jason Wheeler."

Holy crap on toast.

* * *

The two men are probably in their early thirties. I wonder if the FBI deliberately recruits people who have mastered the blank stare because these guys have it down pat.

"I know you," I say to the one with brown hair, Agent Robertson. "I tripped on you in my writing class."

He nods almost imperceptibly and points to the love seat, motioning for me to sit down.

"This might take a while," he says as he glances around my room. He pulls up two chairs, one for him and one for his partner. "We understand you had a run-in with Wheeler your freshman year, and we'd like to understand the details of what happened."

"Sure, but I filed a police report that should contain all the information you need."

Robertson looks briefly at his partner and back to me. "We would, except there's no record of it."

"But... I just spoke to a detective." *Who told you there were some anomalies with this situation but refused to elaborate. Then he stonewalled by saying there wasn't enough evidence.* Shit.

He tilts his head forward. "The department is digitizing its files. It's possible the file was misplaced. It happens."

I swallow, trying to gather my bearings. "Okay, but this can't be about a three-year-old restraining order or the argument Wheeler and I had in class the other day."

Robertson nods again as he whips out a pen and notepad. "We're investigating Olivia Lawrence's disappearance."

I'm glad I'm sitting or I'd have fallen on my ass.

My stomach lurches at the question banging around in my head. It comes out a whisper. "Do you think he's killed Olivia? Like the character in his book?"

Robertson's lips tighten, and his silence weighs heavily in the air.

And all this time I thought Wheeler was threatening me. *Maybe he was. Maybe I was next.* I get chills thinking about all the time we spent alone, working on my book. He could have killed me.

I think back to the conversation I had with Kade. "You know that Olivia's sister thought she was talking to a new guy, right?"

"Her phone records do not indicate any anomalies."

"But what if they were using burners or prepaid phones? People use those all the time when they go abroad."

Robertson doesn't respond, but he jots a few notes in the file that sits in his lap. He asks me about my relationship with Wheeler, how we grew close, when things started to get weird, and when I noticed him stalking me. The hardest part is answering questions about the attack. I must be visibly shaken when I'm done because I almost sense sympathy in their eyes.

The agents appear to be wrapping up the interview when it hits me.

"Oh my God. Brigit." I've been so wrapped up in my stupid book and Wheeler's creepy phone call, I forgot about meeting up with her this week. "You need to make sure she's okay. You have to go now!"

The agents look at each other and one gets up and grabs me a glass of water.

"Slow down," Robertson says, handing me the drink.

"Brigit is the freshman Wheeler has taken under his wing this year. He's editing her book, and she told me he's been acting really moody lately. I wanted to warn her about him, but I didn't get the chance."

I try to take a sip of water, but my hand is shaking so badly, I can barely bring it to my mouth. I set it down instead and take a deep breath.

"He taught abroad in London," I say to myself. I look up at Robertson. "Is that how he knows Olivia?"

"We're not at liberty to say, but if you can give us Brigit's contact information, that would be helpful."

By the time the agents get ready to leave, it's midnight. I can't believe we've been talking for almost four hours. I'm exhausted, stunned and more than a little overwhelmed.

As they reach the door, Robertson turns back to me. "I would keep our conversation confidential, and it's a good idea to stay here for a few more days. Until we can take further action." He reaches into his pocket. "Ms. Avery, here's my card. Call me if you think of anything else that might help our investigation." Although he never outright says I'm in danger, there's a warning in his eyes.

When the door closes, when the reality of the situation really starts to sink in, I'm afraid. With shaky hands, I gulp down some water and sit on the couch trying to understand what just happened.

I don't know how long I sit, trying to absorb what's happened tonight, but as I walk into the bathroom to splash my face with cold water, I see my red dress. *I missed Gavin's show.* Crap.

Grabbing my phone, I realize Jenna sent me a text.

Get your ass over here!

I'm about to write her back when I notice the attachment. As the picture opens, I see the red hair.

Shit. It's a photo of Angelique and Gavin standing side by side, laughing.

Okay, that doesn't mean anything, just that she was at his show. *And you weren't.*

I leave a brief message for Jenna, who doesn't pick up. If she's still out with Ryan, it's possible she can't hear her cell ringing.

I grab my coat and run out the door because there's only one person I want to see right now.

* * *

As I knock on Gavin's door, I start to wonder about what led Robertson's investigation to Wheeler. Kicking myself for not asking more questions, I realize how long I've been standing here. I smooth down my dress. Although I didn't go to the show, hopefully I still look presentable.

I check my phone. It's 1:30 a.m. Maybe no one's home. Gavin might have gone out with Ryan after their gig. It's probably totally obnoxious that I'm here anyway.

I start to turn back toward the elevator when I hear laughter from within his room. Female laughter. My stomach knots.

Then the door opens.

And my heart free-falls out of my chest.

Angelique answers only wearing a t-shirt, one of Gavin's. She eyes me coolly and runs her hand through her tangled long hair. Her lips are smeared with what used to be lipstick, and black mascara rings her eyes. She looks like she's been... *Oh, God.*

"Cat got your tongue?" she asks with a smirk. "Guess you're looking for Gavin, huh? Well, he's busy."

Behind her, a voice calls for her. "Angie, who's there?"

He calls her Angie. He calls her Angie, and he fucks her. Guess he got tired of waiting.

I don't wait for her response before I bolt for the stairs, going as fast as I can in heels. I stop a few flights down and sob into my hands.

Maybe I did this. Maybe I drove him to her. But that doesn't make the cleaver in my heart hurt any less.

Chapter 27

How do you prepare for a national interview after discovering that your boyfriend is sleeping with his ex?

He's not your boyfriend. You were on a break, remember?

I dry off another tear.

Whatever. He told me to wait. No, he begged me to wait and swore he wasn't sleeping with Angelique. *But you let him think something was going on with Daren.* But all he had to do was tell me what he was doing in Rhode Island, and I said I'd explain.

I continue arguing with myself as I drink my first cup of coffee. It's still early. I have a couple of hours before I need to meet my publicist and attorney downstairs.

My eyes are bloodshot and puffy, and I would kill for one of my blue pills, but they're back home. Guess the Regent Hotel doesn't come fully stocked with meds. So I opt for the next best thing. Room service.

"Yes, this is the Vega Suite." My voice is hoarse, and I cover the phone to cough. "I'd like an ice cream sundae with chocolate syrup, a rum and coke, and a plate of chilled cucumber slices." The silence on the line makes me wonder if there's a problem with the connection, but then the woman realizes I'm serious and tells me it'll be up in fifteen.

After a shower where I cry some more, the food arrives. I take a few half-hearted bites of the sundae, place slices of cucumber on my eyes and sprawl back on the bed.

God, how many times will I do this to myself? Let myself get crushed by a guy? Salty tears stream down my face as I think about how much he's hurt me. *It could have been worse. You could have had sex with him.* The insidious thought that if I had slept with him, I wouldn't be here alone right now, haunts me. I can almost hear my mother saying those exact same words she told me years ago.

I think of all the times Gavin and I snuggled in bed together, talking, touching, falling asleep together. *And now he's doing the same things with Angelique.* Of course he wanted to have sex. What twenty-one-year-old male doesn't? But I thought we had more. And I was so close to going all the way so many times. Not that my body needs to be hermetically sealed because I definitely wanted to take that step with him, but I feared this very situation. Being with a man who would be unfaithful. Having my heart broken. Falling apart.

Well, I'm not going to fall apart. Fuck that. I've come too far to have a man rip me to shreds. I'm not going to let myself dwell on this. Not right now. In about three hours, when I'm done with my interview, I plan to curl up in this bed and cry some more so that when I see him next week or the week after, I won't look like I want to die, like he's eviscerated my heart, even though he has. I'll be stronger than that.

Trudging back into the bathroom, I place my rum and coke on the counter and spread out my makeup. Using lots of concealer and eyeliner helps hide the fact that I've been up half the night crying. I get out my iPhone and earbuds and blast some music. By the time I'm dressed in a pair of black pants and a gray blouse, I think I'm put together enough to do this.

* * *

On the ride to the news studio, my attorney Kate, an intense-looking woman in her early thirties, goes over a few topics I should try to avoid and some standard types of comments to get the reporter to back off. Although she's not pleased I won't let her do the interview with me, she says this early in the media cycle, it's probably good to "not look lawyered up."

I don't care how it looks. I just think having her sit next to me during my interview will make me nervous.

My publicist Maeve, in contrast, looks pleased as a petunia to have me doing something to market my book and simply says that any attention is good attention.

I don't mention the FBI's visit last night to either of them. That's a hurdle for another day.

When we get to NBC, I'm briefly introduced to the anchors before I'm escorted to a seating area with two small couches that face each other. Maeve and Kate stand off camera. The reporter who sits across from me looks young but polished. I've seen her around campus. Her long, black hair is swept back into a mock bun, and she looks stunning in a pinstriped suit.

"Hi, Clementine," she says, reaching out to shake my hand. "I'm Madeline McDermott, but my friends call me Maddie." She lowers her voice. "I heard *The Today Show* wanted to fly you to New York to be interviewed by Matt Lauer tomorrow morning, but you preferred to be interviewed by a BU intern." Her flawless face scrunches up in confusion.

Maeve almost had a heart attack when I explained this point was non-negotiable. If I've learned anything from my mother it's that you can make demands when you're in demand. In the scheme of things, I don't think this is such a big deal. But I see why this perplexes Maddie.

"I've gotten a few breaks professionally, and I thought I could pay it forward and provide one for someone else."

I think back to how my book sales took off in the first place. A blogger with a huge following stumbled across *Say It Isn't So* and loved my story, so she shared it with her fans. The next day my novel began jumping up the charts.

Maddie smiles brightly. "Well, I can't thank you enough."

"I've seen you cover stories around campus, so I know you're good at what you do."

Her head tilts to the side as she appraises me. "I think you might be my new best friend." She laughs, and I return the smile.

A guy behind a giant console adjusts the lights, and after a few minutes of clipping mics to our blouses and making sure they're picking up the audio, he explains how the New York station will cut to our segment.

My heart slams into my chest, and, strangely, I think of my mother who is a combination of steel and stone when it comes to situations like these. With that in mind, I take a deep breath and brace myself for what's to come.

"We're on in five," the camera guy says as he counts down on one hand, finally pointing to the red light that indicates we're live.

On a monitor, I see the New York host introduce the story before the screen splits to show Maddie next to him.

She takes a deep breath, which she holds briefly as she stares back at the camera. Then, as though she's done this a million times, she starts talking in a broadcast voice, which is smooth with a kind of melodic cadence.

"I'm here with Clementine Avery, the Avery International heiress, who's been in the headlines this week because her identity as the elusive bestselling author known as Austen Fitzgerald was recently revealed during a heated discussion in one of her writing classes. Clementine, it's great to meet you."

"Thank you for having me, Madeline."

"Is it true that until now, none of your professors knew who you were?"

"Only one professor who helped me edit my book three years ago knew that I wrote under a pen name."

"Young Adult author Jason Wheeler? The son of the former Rhode Island governor Richard Wheeler?"

"Yes."

She sits up just a bit straighter and glances down at her note cards.

"As I understand it, Wheeler criticized your book and accused you of plagiarism during your creative writing class when you revealed that you are Austen Fitzgerald. What do you have to say about his accusations?"

"I'm suing him for slander. I have two years' worth of writing journals and diary entries to prove that what I wrote is mine. Did he suggest that I tweak a storyline or reword certain things? Absolutely. But to claim that those ideas are anyone's but my own is ludicrous."

Out of the corner of my eye, I see my attorney giving me the thumbs up.

Although I'm nervous, I speak slowly, deliberately, like we have all the time in the world. That's how powerful people talk, like they are confident you want to hear what they have to say and nothing will rattle them. Maybe the years of growing up with my screwed-up family will pay off after all.

"Why do you think he would criticize you so publicly?" Maddie leans forward, tilting her head slightly.

"I believe he wanted to make me miserable, to inflict emotional distress. He knows I cherish my privacy, and I doubt he thought I'd call him on his lies."

"You make it sound like he had some kind of vendetta against you."

Taking a deep breath, I nod. "During my freshman year, Jason Wheeler wanted more from our relationship than what I was willing to give. I saw him as my mentor, and he was interested in something more romantic. I think this is his way of getting back at me."

She raises her brows but doesn't continue with this line of questioning.

"In your book, the main character is the daughter of a wealthy family who falls in love with the star quarterback at her school. The boy cheats on her with her best friend and breaks her heart. I know this is a fictional book, but the similarities to your life are striking. You dated Daren Sloan, who now plays football for Boston College and is in contention for the Heisman trophy. He's engaged to Veronica Rogers, who used to be your best friend in high school, and you're the daughter of the heiress Jocelyn Avery, who is the president and CEO of Avery International."

And there it is. My worst nightmare. My whole life spilled out before me. I take another deep breath. I don't know where to start.

"Was there a question?" I ask with a laugh. This is what my mother would do. Pretend like the Hiroshima bomb is simply a gnat in her salad.

"Well, did Daren cheat on you?" Maddie furrows her brow and leans forward again. "Is this story based on your relationship?"

"Maddie, I didn't set out to write an autobiography, so while I might have used aspects of my own life as inspiration as any writer does, I can unequivocally say that this is a work of fiction. Yes, Daren and I dated in high school, but that's where the comparisons stop. We broke up because we grew apart, but he remains a dear friend. I wish him and his fiancée the best."

Breathe. Breathe.

I make deliberate eye contact and smile. Maddie seems surprised by my answer but nods. She probably thought I'd rip into Daren. Even if he and I hadn't recently made amends, I could never publicly humiliate him.

"What about your mother? In your book, the mom wanted her daughter to sleep with her boyfriend, claiming that sex was the way to keep a star athlete satisfied. Is that what happened with your mother? And are you estranged because she wanted you to be a spokesperson for her fashion line and model her clothes, but you refused?"

Fuck.

I consider my words carefully.

"Jocelyn and I are not close. Anyone can tell you that, but I'm not going to speak disparagingly about my mother. I will say that she's a leader in her industry and has worked hard to get where she is today. I admire her many successes. Furthermore, our family continues its decades-long friendship with the Sloans."

I didn't come here planning to defend my family, but this is my business, not the public's. And maybe what I said was wishful thinking, but my mother knows what she did, and that's all that matters to me.

Maddie thankfully switches gears to talk about sales, explaining how I took advantage of the ebook format, noting that I managed to sell well without the help of a big publishing company.

"Now that this is being sold in hard copy," she says, holding up my book, "I'm told stores can't keep *Say It Isn't So* on the shelves. Why do you think readers love this story so much?"

"Your guess is as good as mine." I shrug, feeling self-conscious. "I'm still surprised anyone wants to read my book. I was going through a lot when I wrote it, and I think it portrays an honest depiction about what happens when you have a broken heart and that resonates with people."

She smiles, and I get the impression she's asked all of the tough questions.

"You're a *New York Times*-bestselling author, and you're not even out of college. What's on the horizon for you? Are you working on anything right now?"

"Yes, I'm writing a romance novel, which is a departure for me. It's about a freshman in college who falls in love with her RA."

"Now, is this a true story?" Her eyes twinkle with interest.

"Hmm. I have to tread carefully." I smirk back, managing to

elicit a laugh from her. "The love interest, Aiden, is inspired by someone I know, but he was never my RA."

"Are you dating the real-life Aiden right now?"

Damn it. She's good.

"I was," I say slowly. Maddie raises her brows, and I swallow. *Just say it. Be honest about how you feel.* "But we're not going out any more, which is unfortunate because I'm kind of in love with him." Holy Christ, did I say that out loud? I look down, embarrassed that I actually admitted it. On live fucking television. I'd like to faceplant into the carpet and only barely manage to keep myself upright.

She touches her in-ear monitor and nods.

"I'm sorry, we're out of time. Clementine, I've enjoyed talking with you. And to Aiden, whoever you are, you need to give this girl her happily ever after. I'm Madeline McDermott. Back to you in New York."

The red light clicks off, indicating the cameras have stopped rolling, and I sigh, relieved it's over.

Maddie pops out her in-ear monitor and her calm demeanor disappears. Her blue eyes go wide, her mouth drops open and her hands fist into her hair. "Holy shit. That was amazing."

I laugh. I doubt Matt Lauer would have had the same reaction to interviewing me.

"You did a great job," I manage to say. I tuck my hands under my thighs to hide the trembling.

She leans over and whispers, "Sorry about all those personal questions. The network sent me a dozen really, really invasive ones I tweaked because I couldn't bring myself to nail you with them."

"I appreciate it. I know you went easy on me."

She gets up off her couch and sits next to me. "Can I ask you something? Totally off the record?" I nod, realizing I'm light-headed. "Who's the RA? I'm wondering if I know him."

I mull it over. Maddie could have shredded me on live, national television but didn't. *The relationship is over anyway.*

I whisper back, "Gavin Murphy."

"As in front-page writer for the *Free Press*? And total hottie?"

"That would be the one." She fans herself in appreciation for his looks, and I smile sadly. "I know. Tell me about it."

"I thought he was dating that mean redhead." Maddie crinkles her nose, and if I didn't like her before, I certainly do now.

"Yeah, he was or he is. I don't know." They could just be sleeping together, which is worse.

Maddie frowns. "You look like you could use a drink. Can I get you one? To say thanks?"

"Absolutely."

So what that it's not quite 10 a.m. yet? I've had one hell of a day.

Chapter 28

Three drinks later, I am officially shit-faced. Maddie and I are sitting at the bar of my hotel, realizing that we need to eat something, when Jax and Daren walk in.

"I'm pissed at you," my brother barks as he approaches.

I giggle. "Get in line." I order two beers for the guys, knowing they'll want to join us.

"Why didn't you tell me you had an interview today?" Jax asks. "Why do I have to hear everything from your roommates?"

Daren elbows him. "Dude, lay off."

I wave a finger. "Jax, you had a game yesterday. In a different state. I thought you were busy." I hiccup so hard it hurts, which makes me laugh. "Have you two met Maddie? Maddie, this is my asshole brother Jax, and this is his asshole best friend Daren." I wave back and forth between them.

She turns to look at me, obviously shocked that I was telling the truth when I said Daren and I are still friends. Jax barely glances at Maddie while Daren can't seem to stop staring at her, which is no shocker because she is gorgeous.

"Take a load off. Have a drink." I grab Maddie's hand, yank her off the stool, and wander to a table that can accommodate four. The guys sit down across from us.

"Thanks for not making me sound like a douche in your interview," Daren says to me, making me grin.

"Not a problem. It's bridge under the water." Shit. That's not right.

Maddie's cell buzzes, and she grabs it, putting it right up to her nose to read the incoming text.

Daren motions to my drink. "Have you eaten today?"

"I had a delicious bite of a chocolate sundae this morning, but otherwise, no. I don't think the rum and coke I had at dawn counts as food, huh?"

He calls over the waiter and orders several things while Maddie excuses herself to make a call. A minute later, she runs back.

"Sit down," she tells me, making me crack up.

"I am sitting. You're the one standing."

She realizes her mistake and shakes her head. "Okay, shut up," she says even though no one is talking. "Jason Wheeler was just arrested for kidnapping."

* * *

The news reports that FBI agents kicked in Wheeler's door at ten this morning, arresting him for the abduction of Olivia Lawrence. Daren has the bar turn on the flatscreen, and we watch the coverage in silence.

The camera rolling from the street in front of Wheeler's mansion shows a gated driveway and ten-foot hedges that wrap around an expansive property. The blue and red lights of police vehicles flash up and down the street as neighbors watch in strange fascination.

I keep waiting to hear the gruesome details, bracing myself for the worst. I think about all of the homicide shows I watch and how authorities always expect a kidnapping to result in murder after forty-eight hours. I feel ill, hoping that in the end it wasn't painful. *Maybe now she's at peace.*

And then the most amazing thing happens.

A girl with tangled, long brown hair and pale skin walks out of Wheeler's house.

Olivia is alive.

Everyone in the bar cheers. Tears stream down my face as I watch her reunite with her family. My heart throbs as I think about what this is going to mean to Kade.

He picks up on the second ring.

"Kade, did you hear the news?" I sound out of breath.

He's quiet. "Yeah. She's alive." He sounds choked up, and I give him a minute.

"It's going to be okay, buddy. She has a long road ahead of her, but I'm sure she's going to need some good friends."

He doesn't hesitate when he says, "I plan to be there for her."

"Call me if you need anything. I mean it."

He takes a shaky breath. "You've been amazing through all of this. It makes me feel like a bigger asshole for all the dumb shit I've said to you over the years."

I laugh even though it makes more tears tumble down my cheeks. "Here's to new beginnings. I'm tired of letting the past determine my future. It sounds like you are too. Maybe we can help each other with that."

Glancing up, I see Daren smile at me, and I return the look and reach out and squeeze his giant hand.

"Thanks. I needed to hear that," Kade says.

When I get off the phone, Daren laughs. "You've turned into a big softie."

"Shut up. If you tell anyone about that conversation I'll shank you with my toothbrush, and you won't be the big football hero anymore. You'll be the guy who got beaten up by a girl."

His grin widens. "There's the feisty little girl I love."

I scowl, half-heartedly I admit, and give him the finger. His laughter grows, and eventually I give in and giggle.

Daren gets everyone a round of drinks to celebrate as my phone starts lighting up with messages. I talk to Harper to let her know where I am and that I'll be home in a couple of hours, and then Gavin starts texting and calling. And calling.

"Are you going to get that?" Daren asks after the fifth call.

"Nope." I peel the sticker off his beer and flick it at my brother across the table.

"But isn't he the one you talked about in the interview? The one you—"

"Yes, but that doesn't change things." It doesn't change the fact that he slept with Angelique. And probably lied about it. And broke my fucking heart.

"Don't you want to see what he wants? Maybe he—"

"Daren, I'm pretty sure what he wants is a five eight redhead."

Daren sits back in his chair, finally understanding what I'm saying.

My head is starting to hurt. I guess downing half a bar will do that. Now that I've eaten, though, I'm sober enough to make it back to my room.

Grabbing my purse, I stand up. "I've got to go pack. Guys, can you make sure Maddie makes it home okay?" They nod, offering to drive her back to campus.

I give Maddie a hug, and we agree to go for drinks again soon. Jax puts me in a headlock until I punch him in the ribs, and Daren kisses me on the cheek and says I'd better come to a game soon before he kicks my ass.

I take my throbbing headache back to my hotel room, and even though there's a crater in my chest the size of Idaho from what happened last night at Gavin's, I know I'm resilient enough to survive.

* * *

Dropping my bag by the door with a heavy thud, I watch as Jenna and Harper hop off the couch and run toward me, engulfing me in hugs. Ryan waves hi and stretches out his arms thanks to the space the girls vacated.

"We're so relieved you're okay!" Harper says in a rare show of dramatic emotion.

"It wasn't like Wheeler was lurking right outside my door," I say, trying to calm them down. The truth is, I don't know. He could have been stalking me. I think back to the times I smelled clove cigarettes on our front stoop, and it makes me wonder.

"By the way, you were brilliant this morning." Harper smiles encouragingly. "You were so poised and confident. I was really proud of you."

"Thanks. The reporter didn't grill me as much as she could have."

"Girl, what happened to you last night?" Jenna asks, her forehead knitted together.

Taking off my coat, I decide I can talk about what happened now that Wheeler has been arrested.

"The FBI interviewed me for about four hours. They wanted to know everything that went down with Wheeler, what I knew about him, when we met. It was intense." I glance over to Ryan. "Sorry I missed your show. I really wanted to come. I was dressed and everything."

He waves it off. "Not a big deal. You've seen us play plenty of times."

Yes, but I've never seen Gavin.

"I've had a long day, so I'm going to unpack and take a shower." My head still hurts, but it's faded to a dull ache.

"Hey, why aren't you calling Gavin back?" Jenna asks. "He's been looking for you. He's called me like three times."

"Well, he can deal with it." I grab my bag off the floor and head for my room.

"Clem, don't you want to talk to him?"

I turn back to her, anger and hurt suffocating me.

"Not since Angelique opened his bedroom door last night just wearing his t-shirt, looking freshly fucked."

I look from Harper to Jenna to Ryan whose mouths all drop open. With that, I walk into my bedroom and shut the door.

Chapter 29

The knocking is forceful, jarring me from my sleep. After I got home from the hotel this afternoon, I took a scalding shower, and between that and all the booze I drank, I'm really out of it. Stumbling out into the living room, I wonder where everyone has gone. The lights are off. *The girls probably went out for a late dinner.*

The knocking starts again, and I barely open the front door before Gavin is barreling through it, pulling me into his arms. I stand there, stiff, wondering if I'm actually dreaming.

"Baby, I wasn't with Angelique last night. I never cheated. You need to believe me."

My body says that I am currently being hugged by Gavin, but my head is throbbing, so it's possible I never made it home from the hotel and am passed out in the gutter somewhere.

It takes a few heartbeats to realize that, yes, I am awake, and yes, Gavin is still here, holding me. Pushing hard against his chest so I can look at his face, I stare back, doing my best to look impassive. I might have declared my feelings for him on national television, but it doesn't absolve him of fucking Angelique. The thought of him touching her, of them touching each other, disgusts me. He must see the rage and hurt in my eyes because he says it again.

"I did *not* sleep with Angelique." His voice is so forceful that it gives me pause, but before I can speak, he grabs my hand and yanks me out of my apartment. "Come on."

He's running down the stairs, dragging me behind him. Thank God I'm wearing clothes. I tug on him to let me go, but he tightens his grip.

When we reach the bottom, Gavin points. In the vestibule of my building is Angelique. A very pissed-off Angelique. He pulls me to her before I can protest, but the sight of Angry Red turns my stomach.

"Tell her," he says.

Angelique blinks lazily and looks away.

He inches closer to her, all the while holding my hand. "Fucking. Tell. Her. Now."

Angelique crosses her arms and tosses her head back. "Honestly, Gavin, have some shame. I've never seen you so worked up over a girl."

"I certainly never was over you."

That gets her attention, and she glares back.

"Tell her, Angelique, or so help me I'll never write for you again."

Angelique's eyes skim over me, and with a resigned shake of her head she sighs. "I wasn't with Gavin last night. He and Mark swapped floors, so I was, uh, hanging out with Mark."

"Tell her why you were wearing my clothes." His voice is laced with warning.

She looks at him and rolls her eyes. "God, you're whipped." His eyes narrow at her. "Fine. I spilled something on my shirt, so I grabbed one of yours."

"So we're clear, you hooked up with Mark last night, not me." His eyes are fire, his voice rough.

"Yes, dickhead. I hooked up with Mark. Can I leave now?"

"Tell her why we went to Rhode Island."

She grabs a long lock of red hair and twirls it between her perfectly manicured fingers. "We were investigating Wheeler."

"Thank you. Now leave."

The dismayed expression on Angelique's face dissolves into open hostility a split second before she exhales in disgust and storms out of my building, the door slamming behind her.

I stare after her, a little dumbfounded.

"Hey," he says, nudging me. "Let's go talk. There's more."

* * *

How could there possibly be more? Gavin takes my hand and walks me back upstairs. I follow, quiet, trying to make sense of the last five minutes of my life.

When we get into my apartment, I turn on a few lights and sit at one end of the couch, pressing myself as far as I can into the corner. I grab the green throw pillow and squeeze it.

Gavin sits next to me, leaving a little space.

"I need to tell you everything, so you understand."

My head is still trying to process what Angelique said when he gently touches my face, startling me.

He shakes his head, looking almost hurt that I reacted to his touch by flinching. Pulling me against him, he kisses the top of my head and holds me several minutes. I find myself taking slow, deliberate breaths, trying to relax. *Gavin didn't cheat. He didn't lie.* The thoughts racing through me send a pang through my chest at my own distrust of him. At my doubt. But even though I know the truth, I'm still shaken.

I think I'm in shock, the toll of what's happened over the last few weeks slamming into me. Gavin seems to understand, and he runs his hands down my hair with soft, light touches that reassure. I pull away so I can see him. He looks exhausted. His brows are furrowed, pinched into a V on his otherwise handsome face.

"Clementine, don't get mad, okay? I want you to hear the whole story."

I look at him wearily, but he doesn't wait for my response.

"After seeing what happened with you and Wheeler at the student union, I felt like I needed to do something to protect you." He licks his lips and closes his eyes briefly. "I thought I could find some dirt so he'd have a good reason to stay away from you. I have a friend who works in the HR department who let me take a peek at his employment file, and I noticed a strange letter from a university in Rhode Island.

"At first, it looked pretty standard, a letter confirming his attendance, but then I noticed it had two different names on it. In the subject line, it said Justin Whitmire, but in the body, it said Jason Wheeler, which made me curious. I dug more and found that his family donated five million dollars shortly after he transferred to a different college mid-semester. That *definitely* piqued my interest. Enough to troll through some of the school's message boards and find rumors about a girl who said she'd been raped by another student around the same time. But there was nothing about it in the press. The police didn't have a record of it either."

He squeezes my hand gently. "Considering what you went through with him your freshman year, I thought this warranted a deeper look. I spoke to my managing editor about going to Rhode Island to investigate further, and Angelique overheard and demanded that she come with me. I wanted to handle it on my own, but my boss agreed she should come, and that was the end of the discussion. "

Sighing, he shakes his head. "We were about to knock on the dean's door to ask if Wheeler was in any way connected to the girl who claimed she was raped when the FBI interceded. They feared we'd somehow jeopardize their investigation of Olivia Lawrence, so we were told to back off. Now, as a member of the press, I'm under no obligation to do that, but the agent..."

Running his hands through his hair, his agitation evident, he sighs.

"Agent Robertson knew who you were. Knew about us. I wasn't going to disclose your connection to Wheeler, but the FBI already knew." He shakes his head in frustration. "Robertson said Wheeler was possibly a sociopath, and that if he really viewed me as a threat, as someone who might get in his way, he might take it out on you."

"Which is why you became so distant." I can barely say the words.

"Yes."

His eyes are so full of worry and regret that everything I've been bottling up, all of the feelings I've been trying to block, come rushing back to me. I have a hard time swallowing.

His jaw clenches. "I don't know if you want to hear this, but my *Globe* editor told me the FBI found surveillance photos Wheeler took of you running at night. He had a whole wall of pictures of you at his house."

"So he *was* stalking me?" My words come out a whisper.

"Yeah." Gavin closes his eyes briefly, and when he opens them, I see the dread on his face. "I don't know what I would have done if that sick fucker had hurt you."

He pulls me to him and wraps his arms around me. I nuzzle against his neck, too overcome to say anything.

Gavin kisses my cheek. "I'm so sorry I couldn't tell you the truth. It was killing me that you stopped trusting me."

My eyes sting with tears. Wheeler could have attacked me on any given night. My body shudders against Gavin's chest. In my head, I hear that Beatles song about killing the girl, and I can't hold back the sob that erupts. Everything from Wheeler's threats to Angelique in her underwear totally unhinge me and hot tears stream down my face.

"Darlin', don't cry." He hugs me tighter. "I'm so sorry for all of this. I was trying to make things better for you with that asshole."

He holds me while I weep, soothing me with soft words until the tears stop.

"I was waiting for the FBI to arrest him, which I thought would happen sooner, and then it didn't help that Angelique started antagonizing you. She's pissed because I wouldn't let her write the article that the newspaper is publishing this week."

A small tremor runs through my body, a deep breath I'm finally able to take.

"Why can't she write it?" I ask, muffled by his chest.

"It's a conflict of interest. I can't write it because of my connection to you and the fact that I threatened Wheeler. Angelique shouldn't do it either because she isn't unbiased. She obviously doesn't like you. I told our boss that and recused both of us last week."

Pulling back from him, I wipe my cheeks. "I don't understand the significance of Wheeler's name. Is he also Justin Whitmire?" I sniffle and reach for a Starbucks napkin on the coffee table.

Gavin's eyebrows pinch when he sees me. I'm probably red and splotchy. I smile weakly, and he takes my hand.

"He was known as Justin J. Whitmire growing up, but after his mother died when he was in high school, his uncle, who was the governor at the time, adopted him. But Wheeler didn't change his name until after he transferred from that college, presumably to distance himself from those rape rumors."

I sit there, absorbing everything.

Maybe I can put Wheeler behind me now. For good.

Part of me is overwhelmed by the past few days, but more than anything, I'm grateful. Grateful for this wonderful guy sitting next to me.

I glance up and Gavin smiles, and it feels like the clouds have parted. He pulls me to him for a soft kiss.

"I've missed you," he says against my mouth.

That's when I realize what I want to tell him, what I need to tell him. I push on his chest. "Nothing is going on with Daren."

"I know." One side of Gavin's mouth tugs up in a half grin. "I ran into him this morning coming back from the *Free Press* office. I guess he and your brother were stopping by your apartment to talk to your roommates." Gavin ducks his head and laughs. "Daren asked me why I was breaking your heart and told me that if I didn't get my head out of my ass, he'd take it out for me."

"Oh, Jesus. I'm sorry." I lean back and cover my face, completely embarrassed. "He used to be really protective when we were little, and since we made amends, he's been going a little caveman on me. I'm scared to ask what else he said."

Gavin rubs my cheek, like he's trying to savor the fact that we're finally able to talk again. "Just that he would have, and I quote, 'given his left nut to have you express your feelings about him the way you did about me,' and that if I was smart, I'd do whatever I could to win you back." His lips turn up into a smile. "I guess you weren't very expressive when you were in high school."

My fingers run over the buttons on his shirt. "That's putting it mildly."

"I know. I read your book."

That's when my heart stops. I'm pretty sure that blood flow to my brain has also ceased.

"Clementine, breathe." He chuckles again and brings my face closer to his. "You're a phenomenal writer. Your novel had this beautiful dark humor mixed with some really poetic elements. I mean, it made me want to beat the shit out of your ex, but since he started trying to be noble, I can't really hold a grudge." He leans down and kisses my forehead. "I'm sorry you had to go through all of that."

I squeeze him tighter, half afraid that if I let go, he'll disappear. He shakes his head. "Then I got this phone call from Ryan who started swearing at me because he heard you saw a half-naked Angelique in my room, and that's when I hunted her down so she could explain what happened." He clears his throat. "I can't imagine what you were thinking after seeing her last night. God, I still feel fucked up over that."

"It's okay. I should be the one to apologize for not trusting you."

He shakes his head as he runs his hands down my arms. "I don't blame you for that reaction. I would have felt the same way, and it was unfair of me to ask you to blindly believe me. But honestly, I wasn't sure what to do."

I can't get over Gavin, how he tried to help me, how far he went to protect me. He starts to grumble again about what happened last night, and I twist in his arms to look at him eye to eye.

"Shut up and kiss me."

Tilting his head, he smirks. "Has anyone ever told you that you have a way with words?"

I raise my eyebrows. "What happened to the shutting up and the kissing?"

That does the trick.

<h1 style="text-align:center">Chapter 30</h1>

It's late, past midnight, but neither one of us is ready to say goodnight. We're sprawled across my bed. Gavin is leaning against the wall, and my head is in his lap as he plays with a long strand of my hair.

"It seems like it's been ten years since we spent time together, but it's only been a couple of weeks since our date." My eyelids are heavy, and I wonder if I'm making sense.

"I'm thinking it's time to take you on another." Gavin leans down to nibble on my neck. He seems to sense that we need time to reconnect, so even though I think we're both dying to be together *in that way*, neither of us pushes things beyond kissing.

"You were a pro today, in your interview," he says against my skin. "I've interviewed hundreds of people, and when shit is really on the line, they get nervous and it shows, but it looked like you had been dealing with the press your whole life."

My chest fills with pride that he thinks I did a good job. "Honestly, I was scared out of my mind." Just thinking about that interview makes my palms sweaty.

"You didn't show it."

"I don't show a lot of things. I don't know if that's good or bad."

He leans back far enough so he can look in my eyes, and a mischievous grin spreads on his face.

"My favorite part was how you said you love your sexy RA." Oh God! How can he say this to me, especially since I have no idea how he feels? "And I fucking love that this makes you blush." Gavin runs his finger from behind my ear, down my neck and across my collarbone.

I sit up to face him because I can't let him get away with this.

"Who says I was talking about you?" I tease as I bite my lower lip. He leans down so he's an inch away from my face, and I run my hand through his thick hair. "And I definitely don't remember saying a damn thing about the RA being sexy."

Gavin grins, scooping me up and over his lap to lay me next to him before he props himself on one arm. I laugh as he grabs me again, pulling my body flush to his.

"Baby, I'd have to be for you to give me the time of day." The smile is still on his lips as he kisses me, but when he pulls away, he looks serious.

Clearing his throat, he says, "You must know by now that it's mutual." My stomach clenches and unclenches, and then he says it, the words I've been wanting to hear. "I'm in love with you, Clementine. I have been for a while, but I didn't want to say it and freak you out. I've always liked you, even when you were trying to scare me off by singing Amy Winehouse songs."

I smile, a supernova bursting inside me. He sinks down deeper into the bed, and I turn to him so that we're nose to nose.

He shakes his head. "But you said it on national television, which is the coolest damn thing anyone has ever done."

I reach up and touch his face, which is rough against my palm. I lean in for a kiss, and it's chaste and simple and, for some reason, the loveliest one we've shared.

"You might ruin it for me," I murmur, savoring the way his lips linger on mine.

"Ruin what?" He brushes the hair away from my eyes.

"I might never be able to date another man."

He leans over and grazes my earlobe with his teeth, sending warm shivers down my arms. "That's the plan."

I giggle as the heat of his breath warms me. Laying my head against his chest, I sigh. "Will you stay here with me tonight? I kind of miss you, and I hear you're pretty good at spooning."

He laughs, his grasp around me tightening. "I thought you'd never ask."

Lying wrapped in his arms, listening to him breathe and feeling his heartbeat, is kind of mesmerizing. After a while, it makes me so relaxed that I blurt it out.

"I'm on the pill now." I cringe hearing the words, and he stills.

I glance up, almost afraid of his expression. His brows are pinched as he traces the edge of my shirt.

"Baby, don't take this the wrong way, but I want you to trust me, to trust us, before we go that far." He runs his hand through my hair, holding me to him. He looks away, almost shyly, and grins. "To be honest, you're not the kind of girl a man can love just a few times." He brings my face to him, running his nose along my jaw, and he takes a deep breath. "I want us to have a future, I want you to be mine, and I'm willing to wait as long as you need to get there."

If I ever doubted wanting to take *that* step in our relationship, I don't now. I wrap my arms around his muscular chest and sink back down, letting my leg tangle over his like he's my own personal body pillow.

"I trust you. I'm sorry I didn't before, but I do now."

Daren broke my heart, and Wheeler shattered the last few threads of belief that men were even the least bit trustworthy, but Gavin has shown me it's possible. With my meeting with the dean in a few hours and the crazy media storm resulting from Wheeler's arrest, tonight might not be the right time, but I will find the perfect moment to show Gavin that I mean it.

I close my eyes as I snuggle against him, a smile on my lips, never more sure of myself or him.

* * *

Waking up for a meeting with the dean would be enough to make me lose my Cheerios if it wasn't for the fact that a delectable man is in bed next to me.

Gavin's thick hair dips across his cheek as he lies here, and the high planes of his face are marked by stubble. I let my eyes trail down his body. Even though he's asleep, his biceps strain against his t-shirt.

Good lord, he's sexy.

I still can't believe I haven't ripped off all of his clothes and bedded him already, and even though in the movies, the couples always have this great makeup sex, we had way too much shit to talk about last night. When we finally go there, I don't want it tainted by that psycho Wheeler or that bitch Angelique. It will be about us. Only us.

I slide out of bed for a quick shower before I dress in a pair of black slacks and a long-sleeved pinstriped blouse. Twisting my hair up into a messy bun, I slide two hair clips through to secure it before I dab on a little makeup.

My foggy brain tries to get in the game. Staring into a steamed bathroom mirror, I give myself the *Rocky* pep talk, the one where I hear *Eye of the Tiger* and visualize myself knocking out my opponent. It's cheesy, I know, but it helps. Jax and Daren were insane for stupid jock movies when we were kids, and I'm a veritable expert now. *Friday Night Lights, Jerry Maguire, Rudy, Remember the Titans*—I've seen them all. But I go with the *Rocky* theme because that's the best one, and I close my eyes and try to envision what I want to say to the dean.

It comes down to this: I shouldn't be afraid. Wheeler was arrested. That should speak volumes about his credibility, but his allegation that I've somehow cheated is still out there, and I'm dying to put it to rest and prove my innocence. Thinking about it, that smug look on his face as he tried to unravel my career in class, really pisses me off.

I get lost in these thoughts, and when I look back in the mirror, I'm surprised. I don't look scared. If anything, I look confident. Intense. *I can do this. Just like my interview yesterday, I can do this.*

Gavin is stretching awake when I step into my room.

"Hey, sleepyhead." I bend down to peck him on the cheek, and he grabs me and yanks me down onto the bed, making me squeal.

"Clementine," he growls, "you look like a hot teacher." He kisses my neck, and for about sixty very happy seconds, I forget where I need to be in half an hour. "Fuck, you smell good."

Grinning like a school girl, I push him off me and get up.

"You, sir, are not helping me at all this morning." I trot over to my bureau and re-tuck my shirt before I pull out a pair of small gold hoop earrings. I sense him watching me as I put on my jewelry.

Gavin gets up and stretches lazily, his shirt lifting to show a tantalizing strip of taut muscles just above his low-rise jeans. I angle myself to watch him in my mirror. In truth, I can't take my eyes off him. He catches me staring and winks at me, and what I wouldn't give to be able to crawl back into bed with him.

He shrugs on his hoodie, places his hands on my shoulders and kisses the top of my head. "So, I'll see you in a bit."

I turn and look at him, confused. "I have my meeting with the dean, remember?"

"Yes, and I'm going with you, or at least I'll wait for you while you meet with him."

"Don't you have class?"

"This is more important." He places one light kiss on the tip of my nose and then heads out the door. "I'll meet you there."

* * *

My heels clatter along the hardwood floor of the dean's office as my attorney and I exit. On a bench across the hall sit Jenna, Harper and Gavin. I grin at the sight of my best friends here to support me.

"It must have gone well," Harper says, jumping up to hug me.

"The dean is still going to review Clementine's journals, but he said it was to confirm his belief that she did not plagiarize," Kate says as she reaches into her purse for her phone. "Without Wheeler here to specify what he feels she lifted, this should be an easy case to dismiss. The school wants to put this to rest."

Of course Daren made my attorney come to this. I told him I could handle this by myself, but he said he didn't want to take any chances.

I find myself in Gavin's arms, and I'm so relieved to have this behind me, I could cry. I take a few deep breaths to calm down and turn to Jenna.

"Professor Marceaux spoke to the dean about my work. She stood up for me."

Kate interrupts. "Actually, Marceaux was one of *three* professors who raved about this girl's writing."

Embarrassed, I look down, but Gavin tips my chin up to him. "Of course they did."

He leans down to kiss me, and I could melt right here in the hallway.

"Let's grab some brunch to celebrate," Jenna says, looping her arm through mine and prying me away from Gavin.

By noon, the table at the diner has emptied, leaving only Gavin and me, which kicks off a week of coffees or lunches or quick snuggles for us between classes. It's almost as if he's afraid that if he doesn't maintain constant contact, I'll disappear, which has me thinking about how exactly I plan to reassure my amazing boyfriend. Of course, one thing comes to mind.

Chapter 31

Early Friday evening, I descend from the climbing wall into Gavin's open arms.

"Gross, hon, I'm hot and sweaty," I say, pushing out of his hug, which only seems to encourage him.

"Maybe I like you this way," he whispers, lifting me off my feet.

Giggling, I kiss him as he lets my body slowly slide down his. Trying to ignore the desire that pulses through me, I attempt to focus on something practical. "Want to grab a bite to eat?"

"I can't. I have band rehearsal at Ryan's. You still planning to come tomorrow night?"

Missing his show last weekend still makes me feel bad. I can't believe I've never seen him perform. The fact that he was so understanding about why I missed it doesn't make me feel any better.

"Hell, yes, I'm coming." The guys are playing a big Halloween bash at one of the frat houses.

"Are you planning to dress up? You know it's a costume party, right?"

"Yeah, Jenna said she'd get me something to wear." Shit. I could end up looking like a pole dancer if I'm not careful. "But thanks for reminding me."

When I get home, I think the pole dancer concept was probably a conservative inspiration for the strips of fabric Jenna has left on my bed.

"Jenna, get in here!" I yell. The sound of her fuzzy slippers crossing the hardwood floor stops in my doorway. "You must be doing crack if you think I'm wearing this tomorrow night."

Dani joins her, and they look at each other and laugh.

"Yeah, I know. I'm totally kidding. Just wanted to see what you'd do." Jenna is still grinning when she hands me a brown paper bag.

I purse my lips, hoping this will be an improvement. Opening the bag tentatively, I reach in and pull out white spankies, a short orange skirt and a cropped top that says Tigers.

"Go Tigers!" Jenna jumps up down and does a little dance straight out of *Bring It On* that makes me laugh. "I have your pom-pons in my room."

I bite my lip, wondering if I could pull this off. This outfit is pretty revealing. I'm not sure I want to waltz around a frat house in spankies, but Jenna, sensing my reluctance, sidles up to me and throws her arm across my shoulders.

"Your man is going to think you're so super-duper hot, he's not going to know what to do with himself. Trust me!" She nods her head dramatically.

"Really?" I hadn't thought about that. I guess I do want to look good for Gavin. "What are you going to wear?"

"I'm dressing up as every guy's wet dream." She shimmies seductively, and her mini-me Dani grins.

"Eww, Jenna." Covering my ears like what she says is painful, I scrunch my face. "Do I want to know what that means?"

Jenna looks at me like I'm an idiot. "Princess Leia, you know, in that gold bikini slave outfit." I nod like this makes sense. "Oh, and don't forget the best part! The handcuffs!"

"Because she's captured by Jabba the Hutt until Han Solo rescues her," Dani explains.

I roll my eyes. Sure, that's why Jenna needs handcuffs.

* * *

The basement of the fraternity house is packed with people. Everyone is carrying a red or blue plastic cup that's spilling over with beer. I know because it keeps landing on me.

"Sorry, sweet thing," one very muscly guy says as he splashes me with Budweiser. Gross.

I shake my arm to get it off, and Jenna laughs.

"What's so funny? The fact that I'm getting doused in cheap beer?"

"No, the look on Gavin's face when that guy started talking to you." She points to the other side of the room where the guys are setting up their gear.

"What do you mean?"

Gavin is on the makeshift stage helping Kade assemble his drums.

"He looked protective or maybe jealous. Probably both. It was precious."

She holds up her cup to toast. I give her a look and clink my plastic cup in return.

Jenna looks gorgeous tonight. Her hair is twisted into a complicated braid that hangs over her shoulder. Only she could pull off extensions. And she's totally rocking the slave outfit. I'd be mortified to have that much skin exposed, but she looks comfortable and doesn't seem to mind that most of the male audience is checking her out.

I felt a little silly dressing as a cheerleader, but once I got here and looked around, I realized my costume is pretty tame. There are devil girls, naughty nurses, and a whole assortment of girls in lingerie. In contrast, I actually look a little wholesome with my hair pulled up into a high ponytail.

When Ryan takes the stage, he's changed out of his Han Solo

costume and is wearing a fitted black t-shirt and jeans. Glancing over at Jenna, I laugh.

"Do you ever get tired of eye-fucking your boyfriend?"

Her brow perks up.

"Do I look like I get tired of eye-fucking my boyfriend? Besides, you should talk. Looks like you're about to eat Gavin whole, although he does look pretty scrumptious tonight."

Gavin showed up tonight dressed as a football player. I spent four years trying to get over a jock only to find out that Gavin was the starting QB at his old high school. Figures. And Jenna is more than pleased with herself that she was able to coordinate our costumes to surprise me. Before Gavin got on stage, though, he took off his shoulder pads and jersey and is wearing a t-shirt with those snug white football pants that make him look delectable.

Girls start squealing when Ryan grabs the mic and introduces the band. I have to admit he's pretty cute with his blond hair all spiked up, but then Gavin starts strumming, and everyone goes crazy and pushes forward. By the time Kade kicks in with the drums, this place is insane.

It's a fast, driving beat, and Ryan croons into the mic and owns the stage, strutting seductively. A girl next to me audibly gasps when he looks in our direction. I might tease Jenna about how much she ogles Ryan, but he can't keep his eyes off her either. I'm almost embarrassed to watch them, but two years of accidentally walking in on them screwing on every surface imaginable has almost made me immune.

When Gavin kicks in for the harmony, I almost lose it. His voice is deeper than Ryan's and rougher. He sounds more primal. Sexier. When he looks at me, I fan myself, and he winks. *I can't wait to get him home.*

Jenna and I start dancing, and I'm lost in the music, in the way Gavin harmonizes with Ryan, until a flash of skin catches my eye. In the front row, some girl... she... she...

People are swaying and dancing, and I'm stock still.

"Hey, it's okay." Jenna wraps her arm around me. "Girls flash the guys at every show. They're used to it."

"Uh, I'm not." I'm so fucking not.

Jenna nods like she has a secret to tell me and leans in to whisper, "That's why you should *always* come to the shows and be sure to give your boy a show of his own afterward." She lifts her hand and makes a crude gesture against her mouth.

"Jenna!"

She laughs and grins wickedly. I shake my head, embarrassed.

My roommate might brag about sexing up her man after his shows, but I know they're deeper than that, and I think Gavin and I are too.

When the clapping dies down, Ryan grins. "Thanks for the love, but I need to warn you, ladies. I'm not responsible for what my girl over there does if she catches another eyeful." He laughs into the mic, and everyone laughs with him.

After another half hour, we're good and sweaty from dancing, and I'm sporting a decent buzz. Jenna and I keep giggling, watching our beautiful boys perform, and I have to warn her a couple of times when she gets dangerously close to flashing her Jabba the Hutts.

The music stops, and Ryan shifts to the side of the stage and picks up another guitar as Gavin walks up to the mic. He clears his throat and grins. "This one is for Clementine, that hot cheerleader over there. It's called *Golden Girl*."

He nods toward me, and I could drop dead. Everyone turns to stare at me as Jenna yanks on my arm, jumping up and down.

Gavin reaches for a smaller acoustic guitar and starts strumming.

Holy crap, he wrote me a song.

It's a ballad. As moody chords fill the room, I think back to my birthday and how I hid behind the lyrics of a song. Or the night we sang at the dorms and how much I hoped he was feeling the words we were singing as much as I was.

His eyes lock with mine, and the heat behind them makes me grab on to Jenna's arm for balance. And then he starts to sing.

Golden girl, you've put a spell on me,
    With whispered words that I can see
    I can't walk away after all of this
    You sealed my fate with that first kiss

Golden girl, you have no idea
    You've put a knockout spell on me
    Golden girl, I can hardly breathe
    I can see it, what we can be... Golden girl

Golden girl, I've got those lips memorized
    You know I'll never say goodbye
    Cause your name is carved into my heart
    I've loved you, girl, right from the start

Golden girl, you have no idea
    You've put a knockout spell on me
    Golden girl, I can hardly breathe
    I can see it, what we can be... Golden girl

Golden girl, I'm lost up in that smile
    You feel so perfect, you feel so right
    I won't lie, I am addicted to you
    You've got my heart in your hands, yes you do...

· · ·

Don't try to fight it
    I won't walk away
    I cannot deny it
    I got a thing for you, baby
    Don't try to fight it
    I won't walk away
    I will never hide it
    I promise I'll stay

Golden girl, you have no idea
    You've put a knockout spell on me
    Golden girl, I can hardly breathe
    I can see it, what we can be... Golden girl

When the music stops, the crowd starts cheering, and some blonde in leopard-print lingerie leans over to me and yells, "How did you snag Gavin Murphy? I'm so jealous!"

Jenna is grinning, screaming for the band, but she takes one look at me and stops. "Are you crying?"

"No," I say, sniffling, trying my best to hold it in.

"Oh, man. You have it just as bad, huh?" She hugs me and I nod. "Does this mean I have someone to come to all of their shows with me?"

"Hell, yes. Especially if he's going to write me songs. God." I dab at the corners of my eyes, trying not to mess up my mascara.

Jenna looks like she's debating something when she whispers, "I don't want to make you feel bad about this because I know you had a lot going on, but he sang this song for you last weekend."

But I wasn't there. Shit.

As the weight of that sinks in, I'm overwhelmed.

He was going to tell me he loved me first.

Chapter 32

When we reach my front door, Gavin stops like there's an invisible force field, zips up his hoodie and tucks his hands into his pockets. I open the door, waiting for him to follow, but he doesn't. The night is cold, and wisps of his breath float into the breeze.

Oh, I get it. He's trying to be a gentleman, to have restraint and not take things too far. *Uh, yeah, screw that.*

I'm on a step above him, but he's still taller. With my hands on my hips, I tilt my head and narrow my eyes at him. "Get over here."

He leans in an inch, and I grab both sides of his hoodie and yank him to me hard so that we're nose to nose.

"You wrote me a song."

The grin that erupts on his face takes my breath away. When girls describe a guy as having a panty-dropping smile, it's always made me roll my eyes, but not tonight because, hell yes, this boy could get me to drop my drawers in a heartbeat.

"Did you like it?" he asks, and oh my lord, he looks shy.

I nod slowly and nibble seductively on my lip, or at least I hope it looks seductive and not like bad 70s porn, but given the way he's staring at my mouth, it has the intended effect. "Yes, and I have a surprise for you too." And, oh, do I!

Grabbing his hand before he has a chance to ask any questions, I push the door open and pull him in behind me.

My heart is a jackhammer in my chest, but I try not to let fears about my inexperience overwhelm me.

No one is home, which is perfect. I drop my bag by the couch and head to my room, my fingers still linked with his. I stop at my bedroom door and turn to face him.

"I need you to go get something out of the fishbowl."

Gavin tilts his head. *He must not remember.* I grin, almost unable to keep it together. "Go to the bathroom and grab a couple of packages out of the fishbowl. Go."

I shoo him with my hand, and he looks at me like I'm crazy but complies, walking into the bathroom and turning on the light. The fishbowl is up on the third shelf, so it's possible he's never seen it.

Slipping into my room, I flip on my stereo before I toss a scarf over my lamp to diffuse it. When I turn around, he's in my doorway. He has something clutched in his hand, and he's staring at me. Intensely.

I thought he'd run back in here and rip off all of my clothes, but he hasn't moved a muscle. *Okay.* Guess I have to make the first move. Kicking off my Chucks, I smile before I pull him in and shut the door.

"Gavin? You okay?"

His eyes tighten, and his lips turn into a devilish grin, one I'd like to lick, but I decide to play his game, the one he started on my front stoop.

"So you're kind of a good boy," I say with mock judgment. I open his palm and take the condoms, tossing them on my bed. "Always following all the rules. Not wanting any conflicts of interest." Unzipping his jacket, I look at him with a little pout. "Am I a conflict of interest, Gavin?" I don't stop undressing him as I wait for his answer.

"You are, darlin'." His voice is breathy and deep. "Because I usually play it safe, and you're anything but." I don't know that I'd categorize Angelique as safe, but she was a journalist, so they must have had a lot in common.

"Hmm. That's distressing." Pushing off his hoodie puts a small smile on my face. "Maybe I could say something to make you feel better." I tug his shirt off before angling him deeper into my room and pushing him onto the bed. "I can't believe you wrote me a song. I *love* it. In fact, I might have to show you how much I love it."

His green eyes smolder beneath those lusciously dark lashes, making the blood rush to my cheeks. Realizing how convenient this teeny cheerleader skirt is, I sit astride him. He licks his lips, and deep hot desire for this perfect man burns in my belly.

I'm on shaky territory here. So outside of my safe zone. But I think about Jenna and how she always goes the extra mile for Ryan. *I can do this.* Because I'm in my pep-talk mode, I hear the theme to *Rocky*, which is all wrong and does nothing to get me in the mood. I shake my head, trying to get Sylvester Stallone out of my mind when Gavin runs his hands up my thighs.

Now that gets my attention. I grab his face between my hands and press myself closer. He hasn't shaved, and I love the roughness of him on my skin.

"Baby, we don't have to do this ton—"

I put my finger on his lips for a moment before I place my hands on his chest and push him down. Hovering over him, I reach up and pull out my ponytail, letting my long hair cascade around us.

"Do I look like someone's holding a gun to my head?" If I didn't know him better, I'd think he didn't want to do this. But doesn't every guy want to have sex? Doubt rears its fugly head. Is it possible he doesn't want to sleep with me? Shit. I don't want to throw myself at him.

He must see it in my eyes.

"Clementine."

I'm starting to scoot off him when he grabs my wrists and pulls me down so that I collapse on him, hip to hip, belly to belly. But I already burn with the sting of rejection, and I start to wiggle away. His grasp on my arms tighten. "Stop. Of course I want to. I just don't want you to think that you owe me anything."

I stare at him, silent. He arches his head so he can kiss me, but I don't kiss back, which makes him growl.

"I want to fuck you to next Friday and back again. Does that make you feel better?"

Staring, a little shocked and wide-eyed, I burst out laughing, and then he rumbles beneath me, laughing too. Thank fuck he didn't say he wants to make love. I would have shot myself.

"Yes, actually it does." I prop myself on his chest, and run my fingers in imaginary lines on his skin.

There's enough light in here so I can see this masterpiece beneath me, all chiseled muscle and taut lines. Finally, I rest my chin on my hands and look down at him. "Well, if we're making sure to clarify everything tonight, you should know that I have some requirements." His mouth tugs up slightly as he waits to hear my demands. "If you want this to work, I have three rules."

He nods slowly, amusement flickering in his eyes.

"One, no more lies or omissions. I don't care if the president of the United States is fucking his entire staff and you have the inside scoop but you're sworn to secrecy. You tell me."

He smirks. "Fine."

"Two, no snuggling with groupies—ever—and no more overnight trips with Angelique or I will break your hand, the one you use for self-satisfaction."

His grin grows. "Deal." His arms tighten around my waist as his legs open, dropping me between his thighs where an unmistakable hardness greets me.

"And lastly," I say, leaning down and stopping just before our lips meet, "never let go."

The expression on his face is the only indication that I've negotiated my third sticking point before he flips me over onto my back. I'm lying here breathless, thinking he's going to devour me, but he gets up, and for a scary half second, I'm worried he's leaving.

My heart races, and I sit up only to realize he's undressing. His shoes hit the floor, one after the other, before he stands next to the bed. He changed out of his football pants after the show—he said he was cold, but I think it was so girls would stop grabbing his ass.

I watch as he unbuttons his jeans and lowers them over his sculpted hips, revealing those amazing V muscles that lead down to his Never-Never Land. Holy shit. He's a delicious morsel in nothing but a pair of boxers.

Trying to reciprocate the sexy, I sink back into bed, tucking my hand under my head and sticking my chest and hips out the way models do, and hope I don't look like an idiot. But his eyes pass over me slowly, appreciatively.

"Damn, you're gorgeous," he says as he crawls up my body, staring hungrily.

"If I told you I loved you right now, would you think I was using you?" I ask, half teasing. Running my fingers through his hair, I whisper in his ear, "Because I do. I do love you." He brings his mouth to mine, his tongue gently pushing into my mouth, his hands running along my body, driving me insane with desire.

I thought I loved Daren, and I did in a butterfly-and-hearts kind of way, but it was nothing like this. This is an asteroid shower on a summer night. A tidal wave crashing onto the breakers. Falling over the edge of Niagara Falls in an inner tube. Because I have fallen, irreparably, for Gavin Murphy.

"You might not be able to tell, but I love you too, crazy girl," he says amusedly against my mouth. "I've wanted you for a long time."

His hand ducks beneath the fabric of my shirt, and I push him back slightly so I can tug it off, leaving me in a hot pink push-up and my little skirt.

Gavin runs his finger along the strap of my bra, down to the cup and across the top of my breast until he reaches the clasp where he hesitates. His eyes meet mine and I nod. My skin instantly tightens in the cold room.

His hands are reverent as they smooth across my bare skin. I push my chest into him, and he grips me, sliding his hips between mine. I wrap my legs around his waist and wiggle against his hardness, hoping to get a little friction on the part of me that's throbbing like it's disco night.

He stops and grins. "I have something for that."

I watch, open-mouthed, as he descends down my body, kissing and touching and nipping until he reaches my spankies, which he slides down along with my lacy undies until I get them off.

He kneels between my legs, and I'm lying topless with my skirt hitched up around my hips, trying not to squirm as he looks at me. And oh, good God, does he look. My heart is pounding, and I'm not entirely sure I can breathe.

"Are you up for a different kind of third base?" He grins so big, I might have a heart attack. I realize we're back to baseball metaphors as he lowers himself to my thighs. He takes my legs and drapes them over his shoulders, opening me up more.

Sweet Jesus.

Gavin's hot breath hits my skin first, and his mouth on the most sensitive part of my body has me gripping the bed and writhing. I wasn't expecting this. I know some guys don't do this, but it's fan-fucking-tastic. My eyes damn near roll back in my head as his tongue slides slowly against me, teasing and caressing. But when he slips in a finger, my body lifts off the bed. I grab his hair as his stubble rubs along my thighs, and my toes curl along his shoulders. I hear a moan, then another. Then I realize I'm the wanton moaner, lost in an explosion of light and sensation as a climax shatters me. I'm not sure how long I'm shuddering before I catch my breath.

Gavin crawls back up me with a very self-satisfied look on his face. I pull him down to me and kiss him, too out of it and euphoric to be embarrassed by the taste of myself on his lips. I hear the tearing of a wrapper and realize he's taking out a condom.

"Show me how to do that," I murmur sleepily. Did I really just ask my boyfriend to show me how to put on a condom? I don't recognize the naked girl lying here in bed asking such questions.

Yes, I've purchased condoms and practiced safe sex the one time I went there, but the act of putting it on seems perplexing. Hello, it's a body part I don't have.

"Okay." He smiles, rolling over and placing the circular disk in my hand. "Come here."

I struggle to sit up next to him and finally get my first good look. He's at full mast, saluting me proudly, and my eyes bug out, making him chuckle.

"Honey, I don't think you're going to fit," I say nervously. Sure, we've messed around, but I've never gotten a really good look at him *down there.*

Smirking, he kisses me on the forehead and lies back. He takes my hand, placing it on the crown, and helps me roll on the condom. As my hand moves against him, I have to admit I love his velvety, rock-hard man parts.

When he's locked and loaded, he looks up and we stare at each other.

This is it.

Gavin clears his throat. "Get on top." His raspy voice sends shivers down my arms. "That way you can control it. I don't want to hurt you."

My face must be on fire right now, and I blurt, "But I don't know what I'm doing." It's true. I don't. My one-night stand was quick and unpleasant. It was nameless, faceless rebound sex, and

I've mostly blocked it out of my mind. Suddenly, though, I wish I wasn't so clueless.

He smiles sweetly. "Babe, I think you can figure this out."

Oh God. Oh my God. Trying not to freak out, I straddle his hips.

"I'm still wearing my skirt," I giggle. I'm clearly anxious as all kinds of random things are shooting right out of my mouth.

"Yeah, it's hot. I've always wanted to bang a cheerleader."

I swat at him, and he laughs, grabbing my wrists and pulling me down to kiss. He laces our fingers together as he whispers how much he loves me, that I'm his dream girl, that he has more songs for me. My heart melts as does some of my hesitation.

He's rock-hard beneath me, and when I wiggle, his eyes darken. Wanting to make him feel as good as he's made me feel, I glide across him slowly, which he must like because he grips my hair. I tighten my thighs, and he groans. All of this friction has me throbbing again, which is crazy because I just had a totally mind-blowing orgasm five minutes ago.

After a little more grinding, I decide to take the plunge and angle him at my entrance.

He clears his throat. "Baby, are you sure? We don't have to. I'll wait as long as you need." His voice is clipped and husky, and everything about it says he wants this as much as I do.

"God, *yes*, I'm sure."

He chuckles and grabs my thighs as I slowly push down. The farther I get, the more intense Gavin looks. It pinches at first, but it's the only thing that helps the throbbing, and I want more. Finally, I can't stand it any more, and I let gravity pull me down. I instantly topple over onto him, unable to deal with the fullness.

"Jesus, baby. You're so tight," he groans. I would blush ten shades of red if I weren't already flushed from our recent activity.

I don't budge at first. I can't. His hands run down my back like he's soothing me, and I close my eyes, our naked chests panting against one another. We're hot and sweaty, and this is, hands down, the most intimate moment of my life.

I manage to lift my head. The look in his eyes tells me he loves me, tells me I'm beautiful, and I put my lips on his to reflect those same emotions. Before I know it, I'm moving again. I'm slow as I try to acclimate to him, and it hurts a little, but after a few minutes his body feels so right pressed into mine.

Watching Gavin watch me is hot. His eyes are hooded as he tightens his grip on my hips, and I start to lose myself in the sensation as it builds again.

When he cups my breast, I arch into his hands, appreciating the ripples of electricity that head south, but as he thrusts his hips up, I gasp, putting my hands on his chest to steady myself. Whoa! Is he supposed to be able to knock the wind out of me by jutting his hips?

Sitting up again, I start to move, and his hand lowers to my core, rubbing me in small, slow circles.

With that shattering sensation beginning to tease me, I start to tense, and I can tell Gavin is close too because he's thrusting again, harder, deeper, but now it feels right, now it feels good, *so* good, and I tell him because I can't help it. He rubs me a little faster, and I. Lose. My. Mind.

I scream as bliss washes over me, slumping down as he thrusts a few more times, tensing and tightening his arms around me as he finds his release. He finally stills, all of his muscles taut.

We lie there, panting, connected. The after-sex glow? I've got it. The sex-god boyfriend? Yup, that too. The head-over-heels feeling of love? Definitely.

When did life get so good?

* * *

With heavy lids, I wake, craning my neck to see that it's only 7 a.m. I drop my head back down onto the pillow as a warm arm reaches around my waist and pulls me back, and Gavin's delicious body contours perfectly against mine.

"You're too far away."

I love the way his voice is raspy first thing in the morning. I love that he's here with me. Well, I... I love him. I turn in his arms and lay my head on his chest.

"I'm sorry we broke up," I say, still feeling like shit that I didn't trust him. I've been meaning to tell him this all week.

He laughs softly. "Babe, we never broke up." He strokes my back and kisses the top of my head, and we lie there in the early morning light, tangled together, listening to the rustling of the trees outside my window. "Hey, does this mean you'll go running with me now?"

Laughing, I snuggle closer. "Yes, we can go running." Uh, but not today. I have to make sure I can walk first.

My room smells like Gavin, his clothes, our bodies, and the memory of what we did makes me giggle.

"What?" His fingers trail down my arm, making goosebumps leap out on my skin.

"I was thinking about last night."

He stills, and I look up to see him frown. "Baby, nothing I did to you last night should make you giggle." But then he grins. "Hey, who knew you were a screamer?"

My face falls, and I gasp. Gavin closes his eyes with that smug expression still lingering. I stare, horrified.

"If you hadn't tried to impale me with your superhero-sized man junk, I wouldn't have screamed."

He breaks out laughing, and I shush him, afraid he'll wake up my roommates.

"Superhero, huh?" He's grinning like an idiot.

"Yes, jerk." I brush a few strands of hair off his face.

"Have I told you that I love you? You just made my decade."

"Men and their penises," I mumble before I curl against his chest.

He pulls me closer—fitting his thigh between my legs, pressing my chest to his—and whispers, "That was the best game of baseball I have ever played." He moves the hair off my neck and presses his lips to my skin.

The smile on my cheeks might break my face. "Really? I wasn't horribly awkward and inexperienced?"

"Nope. It was even better than I imagined." His mouth is still working its way down my neck.

I push him away. "So you imagined this? Like, a lot?"

He licks his lips, and that look in his eyes could melt titanium. "What do you think?"

I lean down to kiss that delectable mouth, which only makes me want more. "I think you've been a bad boy." I nibble on his lower lip, and he groans. "And I think you might need to be punished." His eyes dart to mine. I'm sure I'll be sore as hell in the full light of day, but screw it. You only live once.

I clear my throat. Trying to sound in control and demanding, I say, "And don't think you're going to get off easily." Surprised by my own double entendre, I smirk as I nestle my hand against his sinfully carved hip and squeeze. "Time to run the bases."

When I slide my body over him, his eyes widen ever so briefly before his lids shutter closed. He inhales deeply, and I love that I affect him this way. Judging by what he has pressed up against my stomach, I dare say he's hot and bothered. Good. That makes two of us.

As I lean in closer, he flashes me that grin. "Have I ever told you how hot it is when you talk baseball?"

I've never understood couples who can't get out of bed. Until now.

I give him a devilish grin. "Wait 'til you hear me talk football."

Chapter 33

Three weeks later

GAVIN

Of course. Of course she plays beautifully. Through the glass, I see her small hands gliding over the keys of the piano. Clementine's been coming down to practice for the last week so she can prep for Carly's fundraiser. When she gets to the chorus, she tilts her head, and her long hair cascades over her shoulder, and as though she realizes I'm spying, she stops.

I tap on the door, and she stiffens. I know what she's thinking. She's afraid I heard her play, afraid that she sucks because she thinks she sucks at everything, which couldn't be farther from the truth. That's why I call her my golden girl. She has too many talents for her own good. Well, except math, but that only means I get to tutor her, which is a bonus in my book.

Her hair is darker now than when school started, but in the sun, her blonde highlights make her glow like an angel.

Yes, I'm so ass-over-head in love with her I can't see straight. But I don't tell her that. I have too many fears about freaking her out and losing her. Damn. I have nightmares about it. I'm not about to tell her that either. After what she went through with Angelique and that sick fuck Wheeler, I don't want her to worry about anything else. I know she has a lot on her mind as she finishes her new novel.

"Hey, babe," I say as she opens the door to the practice room. "You sound great."

Her eyebrows lift and her lips purse before she flicks me in the arm, making me laugh.

"I thought you said these rooms were soundproof."

God, she's even more gorgeous when she's pissed.

"I said they were *mostly* soundproof." I flash that grin I know she loves, and her icy exterior melts a little. Then I go in for the kill, kissing her on the forehead, and once I have her up against my chest, I don't let go. That's when she sighs and wraps her arms around my waist. "So you have boxes you need help with?"

Clementine nods against me. I'm not sure if that's code for some kind of naked activity, but I try not to let my mind wander in case she really just needs a mover. I've been trying hard to not be a big boner around her, which is difficult since about everything she does is sexy. Only she doesn't know it. That's why she's irresistible.

But I want her to know that our relationship is about more than sex. So I told her as much. That was a great discussion. She ended up yelling at me, telling me she was afraid she was defective and she wouldn't blame me if I didn't want to sleep with her again. *As fucking if.* I'm not entirely sure how a goddess like Clementine ends up with one ounce of insecurity, but it's my main mission in life to make her understand that she's extraordinary, inside and out.

"Are we still meeting up with Olivia and Kade for dinner?" she asks as she slips her hand in mine.

"Yeah, he texted me the address of the restaurant this morning."

Olivia has taken the semester off to recover from the trauma of what happened this fall, but she talks constantly to Clementine and Brigit. I think they've formed a kind of support group that's helping the three of them get through this. Agent Robertson told Olivia's family that Clementine helped piece together some of the missing parts in their investigation. Like the fact that Wheeler had access to a yacht, which is why no airline had any record of him returning stateside in July.

Although authorities added rape to Wheeler's charges of kidnapping, to see the way Olivia is handling everything, you'd never know he held her captive in his guest house for almost three months. She says she's just grateful to be alive and doesn't want him to take anything else from her.

So far, the identity of his first rape victim–the one he attacked when he was in college–hasn't been made public, but I've heard through the grapevine she is preparing to testify against him. And because of all the photos Wheeler took of Clementine, the district attorney tacked on stalking charges, which could add another five years to his sentence when that asshole is found guilty.

I know it bothers my girl to have her name dragged through the media because of Wheeler, but she says if Olivia can handle it, she can too. And fuck if I don't love her more because of how brave she's been through all of this.

Olivia and Kade have been hanging out, and even though he realizes she won't be ready for anything serious for a while, he says he wants to wait and see what happens with their friendship. I've never seen Kade try so hard to not be a dumbass. Olivia's disappearance really changed him. Clementine and Kade are even tight now, which is shocking to everyone who knows them because their fights are legendary.

When we get to Clementine's apartment, there's a box out in the living room with her name written on the side. I recognize it as the one her brother brought over a while back.

"Is this the box? Do you want me to get rid of it?"

She shakes her head and pats the seat next to her on the couch.

She's biting her lip. Clementine does that when she's nervous or afraid. It's adorable. And sexy as hell. *Focus, Gavin. The girl clearly doesn't want sex right now.*

Tilting her head down, she glances up at me and smiles shyly. Man, that smile. For a girl who tends to scare most men, she's surprisingly shy, unsure even. Thinking about her like this makes my chest hurt. I know—I'm going to lose my man card at this rate.

"You're always saying you want to know me better, so I thought we could go through it together," she says, swallowing.

"Sure. Sounds good." I try to sound chill when I respond, but I know this is a big deal for her. She's breathing harder and fisting her hands at her side. I remember the argument she had with Jax when he brought it here and can tell she's about to lose it.

Finally, I can't stand one more second like this so I reach over and pull her into my lap. She laughs, surprised. I kiss her neck slowly before I reach down to her waist and wiggle my fingers against her ribs.

"Gavin! Don't tickle me! Damn it." She tries to get up, but I throw her down on the couch. She's laughing, and she's pissed, and fuck, I love her.

She pauses, mid-gasp, and reaches for my shirt, yanking me down to her.

But before my lips reach hers, I stop. "No, I'm not your sex toy. We have to open your box first."

She snorts. "You know that sounds sexual, right?"

"Baby, I'm trying to incentivize you to stop freakin out."

"By using your body?" She can't hide her amusement.

"We could go with chocolate or a latte, but you seem to like my body."

Her tongue peeks out between her teeth, and her hair is fanning out beneath her. Then she rakes her fingers down my chest as her eyes pass over me languidly. "I *love* your body."

I'm having a difficult time focusing on the goal here. I clear my throat and try to think about who won the World Series last year and the year before that and the year before that. When I think I can construct a coherent sentence, I kiss her nose and pull her up.

"You can use and abuse me any way you want after we get the box open. It's not a big deal. Just stuff from high school. Everyone has junk like this." I know that she didn't date for years over all the shit that went down her senior year. Sorting through this will be therapeutic, which gives us a better shot of making it for the long haul, so I have to stay focused here because this girl is most definitely my long haul.

"Really?" She looks hopeful.

"Yup. My mother saved some flowers she gave me when I graduated and it grew mold."

She giggles. I'm always surprised by how little it takes to make her laugh.

The box is still sealed with clear packing tape, so I grab my keys and run it along the length before she gets a chance to get scared again. I look in and shrug.

"See, yearbooks and photos. Nothing major."

She peeks into the box. Then at me. Her shoulders relax and she smiles, interlacing her fingers through mine and plants a kiss on my cheek, and I don't know if winning a Pulitzer could feel this good.

For the next hour, she pulls out books and photos and knick-knacks. I grab a picture from homecoming and one from prom and set them side by side. It's like the before-and-after photos of a car wreck. In the first, she's glowing, all smiles and charm. She's in a crowd, but it's like she's the center of it, as though the force of her gravity is pulling everyone toward her. In the second photo, she's posing with a couple of friends, but the light has gone out of her eyes. She's mechanical, stiff, hurt.

Her movement next to me catches my attention as she flips through her freshman yearbook. She covers her mouth because she's embarrassed about her hair when she was fourteen, and I laugh when I see it because she looks like a tiny supermodel. Right now, she seems so relaxed, like the past doesn't consume her anymore. She smiles, and it's blazing and brilliant.

My heart thumps quickly as I realize I have the "before" girl sitting next to me on the couch. She's full of light and energy and boundless determination. I mean, who writes two books in college?

Her professor, Marceaux, the one she says tortured her to write about intimacy, loved her submissions in class and not only plans to edit Clementine's new novel for publication this winter, but she wants her to guest-lecture next spring. If I didn't love her so much, I'd be jealous.

And at least there's an upside to the Wheeler bullshit. After he outed her in class, her book sales for *Say It Isn't So* skyrocketed. Not only can she pay off her school loans, but she'll have something left over. She's already had a full-time job offer at the campus bookstore, but I'm trying to talk her into taking next year off from everything to write. I know she wants to dust off some of her other story ideas and polish them up for publication. I want to help her do that.

"What?" she asks, looking at me puzzled.

"What do you mean, what?"

"Why are you staring at me like that?" She looks at me sideways, and I wonder if she knows she owns my ass.

This is it. This is the right time. "What are you doing for Thanksgiving? I was wondering if you'd like to spend it with me in Connecticut."

Her mouth opens into an "o" and she inhales deeply. She's quiet. For too long. Shit. Maybe this is too soon.

"You mean with you and your family?"

"They might be there." I look up at the ceiling and shrug. "Someone has to cook the bird, and I'm sure as hell not gonna do it."

She lets out a nervous laugh. Taking a long strand of hair

between her fingers, she suddenly gets interested in the very tip, like she might have an errant split end.

I know this is new for her, being in a relationship. God, it's new for me. I've dated girls, girls I actually thought I was serious about, but everyone pales in comparison to Clementine. Sometimes she makes me feel like I could forget how to tie my shoes if I'm not careful.

That thing in my chest, my heart, beats a little erratically as I wait for her to say something. I let out a breath I didn't realize I was holding and scramble for a little more footing.

"You know, if you're not up for it, no biggie."

"No, no, I would love to meet your family." There she goes, biting her lip, giving me that shy look. "I was thinking, though, that maybe you could come with me. To see mine." Her big blue eyes are wide as she studies my face.

I don't breathe. I'm not sure I even blink.

She nods, understanding my confusion. "My father called, and he's in town for a while and wants to see me. I told him I wouldn't visit if my mother was there, but he said it would only be Jax and me. But I'd like for you to come too. If you have the time."

I know what this means. She hasn't been home since high school, and she's asking me to go with her. If my girl wants me there, damn straight I'll be there.

"Of course I'll go with you." I lean over and rub my nose against hers as I lace our fingers together.

I think back to our freshman year and wonder what would have happened if she hadn't taken that leave of absence and I had asked her on a date like I planned. Except I came to class that day to find her seat empty.

Her eyes flutter closed, and just like that, she's too far away.

Wrapping my arms around her, I lift her onto my lap so that she sits astride me.

She squeals, but her laughter quickly fades as she nestles closer and grips my shoulders.

Her breath quickens and her blue eyes darken. I tangle my fingers through her long hair, gently tugging her to me until our mouths seal together.

She sighs against me, and I feel it too. How right we are together.

Because I know that there is nothing on this planet as perfect for me as this woman.

And you can bet your ass I plan to give my girl a happily ever after. Starting right now.

Bonus Scene 1

*This scene was originally called "My Kind of Girl" and printed in the F*cking Awkward anthology.*

CLEMENTINE

You can do this.

These people probably think I'm crazy, sitting here with my lips tugged over my teeth like I'm pretending to be someone's granny who lost her falsies.

The sounds of the student union rush around me as I try to visualize what I'm going to do to my boyfriend tonight.

Because I need to visualize.

I *so* need to visualize.

Which sounds stupid. Any nimrod with a mouth can give a blow job.

Except I want this to be good for Gavin.

Really good.

Like I'm studying for a final, I mentally review the suggestions my roommate Jenna gave me this morning. Lick the tip because it's sensitive. Provide some suction. Get my hands into the action. Use spit to lube it up.

I try to shake off the heebie jeebies I get from the idea of spitting on him. I mean, I'm putting the man's jungle rod in my mouth. I suppose I can live with a little spit.

And Jenna said that no matter what, I cannot nick his dick with my teeth.

"That's the number one rule of blow jobs," she emphasized. "NO TEETH."

Taking a deep breath, I bundle up in my down coat, gather my things and head to his dorm. *I can do this.* It doesn't matter that I've never had a penis in my mouth before. I know Gavin doesn't care that I'm inexperienced.

Truthfully, I don't think I do either... except that he's damn good when he goes down on me, and I think I should reciprocate.

We've been dating since last semester, and despite our ups and downs and as scary as this sounds, I'm starting to think he's The One.

Because he puts up with my crazy and doesn't seem to mind that I'm kind of an asshole on a good day. And he's sweet and loving and so fucking sexy. But more importantly, he's my best friend.

So it doesn't matter that the idea of coming eye to eye with his male anatomy freaks me out a smidge. I love him and want to get over myself.

Bubbles of nervous energy surge in my stomach as I ride up the elevator eighteen floors to his room. When I get there, I pass two freshmen boys who look me up and down like little creepers.

Ignoring them, I head to Gavin's room. His door is open, and I take off my coat and wait for him to notice me.

The only light filtering in from the window casts him in shadow.

He's sitting on his small bed, strumming his guitar, looking so damn handsome everything in me clenches. He's wearing jeans and a Celtics t-shirt, no shoes or socks, and his dark hair hangs in his face, covering those magnetic eyes.

He's built like a running back—tall, broad and fit. Graceful in a way that conveys his athleticism.

When he looks up, he shoots me one of those killer smiles that make me weak-kneed.

"Hey, darlin'."

That never ever gets old.

Before I can say anything, he's setting aside the guitar and stalking across his small room to sweep me off my feet.

Literally off my feet.

I giggle in his arms, tossing my bag and coat to the floor before I wrap my arms around his neck. A second later, he's kicking the door shut and pushing me against it, but he does it so fast, my breath catches in my throat.

I stare up at him, feeling light-headed and off-balance.

Sometimes, I need to pinch myself when we're together so I can appreciate that he's real. And he's here. With me.

And this gorgeous specimen of a man actually loves me, the unlovable.

Well, until recently, the unlovable. I'm working on having a better self-image. Thanks to Gavin.

His arms tighten around me, and like a ship to its moor, he rights me, straightening all of my twisted emotional parts until my anxiousness melts away.

Especially when those lips touch mine.

His stubble is rough against my skin, and I settle my palm on his cheek.

The kiss leaves me breathless.

Clearing my throat, I whisper, "I feel like a deviant for corrupting the resident advisor."

"You are a deviant. I was such a good boy before you came along."

Laughing, I run my fingers through his thick hair, but when our mouths connect again, my laughter stops.

Hot, wet sweeps of his tongue in my mouth have me eager to tumble into his bed with him.

Except it's Friday night. In the dorms.

"Babe," I murmur against his mouth. "Should we wait? What if those kids in that corner room get drunk again?" Last weekend, he had to rush another poor slob to the hospital with alcohol poisoning. *I really can't wait until we graduate in May.*

"Nah, I've already warned them that if they interrupt me having sex with my hot girlfriend *again*, I would make their lives miserable."

I smack his arm. "You did *not* say that."

"I told them I was studying for a test." His eyes gleam with humor. "You're the subject, and I need lots and *lots* of practice. Gotta get this right. Don't want my GPA to suffer."

"We can't have that."

"Think you could tutor me? *All* night long?" Those dimples pop out, and my stupid little heart goes pitter-patter.

I smile back like an idiot.

Until I remember what I want to do tonight, and my stomach sinks. Because what if I do it wrong? What if I give him a *bad* blow job? Biting my bottom lip, I look away.

"Hey, what's wrong?" Concern tightens his brow.

I swallow and then nearly choke because I'm thinking about swallowing. Later.

Oh my God. Am I going to swallow? Clearly, I haven't thought this through.

But spitting afterward seems so rude.

Except I *might* need to spit on him to lube it up in the first place?

Jesus Christ. This is giving me a headache.

As much as I'd like to forget all musings of the spit-and-dick combo, the issue gives me pause. It's not like Gavin's ever raced to the bathroom to rinse his mouth after he went down on me. Although, really, I wouldn't object because I could see how—

"Clem, where'd you go?"

See, I always have to make things awkward. I can't be sexy and smooth and get the man in bed and turn him on. No, that would be too easy.

I stare at his t-shirt and twist my finger in the neckline of the fabric. Here goes nothing. "Can I give you a blow job?"

His chest stills under my palm, which freaks me out because why isn't he saying something? I just offered to put his member in my mouth.

There's some alliteration. *Member in my mouth.* Say that ten times.

Ugh. I just cannot do sexy, can I?

My face burns like I've just been scorched under a Caribbean sun.

He squeezes me. "Hey." His voice is deep and rough. *Like how he sounds when we have sex.* Chills break out on my arms.

He lifts my chin, and those green eyes search mine. "You don't have to do anything you don't want."

"But that's just it. I want to do this for you." My chest is heaving because I'm screwing up everything so badly. "You... you're always so giving in bed," I whisper. Seriously, he makes me come really hard. With his hands. His mouth. His monster-sized man muscle.

Except I don't think a penis is an actual muscle. More like tissue. And nerves. A lot of big nerves.

But again, I digress.

His lips descend to mind for one brief, sweet kiss, and when he leans back, mirth dances behind his eyes.

"Baby, you can do whatever you want to me, whenever you want, with any body part you want. But don't ever let this shit stress you out. What we do together should be fun and turn you on and make you relax. It should be about how much I love you and how good we are together. That's it. Plain and simple."

Honestly, could he be any sweeter?

I nod, still embarrassed but also really grateful to be dating such a great guy. And I want to show my gratitude.

"I love you too." Saying those words doesn't feel foreign anymore. Because, God, I do love him.

Leaning up on my tiptoes, I thread my fingers through his thick, wavy hair and nibble on his bottom lip. "So that's a yes? I can go down on you? Even if I screw it up?"

"I'm at your mercy, woman. Do what you want." He grins at me, and it pierces my heart in a bittersweet way that tells me I'll only be this in love once, and I'm a lucky girl to be in love with Gavin Murphy. But I'm even luckier to have him return that love.

Surprisingly, I'm not totally terrified by our relationship anymore. And after being disappointed by so many people in my life, allowing myself to feel this much emotion seems monumental.

I let those feelings wash over me and stare at him, a shy smile on my lips.

"I want."

Suddenly, the jokes are over, and he has me up against the door again with one hand in my hair and another on my leg that he hooks around his hip. His hard length strains against his jeans and presses across my belly.

Wow, so I guess he *does* like the idea of me heading south. His enthusiasm gives me courage.

I breathe him in, his crisp citrus body wash and the warmer scent of his skin. Gripping his jaw, I bring his mouth to mine but stop just before our lips connect. When I brush my nose against his, he tries to kiss me, but I pull back.

"Nuh-hu." Slowly, I lick the seam of his lips, and he growls and tightens his hold on me until there's no way I can fight him.

Laughing, I give up trying to tease.

He smirks and hoists me up until my legs wrap around his waist. He's hot and hard everywhere.

His kiss is decadent. Long licks into my mouth punctuate the slow grind of his hips, and I'm desperate for more.

I tighten my thighs around him, searching for relief. Needing relief.

My head lolls to the side, and his mouth goes to my neck and sucks my sensitive skin.

"Bed. Now," I gasp. Because I still have my mission, and if I don't take back some control, I'll lose the courage to do this.

In a flash, he turns and tosses me on the bed like I'm a rag doll, and I laugh as I bounce around. I love that about our relationship. Sex is *really* hot, but fun. And that helps me step out of my comfort zone.

He shucks off his t-shirt, and I soak him in. So many muscles. So much hardness. *Yum.*

I kick off my shoes and slide off my t-shirt and jeans, knowing full well he's watching me.

When I'm in my sheer bra and undies, his broad shoulders fill my vision as he moves to the side of the bed.

"You're so fucking sexy," he whispers as he reaches behind my neck.

Funny, I was about to say the same thing about him.

Those brilliant green eyes stare at me through thick lashes. His dark hair is sticking out at odd angles, his lips are wet, and a devilish smile tilts his lips.

Returning the smile, I kneel on the bed and run my hands over his shoulders. Over his sculpted chest. Down his sexy stomach. Until I reach the big bulge in his jeans, which I rub slowly before I unbutton his fly.

His nose dips into my hair and his hands are on my breasts, but I tug him down to sit next to me. Then I slide to the floor and nestle between his legs where I unsnap my bra and let it drop down my arms.

Those green eyes widen as I push him onto the bed. Lightly, I scrape my nails down his chest as I kiss my way down his taut stomach.

He takes a deep breath as I nuzzle against his skin and pop open the last button.

My heart is thudding in my chest, but I ignore my nerves and scoot his jeans and boxers down. He angles his hips to help me, and then I'm eye to eye with Little Gavin.

Except he's not so little.

And when I palm him, he swells in my hand. *Hello, Big Boy.*

I squint back at him.

He's actually really pretty if dicks could be considered attractive. Thick and innately masculine. Tall and smooth and strong. *Definitely sturdy.*

Part of me wants to ask how Gavin likes it, but the other part fears saying something stupid and breaking the mood. He's obviously turned on, so I decide to forge ahead. Besides, alluding to the fact that other girls have traversed this path before me makes me want to stab someone with a dull pencil, so I suppose it's best to avoid the topic.

From what we've done together so far in the past, I know he likes a firm grip and a steady tempo. So I pull him in long strokes before I lean in closer. His body shifts, and I realize he's leaning up on one arm to watch.

And right now, with his eyes trained on me, his mouth slightly open, I can see how much he wants me. It's a heady feeling.

His hand thrusts into my hair as I dip down and swipe my tongue slowly over his crown.

"Fuuuuck," he groans, his grip tightening.

I rub him across my lips before I take him into my mouth. He tastes a little salty and smells like clean man. And... surprise of all surprises, I like how he feels against my tongue. The feminist in me doesn't even mind that I'm kneeling at his feet because he's done the same for me many times. And I want to return the favor. I want to make him feel as good as he makes me feel. I want to show him that I love him.

But also, I realize, I do this for me.

Sucking him in deeper, I moan, enjoying how turned on I'm getting from this. My nipples are hard, and my undies are a lost cause.

"That's it, baby. Suck a little harder."

My pulse races when I hear those words. I turn up my eyes up to him, my hand pumping in earnest.

His chest is rising quickly now. Everything about him is strung tight. I scrape my nails lightly down his thigh, and his eyes darken.

Yeah, I like this too.

I pull him out to explore him with my tongue. He glistens in my hand, and I take a long lick up the length of him. And there's a lot of ground to cover.

He watches, his eyes molten while he strains in my palm.

And then I lean close and take him down the back of my throat.

"Oh fuck." His words, not mine.

I come up with a gasp, but before I can go down again, he's pulling me into his lap. His kiss is frantic, and I feel him reach for a condom.

Ten seconds later, I'm on my back.

"Why...why didn't you... Let me finish?" I pant as he seats himself between my thighs, pushes aside my thong and thrusts into me. I arch up and close my eyes, feeling so good and full when he sinks deeper. He bites my neck, making me shudder.

"Because I need to be inside you. Need to feel this. Wanna feel you come on me."

Oh god.

I wrap my legs around him while he reaches between us and rubs that spot.

My head tilts back, and my eyes close as he pumps harder, heightening the intensity.

The room is awash in our groans as he pushes us both to the edge. With one more thrust, everything in me tightens to that singular place between my thighs, and I come hard, digging my heels into his ass. My head thrashes, and I think I yell a few curse words.

A second later, he pulses and follows with his release, letting out a deep moan that sends shivers all over me.

Who knew it was so hot to hear a man come?

We stay twined together, panting and sweaty on his small dorm bed.

We're just barely catching our breath when he rolls us to the left. I figure he wants me on top, so I let him pull me along, except he keeps going. *And going.*

I let out a scream as we tumble to the floor. Still fully connected.

"Holy shit," he groans beneath me. "Guess I overestimated the size of my bed."

After a moment, I start to laugh. "Are you okay? Did I break your dick?" I laugh harder, and he squirms underneath me, his body quaking with laughter. Actually, *everything* quakes. "Honey, really, are you okay?"

"You don't want kids, right?" he grunts out.

"Aww." I slowly disengage from our locked and loaded position. My knees are scratched from the hideous low-pile carpet. But aside from that, I'm okay. *At least I wasn't chopped in two by his monster-sized mansicle.*

Although... my girlie garden is definitely sore.

Once I've untangled myself from his limbs, I straddle his stomach but try to keep my weight off him. "I'm so sorry. Are you okay?"

"If I had to pick how I die, balls-deep in you is the way I'd go."

I snort laugh. Apparently, falling off the bed has made him ultra honest. He pulls me down to him until we're naked chest to naked chest again.

He clears his throat. "But, uh, you're not planning on us having kids, right?"

Whoa. That's some major "we're definitely ending up together forever and ever and having a dog and a house and a family" kind of reference.

What's crazy is I think I want that. But more shocking is the realization that it doesn't scare the shit out of me.

I kiss him. Just a soft brush of my lips against his as I caress his jaw. "I don't know." I swallow the lump in my throat. "I might want kids. If they have your eyes."

He smiles, and it's wide and brilliant and makes me forget we nearly died two minutes ago.

It's my turn to clear my throat. "Plus, you know, I could always kiss it and make it better."

He laughs again. "Isn't that what preempted our near-death experience?"

I nuzzle against him and ignore the fact that we're on his dorm room floor. "Like you said, it's one hell of a way to go."

That gets me a low rumble of satisfaction, which makes me smile.

With a few more groans, we peel ourselves off the floor and clean up in his en-suite bathroom—one of the small perks of being the RA—and get ready for bed.

Internally, I high-five myself for my newly acquired BJ skills. Gavin enjoyed himself, and I didn't bite him or end up with something icky in my hair or eyes. *Bonus.*

And except for the death roll off his bed, it wasn't terribly awkward. Even better, there weren't any interruptions.

"Thank God it's quiet on the floor tonight," I whisper a few minutes later, once we're curled up together in bed.

He's quiet. "It's Friday, right?"

I nod and snuggle closer.

He makes this noise in the back of his throat and sits up with a frown.

"What's wrong?" I ask. Glancing at the clock, I realize it's not that late. Only midnight.

"It's too quiet." He tosses on a pair of sweats and a t-shirt and shuffles into his running shoes.

Even fully clothed, he makes my mouth water. Especially when he looks over at me with that disheveled mop on his head and woos me with those dimples.

Leaning down for a kiss, he mumbles, "Maybe everyone is out partying, but I should make the rounds to make sure no one is passed out, drowning in vomit."

I shudder at the thought, but I love that he cares about the kids on his floor. Well, they're not kids. They're all eighteen or nineteen, but they seem like kids sometimes with the dumb things they do.

"I'll come with you." I reach for his flannel and throw it on sans bra. This is me living life on the edge. Then I slide on my jeans, forgoing my wet underwear because *ew*.

His hand is on the door while he waits for me. "Thanks, babe. I like when you keep me company."

My silly heart sighs.

I'm busy staring up at him like a lovesick school girl when he wraps an arm around my shoulder and opens the door.

A round of applause has me stopping short and jerking back.

What. The. Fuck.

Four freshmen guys are sitting on the hallway floor, sporting shit-eating grins and snacking on popcorn. One by one, they proudly hold out a number on a sheet of paper. *Ten. Ten. Ten. Nine point five.*

The last douchewad smiles like a moron. "Thought you guys needed to work on that dismount."

My face burns. Those little shits were listening to us having sex? And *rating* us?

That's when I realize our mistake. We usually turn on music or the floor is so loud with TVs blaring that we've never had to worry about eavesdroppers.

I'm about to tell them to fuck the fuck off when Gavin laughs and pulls me closer to kiss my forehead.

Then he turns to them with a shrug. "We were studying. *Really* hard." How he says this with a straight face, I'll never know. The boys snicker, and Gavin continues nonchalantly. "Besides, I love Clementine, so how we *study* with the door closed is none of your damn business."

Aww. I love hearing that he loves me.

His eyes slide to me briefly, and then back to the guys. "Okay, losers, go get a life. I'm pretty sure my girl is about *this close* from shanking the four of you, so if you value your manhood, I'd run."

Those little dicks take one look at my expression and scuttle back into their rooms with nary a word.

I turn to Gavin with an evil grin. "You do know me well. Shanking would've been my punishment of choice."

Leaning down, he kisses my lips and then winks. "My kind of girl."

Bonus Scene 2

This scene takes place right after the Kissing Madeline epilogue, and there's a minor spoiler ahead if you haven't read that yet. This is for all of the readers who asked for more Gavin & Clem!

GAVIN

Want to know the worst thing that could ever happen in your life? Here it is.

Step one. Marry the girl of your dreams. For me, there was always only one person who met this criteria. Clementine Avery. The sweetest, most amazing, beautiful smart-ass I've ever met.

Step two. Get your drop-dead gorgeous wife pregnant with twins. Twins! This has you thinking you're a superhero and have sperm with Titan-like strength that charged up her body to create two human beings. So far so good, right? You tell yourself you're the boss. A bad ass. A god among men.

Step three. *This is the part that kicks you in the balls.* You're skipping along, thinking you can do no wrong... until you come home from work and find that lovely creature hunched over the toilet, sweaty and pale while she retches because the pregnancy makes her so sick, she can't even make toast. Toast!

"Oh shit. Baby." I gently scoop her off the cold tile floor and hold her to my chest where her fingers dig into my shirt.

"I smell like puke," she says with a whimper.

I brush her golden hair from her sweaty forehead. "I don't care."

Sitting on the edge of the tub, I place her on my lap and reach over for a washcloth and wipe her face.

Puffy blue eyes stare up at me. Her lower lip quivers.

"It'll be okay," I whisper. "You're doing great. The doctor said the morning sickness should let up soon."

"This isn't morning sickness. It's fucking six o'clock in the evening. I could deal if it were morning sickness."

I kiss her before I remember I shouldn't. But no way can I wipe my mouth because Clementine will freak out more.

Her eyes pop up to mine because she knows I hate puke. She studies my face, and after a moment, her lips turn up into a smile.

"You love me, don't you?" she asks, almost shyly.

We've been married for two and a half years, and she still blushes.

"Of course I love you. You're my wife. You're carrying my children." *I'd sacrifice life and limb for you.* I kiss her forehead. "You're my golden girl."

It's possible I'm not a fair judge, but I happen to think I have *the* most amazing wife. In fact, my friend Daren and I have a bet to see who has the perfect wife, Clem or his wife Maddie. The girls think it's hysterical. And secretly, I know they're both vying to win.

As luck would have it, Maddie is also pregnant. But I get extra points because we're having twins. A boy *and* a girl. *See, super sperm.*

The girls don't know this yet, but the goal is to see which of our families can have a basketball team. Two down, three more to go. If you're counting, we're ahead here.

Clem's arms wrap around my neck, and she sniffles.

Tucking a strand of hair behind her ear, I kiss her temple. "Think you could eat a little Cream of Wheat? I can make it next door."

"I hate that you have to go to the neighbor's house to microwave something."

"I was going to make it on the stove. Not the microwave."

Her arms tighten around my neck. "Really?"

"Yes, really. No lumps for you."

She hates lumps in her hot cereal, and if you microwave it, you end up with lumps. *No bueno.*

Before you go thinking I'm a dick for offering her Cream of Wheat, you should know it's one of the few foods she can stomach. That and sourdough bread for some reason. She just can't deal with the smell—of anything. We had to buy scent-free soap and shampoo. Scent-free detergent and fabric softener. I even have to run down to Starbucks to grab coffee because the smell of my favorite beverage percolating turns her into the *Exorcist.*

I hate torturing my woman because I know she misses coffee, so I've cut back and only drink it at work.

And let me just say nothing—no convenience, no snack or beverage—*nothing* is worth making her sick.

Clem kisses my neck, and my dick goes to full mast, which she can probably feel on her thigh. But with all of the nausea, I can't exactly break out my sexy-time moves on my wife.

"I miss you," she mouths against my skin.

My eyes clench shut.

Here's the Catch 22. She's sick *all the time.* Like every five minutes. But the hormones also turn her into a sex kitten. Yes, my wife—my sweet, lovely, incredibly hot wife—is a total nympho.

Now that she's pregnant, what had been a gorgeous body is now downright sinful. Because there's a little more of her to love.

Those slender hips? Just a bit curvier. That hot-as-hell ass? A little rounder. Those beautiful breasts? A *lot* bigger. This is where I thank Jesus, the Easter Bunny, Santa, that rock climbing wall at BU—whoever or whatever is responsible for her body. Thank you, thank you, thank you.

However—and here's the kicker—we can *never* act on those urges because one minute, we're ripping each other's clothes off and the next, she's hurling into the trash can.

She curls up closer and giggles. "Did I give you a boner?"

Clem thinks dicks are funny. Until mine is pounding away and she's screaming my name. Then it's not so funny.

"You know you did," I growl.

A listless sigh escapes her. "I wish I could give you a blow job at least."

My cock is all for it. Until I think of the projectile vomit that's likely to ensue. "Hmm. Me too, babe." *God, me too.*

Her soft hand runs through my hair. "Maybe we could try having sex later?" she whispers. "The nausea usually goes away around nine or ten at night."

By then, she's usually crashed in bed with one arm hanging off the bed and a little drool coming out of her mouth. Yeah, she's adorable.

I'm about to talk some sense into her, but one look at her hopeful expression, and I can't do it. I'll suffer the worst case of blue balls known to man to make this girl happy.

"Your place or mine, hot stuff?" I kiss her nose.

"Really?"

Yes, it's crazy. My wife is begging me to have sex.

"Whatever you want." Just... *please don't vomit.*

By the time we crawl into bed, the prayer is etched in my brain. *Please. Don't. Vomit.*

Two months is a long time to go without sex when you're married to someone this amazing. But I've found I really miss sex, not when we're in bed, but when we're chatting about literature.

She starts talking about figurative language, and I'm a goner. Shut up. Don't laugh.

Tonight, she's wearing this thin little t-shirt that's snug around her breasts. The kind that's soft and nearly see-through, so I have a great view of her rosy nipples. Her legs are bare, and she's sporting white lace bikini underwear. When we first got married, she told me if I ever wanted to get laid, I could never call them panties. Not sure why that grosses her out, but I don't need to be told twice.

I collapse in bed and pretend to snore, and she smacks my ass.

"No fucking way. We are doing this," she barks.

Laughing, I roll over and grab her, and she squeals. I start to tug her down to me when I remember I need to be gentle. The girl is four and a half months pregnant, and although she has a little tummy, if you didn't know her the way I do, you probably couldn't tell. It's easy to forget.

Slow down. You can hurt her or the babies. Fuck.

She stops mid-laugh and frowns. "What's wrong?" Those blue eyes study my face, and before I can answer, her lower lip juts out. "It's because I'm a whale already, isn't it? You don't think I'm attractive anymore."

"What?" Seriously, what is she talking about? "Darlin', nothing could be further from the truth."

And then the tears start. "I can't fit in any of my jeans anymore."

"C'mere." I tuck her to me and smooth down her mass of golden hair. "You look fucking perfect to me. Do you hear me? Perfect. I've had a massive erection for you since I got home. Would I be sporting this kind of wood if you weren't the most beautiful, sexy creature I've ever seen?" I grab her hand and place it between my legs. "Exhibit A."

Clem sniffles and blinks back a few more tears. "Really?"

"Yes, really. This is all for you."

She strokes me, and I grit my teeth. It's been *way* too long.

"Hey, I'm not feeling nauseous."

"Oh." *Wow. We might really do this.*

"I'm just feeling emotional. Because I want to have sex with my husband and I'm afraid I can't."

The tears start up again.

No no no no no no.

"Hey." I nibble on her ear. "How about I kiss it and make it feel better?"

Her chest stills, and I dip down to her neck and open my mouth and suck lightly until her pulse kicks up.

She gasps. "That... that might work." She sniffles again, and I will myself to go slowly. Even if I die, even if my balls explode in the morning because we couldn't get there, I will make my wife feel better.

But before I kiss my way down her body, I get up and kick the bedroom door shut.

What? Did you think I was going to share all the details about how I have sex with my hot wife? Fuck, no. She's *my* sex kitten. Go find your own.

From the Author

While *Dearest Clementine* is the second book I wrote, it's the first one I had the guts to release. It took me eight months to write, and during that time, I listened to Amy Winehouse's *Back to Black* album nonstop. Even now when I think of this book, I think of that album. On the day I clicked publish, I was so freaked out, I thought I might puke. (Thankfully, I did not!)

Inspired by my time as a student at Boston University, *Dearest Clementine* features one of my all-time favorite settings. Boston is a town near and dear to my heart for so many reasons. I loved living in Warren Towers as a freshman and Bay State Road my subsequent three years. The two lovely girls I lived with (who are still two of my dearest friends) were seniors my sophomore year and inspired the dynamic between Clementine and her roommates.

Since I write linearly, I wanted to begin this book with my first welcome to BU, which was dorm life in Warren Towers. I cried the first night there after my belongings didn't arrive on time, which forced me to sleep on towels that I draped over the sketchy mattress. I had moved half-way across the country, didn't know a soul in Boston, and hadn't a clue what the future might hold. That night, I wasn't sure I'd made the right decision.

Starting the story with Clem sitting in that dorm room as she struggled to think of a new book idea in some ways captured my hopes as a new college student. At its heart was the idea that all of my dreams were possible *if* I chose the correct path. It was an electrifying (and terrifying) idea.

I used many of my experiences in college as the backdrop for Clementine—running along the Charles, eating lunch with friends at the student union, and even having an RA who helped a student who broke her leg in the middle of the night.

The Landsdowne Street club we loved at the time was called Venus, and a friend knew the bouncer, who let us in without IDs. One night, another friend got carried home from Venus by a guy from our dorm. We were lucky he was super nice and that the security dude in our building didn't bounce us for being idiots. (In retrospect, that was scary. Don't do the dumb shit my friends and I did when we were nineteen!)

Ultimately, my four years at BU were some of the happiest (and craziest) of my life. I'm so grateful for the time there. And while I didn't meet my husband while I was a student, I met him shortly after graduating. My almost college sweetheart and I are about to celebrate our 26th wedding anniversary!

Side note: My husband is a songwriter who's had music on hundreds of TV shows, and he inspired Gavin's musical abilities. I majored in journalism and later taught it, so that's what inspired Gavin's work on *The Daily Free Press*.

Writing *Dearest Clementine* was also my escape. At the time, my twins were very ill, and I spent months in the hospital with them. I realized I needed something that could bring me hope, something that would help me stay strong for my kids, and writing became that outlet, along with consuming an absurd number of romance novels.

Today, I'm a self-proclaimed romance junkie. I love consuming it and writing it, and I'm so grateful for the readers who picked up my first published novel and gave an unknown author a chance. This special edition is for you!

Keep flipping!

I hope you enjoyed *Dearest Clementine*! Keep flipping to read Jenna & Ryan's story.

The Girlfriend Games

About The Girlfriend Games

I never thought I'd find myself pole dancing to help a guy I hate win money to help his injured brother. But that's how I end up getting carried—koala bear-style in a bikini—around an outdoor obstacle course in the dead of winter by Ryan Hunter.

Somewhere between being dragged through mud and double-fisting vodka shots, I realize he's not the arrogant jerk I thought he was in class.

And when we have to spend the night squeezed together on a tiny bed, I find out we're *very* compatible in other ways.

Playing the part of fake girlfriend for forty-eight hours won't be a problem.

But letting Ryan go afterward might be.

'Twas not into my ear you whispered but into my heart.
'Twas not my lips you kissed, but my soul.
— Judy Garland

One

JENNA

Of course it's a C. Story of my life.

It doesn't matter that I started working on this assignment as soon as I got it or that I busted my bum to do a great job.

I glare at the red letter that looks like it might've been written with the blood of small children. Knowing Professor Dalton's teaching assistant, it's not entirely implausible. I swear Mallory, the TA, took one look at me and hated me on sight. I could see the words forming in her pointy little head on the first day of class. *Blonde. Pretty. Stupid.*

It's no secret I'm not a rocket scientist, but I hate that people assume I'm an idiot without ever speaking to me.

My mama always tells her friends I look like a cheerleader. In most of America, that's a compliment, but in Boston—brainiac central—it's not.

People always say blondes have more fun. Well, not in Psychology of Human Sexuality.

The rowdy male laughter a few feet away makes me roll my eyes.

Let me rephrase that. Blondes have more fun—if you're a dude.

The annoyingly good-looking guy who sits next to me high-fives his bro, the other douchebag in my row. I don't have to look at their essays to know they got better grades than I did.

The gods of alphabetical order have a sick sense of humor.

In eighth grade, I had to sit next to the kid who hadn't learned to use deodorant yet and rarely changed his pants, so every time he walked by, I had to smell his stinky ass.

In high school biology, I had the pleasure of sitting next to a mini-Bill Gates, which also underscored my gross ineptitude in science. Although he was a nice guy, the food that got trapped in his braces made me slightly nauseous.

And now, my sophomore year in college, I have the honor of sitting next to Mr. God's Gift to Women, also known as Ryan Hunter, Boston University's resident manwhore.

He's blond, blue-eyed. Slender but muscular. Smells like the summer rain. You can't miss him. He's the one who has a flock of girls hanging off his every word like he's the next Justin Bieber.

Ryan's in some stupid band. He sings. *Whoop-de-do.* For some reason, this makes women lose their ever-loving minds—and undergarments—when they're around him.

Most girls would kill to sit next to him in class, but every time he flirts with our TA and she moons back at him, I only barely restrain myself from committing two homicides.

Because *some of us* have to work hard to get good grades. Or, in my case, passable grades.

A weary sigh leaves me as I get out my syllabus and study the next assignment, which requires us to analyze the use of phallic imagery in a series of 90s print ads.

I reach into my bag to take notes, but I can't seem to find my pen.

Ironically, even though this class is killing me, I still enjoy it. Truthfully, I want to push myself to be my best. Even if my best is just a C. I might've partied hard last year, but this summer I averaged out how much each daily class costs, and that lit a fire under my mediocre ass. The cost of higher education is no joke. And since my step-father is footing the bill, I started to feel guilty every time I slept in because I was hungover or too tired to get up.

As Mallory starts writing on the board, someone taps my shoulder.

A velvety smooth voice says, "Hey, princess, you dropped your pen."

I still. Ryan and I have never spoken before even though our desks are twelve inches apart.

My eyes shift to his open hand, where I spot my pen, and then I look up at his face. His stupidly gorgeous face.

Ethereal sky-blue eyes stare back. Disheveled dirty blond hair stands in every direction, looking both negligent and terribly sexy.

I'm completely derailed by those long lashes. By his chiseled cheekbones and the way his bottom lip pouts slightly.

Until my poor misdirected brain finally registers what he said.

I've sat next to him for months. Every day, the TA calls out our names. 'Jenna Gentry' comes right before 'Ryan Hunter.' Is it that difficult to learn someone's name when you're sitting next to her for the entire semester?

Somehow I manage to not growl. "Do girls get off on your little pet names for them?" Internally, I cringe at how my Southern accent is so strong. When I get nervous, it gets worse.

He stifles a laugh and licks his lips. His incredibly sexy lips.

Asshole.

Holding a hand over his mouth so Mallory doesn't see him talking, he whispers, "Honestly? I'm not sure if it's the pet names, my magic hands, or my big dick, but girls always get off."

I let those words sink in and barely restrain another eye roll.

Instead, I smile and bat my eyelashes as I hold my finger up to my open mouth suggestively.

And then pretend to gag.

I'm not sure what I expect his reaction to be, but not the laugh he tries to muffle, or the wide smile he gives me afterward, or the way he studies my face like he's trying to memorize it. And I'm definitely not expecting the chills that break out on my neck and travel straight to my nipples.

"Miss Gentry, care to answer my question?" Mallory calls out from the front of the room.

Dang it, Ryan. The *one day* our TA calls on me, and I have no clue what we're talking about.

I swallow and flip through my syllabus like maybe whatever the hell she was saying is tucked away between the pages.

Ryan clears his throat. "Sex sells. That's why phallic imagery is so popular. From subliminal images in vodka bottles to naughty ice cream cones and double entendres, people are intrigued."

She nods toward him, an amused smile on her lips. Her hands smooth down her pencil skirt. "Interesting. I enjoyed your last essay, by the way."

Oh, puh-lease! What could he have possibly written in that essay? How to fuck a girl doggie-style while doing a bong hit?

For the next sixty minutes, I stew in irritation. The minute class is over, I bolt out of my chair. I'm out the door, down the hall, and halfway out of the building when I get yanked to a stop.

Ryan lets go of my elbow and holds up his hands. "Sorry. Sorry. I, um..." He rubs the back of his neck. "I didn't mean to be a dick in there. I just wanted to talk to you. We never seem to get a chance in class."

I stare up at him, hating how he somehow blocks out the sun behind him with those wide shoulders. No guy is supposed to be this good-looking in a torn flannel, jeans and combat boots. Doesn't he know grunge died in the nineties?

"You mean I don't fall all over myself to talk to you?"

He chuckles. "No, I mean—"

"Ry-annnnnn." A chorus of girls whine his name. Three stunning brunettes in matching sorority sweaters shimmy up to him, and two loop their arms through his. They remind me of those little charms you stick on a bracelet when you're ten. Except Ryan is the bracelet.

"Hey, ladies," he says amicably, making no effort to disentangle himself, before he looks at me expectantly, like he thinks I have the time or inclination to finish our conversation. Was he hitting on me a minute ago? And does he genuinely think I want to go out with a guy who looks like he might break into an orgy at any minute?

Not that I blame him because these girls are beautiful, and they probably have higher GPAs than I do. If I were into women, I'd be all over that.

I glance at his new friends and pat him on his ridiculously hard chest. "I'll see you around, rock star."

His mouth opens, but before he responds, I turn and head to my next class. Because what's the point?

Judging from how much Ryan sets me off, you'd think I hate men. I don't. In fact, I *love* men. I love their bodies and roughness. The gruff edge to their voices. The hardness of their muscles. Their clean sweat and dirty mouths. Alpha males, beta males, book boyfriends—all assortments of men. I swear, I popped out of my mother ready to fall in love. I had my first boyfriend in kindergarten, my first French kiss in seventh grade, and my first sexual experience junior year in high school. I did it with a boy I would have sworn I'd be with forever. Alas, soulmates we were not, and we only lasted through spring break.

But I believe in love. Epic, sweeping, it-hurts-so-good-I-can-hardly-breathe love.

While I might be average at many things in my life, I've always promised myself I'd never be average at love.

So while Ryan Hunter might make most girls shiver with

delight, I'll never settle for someone who wants to bang and bolt. A great fuck and cuddle with a side of Netflix? Sure. I'm not against having fun. But I'm an expert at identifying the love-'em-and-leave-'em type. After all, I've had a lifetime of experience dealing with the fallout after a guy takes off.

I don't have to be a genius to know Ryan's not the man you pine after if you want epic love. Especially when staring into his eyes reminds me of the time I tripped on our family vacation to the Grand Canyon and nearly dove headfirst to an untimely death.

No, he's the match you light when you want to go up in flames.

So no way will I entertain the idea of Ryan Hunter.

Why play with fire when it always ends in ashes?

Two

RYAN

I'm not exactly sure what just happened.

Jenna's sun-kissed blonde hair whips in the wind as she stalks off. I stare at her retreating form until something tugs at my arm and I realize the Delta girls are waiting for me.

I'm still processing that Jenna hates me even though today is the first time we've ever spoken. In fact, she wrinkled her nose at me like I disgust her.

Sometimes I forget not every woman wants me for something. Most look at me with hunger in their eyes. The game is trying to guess what they want. A song about them? A backstage fuck? The debauchery that's supposed to go hand in hand with hooking up with a musician?

I want to tell them it's not worth it. That this shit will taint your soul. Besides, my drug of choice—ninety minutes on stage—will always come first.

Jenna's smart to run the other direction.

Hopefully she doesn't realize this, but sometimes I just stare at her in class. I could do it all day because she never looks at me, not even when she has to pass me an assignment. Except for the first day of class where our eyes locked and heat seared down my spine, she's never given me the time of day.

Of course I know her name. I memorized it at the beginning of the semester. It was impossible not to. Her big hazel eyes are goddamn mesmerizing. The fact that she's funny as fuck and the most gorgeous woman I've ever seen is a bonus.

I haven't a clue why she looks like she wants to jab me with something sharp, but it's probably for the best. If we ever did go out, she'd probably shit a brick if she saw what groupies at my shows do.

The sorority girls look sad I'm steering them down Com Ave toward the student union and not somewhere private. But I'm still bothered by Jenna's reaction. Still thinking about her hypnotic eyes and the way they pierce me with derision.

I'm usually the guy who doesn't give two fucks what people think, but for some reason I care that Jenna looks at me like I'm disgusting.

I'm not used to that reaction here. Back home? Well, that's a different story.

There are only a few things I've prioritized in my life: Getting the hell out of that trailer park in Philly, writing music that means something to me, and not letting fear control my actions. If there's a high dive, I want to jump off it. A rollercoaster? I want to ride it. Because if I don't face my fears, all the crap I've boxed up—all the thoughts that I'll never be good enough to make it—will come surging back.

I'm not the guy who can afford a school like Boston University. My family can barely pay for Spam and day-old bread. I'm here because I'm sure as fuck not gonna let my little brothers grow up in the same squalor I did.

But see, I'm not here on a music scholarship. If I was that good, I'd be attending Berklee down the road. I'm at BU for two reasons.

One, my counselor in high school had gone to BU and loved it. He made it sound like nirvana, with collegiate-sounding dorms like Warren Towers and Shelton Hall, and he said I'd meet people in this town who could change my life. The second reason is because I'm a decent test-taker, and for some reason, the good people at this university took pity on the poor kid who grew up wearing clothes from the Goodwill.

Yeah, I put all that shit in my college essay. How we slept in the basement of the nearby church on cold nights because our trailer was an ice box. How I stole food from the grocery store so I could feed my siblings. How my mom cried at night because she couldn't pay the bills. Everything that makes my gut ache if I think about it too long.

Even with the scholarships, I'm still barely scraping by, especially with how tuition goes up every year. I'm so damn sick of barely getting by. I'm so tired of feeling like I'm living on borrowed opportunities.

When I got the call from my mom two nights ago, I wanted to cry right along with her. Hearing she can't afford rent, much less groceries, makes me desperate. Makes me consider packing my shit and going home. Because it's not fair that I have all the food I can eat in the school cafeteria while my family goes hungry and struggles every single day.

I send them whatever I can afford, but it's not enough.

My cheap flip phone rings in my back pocket, and I excuse myself from the table at the student union to take the call from my cousin Sean. He takes classes at Bunker Hill so he can have a reason to be in Boston to play in my new band. He wanted us to go to New York, but it's even more expensive there, and I hoped to avoid living up under a bridge in the Bronx. I never told him I love Beantown and its reputation for academics. He'd laugh his ass off if he knew I liked school.

"Hey, man. Give me some good news. I need it today." *Please.* I'm out of shit to sell unless you count my blood. That's the only thing I have left—that and my guitar and a few amps. While our shows do well, we only book about one a month, and when you split that between four guys, it goes fast.

"I got you." He laughs.

The tension that's been clawing at my throat for the last forty-eight hours finally subsides. "Awesome. What is it? Another loan?"

He doesn't answer right away. "Not exactly."

I rub my hand over my face. "Nothing illegal, right? I'm not gonna steal anything or hurt anyone." Everyone knows my cousin is one stupid decision away from being the inspiration for a Quentin Tarantino film. Except once in a while, he comes through on something legit.

"Relax. This is right up your alley. Remember that rich prick Hamilton?"

It takes me a second to place the name. "The guy who lives like a sultan on the other side of town? Over in Cambridge?"

"Yeah. Hamilton York Pembroke the Third," he says like he's some snotty butler. "Well, you're never gonna believe the shit he has going on this weekend."

By the time I get off the phone, it's dark outside. My cousin's solution to my problem is a long shot at best. But when I get another call from my mom, I know I don't have another choice.

As I walk through campus, not a star shines in the sky even though I keep searching for one. My breath rises up like steam in the frigid air, and I huddle in my hoodie.

Over and over, I remind myself why I'm doing this. Why I'm trying to make it and forge a better life.

But inside, I feel like the worthless piece of shit from the trailer park. Like attending a nice university in a beautiful city is just window dressing. Because if I can't help my family, what's the fucking point?

Three

JENNA

For all intents and purposes, Alex is perfect. He arrives on time for our dates. He's sweet and cuddles but doesn't smother me. We talk just enough that I don't feel like I'm doing the walk of shame the next day, but not enough to think this —whatever we've been doing for the last few months—is serious.

And it's been nice. Not earth-shattering. Certainly not epic. But not bad as far as friends with benefits go.

Except tonight I'm not feeling it.

We're sitting on his bed, but instead of getting naked, I toy with a loose end of my hair and stare at his desk, pissed that I'm still thinking about Ryan Hunter and those infuriating blue eyes.

"You okay? You're quiet tonight." Alex rubs my shoulder, and I fight the urge to smack him away.

"Yeah, I'm fine. I guess I have a lot on my mind." I don't have the heart to tell him I'd rather be at home wearing sweats, curled up with my Kindle reading something smutty.

"We could do this another time."

Relief hits me, and I nod. I'm definitely not in the mood for sex even though it's been a few weeks since we've hooked up.

I tell him I'm heading home, so he offers to walk me. It's past one in the morning, and Bay State Road is dark as we trek from his dorm room near Kenmore Square.

When we reach my brownstone, he's pulling me in for a hug when I finally let it out.

"I don't know if this is working for me," I whisper, not wanting to hurt his feelings. Until my run-in with Ryan yesterday, I hadn't realized things with Alex had gone south.

Because I had hoped Alex and I would turn into epic.

But all we did was fizzle.

He sighs, his arms tightening around me. "I kinda figured."

"But we had fun, right?" I mumble against his chest.

"A blast, babe."

The fact that he doesn't seem too disheartened tells me we're in the same place. This was nice while it lasted, but I'm realizing I'm not into casual sex, and that's all Alex and I have been about.

I want something more. Something substantial. And this isn't it.

The squeal of tires makes me turn in Alex's arms as a car screeches to a halt across the street. The door opens, and music blasts from the speakers. People stumble out of the vehicle, and a half-dressed co-ed swan-dives across the lawn in a fit of giggles.

A guy stumbles behind her and helps her stand. Irritation pricks my skin when I realize it's Ryan. He's joking with his friends as he backs away from the vehicle toward the brownstone kitty-corner from ours. Does he live across the street? Or maybe his date does?

Really, Jenna? Who cares?

"Someone's having fun tonight," Alex mumbles, amused.

That's Ryan. Mr. Good Times.

I let go of Alex. "Thanks for walking me home. Stay in touch, okay?"

He yanks me into a bear hug, lifting me off my feet, and I laugh as he whispers into my hair, "Damn straight I'll stay in touch. You're awesome, Jenna."

I wave as I trudge up the steps to my brownstone. Across the street, a burst of laughter echoes on our quiet street as another girl bolts from the car and plasters herself to Ryan. Jealousy, like a hot knife, slices through me.

How in the world can I be jealous over a guy I don't even know?

Four

RYAN

When I see her, everything stops.

I don't hear the giggling girls or the purr of the car engine or even my own heartbeat.

Just Jenna.

In the arms of another man.

My jaw tightens as I will myself to look away.

I help my friend up to her room before heading back downstairs, pissed that all I can think about is a woman who obviously hates me.

Five

JENNA

"Why do you sound like an angry bear?" my roommate Harper asks from the couch in the middle of our suite.

We live on the third floor of our brownstone and are lucky enough to have our own rooms, but we share a small common area and a bathroom.

I squint at my laptop, hoping the list disappears. "Because I just got my new group assignment for Human Sexuality."

Our groups get shuffled around every month, and of course, Ryan is in my new group.

"I thought you loved that class."

"The professor is great, but I hate my TA, and my small groups are hit-or-miss," I grumble.

Our other roommate Clementine sets down the book she's reading. "I can't believe you sit around talking about body parts. I'd be mortified discussing that shit in a room full of horny college dickheads." She cringes.

I usually try to be pro-men with my roommate because she's

had some terrible experiences, and I don't want to feed into that since I generally love the opposite sex, but she has a good point.

"It's not always that bad. Except the other day, the professor broke out a banana, a small cucumber, and a baby carrot to discuss penis size and micro-peens, and it was chaos."

Harper chuckles. "Is there anyone in particular who has you looking like you'd rather suck a lemon than go to this group discussion?"

I nibble my lip. "Yeah. This guy Ryan." I fill them in on my annoying classmate, and when I'm done, Harper raises her eyebrows.

"You're awfully intense about someone you barely know. Are you sure you don't have a little crush on him?"

I feel heat crawl up my neck. Leave it to Harper, whose dad is some famous psychiatrist, to go there. "I do *not* have a crush on Ryan Hunter."

Nope. No way. Not at all.

Six

JENNA

"Where were we?" Sabrina asks as she shuffles the stack of papers in front of her.

Keith waggles his eyebrows. "I believe we were discussing the clitoris."

He says it so loudly, everyone in the library turns to look at our table. I keep my face impassive even though addressing sex in public is new for me. I'm a Southern girl, born and bred, and if I ever said anatomical words in front of my parents, they'd have an aneurysm. Which is why I took this class in the first place. I don't think people should feel ashamed of their bodies.

Ryan half coughs, half laughs across the table. "We're suppose to discuss the female orgasm and whether an emotional connection is needed to do the deed, and then write a reflection."

Sabrina gives me a look as though she expects me to take the lead on this. Fine. Screw it. What's the big deal? Orgasms are natural. There's no reason to be embarrassed.

I clear my throat. "The female orgasm is about more than

achieving a climax. A partner can do all of the right things, touch you in the right way..."

"Assuming he knows where your clit is," Sabrina mumbles, and I chuckle.

"Right. So your partner might know exactly how to rub the genie lamp, but without some kind of connection with the other person, sometimes it's hard for women to come."

There.

I take a breath and look around the table.

Keith is busy whispering what I'm assuming is something dirty to Sabrina, but Ryan's attention is riveted on me. He shifts in his seat. "What about casual sex? Are you saying that women who only hook up don't get off?"

"I'm saying it's different for every person. Can some do one-night stands and leave satisfied? Sure. I mean, I guess. But I need..."

I stop, realizing what I was about to say.

Ryan's voice gets low and gravelly. "What do you need, princess?"

My face gets hot, and I see the challenge in his captivating blue eyes. "More than a big dick and a pretty face."

He looks like he's about to say something when Keith pipes up. "Inquiring minds want to know, ladies. Is it easier to come with oral or do you just need a good dicking?"

I roll my eyes. "Bless your heart. You must think you're good at the 'dicking' part."

Ryan laughs, and Sabrina's face gets pink, and she waves her hand at me like she expects me to give Keith an actual response.

Oh, for fuck's sake. "How should I know? I've never had oral. I've only given it," I mumble. Giving blow jobs in high school is like a rite of passage.

I finally brave a look at Ryan, and he smirks. "You need to date better men."

"No shit."

He opens his mouth, but his phone cuts him off.

Sabrina scowls. "You're supposed to turn off your ringer in here."

Ryan holds up his hand and takes the call. "Mom, what's up?" He gets up and stalks off without another word to us.

Sabrina shrugs. "Guess we're taking a break." She looks at her phone. "Let's regroup in ten."

I grab my purse and head for the bathroom. When I get in there, I look at my flushed face and rub my sweaty palm across my cheek.

My God. Is Harper right? Do I have a thing for Ryan?

Because I will not compete for that man's attention. I won't play the pick-me game with his groupies. I watched my mama do that with my father when he had an affair, and it whittled away her confidence. Thank goodness for my stepfather. He's a great husband and restored my faith that good men are out there. He always treats my mama like a princess.

I jerk to a stop. *Is that why it bothers me so much when Ryan calls me a princess? Because it feels like mockery?*

After I go to the bathroom and wash my hands, I head out, pausing to throw my empty water bottle in the recycling bin.

"But he's okay?" Ryan says in a hushed voice around the corner. "Mom, don't worry about the hospital bill. Just take care of Denny. Let's look on the bright side. All he broke was his arm and not his scrawny neck." He's quiet a moment. "Mom, don't cry. It'll be okay. My little brother's tough. And I promise I'll get you some money by Monday. Trust me. They won't turn off the lights. You'll pay those bills on time. As for the hospital... see if we can cover that in several payments."

My feet root to the ground at the distress in Ryan's voice.

"I wish I could come home for the holidays too, Mom, but those plane tickets are expensive, and I don't think Sean's van will get us home and back again."

Before he catches me snooping, I speed-walk back to our table. When he returns a few minutes later, I'm suddenly self-conscious about my designer bag and expensive jeans. About how much I spend on makeup and beauty supplies and clothes. About the way I throw around money. Shopping is one of my favorite pastimes. My stepfather makes a good living, and he's always been generous with me and my sister.

Ryan's quiet when he rejoins us. We all write our reflections, but I catch him looking out the dark windows more than once, worry etched all over his handsome face.

Something uncomfortable unfurls in my chest.

It's shame. Shame for judging the man when I don't really know him at all.

And if I'm being honest with myself, I'd like to know him. The real Ryan.

Not the rocker dude who struts around campus with fangirls hanging off his arm.

But the guy who sends his mama money and makes sure she can pay her bills.

Seven

RYAN

I pace outside Becky's brownstone and hit call again. Five rings later, she finally picks up. Thank God. I'm out here having a heart attack.

A scratchy voice answers. "Hello?"

"Becky? Hey, are we still on for today?"

"Ugh, Ryan, I'm so sick."

My heart drops. I close my eyes and drop my head back. When I can breathe again, I tell her I hope she feels better and call Sean. "Becky's got the flu and can't make it. What the fuck do I do?"

"Relax, dude. There are probably a dozen girls you could take."

My cousin doesn't get it. "Bro, I can't take just anyone. Did you see the list of activities I printed out? It's called the *Girlfriend* Games."

"What if you call one of the twins?"

I dismiss his suggestion outright. "I need someone who won't read into this. Someone who won't just get drunk and fuck off the competition. Someone who won't think I'm looking for a relationship." Becky is a former friend-with-benefits. She knows what I'm about and won't think I'm asking for more.

After what happened with my ex, I'm gun-shy about getting into another relationship, which is why I like to keep things casual.

My breath steams in the cold air, and I zip my hoodie. Winter in New England requires down coats and thermal clothes, shit I can't afford.

He laughs. "Good luck. You'd need someone who isn't half in love with you."

Someone who isn't...

I stop pacing.

"You're a genius. Talk to you later." I hang up and stalk down the street as I scroll through my phone. It takes two calls to classmates before I track down Jenna's number, and when she answers, I want to fall on the ground in relief.

"Jenna, it's Ryan. Don't hang up."

Silence.

"Ryan. Hey."

Shocked she sounds almost pleasant, I almost trip over a crack in the sidewalk. "I need a favor."

"Sure. What's up?"

I'll be damned. Maybe she doesn't hate me and I don't have to beg. "What are you doing this afternoon?"

Eight

JENNA

"Thanks again for doing this," Ryan says. "I'll be there in five minutes."

Click.

Five minutes?

What the heckfire did I just agree to?

My first impulse had been to hang up on Ryan. Then I remembered that conversation I overheard the other day and immediately felt bad. My Sunday school upbringing kicked in, and all I could hear was the Golden Rule: *Do unto others...*

And that got me thinking. If the roles were reversed, I hope someone would lend me a hand too.

So I agreed to go do this thing with him. If it means he can help his family, then I'll set aside my pride for one afternoon.

From Ryan's description, today's activities sound like the drunk Olympics. Which could be fun. Who knows? I'll try anything once. I partied way too hard last year and have mostly put that behind me, but maybe I can put those skills to good use today.

Realizing I only have two minutes before he gets here, I run around my room and throw a few things in my favorite Dooney & Bourke duffle bag. After nearly tripping and falling on my face, I force myself to stop and take several breaths because I'm more hyper than my mama's hairless terrier.

I'm going to spend the whole day with Ryan Hunter. Why does that cause my belly to flutter wildly? I close my eyes and pray I don't have a crush on this guy. His ego is already the size of a Buick, and I don't want to be another fangirl who bats her eyelashes at him like a dunderhead.

Be cool, Jenna.

And for the love of God, don't take anything he says today seriously.

It may be called the Girlfriend Games, but you're not his girlfriend.

Nine

RYAN

A few minutes later, Jenna trots out of her brownstone all wrapped up in a puffy pink jacket, toting a matching pink duffle bag. Snowflakes swirl around her like she's a fairy princess in a Hans Christian Andersen story. She smiles, and it hits me like a goddamn lightning bolt.

"Thanks for doing this." I open the passenger's side door to my roommate's car I borrowed.

"No problem."

I run around to the driver's side, briefly slipping on the fresh snow, and jump in. "If we win, we'll split the five K." Twenty-five hundred will pay all of my mother's bills and get her caught up on rent. Maybe it'll help her pay something on Denny's trip to the ER.

Jenna nods, totally chill about the whole thing. It makes me uncomfortable.

As I drive down the street, I feel compelled to make sure she understands. "You're sure you're cool with this? I might have to carry you and toss you and who knows what else. There are half a dozen drinking games and a stripper pole competition." Shit. If she didn't like me before, she'll probably hate me once this is over.

"I got this, Ryan. Don't worry about me."

I nod, grateful she's being so laid-back. I have no idea what caused this shift in her attitude toward me, but it came at the perfect time.

"And, uh, is your boyfriend cool with you doing this?" I don't know why I ask. It's none of my business. I should just shut the fuck up, but curiosity gets the best of me.

Her brow crinkles. "I don't have a boyfriend."

"You're not dating that guy? The one I saw you hugging the other night on your front stoop?"

"Alex? We were a thing for a while, but not anymore."

I nod, ridiculously pleased she's single.

She clears her throat. "What about you? Are you dating one of those girls who swan-dived across the lawn?"

I chuckle. "We're just friends. I'm not dating anyone either."

She gives me a smile that makes me feel like I'm doused in sunlight.

As we head over the Mass Ave bridge, she reaches for the radio. "Is this okay?"

"Sure. Go for it."

She pauses on an indie station and starts humming to Elliot Smith. I smile because she can't sing for shit, but she doesn't seem to care.

I motion to the radio. "I love this guy."

"His voice is so melancholy, but it's beautiful. I became obsessed with him after I saw *Good Will Hunting* and couldn't stop listening to that soundtrack," she says as she taps a finger along the passenger window.

"Great movie." To say I'm surprised she and I have anything in common is an understatement.

"'I got her numba. How do you like them apples?'" she asks, deepening her voice, mimicking Matt Damon's famous lines.

I chuckle, enjoying this silly side of her. "That's a pretty decent Boston accent."

She blows on her knuckles and buffs them on her jacket. "I know."

My smile grows, as does my awareness. Grouchy Jenna from class is a snow princess. Perfect. Untouchable. Someone I never really tried to talk to because I figured she was out of my league. But smiling, joking Jenna is a fucking fox who makes me want to see what else she can teach me about the female orgasm.

"So how do you know the people we're hanging out with today?" she asks when the song ends.

"My band played for one of their parties last year, and my cousin got talking to the guy the other day, and he extended an invitation."

"What's the deal with this event? A drunk college Olympics seems really random."

"That's a good way to describe it. Hamilton, the guy who's hosting it, has too much time and money on his hands and tends to throw outrageous parties. I think the Girlfriend Games is probably just a reason to gather all of his friends and drink too much."

We weave through Cambridge traffic, which will be gridlocked soon given the weather.

"I love New England in winter." She sighs as she stares out the window. "The way twinkle lights line every cobblestone street and snow dusts the ground. It's magical."

"Where are you from originally? I hear that Southern drawl." When she talks, it wraps around me like warm honey.

"A small town in Georgia." She smiles, and it sends another jolt of awareness through me. "What about you?"

"Pennsylvania. Philly."

We drive the rest of the way listening to the radio, which I appreciate because I don't wanna talk about Philly. I like that she doesn't try to fill the silence with bullshit.

But it's tough to concentrate on the directions I've memorized with Jenna sitting so close. Her perfume or shampoo or whatever smells amazing. She always smells good in class, but now that we're trapped together in a car, I feel surrounded by her incredible scent.

I shift uncomfortably, hoping I'm not sporting an erection for her all day. I've never been turned on by a woman simply sitting next to me.

The rest of the way I'm thinking about Georgia peaches and wondering if Jenna is just as juicy.

Ten

JENNA

Ryan explained the premise of the Girlfriend Games, but I had no idea it would be like this. There have to be at least a hundred people milling around this gorgeous mansion.

I gawk at the palatial house with huge glass windows that's surrounded by a ten-foot-tall privacy fence. The inside has a mid-century modern feel with sleek, retro furniture.

Some guy named Hamilton spots Ryan from across the enormous living room and shouts, "Dude! You made it!"

He cuts through the crowd and grabs Ryan in a bro hug before Hamilton turns to me. "Never thought I'd see the day when Hunter here settled down. How'd you two meet? At one of Ryan's shows?"

I have no idea what to say. We didn't discuss what we were going to tell people.

Ryan's quiet for a second before he jams his hands in the pockets of his jeans. "Jenna and I have a class together, and I couldn't take my eyes off her even though she never looked my way."

My head jerks up to look at him, and our eyes connect. Does he mean that?

His cheeks go ruddy, and a little part of my heart melts.

Hamilton chuckles as he turns to me. "Well, you two definitely have the chemistry part down. Given that Ryan always seems to have fifty girls lining up to fuck him after his shows, you must be something special."

I flinch at the reminder of who I'm with today.

Don't be dumb, Jenna. Ryan's not here to woo you. This is all part of the charade.

Ryan glares at Hamilton. "Dude, what the fuck?"

"It's true, man. Just saying your girl here must be a winner."

After I steel my determination not to take anything Ryan says to heart, I thread my arm through his like one of his groupies and force a smile. "What can I say? I'm a lucky girl."

Hamilton gives me a wide smile. "I'm glad you guys could make it. Today's activities start with beer pong in the game room in half an hour, and tomorrow kicks off at noon. Find a bedroom upstairs before they fill up, and make yourselves at home. Oh, and don't forget to sign the waivers."

I drop my arm from Ryan's as my eyes widen. This is a two-day thing? And why the hell does he need waivers?

When Hamilton wanders off to greet someone else, Ryan curses quietly under his breath. "I'm sorry. About everything. About Hamilton being an ass. About this being a two-day thing. I had no idea we'd have to stay all weekend." He rubs the back of his neck. "I could drive you home tonight and pick you up in the morning if you want."

"After we've been drinking all day?" But dang it, I didn't bring my pajamas, floss, face wash, or night cream.

Just hearing my thoughts has me rolling my eyes at myself.

Ryan's trying to put food on his family's table, and here I am worried about my nighttime routine.

Buck up, Jenna. It's just one night. "It's fine. We'll survive. We're talking five K, right? Totally worth a little inconvenience. But I sleep like a starfish, so don't complain if I knee you in your goody basket."

He laughs and looks at me like he's seeing me for the first time. "What?"

He shakes his head. "You're not what I expected."

Tilting my head, I purse my lips. "I don't know if that's a compliment or not."

"I don't know either."

We stare at each other a moment before we both start laughing, and he pulls me into a hug. "If I haven't told you yet, I really appreciate you doing this. You have no idea how much it means to me."

I might have some idea.

It's challenging not to melt into his hard body. He smells like sandalwood soap and sexy man. I want to bury my nose in his neck and take a deep breath, but that would be weird. Pressed up against him, I feel so tiny, like he could toss me over his shoulder.

I make a mental note about what I want in a future boyfriend. I'm always down for a good tossing.

He inhales and makes a strangled noise. "Fuck, Jenna. You smell good."

I smile against him. "You do too. Now let's go kick some ass and win this fucker."

Eleven

RYAN

Surrounded by ten other girls, Jenna hoots as she nails the ping-pong ball in the Solo cup on the other side of the table. "Drink up, biotches!"

My fake girlfriend dominates the table like she heads a sorority house, but I don't think she's in one. Quarters, beer pong, flip cup —she's kicking everyone's ass.

I lean against a pillar as I watch her in awe. With my partner doing so well, we might stand a chance when it's the guys' turn.

After she wins another round, she trots up to me with a huge smile and bounces on her toes. Her gorgeous face is flushed, and her hair is pulled up in a sleek ponytail that makes me want to fist it and bring her lush mouth to mine.

"How much have you had to drink?" I ask quietly as I brush a loose strand of hair out of her eyes. I want to win, but not if that means Jenna gets sick.

"Three beers, but I'm good to go 'cause I've been chugging water in between, which is why I have to pee like a racehorse right now."

A bark of laughter spills out of me. This girl is the shit. I might be in love.

She leans up and whispers in my ear, "I overheard Hamilton tell someone he's bringing out a huge spread of food and can't wait for everyone to puke later when we're doing the races, whatever that is."

I ignore the flash of heat that runs through me when her warm breath hits my neck. "Good reconnaissance, gorgeous. We'll go easy on the snacks then."

She nods. "We got this."

We're in the lead, but given that the other guys I'm up against look like they're all football players, I wouldn't say this is a done deal. I'm in good shape because I walk or skateboard everywhere and haul amps and other shit to my shows, but these dudes look like they could bench-press me.

I glance down at the beautiful woman by my side. Jenna's petite. Delicate. Like a little fairy with a great rack.

I avert my eyes before I check out her tits again. She has two perky handfuls that have me wondering if her nipples match her pale pink lips. I make an effort to stop fantasizing about pushing my face into her cleavage.

On the last drinking game, most of the other girlfriends are getting sloppy and tripping over themselves, which makes it even easier for Jenna to dominate. When she's done she leaps into my arms with a laugh. I hold her by her cute little ass and smile down at her. Hopefully, she has no idea I just went rock hard. I lift her up to my waist to avoid my dick that wants an up-close-and-personal introduction to her body.

She threads her hand through my hair and pulls me down to her to whisper again. "One of the girls said they're kicking out people who don't look like real couples."

"They probably want to thin the competition." I lean back and stare into her luminous hazel eyes. "Then maybe we should level up. You okay with that?"

Her eyes dart to my lips as I talk, but when she doesn't say anything, I start to backtrack. "You know, it's cool. We can just—"

But she surprises me by yanking me to her mouth.

A groan rips through me. She tastes like malty beer and some citrusy lip balm I want to lick off her.

I'm not sure how far she wants to go, so I let her take the lead. I'm shocked as hell when she opens to me and strokes her tongue against mine.

Fuck. I want this girl. I think I always have. I wasn't bullshitting earlier when I was talking to Hamilton. I noticed Jenna the moment she walked into our class for the first time.

I spin around and press her into the pillar as we kiss. Her arms wrap around my neck as our tongues battle for dominance. But when her thighs pull me tighter to her, I give in and press my cock against her. Fucking heaven.

"Get a room!" someone shouts, and that snaps me back to reality.

Lowering her to the ground, I push my face into her neck. "Need a minute. I can't compete later if all the blood is in my dick."

She chuckles and gently scratches the back of my head, and I groan again. Why is she so perfect?

"Dinner's served! Eat up! You have half an hour to chow down," Hamilton yells, and people start shuffling out of the room.

I finally get ahold of myself and let go of Jenna, who gives me a shy smile and motions behind me. "Why don't I grab us some dinner, and we'll take it up to our rooms? That way we don't starve later."

"That's a great idea." We're gonna have to squeeze onto that twin bed 'cause it was the last one available, and we ended up in Hamilton's little brother's room.

I told Jenna I could sleep on the floor, but she said I was being silly. That we were two adults who were fully capable of sleeping in a bed together and it not getting weird.

At the time, it sounded good. Now, though? Now I'm starting to wonder if I should crash on the floor before this goes too far.

When some drunk guys fall into us, I shove them off and thread my fingers through Jenna's. Before I know what I'm doing, I lean down to kiss her forehead.

I can legit say I've never had the impulse to kiss some chick's forehead before.

But Jenna doesn't feel like "some chick."

Twelve

JENNA

Back down in the game room, which is enormous, Hamilton jumps on a table and points to a huge pile of balloons. "The couple who pops the most wins. My girl and I are gonna demonstrate. Only the ladies can touch the balloon or you'll get disqualified and your team will lose points."

A curvy brunette grabs a balloon, holds it against her ass, and then bends over.

Um.

Hamilton grabs her hips and pounds into her from behind until the balloon pops. Granted, he's fully clothed, but everyone's howling with laughter 'cause Hamilton makes hysterical sex faces.

Ryan curses next to me, and I grab his hand and squeeze. "Just go with it. I'll be fine."

He's been worried he'll weird me out. Maybe it helps we've had class together all semester or that he was willing to give me the bed tonight, but I'm not concerned. I just want to help his mom.

Guilt niggles at me. If I hadn't gone on that shopping spree last week, I could probably give him a few hundred bucks, but I wanted to order Christmas gifts for my roommates and family and get everything delivered in time.

Before I line up next to the other girlfriends, I turn to Ryan. "Don't hold back. If you do, we'll lose. Balls to the wall, you hear me?"

He chuckles. "Yes, my pretty princess."

For some reason, that nickname doesn't bother me anymore. "Let's show these Hahvard boys what we got," I say in a mock Bostonian accent that makes him laugh.

I give myself a little internal pep talk, but nothing prepares me for how intimate this game really is. For the way Ryan's fingers dig into my hips or the way I wish we didn't have this balloon between us when he thrusts or how his hot breath feels on my neck.

I'm flushed by the time it's over even though all I had to do was stand there and hold balloons against my bum.

A quick glance at Ryan makes me blush. My fake boyfriend has a very obvious erection bulging against the front of his jeans, though he's not the only one.

Hamilton, that wily fucker, must know what he's doing because two of the girls start puking in one of the huge garbage cans set up along the perimeter. And one of the other couples wanders off, I'm guessing to try this activity without any clothes.

Which leaves eight couples, since one bailed after the last drinking game.

I avoid looking at Ryan because his handsome face is ruddy, and that's doing things to my insides. I'm kinda embarrassed his thrusting made me wet. Good thing I'm wearing jeans.

But the next competition is worse.

The other girls and I change in the bathroom. When Ryan said I'd need to pack a swimsuit, I thought maybe we'd relax in a hot tub after the competition was over, not compete in an obstacle course.

Ryan does a double take when he sees me. "Not sure how well I can function with you in that bikini."

Inside, I preen like a peacock. But flattery won't win this competition. "Eyes on the prize, handsome."

He's wearing swim trunks, and his taut muscles are things of beauty. I want to revel in his body as well, but too much is riding on our success.

After the couples change into swimsuits, we all head for the sunroom. Seriously, how many wings does this dang house have?

As Ryan and I walk hand in hand, I have a hard time not admiring his lanky, hard body. No wonder girls lose their ever-loving mind around him. He's a total babe.

Hamilton jumps up on a chair. "Now for the good stuff! As some of you may know, my mother's family hails from Finland, where our small town has an annual tradition. It's called the Wife Carrying Championship. Legend has it that this competition dates back to the Vikings." He points outside, where tiki lamps light the backyard that's covered with a large tent. Beneath the tent are kiddie pools, logs, and what looks like a long mud pit.

Holy crap. This is crazy.

My eyes widen as Hamilton and his girlfriend demonstrate how we're supposed to race. He faces her, bends over, and sticks his head between her legs. Then he wraps his arms around her thighs and rises so that she's dangling over his back.

The guys all hoot and catcall. Except Ryan, who looks stressed out.

When I fantasized about him tossing me over his shoulder, this wasn't what I had in mind.

While toting his girlfriend, Hamilton points to himself. "Gents, here's a tip. Have your girls cross their legs in front of you. It helps balance you as you run. And while there are no restrictions on how you carry your woman, I suggest this one, which is a Nordic tradition."

The teams have to *run* like this?

He continues. "You have to make two circuits, and the first team that crosses the finish line wins fifty points." Dang, that's double the total number of points anyone has right now. "And not only will you get closer to bagging five grand, but you'll also win your lady's weight in beer!"

All the idiots around us cheer.

"Now, I know it's cold outside, but I figure this won't last longer than ten minutes, so suck it up. When you get back, head around to this entrance where someone will hose you off. In your rooms afterward, you'll find everything you need to warm up. Now, get your asses out there!"

Does this man really expect us to do this?

Judging by all the couples jogging out into the cold, he does.

Ryan pulls me to his side. "Come on," he says quietly. "Let's get out of here."

He starts to lead me away, but I jerk him to a stop. "We're *not* quitting." We can't quit. His family needs this money. Sure, I'd rather be home, wrapped in my fleece blanket and drinking hot cocoa, but that's not an option right now.

His eyes widen, and he lets out a dark laugh. "You're really gonna let me haul you around the back yard in thirty-degree weather in a bikini?"

"We didn't come this far to quit." I poke him in his hard chest. "And you'd better be fast and win this thing."

I grab his hand and drag him out back to the starting line, which is just a line of lacy bras lying in the dirt. All of the girls strap on helmets.

That asshole Hamilton, who's now sporting a thick winter jacket, yells, "You have sixty seconds to get into position."

Shit. I grab Ryan and turn to face him. "Don't drop me." When he doesn't move, I make a face. "I expect you to bend over and put your head between my legs. And don't look so shocked. I can't be the first woman to say that to you."

He laughs and moves into position. I spread my legs and lean over him as he lifts me into the air. His calloused fingers grip the back of my thighs, and I wrap my arms around his back. He's warm, and I shiver and tighten my grip. His hair tickles my belly. No wonder you're supposed to be dating. This is a really intimate position. My pussy is basically nestled to the back of Ryan's neck, and my face is smushed against his back.

I glance to the side, where one of the other couples gives up trying to get the girl in position. Her boyfriend sets her down, and she leans over and hurls. I pat Ryan on his firm ass. "You got this."

At least the guys didn't drink much tonight because then this game would be impossible. Maybe even dangerous. Even though Ryan's been nursing one beer all afternoon, I'm still apprehensive. Behind me, people are placing bets and commenting on which girl has the best ass.

My heart is pounding when the race gun goes off.

Thirteen

RYAN

I don't have time to think about how Jenna is plastered to my body, ass up, head down. I'm too busy trying to stay in the race.

Since the tent keeps the snow off the ground, it's not as bad as it could be, but there's a layer of frost on everything. All I'm wearing is swim trunks and Chucks, so if we wipe out, it's gonna suck.

Leaping into the kiddie pool, I somehow manage to keep us upright, but the couple next to us goes down and splashes us with ice-cold water. Behind me, Jenna curses.

I want to tell her I'm sorry, for everything really, but there's no time. After I slosh through the first two pools, I jump over a bench and slide into a huge pile of mud.

"Oh, fuck." I'm sure I'm about to fall face-first into it when Jenna flings herself backwards, and that somehow balances me. Or so I think.

We go tumbling down into a pile of bodies because I end up tripping over another couple.

I get up as fast as I can and pull Jenna into my arms, koala bear-style. We don't have time to get into that other position, which was scary as fuck. Even with a helmet, if Jenna went down on her head, I'd never forgive myself.

"This is better," she pants in my ear as she burrows into my neck. As I run, she wraps her legs around my waist.

"Cross your legs behind me."

We're coated in mud and she's slippery, but the other couples are covered in it too.

As we clear the next pool, I realize there's only one more team in front of us. "Holy fuck, Jenna. We're in second."

Her legs tighten. "We can do this! Don't stop!"

I decide not to try any death-defying maneuvers. I'm happy to stay in second place and try to get close to the lead couple. Maybe they'll wipe out.

Which is exactly what happens when we reach the mud pit again, except this time the dude on the ground, some asshole named Bryce, grabs my ankle and catapults me forward.

Jenna screams, and as my life flashes in front of me, I manage to twist and break her fall, but goddamn, everything hurts. "Fuck."

A minute later, Jenna's wide eyes meet mine. "Ryan, are you okay?" She's covered, head to toe, in mud.

I swallow and nod, which is tough when I'm just trying to pull in a full breath. "My dick's okay," I wheeze. "That's all that matters, baby."

She laugh-groans and tries to yank me up. "Hurry. There's just the straightaway. We can do this!"

Staggering to a stand, I have her jump on my back. That way if I fall, I don't have to worry about smashing her to pieces on my way down.

Everyone is cheering, and the carnage of bodies behind us reminds me how close we are to the finish. There's just that one couple in the pit with us, and thinking about how those douchebags tried to cheat pisses me off enough to keep moving.

When I get to the final pool, I turn my head. "Hold on, babe. I need both arms for balance."

"Don't worry about me!" Jenna yells. "Go!"

Somehow, I make it through the pool without killing both of us. The track is covered in water and mud, so I'm not even sure where the finish line is anymore, but I spot Hamilton and head for him by the end of the tent where we started.

I finally spot the line of dirty bras that have now been stomped across. Just a few more feet.

And that's when I trip again and fall on my face.

Fourteen

JENNA

Once I pick myself off the wet grass, I yank off my helmet and crawl to Ryan, who's face down on the ground.

I'm so glad I somehow managed to not land on top of him. My knees are bruised, and blood trickles down my leg, but I'm too worried about my partner to care.

Hamilton, that turd, stands there laughing, and I scream at him, "Help me, asshole!"

As gently as possible, we turn Ryan onto his back.

"Please say something. You're scaring me." Someone hands me a towel, and I wipe his face. When he mumbles something, hot relief floods my chest. I lean closer to hear him. "What did you say?"

"Come.... to my... next show."

I'm overwhelmed with relief. Tears flood my eyes, and I cover my mouth.

He cracks open his eyes and looks up at me. "Is that a no?"

"Ryan, what the hell? Are you okay?" I'm full-on crying now, and he lifts a hand and threads it through my muddy hair, and he pulls me down on top of him and wraps his arms around me.

"I'll live. Are you hurt?"

I shake my head and bawl into his neck.

Someone nudges me with his shoe, and I look up to see Hamilton grinning down at me.

"You guys won the race. Nice job. I just need to weigh you to determine how much beer you get."

I growl. I'm going to kill this dickhead.

Ryan must know I'm homicidal because he pulls me closer to his chest. "Don't worry about it, dude. I'd rather get cleaned up and make sure my girlfriend is okay."

My girlfriend.

My heart swells with happiness, and for a second, I forget we're pretending. That his hugs and kisses this weekend are all for show.

How would it feel to really belong to Ryan? To be at the center of his attention? To be the only one he wants?

I shake my head.

Don't be crazy, Jenna. Ryan won't give up his player ways for anyone.

Not even you.

Fifteen

JENNA

No matter what I do, I can't get warm. After getting hosed off downstairs and taking the hottest shower I could manage, I'm still shivering.

When Ryan steps out of the bathroom, he's carrying some first-aid supplies. "Here. Let's take care of your cut." He's only wearing a pair of jeans that hang indecently low on his slender hips. We were in such a rush to do that stupid obstacle course earlier, I didn't get enough time to appreciate the beauty of the man. His shoulders are wide and sculpted. His chest is built, but not overly so. And his enticing eight-pack leads down to a trail of blond hair that arrows into his jeans.

Surprisingly, aside from some bloody knees, he only has a few scratches on his face and some bruises, thank the good Lord. It could've been so much worse. Although I'm guessing he's going to be sore as hell tomorrow.

"I'm okay." I'm sitting on the bed, wrapped in a comforter. I'm probably getting blood all over it, but I'm too salty at the moment to care.

"Come on, babe. You don't want it to get infected." When he kneels in front of me, I relent.

"Watch your knees."

He nods with a smile. "They're bandaged up."

I stick out one leg from the giant comforter, and he cups my calf. I'm just wearing a T-shirt and panties, but I figure he's already seen me in a bikini, so I don't really care if he catches a glimpse of more.

But now that he's staring up at me, the intimacy of the moment does funny things to my belly. Maybe it's because we're finally alone together.

He dabs some ointment on my torn knee before he gently covers it with two bandages. "You were great today."

"You're the one who did all the hard work. I just hung on."

Shaking his head, he laughs. "Don't forget that you dominated those drinking games earlier, and that's what made me think we had a shot at winning this thing."

"I'm glad my old party ways paid off."

He stares at me for a long moment before he clears his throat. "Are you hungry? Why don't we eat something?"

My stomach rumbles in response, and we both laugh. "That would be great."

He grabs the plates we brought up earlier. I scoot to the head of the bed, and he sits next to me with a groan.

"Did you take some pain relievers? I left the bottle in the bathroom for you."

He nods. "Yeah. Thanks."

We quietly chow down on hoagies. He seems lost in thought, and I wonder if he's worried about his mom.

I search for something to say. "What kind of music does your band play?"

His eyes light up in a way that transforms his whole face. He's a handsome man, but right now, he's breathtaking. "Do you like indie rock?"

"I kinda like a little of everything. I know I'm going to sound like I'm in a retirement home when I say this, but I have a soft spot for classical because I used to dance."

"What kind of dance did you do?"

"Ballet."

"Why'd you stop?"

I hum as I think how to describe what happened. "For one, I never really fit into that scene. When I was little, I was always the kid hanging upside down off the barre, which is a cardinal sin in ballet. Once I got older and learned to comport myself the way I was supposed to, I got hurt."

His eyebrows pull together. "What happened?"

Leaning back, I pull the blanket back until I can stick out my other leg. "ACL tear. I was never really right after that."

"I'm sorry, babe. That had to be tough. I don't know what I would do if I didn't have music."

"Judging by all of your fangirls on campus, you must be good."

He shrugs. "I hope I am. Who knows? Only time will tell, I guess."

I'm surprised he's so modest. It makes me like him even more. "If I go to your show, will you sing me a song?" I tease.

He levels me with another megawatt smile. "Definitely."

I don't know if I should believe him, but I'm having fun flirting.

I yawn and cover my mouth with a laugh. "Sorry. I'm so tired."

"Shit. Yeah, we should go to bed. Who knows what Hamilton is cooking up for us tomorrow."

"Ugh, don't remind me."

We're in the lead by ten points. The second-place team that cheated in the last race can still win if they do well tomorrow. The competitor in me is rankled, and I'm out for blood, so I definitely need my beauty sleep.

Ryan sets our empty plates on the desk across the room and

rummages around in the closet for another blanket. When he starts to spread it on the floor, I shake my head. "What are you doing?"

"I figured you should get the bed."

"You're right. I *should* totally get the bed. But you should share it with me. I know it's a twin, but I'll feel bad if you sleep on the floor." I scoot over and pat the side he was on earlier. "I promise I won't ravish you in your sleep."

He chuckles. "You say that like it's a problem."

I bite my bottom lip and try not to smile. He turns off the lights and slides in next to me with a groan.

"Are you really okay?" I ask softly. It freaked me out to watch him wipe out at the end because he was so still.

"My shoulder is killing me, and my knees are raw, but I'll live."

We're quiet as we settle in and listen to some rowdy people in the other room.

"Ryan?"

"Yeah?"

"I had fun today. With you, I mean."

"I did too, princess."

I shiver again and burrow deeper into the blankets.

"Are you cold?" he asks.

"I can't seem to get warm. I couldn't find a hairdryer, so my damp hair isn't helping."

"Come here. I'll snuggle you."

I swallow as my heart starts to hammer against my ribs. "Do you think that's a good idea?"

"Are you saying that because I'm wildly attracted to you?"

I'm glad he can't see the ridiculous smile on my face. Since it's dark, it's easier for me to be honest with him. "I'm attracted to you too, Ryan," I whisper.

When he doesn't say anything, I start to freak out, but then he wraps his arm over me. "We'll just snuggle. That's it."

I nod and scoot back into him, except I'm still wrapped like a giant burrito. "One sec." I unravel myself and cover both of us with the blanket.

A contented sigh leaves me when he fits my back to his hard chest. "You kicked ass today," he says in my ear.

"I was really worried about you tonight. When you didn't move? I was so scared."

"Ah, hell. You don't need to worry about me, baby. I'm tough. I should've died from tetanus a half dozen times as a kid."

"Why's that?"

He's quiet for so long, I'm starting to wonder if he fell asleep, but then he sighs. "My cousin and I were always crawling over rusty shit. Instead of toys, we'd play with the crap people left behind."

"Left behind?"

"Threw out in our..." He coughs. "Threw out where I lived."

It hits me square in the chest, how differently we grew up. I'm so tempted to tell him I heard about his mama and that's why I'm here, but I know how guys get. They need to keep their pride. Crawling around in mud today was bad enough. I'll mention it another time because I don't believe in keeping secrets.

We're quiet for a few minutes, and then I tell him what's been on my mind all day. "I'm sorry I've been such a bitch to you in class. I don't really have a good excuse. I just got so irritated when our TA would fawn all over you, and then I'd try to ask a question or comment, and she'd look at me like I'm a dumb blonde."

He smooths a rough palm down my arm. "To be honest, that pissed me off too."

"Really?"

"You're smart. Beautiful. I think that intimidates her."

Huh. I never thought of it like that. Not sure if that's all true, or if he's just being nice, but I appreciate it regardless. "Are we going to still be friends next week in class? Or will it be weird, and it'll be like this weekend never happened?" My mama always says not to ask the question if you don't want to hear the answer, but it'll kill me if we go back to how things used to be.

"I think the genie's out of the bottle, Jenna. You're stuck with me now."

I chuckle and close my eyes. "Good. Because I kinda like being stuck with you."

Sixteen

JENNA

I'm not sure what wakes me up, but I'm cocooned in heat, and there's a deliciously hard body pressed to mine.

Ryan.

His big hand is resting on my breast, and his muscular thigh is wedged between my legs.

His breaths are slow and steady, so I know he's asleep.

I sigh and snuggle back into him, and he groans and presses his hips forward.

"Mm. You feel good," he mumbles, his voice raspy.

I arch back because his huge bulge is pressed up against my rear, and I can't help it. That gets me another groan, and his palm tightens on my chest.

Everything south of the border pulses with need, and I'm debating whether I should turn around when his hand slides down my belly. "You awake?" His hot breath raises goosebumps on my neck.

Nodding, I press back again, loving the groan that rumbles in his chest. "Ryan, you're making me horny."

He chuckles. "Back at ya, princess. But maybe I can help with that." He nibbles along my neck, and my nipples go rock hard. His smart fingers pluck them, and I squirm again. "Roll over, baby."

It takes a little maneuvering because this bed is so small, but when I finally get on my back, he leans over me. His hair falls rakishly over his eyes, and he gives me one of those beautiful smiles. There's just enough light streaming from the window that I can see his handsome face.

I reach up, and thread my fingers through his hair. "Are you going to kiss me?"

"Been thinking about doing it for a while."

"We kissed earlier tonight."

"But that was for show. This is just about us."

I absorb his words as I play with his hair. "Is there an us? I thought you were a 'live free and fuck around' kind of guy. If that's what you need, that's what you need, but I have to warn you, I don't do casual. Not anymore."

"Missed your casual dating window, did I?"

I shrug. "It's not for me. I need more of a connection if I'm going to sleep with someone, and deep down, I want something epic. You know, big declarations. Fireworks. Flames. I want to grow old with someone. Be the person my man reaches for in the middle of the night. The *only* person he reaches for. Granted, we might not work out—maybe we date for a little while and realize we're too different—but I don't believe in tasting everything on the table when you only crave one dish." Leaning up, I softly press my lips to his. "Am I scaring you yet?"

Pausing, he tilts his head. "Strangely, no. I like your honesty. That you don't play games."

His eyes burn into mine. They're coal black in the dark room, so I can't tell what he's thinking. "What's it going to be, Ryan? You want to take a chance on this, and we'll have mind-blowing sex? Or should I go to the bathroom and take care of myself? I won't hold it against you if you want to just stay friends."

This time, he leans down and licks my bottom lip. "Is that what we are, Jenna? Friends?"

"Yes, but it can't go farther than this if that's all you want." I palm his handsome face. "And for the record, I'd love to be your friend. You're a good guy, and I'm sorry I didn't see that sooner. I'm working on not being so judgy."

"So... what? You want to date me?"

I chuckle. "Why do you sound so surprised?"

"Just... I didn't think I was the kind of guy you'd go for."

"You shouldn't underestimate yourself," I whisper as I turn to face him.

We're nose to nose, and I run my finger over his rugged jaw. "I'd be honored to be your girlfriend. But we don't have to put a label on it. I just want to agree we won't see other people while we figure this out. Fair warning, though, I don't like girls hanging all over the guy I'm seeing, so if that would be a problem for you—"

"It's not. I've been at this band thing for a long time, and most of those women just want to fuck a musician. It's not really about me. And if I'm being honest, I'm not a fan of easy lays. I like my women a little feistier."

"Feisty, huh?" I smile. "I thought all men lived for that kind of buffet."

He leans forward, and the moonlight highlights his face. Good golly, he's pretty. "Since we're being honest here, you should know I need to fuck after a show. Those sets are ninety minutes of adrenaline, and it goes straight to my dick."

I laugh and reach down between us where I palm the erection straining his jeans. "Poor baby. Are you saying I need to go to all your shows?"

"Every single one," he says as he leans down to kiss me.

I turn my face away and set my hands on his chest. "If I don't? Are you the kind of man who'll grab someone else because it's quick and easy?"

"And jeopardize this with you? What, are you high?"

My smile widens, but I think we need to be really clear about our expectations. "Ryan, if you ever think this isn't working for you, or you'd rather have someone else, just tell me, okay? Don't cheat. I'd rather us be honest with each other and go our separate ways. If you can promise to always level with me, then I'd be game to give this a test run. And I know this is really fast, but I'm a balls-to-the-wall kind of girl and believe in going after what I want in life."

"And you want me?"

"I want you." I lean up to kiss him. "We could be epic."

He smiles against my mouth. "Kinda think we already are, princess."

Seventeen

RYAN

Having a girlfriend is the last thing I wanted, and then Jenna Gentry crashes into my life like a fucking hurricane and proves me wrong.

Staring down at this gorgeous woman, I make myself a promise not to screw this up. Jenna's spectacular looks aside, she's honest and sweet and feisty as fuck. Bonus that she doesn't shy away from saying what's on her mind.

It's weird to think this, but I love that she hasn't heard my band. She likes me for me. Not because I'm some rocker dude she wants to fuck or a charity case from the trailer park she wants to save. I've experienced both of those scenarios, and I'm over that shit. Nothing pisses me off more than pity.

That's another reason why I came to Boston. To get away from everyone who had me pigeonholed as that loser from the other side of the tracks. Trust me when I say there's nothing worse than dating some pretty girl who's too ashamed to introduce you to her parents.

I'm just now realizing how much my ex girlfriend fucked with my head. We got in a huge fight before Prom, and I found out the only reason we dated is because her friends had dared her to "slum it" with me. We were together for almost two years, and she fucking leveled me with one conversation.

After something like that happens, the last thing I wanted to do is have another serious relationship.

But there's something about Jenna that makes me want to take a chance.

When Jenna threads her hand into my hair and gently scratches, I groan. "You know, if you hadn't been so scary all semester, we could've been fucking each other's brains out for months now."

She laughs, and it's sultry and sexy. "Then we should make up for lost time."

Leaning down, I brush my nose against hers. "Been thinking a lot about our female orgasm discussion in the library last week and the fact you haven't ever had your pretty pussy properly licked."

Her mouth drops open in an adorable O. "I didn't say..." She pauses. "I did admit that, didn't I?"

"You absolutely admitted that, and I've been able to think of little else ever since."

She tries to hide an embarrassed smile, and I laugh and hold my hand over my chest. "It would be my greatest honor to do this. What do you say, babe? Can I go down on you and show you what you've been missing?"

As she nibbles her bottom lip, I pray she says yes.

"Only if I can return the favor and go down on you."

Who says prayers go unanswered?

Ignoring the way my entire body aches from wiping out earlier, I settle between her legs and take her face between my hands. "I don't think I've told you this before, but you're so beautiful. I literally can't stop staring at you when we're in class."

She looks down shyly, and it's so fucking sexy. "I hate when girls hang all over you. I think... I think I've been jealous."

My heart swells for this woman. I really dig how vulnerable she's being with me.

Ducking down, I taste her mouth. Kiss her as if we have all the time in the world. "Jenna, you're the only one I see. It's like the world dims when you're around." I tuck her hair behind her ear. "Let's take this slow." Words I've never said to anyone, much less thought. "Let's get to know each other. Learn to trust one another. And we'll go from there."

She sighs, and a beautiful smile tilts her lips. "I'd like that."

We come together in another kiss. It's sweet. Just tasting each other as she cradles me between her slender thighs.

I kiss her until she wiggles beneath me and starts to lift her hips.

When I reach down to grab the hem of her t-shirt, I pause. "Can I take this off?"

She nods, and a second later she's left in a tiny pair of pink panties.

Her tits are things of beauty. High. Perky. With tiny pink nipples.

Leaning down, I stick my face in her cleavage and press her tits to me. "I'm living the dream right here." She chuckles, and I smile against her skin.

She smells so sweet. We both used the body wash in the bathroom earlier, but Jenna's delicious scent still clings to her smooth skin. Are those pheromones making me insane for her? Who knows? But I want to gobble her up.

After licking one nipple a few times, I take it into my mouth and suck with a rhythm that makes her writhe.

I can feel her heat through my jeans. It's slowly driving me insane.

When I can't wait another minute, I make my way down her gorgeous body. Down her trim stomach. Over her pretty mound. Between her slender thighs. Where I make myself comfortable.

I drag my finger over her damp thong before I lean down and brush my nose against her. "Fuck, I'm so hard for you right now."

Glancing up at her, I watch her as I drag my tongue over her. Her hips tilt up and her hands grip the comforter. Little pants lift her chest. Her gorgeous tits heave, and I don't know who I'm driving crazy, her or myself.

"Lift your cute butt."

As I slide down her panties, I get the first look at her smooth, bare pussy and let out another groan. I wanna fuck her so bad, but I have to take tonight slow. I can't just ravish the woman. Jenna's special, and I don't want to rush this. I need to make her feel good and show her I appreciate her.

When I think back to that conversation in the library, there's something I need to know. "Princess, have you ever come during sex?"

She shakes her head. "I've come close, but..."

"But no one has ever gotten you there." It's a crime, honestly. No man should nut if he can't get his woman to the promised land.

"You up for the challenge?" she asks with a laugh.

I take a long, slow lick up her center, loving how she shivers beneath me. Christ, she's delicious. "Abso-fucking-lutely."

The time for talking is over. I dip my head and commit myself to getting Jenna off like it's my only mission in life. I spread her wetness with my finger before I press it into her tight hole. Her legs drop open, and I slowly spear her with a second finger.

Just watching how wet she's getting makes me want to jizz my pants like a randy teen. When it comes to Jenna, my control hangs by a thread.

I glance up her body as I fuck her with my hand, and holy crap, what a vision she is. Her blonde hair is spread all over the pillow, and her head is tossed back with abandon as she shifts her hips. Her gorgeous breasts bounce in rhythm with my fingers, and I suddenly get a vision of coming all over those pretty tits.

Her soft moans get louder, and by the time I spread her pussy lips with my other hand and lick her swollen clit, she's chanting my name.

It only takes a few light sucks before she pulsates around my fingers, arches her back, and lets out a scream.

I smile against her pussy as I lick her through her climax.

She collapses on the bed with a curse that makes me laugh. "Feel good, baby?"

"So good. My God. That was cataclysmic."

With a satisfied grin, I pull myself up from her sweet heaven and slide in next to her. Pull her to me where I hug her and kiss her forehead. After I wipe my face, of course. I'm not a total animal.

She nuzzles into me. Tosses her thigh over mine. Palms me through my jeans.

"It's my turn, right?" she asks as she kisses my neck.

"Not sure I could ever tell you no."

Settling over me, she pops open my jeans, and my eager dick springs out.

"Oh, my." She pauses to take me in. "That's quite the weapon you've got there. Do you need a special license to carry that thing around?"

"You're awfully good for my ego, babe." I might not have much to my name, but I've been blessed with a big dick.

Wrapping her hand around me, she leans down and takes a tiny lick of my tip and gives me a saucy smile. "Maybe I can rock your world like you rocked mine."

I drag my thumb over her bottom lip. "You already have."

Eighteen

JENNA

My bones feel like they've melted together, but I want to make Ryan feel good since he just introduced me to the Holy Spirit. With that incredible orgasm still pulsing through my veins, it's easy to forget my knees are scraped and my muscles are sore from Hamilton's dumb games.

I glance down at the mammoth in my palm and lean down to swipe it with my tongue again. The tip is weeping. Ryan's salty-sweet taste makes me grin against him. Everything about him turns me on. He has this earthy, sexy scent I can't get enough of.

His eyes are glued to me as I lick up his long length to get it good and wet. And then I drag my tongue around his thick crown. His chest rumbles with a deep groan, and his hips thrust up.

Reaching up, I lightly scratch down his chest before I lean down low and pull one of his balls into my mouth.

"Christ, Jenna."

His body goes rigid, and he thickens in my palm, so I take that as a sign I should give his other ball the same treatment.

Yeah, I'm a little bit of a freak, but Ryan looks like he can handle it.

When I let go of his dick to lick my palm, it stands straight up at attention. His cock is perfection. Thick. Tall. Proud.

I take him in hand again and jerk him off as I suck his tip. He might've made me come just a few minutes ago, but this is turning me on again, so I reach down and circle my clit.

"Fuck yes," he grunts. "Get yourself there again."

Tempting, but I have other ideas.

With some of my wetness, I circle him again and really start to pump. Every few strokes, I go deep. It's a sloppy blowjob. Pretty sure it looks like I'm drooling all over him, but Ryan looks like he's loving every minute of it, and frankly, I'm enjoying giving him a show.

His hand grabs a chunk of my hair and moves it out of my face before he fists it. He holds me still when I try to deepthroat him again.

There's a challenge in his eyes that makes me so hot. "What do you want, Ryan?" I ask before I rub him against my lips.

He hesitates. "I wanna cum on your tits."

I'm on board with this. "Switch places with me." I don't have to ask him twice.

He scoots out of bed and kicks off his jeans, which were hanging down his ass, before he straddles my chest.

"Get closer." I put my arms under his muscular thighs and grab his tight ass. "Fuck my face."

He pauses. "You look like an angel, but you're a dirty girl deep down. I fucking love it."

I laugh, and it feels so good to be able to let go and have fun when I'm being intimate with someone. This is what I was missing with my prior boyfriends. I could never let my guard down and be myself, but Ryan makes me feel like I'm safe with him.

Moving closer, he places his tip at my mouth, and I open for him. I press against his back to get him to move, and he takes the hint and goes deeper. His thrusts are shallow, and I appreciate the consideration, but he can be rougher.

I lean my head up to take him deeper. He rests his hand against the headboard and leans forward and sends himself down my throat. Pleased, I groan around him.

"You look so good stretched around me, princess." With his other hand, he traces my top lip. We watch each other as he moves in my mouth.

When he goes deep again, I hold him to me by pressing against his back, and the moment I let go, he backs off. He's grunting and cursing under his breath when he pulls out. I'm gasping for breath, but not in a bad way. Ryan hasn't pushed beyond my limits.

He grips his dick, looking like he's about to explode.

Reaching between his legs, I push my boobs together, and he doesn't need any instruction. He pumps between my tits, and I squeeze myself tight.

After a second, his head tilts up, and his body goes rigid.

"Oh, fuck." He scoots back suddenly just as hot ropes of come shoot across my chest. It lands on my lips and cheeks and boobs. I'm covered in it.

I trace my finger across my chest and bring it to my lips, where I taste him.

He gives me a heavy-lidded, blissed-out smile. "If I haven't told you yet, you're the best thing to ever happen to me."

I laugh again. "Of course I am."

And then we drag ourselves to the bathroom to clean up and take another shower, but this time together.

After another round of incredible orgasms, we snuggle in bed. I have a huge grin on my face as I close my eyes and rest my head on his chest. When he wraps his arms around me, I let out a contented sigh.

I could definitely get used to this.

Nineteen

RYAN

Waking up with a warm, naked Jenna in my arms is almost too good to be true. For a guy like me, good things feel fleeting. Like I'm going to blink, and she'll disappear.

Someone starts banging on the doors with a wakeup call.

Jenna growls and burrows deeper under the covers.

"Hey, gorgeous." I kiss her forehead. "We need to get up."

"Do we have to?" she grouses and squeezes me tight. "You're so cuddly. I don't want to move."

"You feel good too, babe, but we have to get downstairs."

"Ugh. How did Hamilton come up with these dumb games anyway?"

"I think he's just a rich guy with too much time and money on his hands. Plus, his parents go abroad for months at a time. This isn't even the craziest party he's ever thrown. He threw a bacchanal last spring. It looked like an orgy from that show *True Blood*."

Her head pops up, and her blonde hair is tangled on one side

414

and smushed on the other. It's adorable. "Did you bang some girls at the orgy?"

I laugh and shake my head. "I really didn't feel like getting fucked up on drugs and screwing some rando. My band played. It was a great payday, but I wanted to get out of there before someone OD'd or got arrested."

She pats my chest and collapses on me again. "Smart."

When I catch a glimpse at the clock, I groan. "Come on, baby. We'd better get going."

Sighing, she sits up and stretches, the blanket dropping to her waist and treating me to a beautiful view of her gorgeous tits.

I plant my mouth on one and tackle her to the bed. She laughs and shrieks, and I rub my hard dick between her thighs.

Groaning, I stop and drop my head to her chest. "I wanna fuck you so bad."

She threads her hand through my hair and scratches the back of my head. "Soon."

Nodding, I kiss her and drag myself out of bed. I get dressed without looking at her because I don't want to get tempted again.

"Today's the pole dance, right?" she asks behind me.

I drop my head back and press my palms to my eyes. "Just don't make me come in my jeans. That would be embarrassing."

She chuckles. "Isn't that the point, though?"

The bathroom door closes, and I'm grateful for a moment of solitude. This thing with Jenna is intense. What is it she said she wanted? Flames? We're a whole fucking inferno.

I love it, though. At the same time, I'm glad we haven't had sex yet. I need a sec to get my bearings. I'm already crazy about this girl. She's a wild child wrapped up in this angelic package I can't seem to get enough of.

She needs to go to one of my shows. She needs to see how out of control things get sometimes and make sure she can handle it. I have no intention of straying, but if she was jealous of our TA, I'm a little worried how she'll handle my drunk fans.

When Jenna emerges from the bathroom fifteen minutes later, her hazel eyes are rimmed with kohl, but her blonde hair is twisted up in a messy bun. She's wearing tortoiseshell glasses, a modest button-up white blouse, and cutoffs with some Chucks. It's an odd combination, but it works. She's fucking gorgeous.

I pause to take her in. "You're rocking my dirty librarian porn fantasy right now."

Her eyebrow lifts, and she taps her glossy bottom lip. "I can work with this."

We grab our stuff, and I toss an arm around her shoulders as we head downstairs. Before we reach the game room, I whisper in her ear, "Just remember. I want to win, but not if that means pressuring you into doing something you don't want to do."

She leans up and presses a kiss to my cheek. "Thanks, babe, but I got this."

Babe. Oh, I fucking like that word coming from her lips.

The crowd has thinned out since last night, but there are still at least fifty people standing around in addition to the four other competing couples, including that douchebag Bryce and his girlfriend, who are in second place. We have to check our phones today because Hamilton doesn't want today's activities to circulate online.

Everything from last night has been cleared out, but from what I can see through the fogged-up windows, his backyard looks trashed, not that he seems to care.

The female contestants are standing around in string bikinis. I glance at Jenna, who's the only one wearing clothes, but she looks calm, so I'm not gonna worry. Her confidence is hot as fuck. The other girls have everything hanging out right now. Jenna looks almost prim in contrast, and for some weird reason, that make me hard.

Then again, everything about this woman turns me on.

Hamilton strolls to the front of the room and flips on a mic. "Let day two commence!" he yells, and the crowd cheers.

I lace my fingers with Jenna's and squeeze. She gives me a soft smile. I keep looking for hesitation or worry, but she's super chill. If she's not worried, then I won't be either.

Hamilton jumps up on a makeshift stage. "Before the ladies get up here, the gents are gonna give the girls a lap dance. Rules of a strip joint don't apply. Feel free to touch each other. My buddies will pick the winners."

I tally the points in my head. If we lose this and the pole dance to Bryce, he'll snag the five K.

Jenna pulls me to the side and grabs my face between her palms. "We did not get dragged through the mud last night and nearly get pneumonia to lose today, so you get out there and give these people a show. Work me like you're in *Magic Mike*. You got the goods, so don't hold back, okay?"

Fuck, this girl. I kiss her. She'll never know how much this means to me. If we win, I won't have to worry about my mom and little brothers this winter.

The women sit in folding chairs at the front of the room while everyone else stands behind them, and "Pony" by Ginuwine blares from the ceiling.

One by one, the guys grind on their girls. Luckily, football players can't dance for shit. They have no rhythm.

Then it's my turn. Here goes nothing.

Twenty

RYAN

Like any good stripper, first I rip off my shirt, and the crowd howls behind Jenna. She grins and stares up at me like she's thinking about what we did last night, which, for the record, might be the highlight of my life.

As I dance in front of her, she gets into it and sways to the music too.

I spin and drop down to her knees, run my hands over her thighs. Lean over to run my nose down her throat. She reaches up and drags her hand down my chest as I lean back. Her hand doesn't stop when she reaches my jeans, though. The eye fuck she gives me is almost as hot as the way she palms me. Then my little minx winks, and I laugh.

I straddle her lap and hold the back of her chair as I mock-fuck her. I'm sure I look like the other douchebags, but I don't wanna feel self-conscious, so I just focus on Jenna, whose hot eyes are promising all kinds of sexy fun later. She tilts her head up and licks my abs, and my dick twitches. I whisper in her ear, "I'm gonna fuck you so hard later."

"Promise?" she asks coyly.

The look she gives me could light us both on fire.

When the song ends, nobody turns off the playlist, which kicks on "Body Moves" by DNCE, so I sing along with Joe Jonas. I keep dancing, spinning, acting like an idiot, but Jenna's right. We've come too far to back down. Besides, the crowd loves it. Hamilton hands me the mic, and now I'm in my element, crooning to my girl and serenading the room.

"That's no fair," Bryce yells as his girlfriend Annika shoots me dirty looks.

When Hamilton's asshole friends crown Bryce the winner, the crowd boos and starts chanting my name, but Hamilton doesn't care this isn't fair. He smacks my back. "Tough loss, dude. But there's still one more round."

Jenna jumps up and starts to run after him, but I pick her up by the waist and hold her to my chest. "Calm down, princess."

"They totally screwed you over," she huffs. "Even the crowd knows it."

It's possible this was rigged all along. I hadn't really paid attention to Bryce until the last competition yesterday, so I'm not sure if he got a leg up before that.

And his friends might pick his girlfriend to win the last challenge even if she can't dance, which would mean they'll take home the money.

I'm wondering more and more if I'll have to sell my amps and gear to keep my family warm this winter.

I spin Jenna around in my arms. "Don't stress out about it. If we win, great. If not, well, we gave it our best shot."

"This is bullshit."

Hugging her to me, I press my face against her neck. "I'm gonna look on the bright side. At least I'll get to watch you work a pole." And then I smack her ass, which gets me a laugh.

There's two rounds of drinking games for the guys. I come in second in one and third in another. It's not enough to knock us out of contention, but it's enough to give the third-place couple a shot at the five K.

But as I'm coming back from the bathroom, I spot some of Bryce's friends in the foyer having a serious discussion, and it sets off alarm bells in my head. I pause behind a pillar.

"He's got it in the bag."

"What if Annika can't dance?"

"Doesn't matter. Bryce will still win."

Fuck.

Before they see me, I duck down the hall.

I don't have the heart to tell Jenna what I overheard before she competes. It's possible those guys are just drunk idiots talking out their asses. Then again, they did pick Bryce to win the lap dance, and that douche can't dance his way out of a paper bag.

It probably all boils down to Hamilton. I don't know the guy well enough to say whether he'll let his friends cheat for the overall prize. Guess we'll see.

Even though I'm stressed out, when I see Jenna, I'm filled with fondness. It'll suck if we lose. Absolutely. But getting to know this woman has been a prize in and of itself.

"Kick ass up there, princess," I say before I pull her into a hug.

She kisses me and gives me a sassy wink as she walks away. "I got this."

The girls go up to the front of the room where they've installed a makeshift pole.

As I sit here and wait for Jenna to get her turn, I have to admit I'm more nervous for her than I was for myself. I have no idea if she can dance. She said she did ballet, but that doesn't mean she was any good at it. Even if she was, pole dancing is a far cry from twirling in *The Nutcracker*. I just hope this doesn't embarrass her.

Sultry music with a hard beat kicks on, and the first girl walks up to the pole hesitantly. She manages to crawl up it and back down again before she nearly falls on her face and has to be carried off. The second one manages a spin before she gives up and just dances around it.

Then Bryce's girlfriend Annika is up. It's obvious she's been practicing for this. She seems to have a routine that involves shimmying and grinding on the pole. She eventually climbs up it, shimmies again, and slides down, but there's nothing really sexy about her moves even when she accidentally flashes the crowd because her bikini gets untied.

When it's Jenna's turn, she trots up to the stage. While the other girls were dancing, she had unbuttoned her shirt, which is now tied in front. With her cute glasses and Daisy Dukes, I have a hard time not drooling.

Standing there, she kicks off her Chucks, one by one, until she's left in a simple pair of white socks.

A gritty song by Eminem and Dr. Dre comes on, and as she struts to the pole, the sway of her hips match the beat. She gives the crowd a saucy smile, unties her hair, and tosses her glasses. I hoot and holler with the crowd. Even if she's terrible at this, I'm proud as hell. She's so beautiful and confident, and I can't take my eyes off her.

I'm holding my breath as she reaches up behind her to grab the pole, and then she dips her body one way and then another.

Still swaying, she turns to give us her back and rises up on her toes as she leans forward, sending her butt into the air. She's so fucking sexy, I can't stand it. I can't wait to bend her over a piece of furniture and bite her little ass.

A moment later, she's up and spinning on the pole. It looks so effortless. She's a study in long lines and taut muscles. Then she crosses her legs and does this intricate spin that makes her look like one of those Cirque du Soleil acrobats dancing on air. When she comes down in the splits, the crowd roars.

A few sways later, she's on her feet and kicks up one slender leg, and holds the damn thing right by her ear. There's that ballet experience. Mental note for later: Jenna's flexible as fuck.

Tilting forward as her leg goes back behind the pole, she does some complicated move I can't begin to describe, and next thing I know, her legs are crossed on either side of that contraption as she holds her body parallel to the ground. She's facing the ceiling and arches back until her hand drags along the floor as she spins.

Holy shit. She's amazing.

Leaning back, she grabs the bottom of the pole and kicks out one leg while her other foot latches to the top. She arches off the damn thing and then suddenly flings herself upright and catches the pole with her hands.

I sit there, dumbfounded, as she brings down the house.

"Goddamn," Hamilton shouts next to me. "Fuck, yeah, baby!"

It's my turn to shoot the dirty look. He sees my expression and laughs. "You lucky bastard."

Hell, yes, I'm a lucky bastard. Because this gorgeous woman is going home with me tonight.

Twenty-One

JENNA

Holy hotcakes, we won. But there's no time to bask in the glory. With the way Bryce and his friends are eyeballing us, I'm worried they're going to corner us outside.

Ryan and I race upstairs to our room as he tells me about the conversation he overheard just before I competed on the pole.

"So those goons might come after us?" I toss my bag on the bed, fling five grand in it like we just held up a bank, and hop up and down as I change into jeans and slip on my Chucks.

"I'm not sure. Let's take off so we don't find out." Ryan checks the bathroom, tosses a shirt in my duffle, grabs my hand, and we're out the door again as I tug on my coat.

"Shit." He yanks me across the hall and into a closet.

My heart is racing as I press myself to Ryan's back. Outside, I can hear that meathead talking to his buddies.

"I swear they came up here," he slurs. "If we don't get the money, I can kiss that coke deal goodbye."

Of course this is about drugs.

After a few doors slam, it's quiet, and I let out my breath. "What's their plan? To beat you up and take the cash?"

"Pretty much. Yeah."

"Those assholes."

He brings my palm to his lips, where he presses a kiss. "Let's try going out the kitchen, but if we get stopped by those dicks, I want you to keep going. Fling the bag at them and run."

"Are you insane?" I turn him around until he faces me. It's pitch black in here, but I want him to hear me clearly. I poke his chest. "I am not leaving you, you big nut. That's not how this works. We're in this together, so if they corner us, just don't do anything that puts you in traction because I have plans for you later."

He chuckles and pulls me into a kiss so hot, I want to melt at his feet. "Food for thought, princess."

Cracking the door, he peeks out. When the coast is clear, we sneak out to the back stairwell.

The whole time, my heart is pounding. The last thing I want is for Ryan to get beaten up. It's messed up what those dicks are willing to do for cash.

When we reach the kitchen, there are a few staff members standing around. I wave my hand. "We were never here." I fling a few bills from my duffle, and when we reach the backyard, I laugh at the look Ryan gives me. "What? I saw that in a movie once. It looked effective."

"Did you live a parallel life of crime I should know about?" he asks as we slide through the snow, which is coming down steadily.

"I have an active imagination. Maybe that's why I'm a creative writing major."

"That's cool."

"What's your major?" It's funny we're having this conversation as we're trying to escape this bizarre situation.

We're slipping and sliding down the driveway when he tells me he's studying business.

I wrinkle my nose. "How does that work with your music? Shouldn't you be a music major?"

"It's my Plan B. Besides, the number of musicians who get their big break only to blow their advance on stupid shit is so common it's cliché."

When he says it like that, I get it. "Smart. It's good to learn how to manage money and do business-y things." That's stuff I should probably learn too.

He laughs as we pull up to his car and uses his arm to wipe the snow from the windshield. "Business-y things?"

"Shut up. Let's get out of here so you can warm me up."

His smile goes wolfish. "I love the way you think."

Twenty-Two

JENNA

As we wind through Cambridge, I tell him to pull over. "See that parking lot in front of those apartments? Park there."

"Why do we want to do this?" he asks, though he turns off the road.

The moment he stops the car, I'm on him.

"So I can have my way with you," I mumble against his mouth.

He groans, reaches down to push back his seat, and then pulls me into his lap where I straddle him. It's a tight fit, but I don't care.

Gripping my hair, he tugs my head back so he can press wet kisses down my neck as I grind down on him. "You were so hot when you did that lap dance. I might need another performance."

"Jenna, I've been hard since you stepped up to that pole. Where the hell did you learn how to do that?"

I lean back and look down at him. "Remember when I told you I couldn't do ballet anymore? When I was finally able to dance again, I started taking pole dancing classes. But don't tell my parents, because they thought they were paying for aerobics."

He laughs and threads his cold fingers through my hair. "Amazing. You were incredible. Hey, what are you doing Saturday night? I've got a show next weekend. I was serious when I invited you. Wanna come?"

"I'd love to come." I waggle my eyebrows.

We make out until the windows fog, and I start to sweat. I lose my shirt and strip off his. He tugs down my bra and sucks and bites me until I'm so turned on, it's painful. I'm just about to suggest we move to the backseat when someone bangs on the window. I yelp and hold my hands against my chest.

Ryan cracks the window, and I cringe to find a cop. He stares at me, then Ryan. Then back to me. "You okay, ma'am?"

My head does a bobblehead nod. "Yes, sir. I'm great, sir."

He gives Ryan a glare. "You're parhked in a fire lane, kids," the policeman says, his Boston accent thick. "You have exactly thirty seconds to get the hell outta he-ah before I have you towed. I'd be giving you a ticket if I wasn't freezing my ass off right now."

"Sorry, Officer!" I yell as I scramble off Ryan's lap.

He taps again on the window again. "Snow's coming down pretty harhd. Get yourselves home now."

"Yes, sir!" I say as I dangle over into the back seat to get our shirts. "Thank you!"

Once Ryan and I are fully clothed again, we look at each other for a second before we bust out laughing. He starts the car. "What a cockblock."

As we hit the road again, it's getting dark and the snow's getting bad. "Maybe that was a blessing in disguise. I didn't realize how bad the weather was getting."

At least it's Sunday night, so there's not too much traffic, but it still takes an hour for what should probably only take ten minutes.

When he pulls up to my brownstone, I dig around my bag,

trying to find my phone. "Oh, shit."

"What?"

"We never got our phones from Hamilton."

"Fuck." He rubs his face. "I need to call my mom." Groaning again, he closes his eyes and leans his head back. "I'll go back tomorrow to get them."

I nod. "Okay. But hey! Cheer up. We won five grand!" I think it over a moment before I take the stack of cash out of my duffle and hand him the entire wad.

Ryan frowns and tries to hand it back. "Count out your half."

"Keep it. So you can go home for Christmas."

He freezes. Opens his mouth. Closes it. "What are you talking about?"

It's probably time to come clean. "Don't get mad, but I overheard your conversation last week at the library when you were talking to your mom."

When he doesn't say anything, I start rambling. "Airline tickets are so expensive right now, and I thought if you had my half too, it would help, and then you could go home to visit and wouldn't have to worry about your family. That way you could see your little brother. Make sure he's okay."

His whole expression changes in a flash, and his jaw goes tight. "You were snooping on me? Because, what? I challenged you during our discussion? Because I gave you shit in class?"

"What? No." I shake my head. "I was just coming out of the bathroom and heard your voice. I felt bad that your family is obviously going through tough times. But take what we won. This way, your mama can pay the bills, *and* you can head home for the holidays."

He's quiet a long minute. It's getting awkward.

"So this is about pity?" His eyes go glacial as he tosses the money on my lap like it's diseased. "Is that why you decided to step off your pedestal and be nice to me? Because you felt... because you felt bad for me?"

Those words, like well-placed barbs, sting. "I... no. I mean, why is it wrong to want to help?"

His dark laugh fills the car. "I get it now. You thought you'd slum it for a while, huh?"

What's happening here? Where's the sweet guy I spent all weekend with?

My eyes sting. "Ryan, don't be like this. I like you. I think we have a lot in common and—"

"A lot in common?" He spits the words. "What, with your designer clothes and leather bag? I bet your family has a huge house. It's probably nice and warm there right now in the dead of winter, and you never have to worry about bills and whether or not they have enough money to put food on the table. Princess, we have *nothing* in common."

Someone honks behind us, and I flinch. "You're being an ass. All I've done is try to help you and—"

"Maybe I don't want your fucking help."

There's a huge lump in my throat, and my heart is racing. I keep waiting for him to tell me this is a joke, but based how his eyes are narrowed on me, he's pissed.

How did I get this guy so wrong?

Does he really think I'm just a bitchy, spoiled princess?

"Looks like I wasted the entire weekend. Message received. Sorry I busted my ass for you." As I let out a pained laugh, I swipe the treacherous tears that slide down my cheeks and grab my bag. "Have a nice life, Ryan Hunter. Good luck with that chip on your shoulder." When I get out of the car, I throw the money back in his lap. "Merry Christmas, jerkoff."

I slam the door closed and slide around the walkway until I reach the steps to my brownstone. He calls out my name behind me, and I hold up my middle finger before I get inside.

Seriously, fuck Ryan Hunter.

I wish I'd never met him.

Twenty-Three

RYAN

What am I doing? Why am I arguing with her? Jenna's right. I'm being a total asshole.

I leap out of the car and call her name. She gives me the finger before she disappears inside her brownstone.

The car behind me honks again, and I stand there like an idiot. Jesus, how did I screw this up so badly?

"Are you gonna stand there all day or are you gonna move before we both get snowed in?" some guy in a Bronco yells at me.

Reluctantly, I head home. I'll call Jenna tonight to apologize and...

Damn it! I don't have my fucking phone.

I consider turning around, but the streets haven't been plowed yet, and I'm pretty sure I only have a small window of time to get off the road before I get stuck.

It takes me another forty minutes to get down Com Ave and pull into my shitty apartment in Allston. It's cold and empty. My roommates are probably holed up with their girlfriends, which is what I would be doing if I hadn't flipped out on Jenna.

Way to fuck up a good thing, idiot. That girl was nothing but sweet and caring, and you shit all over her.

I collapse on the couch and groan when I think of the look of devastation on her face when I went off on her.

For some reason, I think back to a lecture we had earlier this semester in the Psychology of Human Sexuality. Our professor likes to go on tangents, and that afternoon he shared ways people self-sabotage.

"If you tend to wreck perfectly viable relationships with lying, cheating, or other forms of self-sabotage, you need to take a long look at yourself," he'd said. "These behaviors often stem from a fear of vulnerability, a fear of rejection, or a fear of attachment."

I scrub my face. Guess I'm that asshole.

Never thought I'd be the perfect candidate for therapy, but here I am.

When my cousin blows through the front door an hour later, I borrow his phone to call my mom. I sit on the edge of my bed and dial.

It takes her a second to realize it's me.

"Hey, honey," she says. I can hear the fatigue in her voice. "Why are you calling from Sean's phone?"

"Long story. Listen, I'm gonna wire you the money first thing tomorrow."

"Are you serious?"

"Yup. I got it." She starts to cry, and my gut twists hard. No one wants to hear their mother sob. "It's enough to cover you for a little while. Help you make that first payment for Denny's hospital bill."

And it's all thanks to Jenna.

A deep shame washes over me. How did I get so screwed up that I can't accept a gift from a lovely woman?

My mom sniffles. "Please tell me you didn't do anything illegal to get it."

"I swear."

I'm lost in my thoughts when my mom hums. "Are you okay, Ry? You sound upset."

I blow out a breath. "I just screwed up a really good thing, and I'm angry at myself."

"Is this about a girl?" she asks hesitantly.

We never discuss relationships, and it's awkward as hell, but if someone can be honest with me, it should be my mother.

"Yeah. It's about a great girl."

"Please tell me you didn't cheat on her. I raised you better than that."

"Mom, no. I didn't cheat. I would never do that. Come on."

"Thank God. I was about to bust your ass."

I chuckle and lean back on my bed. "I might deserve a good ass-kicking anyway." I groan and decide to spill my guts. "Remember when I dated Sarah Mattheson in high school?"

"The one who wouldn't go with you to the prom?"

"Yeah. I never told you why." I clear my throat. "She didn't want to introduce me to her parents."

"Why the hell not?"

How do I say this without offending my mom? "She came from a wealthy family, and she didn't think her parents would want her prom date to pull up in Uncle Bill's beater."

My uncle used to loan us his old Ford. It was rusted, and the muffler was loud and blew black smoke out the tailpipe, but it ran.

"What a little brat."

"I suppose I see her point now. We'd be all dressed up, and I'd drive up to her house looking like the hired help. Anyway, we got in a huge fight about it and broke up." I don't mention how she felt sorry for me and dated me on a dare to "slum it" with the poor kid from the trailer park.

I rub my chest. "Anyway, there's this girl in my psych class. She's gorgeous. Funny. Outgoing. Totally out of my league—"

"Ryan Andrew Hunter, don't you let me hear you talk like that again. No one is 'out of your league,' do you hear me? You're a good young man with a big heart and a great personality. You take after me. Of course you have a fabulous personality."

I laugh. "Yes, ma'am."

"Tell me about this girl."

"Jenna is incredible. At first I thought she was a snob, but she's not. She's selfless and sweet. And I totally went off on her and ruined everything after she spent the whole weekend helping me." After I explain what went down, my mom sighs.

"Oh, honey. I'm sorry Sarah hurt you so badly that you're having a hard time dating someone else. I love Dr. Drew. Do you ever watch him? I think he would say you got triggered."

My psych prof has used that term before, and yeah, that sounds about right.

"What do I do to make this right?"

"You owe Jenna a huge apology."

"Of course." I've never groveled for a woman before, but I guess there's a first time for everything. "But what can I do to show her I'm sorry and ask for a second chance?"

She thinks about it. "You should put your talents to good use."

What does that mean?

Twenty-Four

RYAN

The snowdrift outside is so high, I can barely get out my apartment. Classes are canceled, which sucks because I was hoping to see Jenna. I'm thinking I should get her phone back, and that would give me a good reason to go see her. She'll have to open her front door if I have her iPhone.

After I hoof it to the corner to wire my mom some money, I dig out my roommate's car, but I nearly stall out a block away. I doubt there's any way to make it across town, so I decide to wait.

By the next morning, the streets are plowed and classes resume. I finally retrieve our phones from Hamilton's, but no one answers at Jenna's place.

On Wednesday, I get to class early. My leg is bouncing as I wait for Jenna to arrive, but she never shows up. The second class ends, I beeline to her place.

"Hi, I'm here to see Jenna," I say into the speaker in the entryway after I buzz her suite.

"Who's this?" the unfriendly female voice asks.

"Ryan Hunter."

"You're dead to her. Go away."

Click.

Damn. That's cold.

I try again, and that same lovely person answers again. "What part of 'go away' was unclear?"

"I fucked up. I admit that. And I'm really sorry I hurt her."

"You should be, asshole."

"Don't hang up! I brought her phone."

The speaker muffles for a second, and then she says, "Leave it there."

"Someone could steal it."

"I'm coming down now."

Click.

Jesus. I wipe my sweaty hands on my jeans before I pull out Jenna's phone. It's crazy that I'm standing here sweating when it's twenty-eight degrees outside.

Through the giant glass window in the door, I see a little blonde with death in her eyes stomp down the stairs. She swings open the door and crosses her arms. "Why are you still here?"

I hold out my hand. "Hi. I'm Ryan. Also known as the dickhead. I'm here to grovel and plead my case." From my backpack, I pull out a dozen roses. I flick off a few mangled petals and hold them in front of me. "As charming as you are, these are not for you."

Her eyes soften when she sees the flowers, but a second later she reverts back to Wednesday Addams, the Barbie version. "I'm Clementine. Hater of Men. Buster of Balls. Destroyer of Small Egos and Smaller Dicks."

I laugh and then attempt to school my expression when she raises her eyebrow. "Hi, Ball Buster. Please let me speak to Jenna and apologize for my momentous lapse of reason."

"You made my roommate cry. She never cries. She's a ray of

fucking sunshine on the cloudiest winter day. The kind of person puppies love and little birds come out to sing for. And *you made her cry.*"

Hearing that tears up my heart. "I never meant to hurt her. I swear."

She stares at me so long, I shift. Finally, she sighs. "Give me the phone and the flowers. I'll make sure she gets them."

I hand them to her and scramble to make a last-ditch effort. "Jenna is the most amazing woman I've ever met, and if I fuck this up, I'll never forgive myself. Have you ever had 'the one who got away?'" I rub the back of my neck, weirded out that I'm having this conversation with a total stranger. "I don't know how to describe it, but I'm worried Jenna's this person for me, and if I lose her before we even begin, I'm going to have a huge void in my life and not know how to fill it."

I blink, not knowing where that word vomit came from. It's not untrue, though. There's something special about Jenna, and I want to get to know her, to find out if what we have could develop into more.

Clementine's icy demeanor thaws and her eyes go soft again. "Jenna's sick." Her head tilts as she thinks. "Maybe you could get her soup and tissue. Some zinc drops and orange juice. Her nose is red, and she's snotty."

Jenna helps me all weekend, lets me drag her through a wet and rainy obstacle course, and I make her fucking cry and get her sick. I'm such a dick. "Of course. I'll get that now. Will you promise to open the door again?"

Even though she agrees, when I return an hour later with everything Clementine suggested, no one answers.

I leave the food in the foyer and text Jenna. Now that she has her phone, at least I can start apologizing.

I know u don't want to talk to me, so I'm leaving ur soup in the foyer. It's still hot. I hope u feel better. I'm really

fucking sorry, Jenna. I probably don't deserve ur friendship, much less anything else. I hope u'll forgive me and let me make it up to u.

And then I walk away.

Because I'm not sure what else to do.

Twenty-Five

JENNA

I wipe my nose with the tissue Ryan left me and read his text for the millionth time.

"Maybe you should talk to him," says Harper, glancing up from her textbook.

"I'll admit he did look pretty pathetic downstairs." Clementine sniffs. "I suppose he seems sorry. The flowers were a nice touch."

After I wipe my nose, I slouch into my blanket. "Y'all, I hate arguing. And I kinda shut down when people yell at me." Not that Ryan yelled at me exactly. But it felt like he did.

Harper pats my hand. "Doesn't mean you can't work through this. If you really like the guy, maybe he's worth it. But I'd have him explain why he jumped to the conclusions he did before you consider it."

"Seeing how I can't skip class anymore, I'll have to see him eventually."

Clem hands me another tissue. "You had a hundred-and-four-degree fever. I wouldn't describe that as skipping class."

"Well, I was *thinking* of skipping class. I just got lucky with a fever."

My roommates chuckle, and I burrow deeper into my blanket.

I want to talk to Ryan. I miss him more than I'm comfortable admitting.

I'm usually a 'jump in feet first and ask questions later' kind of person, but given how much I like this guy and how badly he hurt me, that's probably not a good idea.

That dressing-down stung, and I'm not over it yet.

Twenty-Six

JENNA

By the weekend, I'm finally feeling better.

And I'm reconsidering things with Ryan. Now that I've had a little time, I can appreciate his apology. I'm reserving judgment until we talk face-to-face, though.

I pull up the website for the club where he's playing tonight.

Three bands are performing. I think Ryan's is Tragic Paradox, which is headlining.

I glance at the clock. My heart pounds when I realize I probably only have an hour to get down there. I bite my thumbnail until it's a little nub.

I growl and drop my head on my desk. I can't handle this. Am I going to be a nervous wreck if I sit home all night?

Fine. I'll go, dang it.

What's the worst thing that could happen? We argue again? He tells me I'm a spoiled little brat, and I knee him in his balls?

Okay, I would never resort to violence.

But I'd think about it.

Crap. What am I going to wear?

I sniff my armpit. Thankfully, I'm fresh from a shower I had this morning. I run around my room and try on three outfits before I settle for a slouchy black sweater that comes off my shoulder, a pair of leggings, and black boots. I go for thin, gold hoop earrings, because those are always in fashion, and a few bangles.

Looking at myself in the mirror, I wonder if he's going to take one look at me, see that rich girl, and write me off. Not that I'm rich exactly, but it sounds like my comfortable life is a far cry from what his family has experienced, and that makes my heart ache.

I take a deep breath. I guess if he sees me as a stereotype, if that's all I am to him, then he's not the man I thought he was.

But would he have bothered with the flowers and soup if that's truly how he feels?

Please don't be an asshole, Ryan.

Except I've never lived my life with fear, and I'm not about to start now. I'll admit I wussed out by not going to class this week. I'm ready to get back to who I know I am deep down.

Since I don't have time to do anything fancy with my hair, I tie it up in a messy bun. Then I swipe on some eyeliner, a little mascara, and pink gloss.

Clementine is studying in the living room when I rush out and motion to my outfit. "Is this okay?"

"You look great. You're going, huh?"

"Yeah." Reaching into my purse, I lightly spritz myself with my favorite scent. "You available later in case I've strangled him and thrown him in a trunk somewhere?"

She chuckles. "I'll bring the shovel."

This is why I love my roommates. They always have my back.

As I open the front door, I tell her to wish me luck.

"You don't need it!" she yells.

I hope she's right.

It's almost midnight by the time I get to the club, which is dark and crowded. Along one side is a long bar. Tall tables dot the perimeter, and the stage stretches across the back.

I grab a mojito at the bar, though I probably shouldn't be drinking since I've been sick, but I'm anxious to to see Ryan.

The bands must be between sets because a guy is up on the stage, messing with the drums. I sit at the edge of the room, next to a rowdy table of girls.

"I'm so getting laid tonight!" a beautiful woman with long black hair yells to her friend. Actually, they look like sisters, possibly twins.

"Maybe he's in the mood for double trouble," her twin says.

Do those sisters really tag-team a guy? Gross.

"There's always a line waiting for him after the show," the third girl says. "Good luck."

"He texted back! He said to come say hi afterward! You know what that means!"

I freeze, hoping I'm not hearing Ryan's booty call making plans to hook up with him later.

She elbows her twin. "Let's go to the front so we can flash him!"

I watch the girls elbow their way to the stage.

A storm of emotions swirls in my belly.

Did I wait too long to talk to Ryan? Is he over me already and back to banging groupies two at a time? Or was he just playing me last weekend, and I was never anything special?

I decide if he can't wait *one week*, then this was never going to work anyway.

Crossing my arms, I silently seethe and think of all the things I'm going to yell at him later if he was just screwing with me.

I'm ordering another mojito when the band takes the stage. A spotlight lands on Ryan's handsome face, and he waves to the crowd. All the females in the audience collectively squeal, and while I'm too upset with him right now to fangirl, I'll admit he looks good up there.

With how dark the room is and the bright lights shining in his eyes, I doubt he can see me. I'm okay with that. I'm curious to see him in his natural element.

He's wearing a black t-shirt and jeans that look so good on his lean, muscular body. Ugh, he's a handsome bastard. And why is a man with a guitar strapped to his chest so sexy? I've never understood the excitement over musicians, but clearly I was listening to the wrong bands.

Tragic Paradox kicks off the set with an up-tempo song. It's a fast, driving beat, and everyone seems to know it. When Ryan starts to sing, chills erupt up and down my arms.

Dang, this man can sing. He sounds like a cross between Joe Jonas and Charlie Puth, but edgier and more rock.

Song after song, he owns the stage. He works the crowd and puts his whole heart into every song. I'm sure the girls are flashing him from time to time because his bassist elbows him to look, but Ryan doesn't make a big deal about it. He just keeps singing.

After several songs, things slow down, and Ryan pulls up a stool and strums. "Have you ever met a woman who knocked you on your ass? Someone who stole your heart from the first hello?"

"Are you talking about me, Ryan?!" one of the girls screams.

He tilts his head and looks out at the crowd. "I wrote it for a very special woman."

Freaking out, I fold my hands against my lips. Is he talking about me? Or am I the biggest narcissist ever and thinking he means me when this is probably just the kind of stuff he says at all his shows?

"This is a new one," he rasps into the mic. "It's called 'Would You Be Here.'" The spotlight is on him as he strums, and the girls in the front row scream. His band doesn't join him. Ryan tilts his head as he plays a hauntingly sweet melody.

"Dancing girl

Sparkling eyes
Wants the starlight
Streaking her sunrise.

Quiet streets
Blankets of snow
Echoes of a place
Only she would know.

Would you be here?
Would you be here?
I'd give it all up now
Just to have you near.

Laughing girl
Secret smiles
Wants a fire
Burning her moonlight.

Quiet nights
Empty space
Left it behind
Gone without a trace.

Would you be here?
Would you be here?
I'd give everything
Just to have you near."

·   ·   ·

By the time he repeats the chorus, tears streak down my face, and my heart is in my throat.

I can't wait to see him backstage.

Twenty-Seven

RYAN

"Great show, man." A dude in one of the opening bands pats me on the back, and I force a smile as I make my way to the greenroom.

I just need a few minutes to myself to clear my head.

I've never had trouble focusing during a gig, but tonight, I couldn't stop thinking about Jenna and wishing she was here tonight. But since she never bothered to text back, I'm guessing this is the last place she'd go.

It took me a while to pack up my gear because people kept talking to me, and now the greenroom is full. My bandmates and fans litter the room, beer and bottles in every hand. I'm debating if I could just bolt, but that's not fair to my guys. I always deal with the money, and I'm not sure any of them should handle our funds right now given they're already drinking.

Bypassing the crowd, I head straight to the small bathroom off to the side. I unzip my jeans to take a piss, which is uncomfortable with the wood I'm still sporting, but I can't really help my body's reaction.

I wasn't joking with Jenna when I told her shows make me hard, but if I wait long enough, it'll go away. Or I can handle it when I get home. Because I won't find someone to take the edge off. Unless she's a feisty little blonde with hazel eyes and an ass-kicking attitude, I'm not interested.

I'm not sure how much longer I can try to pursue her before Jenna gets a restraining order, but I want to give her some time to recover from being sick. Then I plan to play the long game. If a woman is worth it, I'm more than willing to be patient and wait. And everything in me is saying Jenna's worth it.

Bending, I lean forward and place my hand against the wall so I can aim my wayward dick down. I'm mid-stream when the door busts open, the flimsy hook lock falling to the floor, as the twins stumble in.

"Ryan!" the girls squeal.

Fuck me.

And I don't mean that in the physical sense.

"Ladies, I need a minute. I'll meet you outside."

Exhausted, I close my eyes and try to finish my business so I can jam my junk back in my jeans. Of course I have to deal with this shit tonight.

Next thing I know, one of them is kneeling on the sticky floor and the other one is fisting my hair and trying to get me to kiss her.

What the fuck?

Turning my face away, I try to keep my balance to tuck myself away without catching my dick in the zipper when a gasp from the doorway has me looking up.

Jenna's standing there, a horrified expression on her face.

I take stock of how the twins are halfway undressed, their tits hanging out. When that happened, I'm not sure.

"Baby, no," I say as I shove the groupies off me. "This isn't what it looks like."

"I'm not fucking stupid, Ryan. This is exactly what it looks like." She shakes her head, murder in her eyes, as she backs away.

Goddamn it.

I try to run after her, but trip over the twins and land in a heap on top of them. Their cloying perfume makes me cough. "Jenna!"

By the time I scramble up and out of the packed greenroom, she's gone. I rush out and check the back entryway before I try the front of the club, but there's no sight of her.

Goddamn it!

How did I screw this up again?

Because I'm pretty sure there's zero chance Jenna's gonna give me the time of day now.

Once I square away my band's payment for the night, I borrow a car and drive down to Jenna's.

No one answers.

Twenty-Eight

JENNA

Ignoring the looks of the other drunk college students on the T, I let myself cry. I'm not a fan of public displays of heartbreak on the subway, but I can't keep it in. I decide to give myself exactly one hour to purge Ryan from my system before I pull myself together.

Deep down, I know I shouldn't be this worked up about a guy I only really started talking to last weekend, but our connection was intense. I guess I can admit I started developing feelings for him earlier in the semester, but that makes me feel foolish. How can you have feelings for someone you barely know?

I thought we could be more. I thought we could turn into something epic.

And tonight, everything went to hell in a handbasket.

Toward the end of the show, I'd started talking to one of the bartenders. She'd told me to give the band time to break down their gear, and she and I chatted about this new dance studio that just opened up.

I'd been so excited to see Ryan. I feel like a dumbass.

That song had really spoken to me, and I was hoping that…

Well, it doesn't matter anymore, does it?

Nothing could've prepared me for what I stumbled on backstage.

Now I understand what his bandmate had meant.

When I'd asked if he'd seen Ryan, he pointed toward a room off the side and said, "Go get in line. He might have something left for you." I saw a woman there, just outside that bathroom, and walked around her to see what looked like a threesome.

Nausea presses up the back of my throat, and I hold my hand over my mouth. Puking on the subway would suck.

As the T pulls up to my stop, I wipe my nose with my sweater, a very classy move, but I'm too heartbroken to care.

Ryan Hunter has shown me what he's all about, and I'm smart enough to believe him.

Twenty-Nine

RYAN

Fifty-two apology texts later, I wonder if Jenna is a lost cause. Since we don't sit together in our Monday lectures, I know there's no shot at talking to her. During Wednesday's smaller session with our TA, Jenna full-on ignores me.

"Come on, princess," I whisper. "You didn't even read my messages. I swear to God that wasn't what it looked like."

It's like I'm talking to a brick wall because she never turns my way.

Our TA Mallory pauses by our row when we have to turn in our assignments. "That was a great show Saturday night, Ryan. My friends and I stopped by. I had no idea you'd be playing."

Jenna snorts next to me, but when I look at her, her expression is blank as she flips through her planner.

"Anyway," Mallory continues, lowering her voice. "I'd love to know when you play again. Since the semester is almost over and you won't be my student anymore, I was thinking we could get a drink afterward."

Next to me, Jenna growls, and it almost makes me laugh.

I shouldn't take pleasure in upsetting her, but that means she cares, right?

I clear my throat. "Actually, I'm dating someone. I appreciate the invite, though."

Mallory's eyes dart to Jenna, then back to me. She shrugs. "If you change your mind, you know where to find me."

The moment class ends, Jenna flies out of her seat.

Whether she cares or not is irrelevant if the woman never talks to me again.

After my next class, I try ringing her door for the third time this week, but no one answers.

The next night, when our discussion group meets in the library, I'm hoping she has decompressed enough to hear me out, but based on her frosty demeanor when she sits down, I'm gonna get more of the same.

Sabrina scans the assignment, shakes her head, and hands the paper to Jenna, who rolls her eyes and reads it out loud. "We're supposed to discuss the penis and the male orgasm and whether or not an emotional connection is needed to have sex. Good times."

Keith hoots. "Good times is right! I love talking about my penis." He elbows me. "Bet you do too, right? With all those groupies tripping all over themselves to flash you their boobies."

Shit. This dude is not helping me right now.

Jenna taps her pen on the table. "He definitely enjoys that. Don't you, Ryan? Why don't you tell everyone how much you love when groupies deepthroat you in the bathroom right after your shows. And we can tie it into our assignment because we all know *you* don't need an emotional connection to get laid."

Sabrina's mouth drops open, and Keith scoots closer to me. "You lucky fucker. Tell me everything."

The table next to us shushes us.

I glare at Jenna. "That's not what happened. If you had read one of my many texts, you would understand what went down."

"'What went down?' That's an interesting way to describe it."

Her eyes narrow into sharp little slits. "So you're saying you weren't waving your dick in front of the ditsy twins? Who, by the way, were on their knees and had their tits out and ready for your load, just the way you like it?"

Fuck. That sounds terrible.

I scrub my face. Sabrina is wide-eyed, and Keith looks like he wants to make some popcorn.

"Only one of them was on their knees," I say lamely. I don't know why that's what comes out of my mouth, and I regret it the moment I'm done.

"Oh! Excuse me, Sir Dicksalot! Only *one* of them was on her knees." Jenna says it so loudly, the librarian across the room tells us to be quiet. Pretty sure all the tables around us are listening to Jenna snark at me. "By the way, I had the joy of sitting next to them during your set. One of them was texting someone in your band and got invited to say hi afterward. Are you saying you didn't invite them back stage for sex?"

"I didn't text them. It could've been my guitarist, who's hooked up with them in the past."

"But you've hooked up with them too, right? Because those girls seemed really comfortable flashing you their goodies."

Fuck, this is awkward, but if she wants the truth. "It was a long time ago."

She laughs sarcastically. "What does that mean? Last week?"

"Last year." But based on her expression, she doesn't believe me. I'm starting to get pissed this woman won't just fucking hear me out.

Jenna starts to pack up her books. "You don't need me for this discussion. I'll take the zero."

"No, you don't." I reach over and grab her bag like we're playing tug-of-war. "You are going to sit your cute little ass down and listen to me."

"And if I don't?"

"Then I am going to tackle you to the ground and sit on you until you do."

Keith chuckles. "Do it, dude. Do it."

I glare at him. "Shut the fuck up."

Jenna drops her shit on the table, collapses in her chair, and waves at me. "By all means. Let's hear this great excuse for why you looked like you were seconds from jizzing all over two pairs of tits. I'm *dying* to hear the details."

This woman is making me insane. She wants to have this conversation in public? Fine. "I went in there to take a piss, as some people tend to do. I'd been singing for an hour and a half and drank a shit ton of water. I had to drain the lizard, okay?"

Keith laughs again. "I got you, dude. I'm the same way. Sometimes, I just gotta piss so bad."

I press my palms to my eye sockets. If this guy doesn't stop talking, I'm gonna punch him in the face. "I went in there, locked the latch, and was taking care of business when the girls busted in. I told them I was busy and would meet them outside, but they ignored me. I was in the middle of putting away my junk when you came in."

"That doesn't explain why you were sporting an erection the size of a baseball bat."

Keith snort-laughs and tries to high-five me.

Ignoring that asshole, I try to plead my case to Jenna. "Babe, I told you shows make me hard. It's the adrenaline. I can't help that it goes straight to my dick. Which is why I had to lean over so I wouldn't nail the wall with piss. Because my dick wouldn't go down. That doesn't mean I was gonna fuck two groupies in the bathroom when all I can think about is you."

She looks stunned at my declaration. Then sad. She shrugs and bites her plump bottom lip before her eyes fill with tears. "I wanted to tell you how much I loved your songs and how you put your whole heart into each and every one. How that one ballad was so incredible. And then I walked in on that."

I wrote the song for her. I hadn't even had time to rehearse it with the band, which is why I just did an acoustic version.

"Jenna, what can I say to make you believe me? I swear to you, on my mother's soul, I was not gonna hook up with those girls. I wasn't gonna jerk off on their tits or get a blow job or a hand job or any kind of job."

She swallows. Looks down. Wipes her eyes. "Part of me wonders if I shouldn't be so upset since I hadn't responded to you all week. Maybe you thought we weren't together anymore and you could do your own thing. Play stupid games, win stupid prizes, I suppose. Not that I was trying to play a game with you. I really was sick all week, and I was upset from our conversation last weekend when you dropped me off. But the truth is, seeing you there with those two girls hurt me." She shrugs. "I'm just not sure how to trust you now."

I close my eyes, my chest aching. How do I get her to understand?

With a pained sigh, I glance up and see a familiar face across the library and pause. It gives me an idea.

I'm out of options at this point. I'll try anything.

"Hold on," I tell Jenna. "Don't go anywhere, okay? I need two minutes. I think I have a way to prove this to you."

She doesn't look convinced, but she agrees.

Exactly sixty seconds later, I'm back. I motion to the woman standing next to me. "Jenna, this is Abby. She's a friend of my drummer. She was standing in front of you when you got to the bathroom, right?"

Jenna probably wonders where I'm going with this, but nods.

I turn to Abby. "Please tell Jenna what you saw when you got to the greenroom."

Abby looks at me like I've gone off my rocker but agrees. "The twins were drunk, as usual. And I saw one break down the door to the bathroom to get in. Actually, she kinda fell into it with her shoulder, and it flew open. I didn't know who was in there when I saw it. I wanted to use the restroom too, so I was pissed she broke the lock."

"How long were the girls in the bathroom with me before Jenna showed up?"

Abby tilts her head. "Maybe a minute or two. Not long."

"What happened after Jenna took off?"

"You ran after her but tripped over the girls. Which pissed you off, and you started cursing." She laughs. "I don't think I've ever seen you that mad. And when you got back, you kicked the twins out of the greenroom."

"Before I saw you here in the library, did I ask you to say this to Jenna or pay you to do this or anything like that?"

"No." She turns to Jenna. "For what it's worth, Ryan was a sad panda after you left."

Jenna's quiet once Abby leaves. Keith keeps blabbing on and on about how he wants to be in a band so he can have some groupies flash him, and Sabrina looks annoyed. The whole time my heart is pounding as I watch Jenna, who's staring at the table.

I lean down until her eyes meet mine. "Can we talk? Just the two of us?"

Please say yes.

At first, she doesn't say anything. Then she grabs her bag and books and nods.

Thirty

JENNA

Without a destination in mind, Ryan and I head out of the library. It's a quiet night. Snow covers the campus, and it reminds me of his song.

My head feels jumbled. Hearing Ryan's side of things makes sense, and he never wavered or seemed like he was lying. He looked me straight in the eye the whole time.

And I guess... I guess I believe him.

"You okay?" he asks quietly.

"I feel overwhelmed." I finally brave a glance at him. He has his hands jammed in his hoodie. *Why is he wearing a hoodie when it's twenty degrees?* "Where's your coat?" I'm wearing one that makes me look like the Stay-Puft Marshmallow Man, and I'm still freezing.

It's so cold, our breaths rise in little clouds of steam.

He shrugs and looks away. "This is it."

We stand in the middle of Marsh Plaza as I process his words. Things must be much worse for him and his family than I thought for him to not have a coat. When was the last time he had a nice winter jacket? I'd thought he hadn't worn one to Hamilton's because we were in the car the whole time, but obviously that wasn't the case. "You just won five thousand dollars, Ryan. Why didn't you use some of that to get one?"

"I won *half* of that. I've been saving the other half to return to you, and I sent my mom the rest."

He bought me sick girl supplies with funds he doesn't have. The thought makes my throat tighten.

What the hell are we doing out in the cold? This is stupid.

I grab his frozen hand and start marching back to my brownstone where it's warm. I can make him some hot chocolate. Maybe some soup. Cover him with blankets. Before this ridiculous man gets pneumonia.

"Let me get this straight," I huff. "You bought me soup, flowers, zinc drops, and orange juice, and sent your mama half of that money, but you didn't buy yourself a coat?"

When he doesn't respond, I growl and walk faster.

"Are you mad right now?" he asks.

I stop and spin on him. "Yes, I'm mad right now. You're freezing. This is Boston in December. Where the fuck is your coat? You're from Philly. It's cold there too. I'm pissed off, Ryan. Why are you doing this?" Tears spring to my eyes. "Dang it. Now I'm crying. This is your fault."

He wraps me in his arms, and I cry against his chest. "I'm okay, princess. I'm used to it."

He's used to it. He's used to freezing in the winter.

Hearing that makes me cry harder. "I have so much. My family isn't rich, but we have enough. And I feel bad I have all this shit I don't need while you and your family don't even have the basics. It hurts me."

As I cry against him, he kisses the top of my head. "I'm sorry for yelling at you after we left Hamilton's. I was a total asshole, and you were just being your sweet self. I'm just... I'm not used to that kind of kindness. That's no excuse, but I want you to know I'll do better. I promise I won't talk to you like that again."

"If we're going to be together, you have to let me do things for you. I like doing things for my friends. It's who I am. You can't get mad about it."

He nuzzles his cold nose against me. "Does this mean we're okay? That you believe me about what happened Saturday night?"

I nod. "I believe you. And since we're breaking out the apologies, I'm sorry I didn't hear you out sooner. I'll do better too." Grabbing his shirt in my fist, I pull him close and stare up at him. "But listen carefully, Ryan Hunter. I will *never* share you. Not in a million years. I've never thought of myself as a jealous person, but I get positively feral when I think about other women getting their mitts on you."

He chuckles. "Their mitts?"

"I'm not joking. My level of crazy about this can't be healthy. You sing in a band, and you're so sexy up there doing your thing. How am I going to handle all those titty flashers who want to maul you afterward?"

A sweet smile tilts his lips. "Maybe you should just come to all of my shows. Then you'll see you have nothing to worry about."

I sniffle. "You'd really want that?" He mentioned this before, but I didn't take him seriously.

"Of course. I'd love to have my beautiful muse there." His cold hand cups my face. "I wrote that ballad for you, you know." He presses a soft kiss to my lips, and I sigh.

"Can we get out of the cold before you turn into a popsicle?"

He laughs and wraps an arm around my shoulders. "Your place or mine?"

"Mine is closer. Hurry."

Thirty-One

JENNA

We race up the stairs, laughing. I'm not even sure why we're laughing except I'm so excited to see him without all of this horrible stuff between us.

When we burst through the door of my suite, Clementine yelps as she almost gets clipped by the door.

"I'm so sorry!" I hug her, and she patiently lets me.

She watches Ryan warily. "So... he's forgiven?"

"He's not the turd we thought he was."

She sniffs. "I still have that shovel, so if you're not sure..."

Ryan laughs and holds up his hands. "Remind me to never cross you."

"That's a smart decision." She grabs her coat and leans close to me. "I'm just going to grab some overpriced coffee and convenience store snacks. If you have any trouble, text me. I can get back here in under three minutes."

"You're the best." I hug her again. "I'll be fine."

She points at Ryan. "No funny business."

"The only funny business I'll be doling out is the kind Jenna wants."

My whole body heats when I think about what I hope is about to happen. I have a hard time not smiling, and when Clementine catches a glimpse of my expression, she snorts. "Please practice safe sex. I threw those extra condoms in the fishbowl."

And then she's gone.

"Your roommate is scary. But I kinda like her," Ryan says.

"She has a prickly exterior, but I love her. I have a feeling we're going to be lifelong friends."

He grabs me in a hug, and I palm his handsome face. "You're freezing. I'd like to warm you up."

He gives me a lopsided grin. "You can definitely warm me up."

I'm not sure who moves first, but like two magnets that can't be held apart, we rush together. I lean up to wrap my arms around his shoulders. His hand tightens in the back of my hair as he kisses me so intensely, it makes me ravenous.

But then his kisses turn soft. Sweet.

"I've missed you so fucking much, Jenna," he mumbles against me. "It freaks me out, to be honest. I shouldn't need you this much, this soon."

"I know what you mean. I feel like I'm about to go cliff diving." I stare up at him. "So let's jump together." I grab his hand and pull him into my bedroom, close the door, and turn on my small lamp. "What are your thoughts about sharing a twin bed again?"

"As long as you're in it with me, I don't care about the size of the bed."

I shrug off my coat. Toss it on the chair by my desk. Slide off my sweater. All while he watches me.

It's like that, huh? He likes to watch. I can work with this.

After I kick off my shoes, I unbutton my jeans and wiggle out of them. Tug off my tank top. Until I'm standing in a lace bra, booty shorts, and socks.

My nipples are giving him a full salute through the thin material, which does not escape his notice.

Turning, I bend over, making sure to put my ass in the air, and pull down the blankets on my bed. "You just going to stand there?" I ask as I flick off my bra.

He swallows, his chest heaving like he just ran a marathon. His eyes drift over me, slowly moving from my face down my breasts, stomach, thighs, and then back up again.

His voice is rough when he finally speaks. "I hope you don't have plans to walk later."

My breath catches at the need in his voice.

And then I'm in his arms. Tossed on the bed. Scrambling to shove off his hoodie and t-shirt. To unbutton his jeans. Until we're both in our underwear.

I run my hands over his arms and chest. He's so cold, it makes me shiver. I make myself a promise to look after this man. He's mine, and I always take care of what belongs to me.

Nestled between my thighs, he's hard and thick against me. His weight feels so good. I moan as we kiss. I can't get enough of him.

He nibbles down my body. Bites my neck. Sucks my nipples. Licks down my abs. Until he pulls off my undies, spread my legs, and shoves his face between my thighs.

"Oh, God." I arch back as he takes long licks.

"Already so wet, baby."

I squirm against him. "I'm always wet for you." I'm not exaggerating. If I'm with him, I'm in a constant state of arousal, like I'm somehow wired for his frequency.

"Pull your knees up."

I do what he asks and then reach down and spread myself open for him.

"Fuck, that's hot, princess."

Looking down, I watch as he runs a finger around my clit, grazing it, before he sinks into me. He works me over with one finger, then two. By the time he adds a third finger, I'm writhing on the bed.

"Ryan."

His eyes are positively feral as he looks at me. "Touch yourself, baby. I wanna watch you come on my fingers."

Nodding, I circle my clit while he pumps me with his hand. But then that dirty man licks a finger and presses it to my asshole.

"RYAN!"

He chuckles. "Does this feel good?"

I blink, all the sensations swirling through me as he rubs me in ways I've never experienced before. And maybe it's the taboo aspect of this, but yeah. I'm into it. "Don't stop, dang it."

Laughing, he dips his face and does this slow lick-swirl combo on my clit while he fucks me with his fingers and rubs my backdoor until my whole body clenches and quakes. Suddenly, I arch back and come with a scream. My orgasm only intensifies when he goes back to licking me.

"I already... I mean... Oh, God... I'm coming again." The pulses don't stop. I don't know what kind of voodoo magic he's unleashed down there, but wave after wave of pleasure washes over me.

When I'm boneless and so sated I feel drunk, I laugh. "You've fucked me stupid."

He chuckles. "We're not done yet, princess."

Thirty-Two

RYAN

My beautiful woman sprawls on the narrow bed. She tosses her hands over her head in a full-body stretch that makes me want to go down on her again. But then she grabs my arm and tugs me to her.

I smack my lips. "That was just the appetizer."

She laughs and palms my face. "I want all seven courses tonight."

"I aim to please."

All I can think about as I settle between her slender thighs is how there's only the thin material of my boxer briefs separating us.

She leans up to kiss me, and her lips are like a drug. Jenna makes me want things I've never considered before. I've never thought about getting married or having a family of my own or any of that crap, but that's where my head goes tonight. And even though it might freak her out, I want her to know how special she is to me.

Drawing back, I gaze down at the gorgeous girl in my arms. "Jenna, I... I've never had the kind of feelings I have for you for anyone else. I know we're really just starting out, but you've already burrowed deep in here." I tap my chest.

She tangles her fingers through my hair, a shy smile playing on her lips. "I won't even deny that I've fallen hard for you."

Fallen hard.

I've never *felt* that expression before, but I get it now.

When we kiss again, I get a picture in my head. Of me with my girl. Of a few kids running around us on a huge yard. Of a dog barking playfully. The sun is shining, and everyone's laughing. Could that be us some day?

I rub my nose against hers. "Maybe if we play our cards right, you and I could have that forever kind of love."

Her eyes water. "Will you let me take care of you?"

"Never realized I needed that, but yeah. I'd be honored, but only if you'll let me take care of you too. Bring you soup when you're sick. Flowers when you're sad. Kisses when you're lonely."

The smile she gives me could brighten all of Boston in the dead of winter. She taps her mouth. "I could use a few of those kisses right now."

The world seems to fall away when we come together. We make out until she's clawing my back and urging her hips against mine. I can feel her heat through my boxers.

Reaching into my jeans, I pull a condom out of my wallet, but pause before I tear it open. "Princess, you sure you want to do this? There's no rush."

"Ryan Hunter, if you make me wait one more minute to do the deed, I'm going to kick you out of my bed."

I chuckle and roll on the condom while my girlfriend watches my hand with avid fascination. And then I drag it through her wetness before I use my dick to tap her swollen clit. She shivers and reaches up to cup her bouncy tits. Christ, she's fucking gorgeous.

Kneeling, I grab her ankle and place it on my shoulder while I guide myself into her pretty pink pussy. It's a tight fit.

"Jesus, baby." With a groan, I sink deeper and watch her

stretch around me. "You feel so fucking good." I rub my thumb around where we join and then circle her swollen clit. "Can you come again?"

"No, I don't think…" A flush is working up her chest and neck. Her hair is a tangled mess on the pillow.

A wave of pride washes over me. I made her come apart. I made her scream like her soul was leaving her body. I made her writhe with pleasure.

"Don't think. Just feel." I suck my thumb to get it wet and then place it back on her. "I want you to come on my cock."

"I, uh, I don't think I can come in this position. Maybe on top?"

Jenna wants to ride me? I didn't think this could get better, but the thought of her bouncing on my dick makes my balls draw up.

I reach down to strangle my junk so I don't blow. Being with Jenna just feels too good. She's too beautiful. Too sweet. Too fucking sexy.

Once I get ahold of myself, I roll us over while keeping our bodies connected, which is a tall order considering the size of her bed.

The goddess smiles down at me. I reach up to thread my fingers in her hair. Drag her to me. And kiss the fuck out of her.

Our tongues tangle together as I reach between us to grab her breast. I pluck the tight nipple between my fingers until she starts to thrust. Then she sits up and her tits bounce as she really starts to move. Fucking beautiful.

I pat her butt. "Move into a squat."

She doesn't bat an eye. Just shifts positions. I grab her ass and help her move on me, all the while watching her tight pussy stretch around me. It's so fucking erotic.

I reach between us and circle her swollen clit until she's making these little noises that tell me she's getting close again.

"Come for me, baby." Remembering how she shivered when I

tapped her clit with my dick earlier, I tap it with my hand. Soft at first. Then a little harder in rhythm with the way our bodies slap together. Until she squeals and starts to pulse around me.

"Ryan! God, yes!"

Holy shit. The way she's squeezing my cock is insane. "Baby. Fuck, I'm gonna come." When I can't take it anymore, I sit up and yank her to me.

"Oh, Jesus, you're deep like this," she grunts.

She's still quaking around me when I let go. I bury my face in her neck while I bite her shoulder. Lights dance behind my closed eyes as hot pleasure shoots through me as the thought hits me like a thunderbolt—I'm never letting this woman go. Jenna is *mine*.

We collapse in a heap of limbs. She moans and wiggles closer. "Can we sleep like this?"

"Yeah. After I deal with the condom."

We both groan as I pull out. I head out to find the bathroom, and on the way back accidentally flash the other roommate my naked ass. I hold up a hand. "Sorry!"

When I tell Jenna, she laughs so hard, she snorts. "I wasn't thinking with the organ on my shoulders just now or I would've warned you to cover up. It's okay. Harper got a good show."

"Mm." I collapse next to Jenna and let her pull me close until we're twined together again. "I'll apologize tomorrow."

As I lie there, I think about all the things I want to experience with this woman. All the things I want to know about her. All the things I hope we can share. And I wonder if a lifetime is enough to get those answers.

I kiss her shoulder. "Did I bite you too hard? I didn't mean to get carried away."

She runs her hand up and down my back. "It was perfect. I like it a little rough. Something I didn't really know until you."

I feel like a Neanderthal for liking how that sounds.

Closing my eyes, I sleep on her like she's my naked body pillow.

"What are you doing tomorrow after class?" she asks as she lightly scratches her nails in my hair.

"I don't have plans. Why?"

"Because we're going to go get you a coat. And before you argue with me, it's my Christmas gift to you, and if you turn me down, you're going to hurt my feelings, Ryan Hunter."

I smile against her and suck her nipple. "Never thought I'd say this, but I like this bossy side of you."

We talk about what finals we have next week, and she invites me to her study session and promises an abundance of snacks. She doesn't know this yet, but I don't need any incentives to join her.

I lean down to graze her lips with mine. "What did I do to deserve you?"

She gives me a sweet smile and arches up to kiss me. "You won the Girlfriend Games. And you and me? We're the grand prize."

Thirty-Three

JENNA

"Mom! Dad! Come on." I set up the iPad on the kitchen table and dial Ryan.

When I see his face, my heart skips a beat. "Hi, handsome."

"Hey, gorgeous." The grin he gives me promises all kinds of fun when I see him in a few days.

"I want you to meet my parents. They're about to head off to a New Year's Eve party, but they wanted to say hi first."

His eyes widen. "Uh. Okay. Yeah. Cool."

I don't know why this surprises him. I met his mama when we video chatted last week.

Being the persuasive girl I am, I talked him into letting me buy him a ticket home to Philly for the holidays. I found a great deal online, one of those last-minute fares, and told him if the money thing really bothered him, he could help me and Clementine rearrange some furniture to pay me back. Ryan said he was more than happy to help and offered to be my personal slave.

Let's just say moving furniture isn't the only thing on my to-do list.

These few weeks apart have been good for our relationship. We talk every day, sometimes for hours. We brainstormed ways to market his band and new venues to contact. He told me about growing up in a trailer park and all the reasons he left Philly, but how that makes him feel guilty because he wants to be there for his mom. I told him about how my dad cheated on my mom, so I'm sensitive about that sometimes. We swapped stories about our siblings and all the ways they make us crazy. We've even shared what happened in our old relationships, and he told me about that wicked girl who dated him on a dare and then said she did it out of pity.

I've never wanted to punch a woman so badly before. I suppose I should be grateful because now Ryan is mine.

But it helped me understand why we argued after that weekend at Hamilton's. That girl hurt him, but I plan to heal him, one snuggle at a time.

My mama sits down next to me. "Hi, Ryan. It's lovely to meet you. Jenna has told us so much about you."

"It's nice to meet you too, ma'am."

"Oh, please call me Joyce. And this is my husband, Ronald."

My stepdad sits next to her and waves.

I don't know why I'm nervous, but my palms are sweaty, and my knee keeps jiggling. I guess I want my parents to like Ryan.

Because I already know I love him.

When my parents are about to leave, my dad says, "Be sure to come and visit us some time, Ryan. I'm sure Jenna would love to show you around, and my wife makes the best peach cobbler."

"I'd love that, sir."

My mama kisses my cheek and whispers in my ear, "He's adorable. I can see why you're eager to get back to Boston."

Two days later, when I step off the plane, my heart is racing. Ryan said he was going to pick me up. I told him he didn't have to go through the trouble—Logan Airport is a giant parking lot during the holidays—but he insisted.

When I get to baggage claim, I scan the packed room, excitement making me giddy.

The crowd parts, and there he is, wearing the coat I got him and holding a dozen roses. The smile he gives me makes me a little weak-kneed.

My heart races as I run up to him.

He gives me a soft, sweet kiss before he pulls me into a hug, lifting me off the ground. "Missed you, princess."

"I missed you too." It feels so good to be in his arms again. I burrow my face into his neck, and we stand there for a few minutes as he strokes my hair.

"Want to come to my place tonight? I wrote a new song I'd love to play for you."

"Yeah. Can we drop off some stuff at my place first?"

"Sure."

We move hand in hand toward the luggage claim while I smell my roses.

"What's the name of your song?" I ask.

He pulls me into another hug. "'Fallen Hard.'"

I look up at him and smile, my heart beating erratically in my chest. "I can't wait."

"Good." He kisses me again. "Because it's about how I couldn't help falling in love with you."

My eyes sting, and I wave my hand in front of my face. "I love you too, Ryan. I've pretty much been crazy about you since you dragged me face-first through the mud at Hamilton's."

He laughs and squeezes me tight. "Want to hear something funny? When I thought about getting a partner to help me that weekend, I wanted to ask someone who wouldn't read into it. You know, since it was called the Girlfriend Games, and I wasn't looking for a girlfriend. Didn't think I wanted one. And that's what made me think of you. Because you hated me."

I groan and cover my face. "I'm sorry. I was such a brat."

"No, baby." He drags my palm to his mouth and kisses it. "You were exactly what I needed. And the best part is I didn't just end up with a girlfriend. I got a best friend too."

I fling my arms around him. "Well, you're stuck with me now, so this is a good thing."

"The best thing to ever happen to me."

Epilogue

RYAN

The crowd at Madison Square Garden is stomping for an encore, but I'm not sure we have time.

"We should've canceled this show," I grumble as I chug water backstage.

My very pregnant wife, who's sitting on a folding chair next to me, closes her eyes like I've insulted her and shakes her head. "Over my dead body, Ryan Hunter. This has been a lifelong dream of yours." She points to the stage. "Finish the dang show."

It still cracks me up when she calls me by my full name, but now is not the time for humor. "Baby, you're in fucking labor!"

"You'd better hurry up then, huh?"

Jesus Christ. This woman is gonna be the death of me.

My mother-in-law pats my arm. "I'll keep an eye on her. You've got time. I've already called the hospital, so they're expecting us."

Joyce is a godsend. She's holding our three-year-old son, bouncing him on her hip. He's wearing noise-cancelling head-phones and snoozing peacefully. I shouldn't be surprised. The kid could sleep through a train wreck.

My mom pats my other arm and takes my empty water bottle. "Honey, don't antagonize your wife. She's gestating. Get out there and finish. Joyce and I can handle things."

I can't believe I'm about to do another song. This is the last place I want to be right now. Ironic, isn't it?

We've spent the last several months crisscrossing the country on a huge bus for my stadium tour. Tonight is our last show for a while. I need a break, and even though Jenna handles road trips like a boss, the woman needs time to rest and enjoy the new addition to our family. I'm looking forward to pampering her when we get home. I'm clearing all of my nights for baby duty, so my princess can sleep and recover.

My band and I take the stage, and I turn so I can keep Jenna in my sight just in case she needs me.

Glancing at the crowd, I nod at our college friends in the front row, and they smile and clap. They've come down to New York to catch my last show. We're gonna have a full house because my brothers are flying in tomorrow to meet their new niece, and Jenna's sister is visiting in a few days. But it'll be nice to have all the people Jenna and I love in one place for a while.

"We're gonna do one more song, and then I gotta jet," I say into the mic. "My wife and I are getting a very special delivery tonight, and we need to get to the hospital to welcome our baby."

The crowd roars with delight, and I smile, grateful to have these amazing fans. I take a moment to appreciate this incredible accomplishment, something I'm not sure I could've done without Jenna by my side. Yes, I had a dream, but Jenna made me feel like I could achieve it.

Smiling at my gorgeous wife, I strap on my guitar. Sure, we've had our ups and downs. Nothing will test your relationship like being crammed in a small van for weeks on end and gigging in shitty venues. But Jenna always kept me going. Always looking on the bright side. Always making me feel like I could do this.

And when we blew up and I got that first big check, her generous heart humbled me. Do you know what she told me? She said I needed to buy my mom a house. So after I bought Jenna an engagement ring, that's exactly what I did.

"Maybe you guys can help me serenade the woman who helped me get here. She's the toughest person I know. Jenna is sweet and optimistic but also the fiercest mama bear you've ever met. She's a road trip warrior who coordinated my shows for years before we hit big arenas. She's my best friend and the one person I can't live without." I strum my guitar as the band kicks in. "You might know this song. It was my first number one hit, though it took a while to get there. I wrote it for Jenna when we were poor college kids. Help me sing 'Fallen Hard.'"

My fans know all the words, and they scream the lyrics. It's all pretty surreal.

When the last note is over and I run back to my wife, she's crying. "Are you okay?" I kneel before her. "Let's get you to the hospital."

She palms my face. "I love you so much, and I'm so proud of you. I don't want the arrival of our baby to overshadow what you've done tonight."

"This is the single best moment of my life, princess. Tonight's show was incredible, but you and our kiddos are what give it meaning," I say as I rub her swollen stomach, my throat tight from how much I adore this woman and both of the babies she's given me. "And on top of all that, you helped me make my dream come true."

"It's my dream too, Ryan. Everything we've done together. All of the gigs and traveling across the country for your shows? I've loved it all." She kisses me. "Let's go meet our daughter."

My heart kicks in my chest. Jenna is the center of my universe. I don't know what I did to deserve her, but I have a feeling we were always meant to be.

I should text Hamilton to thank him, because I didn't just win a girlfriend that weekend. I won a wife. My best friend. My lover. My everything.

About Finding Dandelion

When soccer all-star Jax Avery collides with Dani Hart on his twenty-first birthday, their connection is instantaneous and explosive. For the first time in years, Jax isn't interested in his usual hit-it and quit-it approach.

But Dani knows better. Allowing herself a night to be carefree and feel the intensity of their attraction won't change anything when it comes to dealing with a player. So when Jax doesn't recognize Dani the next time he sees her, it shouldn't be a total shock. The fact that he's her new roommate's brother? That's a shock.

Dani doesn't regret that night with Jax, just the need to lie about it. Since her roommate has made it clear what she thinks about her brother's "type" of girl, the last thing Dani wants is to admit what happened.

Jax knows he's walking a fine line on the soccer team. One more misstep and he's off the roster, his plans to go pro be damned. Except he can't seem to care. About anything... except for the one girl who keeps invading his dreams.

Despite Jax's fuzzy memory of his hot hookup with his sister's friend, he can't stay away from her, even if that means breaking his own rules. But there are bigger forces at work—realities that can end Dani's college career and lies that can tear them apart.

Jax realizes what he's losing if Dani walks away, but will he sacrifice his future to be with her? And will she let him if he does?

Acknowledgments

My deepest gratitude goes to my husband, who puts up with pizza and takeout so I can write. Matt, thanks for the encouragement to go after a life-long dream. Hugs to my daughters, who make me want to try harder and be better every day. Love you.

I never would've gone to BU and written these stories without my amazing parents who sacrificed so much to get me there. Mom and Dad, thanks for always being my biggest fans.

Kimberly Brower, you're the best agent a girl could ever have. I'm so grateful for your friendship and advice.

RJ Locksley, thanks for your amazing editing skills.

To the authors who encouraged me throughout this series... Whitney Barbetti, KL Grayson, Jules Barnard, and M. Pierce. I'm so grateful for your friendships.

Doris Gray and Jullie Anne Caparas, thank you for starting the Wildcats group for me! Best gift ever.

Wildcats, I love you with reckless abandon. *ass smacks*

Alexis Durbin, Candi Kane, Serena McDonald, and Cristiane Karamanolis, thanks for your enthusiasm and support. I owe you girls a few drinks.

Of course, huge thanks to the bloggers who have supported me in one way or another, especially Aestas Book Blog, The Dirty Laundry, The Literary Gossip, Three Girls and a Book Obsession, Love Between the Sheets, Give Me Books, One Click Addicts, Smut Muffins, Schmexy Girl Book Blog, The Bookaholic Fairies, The Book Bellas, Smokin' Hot Book Blog, Rumpled Sheets, Sinfully Sexy Book Reviews, The Romance Vault, I Bookin' Love To Read, Smut Fanatics, Book Baristas, Literary Misfit, Owl

Always Be Reading, and Teacups & Book Love. There are so many more who shared my books and reviewed. I wish I could tackle hug you all.

Lastly, to my readers... I hope you enjoy this series! Thanks for coming on this ride with me!

xoxo,

Lex

About the Author

Lex Martin is the USA Today bestselling author of Varsity Dads, Texas Nights, and the Dearest series. She writes contemporary romance novels, the steamy kind she hopes readers love but her parents avoid.

She's always been obsessed with writing, starting in elementary school when she would pen short stories and make her father read them. (Afterward, she'd make him take her tests, but he was a good sport and did them without complaint.)

In high school, when she wasn't playing basketball, she wrote emo poetry and worked on the school newspaper.

She later became a nationally-certified high school English teacher and freelance journalist but decided she'd rather write romance novels than tests or city hall articles.

Lex loves coffee, rom coms, pen hoarding, planners, and college football.

She married her almost college sweetheart (they met right after graduation), and she's still obsessed with him, especially when he writes her songs.

She currently resides in her hometown of San Antonio with her husband, twin daughters, a bunny, and their puppy. Drop her a line. She loves hearing from readers.

To stay up-to-date with her releases, **subscribe to her newsletter** via her website, or join her Facebook group, **Lex Martin's Wildcats.**

www.lexmartinwrites.com